Three Wishes

Isabelle Merlin

RANDOM HOUSE AUSTRALIA

Random House Australia Pty Ltd
Level 3, 100 Pacific Highway, North Sydney, NSW 2060
www.randomhouse.com.au

Sydney New York Toronto
London Auckland Johannesburg

First published by Random House Australia in 2008

National Library of Australia
Cataloguing-in-Publication Entry

Merlin, Isabelle
Three wishes

For secondary school age.
978 1 74166 236 8 (pbk.).

A823.4

Cover and internal illustrations by Kerrie Hess
Cover design by WideOpen Media
Typesetting and text design by Midland Typesetters, Australia
Printed and bound by The SOS Print + Media Group

10 9 8 7 6 5 4

Contents

Whenever you see *in my story, there's a post on my blog at* http://fairychild3wishes.blogspot.com

Careful what you wish for

Careful what you wish for. That's always the message in those old stories where someone gets given three wishes. Careful – don't say the first thing that pops into your head . . .

In my mind, it all starts with the blog. I know in many ways that's not really true. It started a long time before that, years ago in fact, even before I was born. But in my mind, it doesn't feel like that. It feels like somehow, before the blog, my life was the same as it had been for the last eight years, since I first went to live with Aunt Jenny after my parents died in the crash. And it seems like, after the blog, things began to get weird . . .

The blog began as an English assignment. Our teacher, Ms Bryce, told us that she thought it would be interesting for us to use 'cutting-edge new media' alongside 'conventional essays and stories'. But she wanted it to be a proper blog, not just the add-on diary kind you have on MySpace or Bebo. It was supposed to have a theme and she was very excited about the project.

Not so most of the class. My best friends – Portia Warren, Alice Taylor and Maddy Fox – groaned and moaned about it. I pretended to moan too. But secretly

I didn't mind at all. I never mind writing, as long as it's creative stuff. I really want to be a writer. A really good, best-selling kind of writer. But I don't like ordinary English assignments much. You know the kind I mean – ones where you have to write about the meanings and messages in books. I can do it okay, but I just don't like it. It spoils good books and makes boring ones even more boring.

I didn't want to set my blog around a serious theme, like some of the ideas Ms Bryce had put up on the board: 'Famous Writers', 'Issues of History', 'Great Journeys' and stuff like that. Or even the humdrum sorts of ideas, like 'My Holidays', or 'My Family History' (that was hardly something I could write about back then anyway, as I knew practically nothing about it). I wanted to do something fun and a bit out there. So I decided I'd do it around the theme of three wishes, you know, the kind given by fairies.

When I was a little kid, I totally believed in fairies. I was sure that by squinting my eyes a bit and looking really, really hard, I would actually see them. I read fairy books and I looked at fairy pictures and I thought and thought about what I would ask for if a fairy popped up beside me one day and declared she'd come to grant me three wishes. I wrote down wishes on little bits of paper and left them under my pillow or under trees or anywhere I thought a fairy might find them. One year, I actually got the wish I'd asked for: a beautiful fairy-princess doll all dressed up in this gorgeous sky-blue dress and bright silver shoes, with gauzy wings and a crown. I knew fairies existed then, because you couldn't find anything like her in the shops. She was special. She was unique. She was fairy magic come to me. Her name was Celestine and I loved her to bits.

But the next year, everything changed. I was at school one day when the principal came into my classroom. She looked very pale. She took me to her office and told me that Mum and Dad had been in a terrible head-on smash with a truck on the highway and that they had died – Dad instantly and Mum on the way to hospital. They'd had no chance, she said, no chance at all. I can still remember how she began to stutter as she spoke and her face looked all crumpled, and how she kept saying, 'Oh, you poor little thing, Rosie! You poor little thing!' and trying to hug me. I remember a fly buzzing around that hot room, and alighting once on the principal's nose. But I don't remember how I really felt. They said afterwards I was in shock.

Aunt Jenny came very soon after and she took me home – to her home, that is. I knew her already quite well because she and my mum Annie, the younger of the two, were very close and always popping round to see each other. It wasn't far, anyway – Aunt Jenny lived in the next street. She looked after me, comforted me and tried hard over the next few years to be both father and mother to me, though it was hard for her. She missed my parents almost as much as I did and she didn't have much money.

My parents hadn't left any money, either. They had good jobs, but they had never been able to save. They loved to enjoy themselves and do fun, extravagant things, like hiring a Rolls Royce to drive to the beach, where we'd have a magnificent picnic, served by a waiter in a tuxedo. Or they might get a joy-flight over the mountains – Dad had his pilot's licence – or buy beautiful clothes or gorgeous toys for me. So they would max out their credit card and just do whatever they felt like, and I loved it. Anything, it seemed, could happen with them. Come to think of it, maybe that's why it was so easy for me to believe in fairies and things like that. My parents sprinkled fairy dust over everything. And it wasn't just to do with spending money, either. They loved each other, and me, really, really dearly, and they weren't afraid to show it and to tell me, over and over again.

So when they died, for me the fairies died too. I couldn't believe in magic wishes any more, because the only thing I wanted during that terrible time was for the accident never to have happened and Mum and Dad and I to live happily together back in our own home. And though I wished it ever so many times, it never came true, of course. Eventually, I settled down to life with Aunt Jenny, and though I missed my parents terribly, as the years passed the ache of their absence grew softer. That was partly time passing, and partly it was because of Aunt Jenny. She's much more anxious than my mum and dad were and sometimes she fussed and flapped, but she was also very kind and loving and I couldn't have asked for a better guardian. The only thing that was a real problem was money. Aunt Jenny worried about that constantly.

Aunt Jenny's a dressmaker, a really good one, but she's a hopeless businesswoman. She's too nice. A soft touch, some people say. She gives discounts to people who could really afford to pay full price. And she makes excuses for people who don't pay on time and who make out they're too skint to pay straightaway. And so money's always tight.

She worked from home, in the back room of our flat, which she'd set up as a workroom. It's a rather nice room, actually, big and full of light, with a couple of tall old-fashioned mirrors on stands, and two tailor's dummies, and beautiful black and white framed photographs of film stars on the walls. Aunt Jenny loves the glamorous actresses of the past, like Grace Kelly, Audrey Hepburn and Marilyn Monroe. There are shelves for the materials, a filing cabinet for the patterns, a table for the sewing-machine and comfy chairs for the customers to sit on when they're ordering stuff. And there's a CD player for the music Aunt Jenny likes to play when she's sewing. It's nearly always from the same era as those film stars – jazz, mostly. I think she'd have liked to live in a world like that, a dreamworld of elegant ease and effortless sophistication. She'd like to have had a design studio catering to those glamorous beauties.

Aunt Jenny makes all kinds of clothes, but she specialises in evening dresses. She's really, really good at those. Slinky satin or full-skirted organza, the latest thing or vintage style, she'd make something gorgeous, with beadwork and sequins and lace and stuff sewn on by hand. She'd love to make mostly the kinds of clothes worn by those classic film stars, and sometimes she can persuade people that's what they should want. But not often. People mostly want things they see in gossip mags, the clothes they see celery-stick-thin modern celebrities wearing. Aunt Jenny gets disappointed – she thinks a lot of modern fashion simply doesn't suit most normal body shapes – but she has to do what the customer wants. And she always makes it beautifully, no matter what she thinks.

When I was little, Aunt Jenny would sometimes use the scraps from some splendid evening dress to make me fabulous costumes for school plays or fancy dress parties or Book Week parades, all those sorts of things. And, as I learned later, it was she, of course, who had made me my Celestine doll . . .

Anyway – getting back to my blog, I'd decided I'd go back to my childhood obsession and write about three wishes. Don't ask me why I returned to something I thought I'd left behind. It just seemed like a good idea at the time. Now I think it's kind of spooky.

The internet's such a weird place. Sometimes it feels to me like a fairytale kind of country. There are trolls and wizards and zombies and people hiding out under false names and others who transform themselves into what they're not. There are all kinds of nasties waiting to trap the unwary and then there are good fairies who make amazing things happen. You can have invisible friends – people you've never met in the flesh. All sorts of odd magic, good and bad, seems to hover there. It was back to the old wishes under a pillow kind of thing – except this time on the web. Maybe that's why calling my blog Three Wishes seemed like a good fit.

When I'd finished setting it up, I thought it looked pretty cool. Ms Bryce did too. She gave me full marks for it. But seeing it up there, in that smart and professional-looking format, made my heart beat faster. What if – you never knew – what if the blog attracted attention from people other than my friends? What about if a publisher saw it, and thought, *Hey, this girl can write, maybe I'll ask her to do a book!* I'd heard of that happening before, that bloggers were discovered by publishers, and their dream of writing a real book came true. I didn't think about it too much, because I knew it was unlikely. But it was at the back of my mind, some of the time at least.

Okay, you might be thinking, what about those three wishes then? What did you write? Well, you can go and have a look at my blog for the full deal – it's at http://

fairychild3wishes.blogspot.com. But basically they were:

1. To win a lot of money in the lottery so Aunt Jenny doesn't have to scrimp and save (we occasionally get lottery tickets but have never won anything).

2. A pair of silver shoes like Celestine's, except in my size.

3. For something exciting to happen to me, because I want to be a really good and popular writer and how can you be that if you just live an ordinary, humdrum kind of life?

In my first post, I'd written, very solemnly, about how you had to be careful what you wished for. 🌹 (Don't forget that whenever I've included this rose, it means you can go and look at my blog, http://fairychild3wishes. blogspot.com, to see what I wrote.) I wrote about the people who made stupid wishes and what happened to them. I wrote about people who didn't think things through. I thought I was safe from that because I had really thought about those three wishes. I didn't want to ask for impossible things. No time-travel or supernatural powers or what have you, just things that might come true. Portia, Alice and Maddy wrote down their own wishes in the comments boxes and I thought their wishes were a good deal more unrealistic than mine. Alice even asked for a magic wand! (Mind you, I used to try out that one on the fairies when I was a little kid – I thought you could then trick them into giving you unlimited wishes.) I believed I'd taken my own advice really rather well, and heeded the warning message of those old stories. What I didn't realise back then was that 'careful what you wish for' isn't really just advice or even a warning. *It is a threat.*

The Snow Queen

It's funny how days that will totally turn your life upside down have no warning label attached to them. There's no red flag flapping on the calendar, no spooky sign that today will be anything other than the usual kind of wake up, get up, go to school, come home on the bus, eat, do homework, watch TV, go to bed kind of routine. It was like that the day Mum and Dad were killed. And it was like that the day the Snow Queen came into my life.

It was a Thursday – March 8 – about three weeks after I'd started my blog. That had been chugging along nicely enough. I'd been posting the odd piece, including a fairy story I'd written. My friends had posted comments on it, and Ms Bryce had said it was very impressive. There'd been one slightly annoying thing: someone calling themselves *Koschei* had barged in on the comments box, saying that 'your wishes have been noted and will be granted'. I'd taken very little notice, though the girls had been a bit indignant about some stranger turning up in our midst. But it just seemed harmless to me, if a little try-hard and stupid of whoever it was. I wasn't to know then that in fact . . .

No, no, not yet. Right now, I'm back to the day when the Snow Queen turned up. It was one of those days where the weather is neither really one thing nor the other. Not sunny, not rainy. It had rained a bit in the night but by morning that had stopped and the day settled into a cool, grey, dull stillness occasionally interrupted by desultory drizzle. All up the kind of day that is best spent curled up with a good book or watching a good movie, or both, preferably with some hot chocolate and marshmallows. If it had been a weekend, that's exactly what I'd have done. As it was, I had to catch the bus and go to school. It was a particularly boring day there, because none of my friends were at school. Portia and Alice were away on a music excursion in the city, and Maddy had a dose of gastro and was at home in bed. To cap it all off, we had a relief teacher for maths who insisted on making us do endless re-runs of some formulas we'd already spent weeks over with our usual teacher. It was a double Maths period, right at the end of the day. Enough tedium, as Aunt Jenny would have said in her funny old-fashioned way, to drive you to drink. But completely uneventful. In fact, you could say every-thing that day, up until the time I arrived home, was a non-event.

The first indication I had of anything being different was the sight of the car parked outside our block of flats. A dark-blue convertible sports car, with a white roof. It was just the kind of thing Grace Kelly might have driven very fast down a road with hairpin bends, in one of those old movies Aunt Jenny was so keen on. It must be one of her customers. Not one I knew, however. I'd never seen that car before. I let myself into the flat and went directly to the kitchen to get something to eat. When Aunt Jenny had a new customer in, she didn't like me interrupting her, so I didn't call out to her or anything. But she must have heard the door slamming, because even before I had seriously begun considering the contents of the fridge, she came into the kitchen.

She looked strange. Pale, her eyes a little too brilliant. My heart lurched as I suddenly thought, *This is just how she looked that afternoon when she picked me up from school, when Dad and Mum died.* I hadn't remembered that image in years. But now, it struck me with a terrible force – and even more so when she spoke.

'Rose,' she said. 'Thank God you're back. There's something . . . something has happened.'

'What's happened? Is it my friends?' I blurted out, imagining, in quick succession, Portia and Alice's excursion bus overturned, or Maddy's gastric illness really being stomach cancer or something.

'No, nothing to do with them. No. Rose, I must tell you . . . I'm sorry that I never . . .'

'Ah! She's back.' A tall woman was standing in the kitchen doorway, with a man hovering behind her. She was dark-haired, blue-eyed and everything about her was polished and perfect, from the tip of her expertly styled hair, waving softly around her ears, to the toe of her smart high-heeled dark-blue shoes. Her clothes were simple – a navy-blue suit with a nip-waisted jacket and a pencil skirt – but obviously expensive. She was one of the most beautiful women I'd ever seen outside the pages of a magazine or the scenes of a film. Flawlessly beautiful, but with something cold and controlled about her. She made me think of the Snow Queen, in Hans Christian Andersen's fairytale. I was always scared by that character – she made shards of glass pierce people's hearts so they no longer acted like warm human beings or cared about anyone.

The Snow Queen looked at me and gave a tiny smile. Those icy blue eyes surveyed me, from tip of messy brown hair to toe of scuffed school shoe, passing the crumpled school shirt and ragged-hem school skirt in between. I don't think I'm exactly ugly. In fact I've been told I'm attractive, though I wasn't quite sure I believed that. But under the Snow Queen's baleful gaze, I felt as though I'd been changed into a sweaty sack of potatoes or something.

'You are Rose Dumerle,' she stated.

To my horror, I found myself stammering. 'Who, er, who wants to . . . to know?'

'My name is Madame Randal. Madame Blanche Randal,' said the woman, and though she spoke very good English, I noticed her accent, now. It sounded French. 'You may call me Madame Blanche, if you wish, Rose. You do not know me yet, but you will.'

It sounded remarkably like a threat. I shot a glance at my aunt. She looked dazed, helpless, almost. I glanced at the man behind Blanche Randal. Unlike her, he was grey and ordinary, wearing a dull suit and a dull haircut. Blanche Randal made a sign to him, and he said, hurriedly, 'Miss Dumerle, I have something important to tell you. It might be wise if you sit down, for it may come as something of a shock.'

'Not here,' said Aunt Jenny, speaking at last. 'Come into the living room.'

She didn't look at me, didn't say anything as she led the way into the living room. I followed, numbly, my brain throwing up all kinds of wild thoughts. Was Aunt Jenny in trouble? Were we bankrupt? Or had she maybe done something wrong? Who were these people? Perhaps they were from Social Services or something, and I would be taken away from Aunt Jenny. I'd refuse. I'd not be taken into care or foster homes or whatever. I'd run away. I was sixteen, not far off seventeen. Old enough to earn my own living. And I was mature for my age, anyway. Everyone said so. I'd start writing professionally. I'd write for newspapers. Magazines. Online journals. Advertising agencies. Anybody. I'd write, and I'd earn money, and I'd help Aunt Jenny out of her difficulties. I wouldn't care about leaving school. It was boring anyway, except for English, and even in that there was too much of that meaning and message stuff.

We sat in the living room, me in an armchair, the two strangers on the sofa and Aunt Jenny perched on the most uncomfortable chair. She had her hands clenched in her lap, and all at once I felt like crying. But before I could say anything to her, the grey man spoke again. He said, 'Miss Dumerle, as I told Miss Flanagan, my name is Joseph Gilham and I am a solicitor working for the firm of Gilham, Gilham and Elliott, in the city. Some time ago, I received a communication from my client, asking the firm to undertake certain investigations. These have led us to you.'

I was beginning to feel really scared now and that always makes me annoyed. I said, rather rudely, 'I wish you'd stop beating around the bush. Why are you here? What do you want with us?'

Blanche Randal gave another of those tiny, chill smiles. She said, 'You are impulsive, I see, Mademoiselle Rose. And your nose, and the colour of your eyes, and the determined set of your jaw – it's your grandfather, all over. No doubt of that at all.'

I stared at her. 'My grandfather? He's dead. He died in a

nursing home just over three years ago.' Pop had been really nice. He could be a bit tedious sometimes with his stories of growing up in the war and how things had changed since then, but he was cheerful and kind and he was also the only other member of our family left, apart from Aunt Jenny and me. My grandmother had died ages ago, long before Mum and Dad did. I didn't remember her at all.

Blanche Randal waved an exquisitely manicured hand. 'No, not your mother's father. Your father's father.'

'My father never talked about his family,' I said, blankly. 'He only said that he no longer felt a part of it. We were his family, he said, and this country was his home. He never wanted to go back.' I stared at her. 'You're from France, like he was. Are you related to him?'

She raised an eyebrow. 'No. I am your grandfather's secretary.'

At first I didn't take it in. I was just so relieved to know that I wasn't related to the Snow Queen. I could just imagine those icy blue eyes shooting a paralysing shard into my heart. Then I realised what she'd actually said. 'My grandfather's secretary?' I echoed. 'You mean to say, my French grandfather is alive?'

'He is ill,' she said. 'A stroke, a few weeks ago. He has recovered well but there is no telling how long it will last. He wants to see you. We will leave as soon as possible.'

I blinked. 'I beg your pardon?'

'I have spoken to your aunt.' She flicked a glance at Aunt Jenny. 'She has already given her consent. She has told me your passport is up to date.'

'My passport?' I said, looking at Aunt Jenny. That was the first time I'd heard I had a passport at all.

Aunt Jenny turned slightly away from the others. She said, very softly, so that only I might hear, 'Rose, I always felt this might happen one day. I knew you'd have to be ready to go at a moment's notice.'

'What do you mean?' I cried. 'You never said anything to me about this!'

She sighed. 'When he was alive, Philippe never wanted to speak about it. But Annie told me that he'd had a big fight with his father and left France, never to return. She said she hoped one day they might make up. She said you had a right to know both sides of the family but Philippe steadfastly refused to be drawn on any of it. He wouldn't even tell her what part of the country he came from. He said he'd gone 20,000 kilometres away from France to forget all of it, forever.' She hesitated. 'She mentioned once that she had a strong suspicion that Philippe Dumerle was not his real name.'

I could feel the blood draining from my face. This was a side of my parents that I had never known. As a kid I had wondered occasionally about Dad's family and why he never spoke about them, but at eight, you don't really think about those things much. He had just one thing from his old home that he'd given to my mother: a little brooch in the shape of a bird, made of black ebony and gilt. I don't think it was very valuable, but it was very pretty. I knew that part of our name, the 'merle' bit, meant 'blackbird' in French, and I always thought of that little brooch as our symbol. Apart from the blackbird brooch, the only thing left from Dad's old life was his French accent. He spoke good English, but he'd always spoken French with me, from the time I was a baby. Even after my parents died, Aunt Jenny made sure I kept up with my

French by sending me to Alliance Française classes. I didn't mind that, it kind of made me feel closer to Dad. And Aunt Jenny wasn't too bad at French herself, as she'd studied it at university. So I was practically bilingual. My French teacher at school said I was very lucky.

But I didn't feel lucky right now. Everything I thought I knew was crashing down around me. I squeaked, 'What do you mean, Philippe Dumerle was not his real name?'

I'd spoken louder than I'd meant to. Blanche Randal cut in, rather scornfully. 'Philippe Dumerle was indeed not your father's real name. Or rather, not his full name. He was born Philippe Auguste du Merle de la Tour d'Argent.'

'Quite a mouthful,' I said, shock making me flippant. 'Philip Augustus Blackbird of the Silver Tower, that means, doesn't it? Sounds like something out of *Pirates of the Caribbean*! Was Dad descended from pirates?'

Her eyes shot cold blue fire at me, as if I'd committed a sin. 'It is a very proud and ancient name,' she snapped. 'If he'd lived, your father would have inherited the family title and estate.' She saw my incomprehension. 'Your grandfather is Count Valentin du Merle de la Tour d'Argent. He is not only from one of France's most noble families, but he is also very well known in his own right, as a writer.'

'A writer!' That was more surprising to me even than the Count bit. I only had a hazy idea of what Counts with bizarre names were about, outside of the pages of Gothic novels or fairytales.

But a writer, that was different! That was exciting. I had always thought my gift for writing had come out of nowhere. Neither Mum nor Dad liked putting pen to paper or finger to keyboard. Aunt Jenny didn't either, though she liked reading almost as much as Mum had.

15

Dad preferred music, and sport, especially sailing and tennis. He only ever read the business pages of newspapers – he worked in a bank – and the occasional *Guinness Book of Records*. Oh, and my school compositions, very occasionally, when Mum pestered him to. He said that when he was a kid he'd start books and never finish them. I thought it truly weird, because once a book had got its hooks into me, I couldn't stop!

'A most respected writer,' said Blanche Randal, sternly, as if I was disputing it. 'A member of the Académie Française, and winner of several literary prizes.'

'Oh,' I said, not sure what all that meant. 'What does he write about?'

'Napoleon,' she said.

I blinked. 'Napoleon? That general who became Emperor of the French and died on an island after he was defeated in a war with the English?'

'Of course,' she snapped, looking at me as though I was soft in the head. 'Valentin de la Tour – which is the Count's writing name – is one of the foremost experts in France on Napoleon.'

'I think Napoleon had short-man syndrome,' I said. I know it was a stupid thing to say, but I couldn't help it. She was so reverent about her employer, it made me feel like being contradictory.

She glared at me. 'Mademoiselle Rose, I hope you will kindly keep such opinions to yourself in your grandfather's presence.'

'Who said I'll be in his presence?' I demanded truculently. 'He's hardly shown any interest in me till now! I wouldn't know him if I fell over him! I'm sorry he's sick, but it's not my business, not really.'

Her eyes flashed. She clasped her exquisite hands together, hissing, 'It is most certainly your business.' She turned to the solicitor. 'Explain, Mr Gilham.'

'Of course,' said the grey man, hastily pulling some papers out of his briefcase. 'Miss, er, Miss Dumerle – I hope you don't mind my still calling you that, your full name – well, I never was much good at French at school.' He caught a freezing glance from the Snow Queen, and hurried on. 'Miss Dumerle, you must understand that the client I referred to before was your grandfather. A year ago, we received a letter from his solicitor in France, instructing us on his behalf. We were to institute a search for his only grandchild, a child about whom he'd known nothing till then. It seemed that he and his son, your father, had been estranged so completely that he had not known of your birth or your parents' deaths. He only found out by chance.'

'It was when I persuaded the Count at last to buy a computer so I could type and store his manuscripts more efficiently,' broke in Madame Blanche. This time her wintry smile had a tiny touch of thaw about it. 'He agreed also to have the internet installed, so he could more easily communicate with his publishers rather than face constant tiring journeys to Paris or waste a lot of time on the telephone. Surprisingly, the Count rather took to the internet, and spent a good deal of time looking at various things. One day, he entered his son's name on Google. He did not get any hits on the real name, but then tried all kinds of permutations. Eventually, he found a small article relating how a Philippe Dumerle and his wife Annie had died in a horrific car crash, leaving an orphaned child.'

'It was then that his solicitor wrote to me,' Gilham

continued on. 'And I began my investigations, which have culminated in us being here today. When I was 99 per cent sure you were the one the Count was looking for, I immediately contacted Mrs Randal, and she came at once, to make the full identification.' He smiled broadly. 'Miss Dumerle, I am delighted to inform you that there is no doubt at all you are the person we have been looking for.'

'What I want to know,' I said, ignoring him and staring defiantly at Madame Blanche, 'is why I should care anything about it. If Dad didn't want to see his father, he must have had a good reason.'

Aunt Jenny had been silent for a while. Now she said, 'Look, Rosie, sometimes misunderstandings arise between two people which they're too proud, or stubborn, or both, to clear up. These things happen in families, and they don't have to be over really bad things. They can be just over stupid little things which get blown up into bigger things, and then time, instead of healing it, makes it worse. People end up not bothering to fix things up till it's too late.' She paused. 'I know Annie really would have liked it all to be cleared up – and in the future, maybe Philippe would have come round to it. But . . . but he didn't get time, you see.'

I looked at her, and saw her eyes full of tears. It made me feel a little shaky. I know how much Aunt Jenny loves happy endings. I was sure she'd think this was one, in a way.

Madame Blanche was watching us both. She said, quietly, 'I give you my word, Mademoiselle Rose, that your father's and grandfather's estrangement was not about anything sordid or unpleasant. It was, as Miss Flanagan so aptly says, a misunderstanding.'

'Over what?' I said, suspiciously.

18

'I think your grandfather wants to tell you that himself,' she said. Her tone changed now, became less crisp, softer, with a hint of warmth. 'The Count is an extraordinary man, but he is old. He does not want to die with regrets on his soul. He believes he was too harsh with his only son, and that he drove him away. Now he would like to make amends, as far as he is able. Will you grant an old man's heartfelt wish, Mademoiselle?'

'Please just call me Rose,' I said, uncomfortably. 'And, oh, I suppose I could go and visit him – if he really wants to see me – but I don't want to live there forever or anything, I don't want to be made into a Countess and have to live far away from my friends and Aunt Jenny.'

'Who said anything about forever?' said Madame Blanche, smoothly. 'It is just a visit – at the moment. You may change your mind, later, of course.'

'No, I won't,' I said.

'There is another thing,' said Madame Blanche, as cool as I was hot. She nodded towards the solicitor. 'Proceed, Mr Gilham.'

'Miss Dumerle, your grandfather is a rich man,' said the solicitor. He sounded rather happy about it. Perhaps rich men paid fatter fees to solicitors, I thought. 'His fortune and his estate are considerable. Before he knew of your existence, he made a will that distributed his property in certain ways. Now he has discovered you exist, he is most keen that his property be left to you – subject to his approving of you, of course.'

'Excuse me?' I said, faintly.

'Isn't it clear enough?' said the Snow Queen, raising an eyebrow. 'If, when he meets you, Rose, he approves of you, then he will alter his will and you will be a very rich young woman one day. And if he disapproves – well, you will just be where you are now.'

'I like where I am now!' I said fiercely. 'I don't care about the old man or his approval or his Napoleon or his pots of money. He can keep them for all I care!'

Aunt Jenny touched my arm, and drew me away, gently. 'Please, Rose,' she whispered. 'Please don't be silly, sweetheart. I think this was meant to be. And I think your parents would have wanted this for you. This is a real chance for you. If your grandfather likes you, then you'll never have to worry about anything again. No money worries, no scrabbling after a dollar here and a dollar there. It's like winning the lottery, Rosie . . . you can't say no to it!'

I stared at her, suddenly remembering the wish I'd made on the blog. The back of my neck tingled. I said, very quietly, 'Then, Aunt Jenny, if that's true I want to give you some of that money – in fact, a lot of it.'

'Don't be silly, Rosie,' she said, her eyes wide. But her lips trembled and I thought of just how hard it had been for her to make ends meet, month after anxious month, looking after me all those years, making perfect clothes she didn't like for people she didn't care for, just so she could pay the bills. I always knew it had been hard, but at that moment I realised just *how* hard. I said, gently, 'Maybe then you'll be able to open your own design studio, and only make what you want to make, Aunt Jenny.'

'Oh, Rosie,' she said, very low, and two red spots appeared on her pale cheeks. It was obvious that already she could see a picture of just such a thing. 'But what . . . what if the old man doesn't like you?'

'Ah, but what if *I* don't like *him*?' I said lightly, and I

20

turned back to Madame Blanche and Mr Gilham, my head held high.

'Okay, I'll go. But I can't promise to like my grandfather any more than he promises to like me.'

The solicitor's lips twitched. 'I am sure such a promise is not a requirement, is it, Madame?'

'No,' said the Snow Queen, surveying me without expression. 'Nothing was said about liking, only approval, Mademoiselle Rose.'

'Are they different to each other, then?' I said flippantly.

She gave me one of her cold-fire glances. 'Most certainly they are. You will have much to learn in the Chateau du Merle de la Tour d'Argent.'

'He has a chateau?' I squeaked, forgetting my blasé sophistication for an enchanted instant. 'A castle? A *real* castle?'

'Indeed,' said Madame Blanche. 'One of the most beautiful in the region, I believe.'

'Oh.' Then I caught myself up again. 'There's one thing. I'd like my aunt to come with me to France. She needs a holiday,' I went on, as Aunt Jenny tried to protest, 'and I'm sure my grandfather can afford it.'

'I'm sure he can,' said Madame Blanche, without a smile, 'but I'm afraid it's impossible, just at present. The Count insists on seeing you alone at first and getting to know you without third parties in tow. Later, it will be possible.'

'Aunt Jenny isn't a third party,' I said, furiously, 'she's my guardian, and . . .'

'Don't, darling Rose,' said my aunt, touching my arm. She glanced at me with her loving, anxious look, then turned to Madame Blanche. 'Very well, Madame. I do understand the position, but I should like to come and see Rose as soon as it's practical.'

'Of course,' said Blanche, with a curl of her elegant lip. 'You will be sent for as soon as is possible.'

I then had the oddest feeling. It was as if I was suddenly the adult and Aunt Jenny the child. Or rather, as if I was a princess and she was a servant, to be dismissed by the princess' courtiers, or something. It made me feel quite disoriented. I saw the Snow Queen's cold blue glance on my aunt's tired face. I cringed, because I knew what the Randal woman was thinking about my aunt. I thought wildly that she had already sent one of those glass shards into my heart and that from now on I would no longer be the old, warm-hearted, innocent Rose Dumerle, but something else altogether, something I didn't even know yet. An arrogant aristocrat's haughty granddaughter. A famous man's heiress, who lived in a castle in France and had servants and a fortune to call her own. I'd stepped right out of my old, comfortable life and into a perilous realm, straight out of a Gothic kind of fairytale, and I had no idea what would happen next.

The silver shoes

The next couple of days were mad. There were all sorts of things that had to be done. Aunt Jenny and I went to the school on Friday morning to tell them I would be away for at least the next three or four weeks. The teachers were cool about it. After all, it wasn't like I was in Year 12 or anything, but only at the beginning of Year 11. I'd be able to catch up later on. Both Ms Bryce and the French teacher, Madame Reilly, were absolutely delighted that I was going to France. (Mind you, we didn't tell them the full story, only that I was going to see my long-lost French grandfather.) They both thought that I would be inspired by my visit.

'You must keep up with the blog,' said Ms Bryce, with a big smile. 'Think of it as a novel in progress. The whole class will be keeping up with your adventures with bated breath!'

I mumbled something non-committal. There was no way I was going to fall in with *that* plan. I was happy enough to post things now and again on the blog – general sort of stuff. But I certainly didn't want the whole class to pore over my life, as if it was some kind of gossip magazine!

On Friday afternoon I went to the travel agent with

Aunt Jenny and the Snow Queen. We booked my ticket, and that was exciting. I'd only been on small planes before, never big ones, and certainly never in business class! Then we organised travel insurance and all the other sorts of boring things you have to do before you travel overseas. That afternoon, Portia and Alice also came back from their city excursion. They and Maddy, who was now recovered from her bug, came round to see me. We sat in my room and talked and talked. They were over the moon about it all. But I swore them to secrecy about all the gory details. I didn't want the whole world to know everything, not until I was sure what I was walking into, anyway.

'You're just so lucky!' breathed Maddy.

'I knew something like this would happen to you. Wish you could put me in your suitcase!' sighed Portia.

'Careful what you wish for,' Alice said. Her brown eyes shone as she put on a woo-woo kind of voice. 'There's real magic around Rose. You might turn into a flea or something. Or a shoe. Then you'd fit in her suitcase.'

Portia crossly flicked back her blonde hair. 'Why do you always have to be stupid, Alice?'

'And why can't you take a joke, Portia?' snapped Alice.

'Can't you two ever stop fighting?' Maddy said. 'Can't you see Rose is sick of it?'

'Who asked you?' said Alice, fiercely.

I listened to their familiar bickering with a hollow feeling in my stomach. Suddenly, I felt as though I was already separate from my friends. They were so excited by the whole story, thrilled with the revelation of my grandfather's identity, the castle and everything, even the Snow Queen. And to them, it was a story. A romantic story come to life. Something that, yes, had touched me with magic.

They looked at me differently now. I wasn't just their friend. I was someone to whom something exciting and amazing had happened. I was like a character in a book or a film.

Portia and Alice had been my friends since the beginning of high school. And Maddy I'd known since primary school, though we didn't actually become friends till Year 5. But now it was like I was becoming a glamorous stranger to them. And that was a lonely sort of feeling. It meant I couldn't properly explain how I felt. I couldn't tell them how scared I was at the thought of leaving the country with the Snow Queen to face a grandfather I'd never even known existed. I couldn't tell them exactly how everything had shifted so that I no longer felt at ease in my own life. I couldn't explain how I felt bad about Aunt Jenny and the way she'd changed, at least in my eyes. She just never stopped talking about it. She had stars in her eyes. She kept repeating how Mum and Dad would have been so pleased, how it was a dream come true, and I couldn't help thinking, 'Maybe she's just glad to be getting her hands on my money,' just as I looked at my friends' bubbling excitement and thought, 'Maybe they just hope to get something out of it themselves.' Horrid thoughts. Thoughts I had never had before.

On Saturday, the Snow Queen insisted on taking me shopping. 'Your grandfather is a most elegant man, and very particular about how the people around him dress,' she said, coolly surveying my messy collection of clothes – a mixture of op-shop, Aunt Jenny's designs, and Sportsgirl-type things. 'It would be preferable to buy you things in Paris, but we won't have time to stop there. I have seen there are a few chic shops in the city here. We will go and choose you some outfits, just to tide you over till we can go up to Paris and properly see to your wardrobe.'

'I prefer to choose my clothes myself,' I said in a strangled voice. 'Besides, I don't want to put you to any trouble.'

She gave me one of her ice-blue Snow Queen smiles, but her voice was surprisingly warm as she said, 'Don't be so defensive, my dear Rose. It is a pleasure for me to take you. I never had a daughter to go shopping with, only a son. And that's not the same at all.'

That gave me a jolt. Somehow I hadn't thought of the Snow Queen as having a personal life. She saw my expression. 'Being the Count's secretary is not my entire life, you understand. Charlie is the other part of it. '

'Will I meet him?'

'He lives in the castle too, so undoubtedly you will,' she said. Was it my imagination, or was there a hint of sadness in her eyes?

'Is he . . . is he little?' I asked.

'No. He is two and a half years older than you,' she said. The hint of sadness – if it was that – had left her face now. 'He is not the easiest of young men. A good deal like his father was. But you will see, when you meet him.'

There was a tone to her voice which made it quite clear she didn't want to answer any more questions. So I didn't dare ask any, though I was burning with curiosity. In what way was Charlie not 'the easiest of young men'? What had happened to his father? And how would he feel about me, the long-lost heiress, suddenly turning up in the wake of his mother?

But the exchange had changed my feelings a little about Blanche Randal. And it made the shopping expedition much less painful than I'd thought it would be. To be honest, shopping with Blanche was actually fun. The unexpected feeling of being able to just go into a shop and know that money was no object, that I could more or less pick what I wanted – depending, of course, if she approved – was liberating. And she was much more flexible than I could have imagined. I had feared she might try to turn me into a clone of herself, with her middle-aged elegance and classic clothes. But it didn't turn out like that at all.

We started with a visit to the hairdresser. My shoulder-length hair was washed and trimmed into a fashionable layered shape, then highlights were added, so that its ordinary brown glowed with honey-blonde lights, and moved and bounced around my face. Then off we went to the kinds of shops I'd never dreamed of setting foot in before. The kinds of hushed places that have no price tags on anything, and where the salespeople look like *Vogue* models. Blanche Randal swept into these rich people's shops as if they were no more intimidating than a chain-store would be to me, and the haughty salespeople just fell over themselves to help us.

Subtly, she pointed me towards clothes, pointing out colours, patterns and shapes. Under her influence, I tried on things I'd never have looked at on my own. By the end of it, I'd managed to acquire a beautiful black coat (it would still be chilly in France in March), a pair of amazing orange trousers that went with a silk shirt of a very pale green, a cashmere jumper in a deep green, some soft cream leather boots, and a striking skirt in op-art silvers and greens. It went with an off-the-shoulder cream blouse that was totally romantic. I had no idea what the whole thing cost, for Blanche Randal paid discreetly with a platinum credit card. But I knew it must be heaps.

The new clothes and hairstyle really did something to me, as if I'd been touched by a magic wand. It wasn't only that the colours brought out the green in my hazel eyes, and the new gold in my hair. Like I said, I'm not exactly ugly, but now – well, I looked older, sophisticated, and yes, even rather French. I was beginning to feel I could truly believe in my new life, my new wealth, my new identity. It was like looking at a glamorous stranger, and it wasn't a bad feeling. I liked it. Looking into the mirror at the new me, with Blanche Randal smiling her wintry approval, I even felt, for a moment, that I might have more in common with her now than I did with Aunt Jenny, or even my friends . . .

After a late lunch – wasted on me, as I was too excited to do more than swallow a few mouthfuls – we went and bought some other bits and pieces: perfume, a cool new watch, a digital camera, cosmetics and a handbag. We also ordered a very smart matching set of luggage, which would be delivered to the flat first thing Monday morning, in time for me to pack.

I was getting seriously used to this money-is-no-object bit by now. I remembered how Portia and Alice had once entered a competition to win a shopping spree. They'd argued endlessly about what they'd pick if they won. Well, this was like that: except that I really had won, and they hadn't.

I'm not the sort of girl who pores over fashion magazines, though you can't live with Aunt Jenny and not know at least a bit about clothes. Like almost any girl, however, I try to look nice. But when you're poor, you don't waste your time pining over things you can't have, or else you just spend your whole life envious and disappointed. Now, things were totally different. I felt a little light-headed, as if I'd drunk a glass of champagne, as I looked at things displayed in shops and thought, I could buy that – and that and that – if I want. I can just say I want that thing, and hey presto, it's mine.

And that was how I found the silver shoes. It was late in the afternoon, just on closing time. We were walking back to the parking station where Blanche Randal had parked her hire car. To reach the parking station, you had to go through an unfashionable part of town, full of two-dollar shops, cheap CD stores and greasy little cafés. The Snow Queen strode ahead, but I mooched along happily, thinking of the goodies I had bought.

I only noticed the shop because of its name. It was called 'Glamour Puss'. On the sign-board was painted an amateurish picture of a glittery cat with false eyelashes and a green top hat. After the swish shops I'd just visited, it seemed so crass and ridiculous that I couldn't help stopping and looking, just for a bit of a laugh.

The shop window was crowded with all kinds of tatty, odd things. Garish plastic jewellery, huge glittery earrings and feather boas in bright colours shared the display with large pink mirrors, diamante tiaras, elbow-length synthetic satin gloves and Edna Everage-style glasses decorated with rhinestones.

'What are you doing, Rose?' said Blanche Randal, rather impatiently. She walked back to me. Her eyebrows rose as she saw what I was looking at. It was clear she was about to tell me exactly what she thought.

But I didn't care. My eye had suddenly been caught by something, not in the display but just behind it, on a little table in the shop. A soft, gleaming silver, with diamante buckles and small heels, the shoes were so *exactly* like the kind of ones I'd wished for, exactly the kind of shoes my doll Celestine had worn, that for a moment I thought I was in a dream or having deja vu. Then I mumbled, 'I'm sorry, but I must have a proper look at them,' and without waiting to hear what the Snow Queen might say, I pushed open the door and entered the shop.

It was small, crowded and so dusty that I could feel my nose tickling. But the silver shoes gleamed alone on the little table. I went over and picked them up.

They were second-hand *and* they must have been very expensive when they were new. They were made of the most gorgeous leather, and the buckles were beautiful. I slipped one of my own shoes off and was about to try on one of the silver ones when a voice said, 'Like those, do you, dearie?'

I looked up. An old woman was standing there, grinning at me. I hadn't noticed her when I came in because I was so intent on the shoes. She was a tiny little thing, with a long nose, a pointed chin and a bouffant pink rinse. She wore a floaty but slightly grubby pink chiffon dress and lots of caked-on make-up. Her hands were thin and scrawny, covered in costume rings and age spots. For a moment, I could only stare at her. She looked so weird, like a cross between a witch and a stick of fairy floss. Then I found my voice.

'I'd like to try on the shoes,' I said.

'Do that, dearie,' said the old woman. Her eyes were very bright and beady black under the pink and purple eye shadow. 'They've been waiting for the right feet. You know that, don't you, dearie?'

Before I could think of an answer, the door banged and Blanche Randal came in, bringing a sudden cold gust of air from the street with her.

'What on earth are you doing, Rose?' she said, after a startled look at the pink apparition.

'I want to try these on,' I said, and slipped on one of the shoes. It fitted like a glove. Somehow, I'd known it would. I put the other on. It was as though they had been made expressly for me. And they looked great. I looked down at my feet, and remembering the old woman's words, thought suddenly of Dorothy in *The Wizard of Oz*, and the magic silver shoes she gets from the Wicked Witch of the East. For a mad instant, I imagined these might be magic too, and surreptitiously knocked the heels together. But, of course, nothing happened. And I felt like an idiot.

The old woman had been watching me. She smiled as if she knew what I'd been thinking. 'There's magic and magic, dearie. May the silver shoes bring true love to you,' she said, very softly so only I heard.

I blushed but the hair stood up on the back of my neck. 'They'll go really well with the skirt and blouse I bought,' I said, a little too quickly. 'And they're very good quality, even if they're not new.'

'That they are, dearie, that they are,' said the pink lady. 'Most glamorous.'

But Blanche Randal said nothing, just gazed at my feet in the silver shoes, her expression quite blank. I began to feel I'd done something to offend her. Maybe I'd proved to her that, despite the new clothes and hairstyle, I was still just a crass Australian girl not worthy of being a French Count's granddaughter. I was expecting her to tell me off. But she just nodded. 'If you desire them, then of course

31

you must have them.' She turned to the pink lady. 'We will take these, please. Kindly wrap them.'

'A good choice, my dear,' said the pink lady, looking at me and not at Blanche Randal. 'You will not regret it. They are shoes fit for a princess.'

She took the shoes to the counter and began to wrap them, rather clumsily, in tissue paper. She put them in a plastic bag. 'That will be ten dollars, dearie.'

Blanche Randal wrinkled her nose. 'They are very cheap,' she observed, scornfully, and took out her purse.

I don't quite know what came over me then, but suddenly I felt that *I* had to pay for those shoes, myself. I had twenty dollars that Aunt Jenny had given me for lunch – money I hadn't spent, because the Snow Queen had insisted on paying. I stammered, 'No, no, let me, please.'

'Well done, dearie,' said the pink lady, as she took the money I thrust at her. She handed me the shoes. 'Well done. You will not be disappointed.' She beamed, showing a very white false-teeth smile.

'Are you ready now, Rose?' said Blanche Randal. 'Or is there something else here that catches your fancy?'

The scorn in her voice was unmistakable. I blushed. 'No, no, it's all right, thank you.' I turned to the pink lady. 'Thank you,' I said hastily.

'No trouble, no trouble, dearie,' said the pink lady, and her beady black eyes suddenly looked very sharp indeed. 'You enjoy those shoes now.' Her glance flicked over the bags I was carrying, then at the Snow Queen who was waiting impatiently at the door for me. 'Good luck, dearie. I fancy you might need it,' she added.

'I'm . . . I'm perfectly all right,' I said, trying to sound haughty, and failing.

The pink lady gave me a little wink. 'Of course you are, dearie,' she said, and I could feel her smiling eyes on my back as I walked out of the shop with as much dignity as I could muster.

Toads and diamonds

Everyone came to the airport on Tuesday night to see me off: Aunt Jenny, Portia, Alice, Maddy and their families. To my astonishment, even Ms Bryce turned up, with her husband and young children in tow. It's always a bit weird to see teachers out of school. When I was a very little kid, I used to think they stayed at school all night, sort of sat on shelves or something with the lights off until it was morning. Like frogs in a drought, waiting underground for rain to make them croak again. Even afterwards when I understood teachers had lives like normal people it embarrassed me to see them out and about, like in the supermarket or something, because they'd always say hello to you and then you'd feel weird mumbling, 'Hello, Miss,' or 'Hello, Sir,' as if you were still in school. Of course, things were different now but it was sort of strange Ms Bryce turning up like that to see me off. She told Aunt Jenny she wanted to wish me luck, but I think it was more than that. She really must have been taken with what had happened to me. Like my friends, maybe my trip seemed like a novel or a film to her. Honestly, I thought with a funny little pang, you'd think they didn't have a life themselves, all these people. And as I caught the Snow Queen's raised eyebrow, I knew she was thinking the same

34

thing. Which made me feel bad. I didn't want to think like her. But I couldn't think like *them* any more – the people I was leaving behind, I mean – either.

But when it came time for us to go through into the passenger area, where the others couldn't follow, I was gripped by a feeling of such fear and sadness that I thought I'd be sick. I clung to Aunt Jenny and hugged Portia, Alice and Maddy in turn and cried, 'Don't forget me, don't forget me, will you?'

'As if,' said Maddy, fiercely, wiping her eyes with one hand and squeezing my shoulder with the other. 'And don't you go forgetting us,' said Portia, sniffing loudly.

'You'll probably meet some gorgeous French guy and not want to come back,' said Alice, glumly.

'Don't be stupid,' I said. 'I'm coming back in a month. Maybe less.'

'Now, sweetheart,' said Aunt Jenny. Her eyes were very red but her voice was steady as she went on, 'Don't you be putting time limits on things. You have to give it the time it needs.'

The others were all looking a bit awkward. Ms Bryce said, brightly, 'Your aunt's right, Rose. You enjoy yourself. Not everyone gets a chance like this.'

'Very true,' said Aunt Jenny. 'And remember, Rose, if you need me, just call and I'll catch the first plane over.' She said this with one eye on Blanche Randal, who just shrugged.

'Of course, if this is necessary, you will be informed at once. Meanwhile, Rose, they are calling our flight. It is time we were on our way.'

So we hugged all over again and promised to keep in touch, and Ms Bryce shook my hand, as did her husband,

and my friends' parents. The little kids just stared. Then, waving and trying to smile, I followed the Snow Queen as she walked briskly into the passenger area. In an instant, the others disappeared from sight, though I heard my friends shouting, 'Good luck! Good luck!'

'You have very good friends,' said Blanche Randal, calmly, as we lined up for passport checks.

My heart was thumping. My hands felt clammy, and my eyes were sore. I managed to croak, 'Yes.'

'That is a nice thing for a young person,' she said. 'If only it could be so for my son.'

'Mmm,' I said, absently. Right now I wasn't interested in her son or her troubles. My thoughts were out there with my friends and Aunt Jenny, and my stomach was churning with fear of the unknown. I had a desperate desire to make a dash for it back through those doors, and say that I'd changed my mind and wanted nothing to do with all of this, that I just wanted to go home and for things to go on as before.

'You are afraid,' said Blanche Randal, after a silence. I started.

'Don't be,' she went on. 'Your grandfather is a formidable man, it is true. But not an unkind one. And everyone will make you most welcome, I am sure. '

'Everyone?' I said.

'The staff, of course. They have been with the Count many a year, and they are most happy that a young member of the family will be returning to the Chateau, and that it will be saved.'

'What do you mean, saved?'

'From whatever was going to happen to it if no heir had been found, of course,' she replied patiently. 'The Count might have left it to the nation, or to an institution. In any case their jobs would have been lost, and their homes too. They have quarters – and very good ones – in the castle too.'

Panic filled me. 'But I'm only coming for a visit, not forever! They know that, don't they?'

'I shouldn't worry,' said Blanche Randal, as the line shuffled forward. She was smiling faintly. 'You do not need to say anything to them about it. They won't expect it.'

I swallowed. 'I really . . .' I began, but then the passport officer beckoned us forward, and I never had time to finish what I was about to say. Which didn't matter, as it would have made no difference at all to the course I was now set on, for better or for worse.

We boarded the plane on time, and took off smoothly into the light-strung night. I looked out of the window as the plane banked and climbed, watching the sparkling city beneath me. The fear was ebbing, replaced by a growing excitement. Down below, the others would be driving home along the dark streets. They'd be little dots on those long gleaming necklaces of traffic down there. But up here we passengers were bound for lands far away, for other places where everything was done differently and where people spoke different languages and looked at the world with eyes that saw different things. Suddenly I felt light-hearted. There was nothing I could do to change my destiny now. I might as well enjoy it. I had wanted something exciting to happen to me, and now it had, and it was time to stop whingeing and panicking about it and be glad.

I looked across at Blanche Randal. Her eyes were closed. But, as if she felt my stare, she opened them. She smiled a little shakily. 'Well, I am glad we're up safely.'

'What?' I said, stupidly, then realised she must have been scared about taking off. It made her seem more human. In fact, I even felt a little superior. I wasn't scared of flying at all. It was fun. Not, mind you, that I'd had much experience of it, just those little planes Dad had hired occasionally, and then once on a biggish plane going interstate with Aunt Jenny for a holiday.

The seatbelt light went off. Blanche immediately went to the bathroom but I stayed in my seat, leafing through the in-flight magazine to see what movies they were offering. Cool! They had heaps to choose from, and I had my own screen, so I wasn't stuck with someone else's taste. It was really comfortable in business class, and I found myself relaxing very easily. The flight attendants came round with drinks and nibbles and menus for what they called supper, and they were all really polite and attentive. It felt funny at first, as if I was a fraud who had got her expensive seat by some sort of trickery and was going to be found out at any moment. But I got used to it pretty quickly!

I watched movies, read magazines and enjoyed my food. The Snow Queen, however, put her seat back into its sleeping capsule, closed her eyes, and went to sleep. But I was far too excited and didn't feel tired at all.

That didn't last. I was halfway through watching a Marilyn Monroe film, one of Aunt Jenny's favourites that I'd already seen many times, *Gentlemen Prefer Blondes*, when I dropped off. I didn't wake till hours later when the plane was beginning its descent into Dubai.

We didn't stay long there, though I would have liked to, because I'd heard that the city was like something out of *The Arabian Nights*. But we were only there to change planes, and a couple of hours later, we were on our way again.

From Dubai, it was only six hours to Paris, and those hours passed quickly enough, watching movies. I was beginning to feel seriously bug-eyed by the time the pilot announced that if we cared to look through the window we might see the Alps to one side and that very soon we would be flying over France. I could feel my heart racing as I obediently looked through my window and saw, down through a band of cloud, a living green map of the country my father had come from, the country he'd run away from, the country of my ancestors, which I didn't know at all except as images in coffee-table books and lessons in textbooks.

'Beautiful, isn't it? Your father must have missed it a great deal,' said Blanche Randal, hitting, in her uncanny way, on the direction of my thoughts.

'He never said,' I muttered. 'He seemed very happy in Australia.'

'At the end of the world.' She said it in French: *'Au bout du monde.'*

'Who says?' I cried, hotly, in the same language. 'Only according to Europeans. But where we stand, it's you who are at the end of the world.'

'As you wish,' she said, her mouth twitching. 'But it was at the other end of the world from his family and his home, anyway. His birth family,' she hurried on, seeing my look. A pause, then she said, 'I am glad you speak such good French. Things will be easy for you – if you try not to be so defensive, Rose. '

I muttered something cross. She laughed softly. 'You are a complicated girl. You speak sometimes toads and

39

sometimes diamonds,' she said, and for a moment I literally had no idea what she was talking about. And then I suddenly remembered the fairytale called *Toads and Diamonds*. I'd read it when I was a kid. There's this fairy disguised as a poor old woman who tests two sisters by asking for water from a well. The older sister is beautiful but bad-tempered and haughty. She's the favourite of her mother. The younger sister is also beautiful but gentle and kind, and she gets treated like a servant. Anyway, the younger sister gives a drink to the old lady and in reward is given a gift – every time she speaks, diamonds and flowers come out of her mouth. But the mean older sister refuses to give the old lady a drink and so she gets punished by having toads and snakes coming out of her mouth every time she speaks.

I didn't like that story much. It made me feel sick. Just the thought of that gunk coming up in your throat. Especially toads and snakes of course but even diamonds and flowers might be awfully choky and might encourage crooks to kidnap you and force you to speak to get more gems out. I mean, that fairy was a crazy old cow. She really didn't think about what she was doing. Or she didn't care. Fairies can be like that in stories.

I was going to say something smart back to Blanche but she had turned away. The plane was beginning its descent again and she was clearly not at ease. So I stewed a bit on what she'd said – was she paying me a compliment, or insulting me, or perhaps both, all at once, and if she saw me as both of those sisters, what did it make *her*? The crazy fairy or something? Blanche Randal's eyes were tight shut again and her knuckles were pale as she clenched her hands on the armrest of her seat. I felt superior again, glorious in my fearlessness and my youth as we came down closer, and now I could see the city of Paris spread under me. I gave a little squeak of excitement as I caught sight of the Eiffel Tower, and then the plane turned sharply away and we were flying low over grey suburbs, landing with thrilling speed on the runway of Charles de Gaulle International Airport.

But the journey wasn't over for us just yet. We still had another leg of the journey to go. Or two, to be precise. A smaller plane to the southern city of Toulouse, where the Snow Queen had told me my grandfather's chauffeur would be waiting for us. The Chateau du Merle de la Tour d'Argent was a short way out of the small city of Albi, which was about seventy-five kilometres from Toulouse and had no airport of its own.

By the time we stumbled out of the Toulouse plane, I was really beginning to feel the jet-lag tiredness lapping at me like a tide that felt as if it was going to get higher and higher till it drowned me. All around, people were only speaking in French. The sky looked different and the air smelled different too. But I could hardly take it in. My mind was fogged up and my throat was thick and I felt as though I was in a dream. Numbly, I followed Blanche as, seemingly reinvigorated by being back on familiar soil, she collected our luggage, placed it on a trolley and strode purposefully towards the place where we were to meet the chauffeur.

And there he was, reading his newspaper, waiting for us. He was a big man, with a cheerful weatherbeaten face, and a bald head under the peaked cap he wore. It wasn't exactly a chauffeur's cap, like in the movies, and he wasn't wearing an actual uniform. But he was smartly dressed, in navy blue, and the cap was also navy blue, with a white peak. It made him look vaguely like a sailor. He smiled at me and said, 'Good morning, and welcome to France, Mademoiselle. I am Louis Vallon, your grandfather's driver.' He extended a hand, and I shook it and said, rather uncertainly, 'Good morning, Monsieur Vallon, and thank you.'

He beamed. 'Oh, you speak such good French, Mademoiselle! Please, call me Louis. That's what the Count calls me. That's what I'd rather be called, by the family.'

'Er . . . yes, Louis,' I said, blushing a little. 'But then, please call me Rose. I'm not used to being called Mademoiselle.'

'As you wish,' he said, smiling. 'Rose is a pretty name. A family name. The Count's mother was called Rose. Rose Marie.'

That was something else I hadn't known. My father had never said I'd been called after anyone. He'd certainly never spoken of his grandmother. But then, he'd barely spoken of his family at all, certainly not to me.

'They say she was a very sweet lady,' went on Louis. 'I never met her, of course, because . . .'

Blanche Randal's voice was sharp. 'There'll be time enough for gossip later, Louis. Rose is very tired.'

'Of course, forgive me,' he said, not sounding crushed at all. 'You will be able to sleep a little on the way, Mademoiselle . . . er, Rose. The car is very comfortable.'

'Thank you,' I murmured, and staggered after them as they walked out of the terminal towards a stately dark blue Mercedes some distance away in the car park. Wow, I thought woozily. Looks a bit better than Aunt Jenny's grotty Corolla, that's for sure. And I suddenly felt like giggling, it all seemed too absurd. Someone was going to pinch me soon and then I'd wake up and find it had all been a dream, like in the stories I used to write when I was a kid and I couldn't think of a proper ending.

Blackbird castle

'Wake up, Rose. We're almost there.' The words reached down through my uneasy sleep, forcing my eyes open. Hell, I felt bad. Limbs heavy, tongue syrupy in my mouth, eyes crusted. I sat up, and looked dazedly out of the car window.

We were coming into the main street of a small village. It was unusual: sort of terraced, with the left side of the street being on a higher part than the right, some grass in the middle, and a small set of stone steps linking the two halves. There were small trees growing along the grassy middle, old-fashioned street lamps, and the houses lining both sides of the street were pretty. All of them were in a similar kind of style: the walls partly ochre-coloured brick, partly whitewashed, with shutters and window boxes and ripple-tile roofs.

'The houses are mostly eighteenth century, though there are a few much older than that,' said Blanche. 'At the time, the Count's ancestor had a lot of the medieval hovels pulled down. He was a reformer, and decided the houses were unhealthy and unsightly.'

'What did the village people think of him pulling down their houses?' I asked.

She shrugged. 'I don't suppose they minded. Besides, he

also pulled down the old castle at the same time and had it rebuilt. In any case, there was no trouble here during the Revolution.' She waved a hand. 'There's a modern sub-division down on the outskirts of the village in the other direction, but this part of the village has been pretty much unchanged for two hundred years. Over there you can see the well. People still use it if there's a drought. Down the end there on the right is the church. And on the left . . .' She smiled. 'Well, you can see for yourself.'

Above the roofs of the last couple of houses on the left side of the street rose a tall pointy tower roofed in a silver-grey slate that shimmered in the rather weak March sun. *La Tour d'Argent*, I whispered to myself, overawed. The Silver Tower . . .

Now we were rolling past the last village house, past a high stone wall over which I could glimpse tall trees and the outline of a large building, though the tower had temporarily disappeared from sight. My pulse raced like crazy. I no longer felt tired. I gripped the side of my seat. This wasn't a dream any more. It was real. Real . . .

We came to a tall wrought-iron gate that was painted a beautiful blue-grey. Through the bars of the gate, I saw the Chateau du Merle de la Tour d'Argent properly for the first time. I could not help uttering a gasp.

'Please, I want to take a photo,' I gabbled, opening the car door before Louis Vallon had time to open the gate. 'I want to have a record of my very first sight of the castle.'

I scrambled out before they could reply, and walked up to the gate. For an instant, I could only hold the bars of the gate and stare. The Chateau, which was set in lovely park-like grounds, was a large square building three storeys high, built of pinkish red brick, with red-and-white

45

decorations around the many windows, and tall French windows leading on to a lovely terrace on the bottom floor. At two corners of the building rose two graceful towers, the main part of which was made of the same pinkish brick, the roof of that silvery slate I'd seen earlier. The steep roof of the main building, unlike that of the village houses, was tiled in the same slate, and between it and the top floor were decorations in stone. The whole effect was charming and light and inviting, not at all like the grim grey fortress I'd half-feared.

At that moment, a plump little bird with glossy black feathers suddenly flew out of the bushes beyond the gate, and landed on the perimeter wall not far from me. It perched there, surveying me for an instant, its gold-ringed black eyes focused on my face. Then it opened its beak, gave a tuneful little whistle, rose up in the air, and flew away.

'See, the blackbird himself welcomes you,' came Louis Vallon's kind voice from behind me. 'It is a good sign, Mademoiselle.'

I murmured something, took my photo and got back into the car, my head spinning, my legs a little weak. And it wasn't because of the blackbird, or what Louis had said. It was because I knew in that instant that I loved the Chateau. Loved it at first sight, sharply, like a beat in the blood, as if I'd always known it. *As if I was coming home, after a long time away*. And that was kind of scary. ❧

As we drew up to the castle, I saw that there was a small group of people solemnly waiting for us on the terrace. All at once, I felt horribly shy. I'd seen this kind of scene in movies before, but never dreamed it would be for me. I felt like running away. But there was no escape. The driver opened the door for me and Blanche, and we stepped out. I hoped she might tell me what to do, but she didn't. She simply gestured at me to walk in front of her.

It was nerve-racking walking up to the terrace under the scrutiny of those many pairs of eyes. I'm still not sure how I did it without tripping over and doing something stupid. I knew they were sizing me up, wondering if the Australian granddaughter was up to much. I was glad I had changed into my beautiful new trousers, shirt and jumper at Paris airport. At least my clothes were reasonable, even if my face was puffy and my eyes red with jet-lag. I reached the line of expectant faces and said, in a rather strangled sort of voice, 'Bonjour.'

'Bonjour, Mademoiselle,' came the echo.

I glanced quickly at the assembled group. There were six of them, five women and a man. The women wore a kind of sleeveless blue coverall over their clothes, while the man was dressed in a stained bib-and-brace overall and woollen jacket, a cap pushed back on his head. I stood there like a fool till Blanche came to my rescue.

'Allow me to introduce you, Rose,' she said, smoothly. 'This is Madame Vallon – she's the cook. And Louis' wife. And this is her daughter and assistant, Samantha.'

It took me a while to work out her name was 'Samantha', as the Snow Queen pronounced the name in the French manner, 'Sarmanta'. Not a very French name, I thought. But I learned later that English-type names were quite fashionable in France now. Seemed strange when they couldn't pronounce them properly, especially anything with 'th' in it.

Madame Vallon was a small, round sort of lady, exactly

what a cook should look like. But her dark eyes weren't jolly. They were sharp and watchful. She smiled at me but the smile didn't quite reach her eyes. 'Welcome to Chateau du Merle. We hope you'll be very happy here.'

Samantha seemed to be in her late twenties. She looked a lot like her father, the chauffeur. Her own smile was broad and genuine as she said, 'We certainly do. If there is any special recipe you would like us to make, please tell us.'

'Thank you, ' I murmured, overwhelmed.

'And this is Madame Collot, she's the housekeeper,' said the Snow Queen, passing on to the next person in the line, a tall thin woman with a sad-spaniel sort of face. She nodded regally at me. 'Madame Collot lives in the castle, like the Vallons. She is ably assisted by Simone Marais and Therese Lacour, who live in the village.' The other two women murmured greetings.

Blanche passed on to the bib-and-brace man. 'This is Pierre Daudy. He's our gardener. He has help a couple of times a week from lads in the village.'

Daudy gave a faint smile. 'When they feel like it, that is,' he said. He had big, knotty hands and a thick neck and looked as strong as a bull. 'Welcome, Mademoiselle Rose. It's good to see another young face in the place.' At least, I think that's what he said. He had quite a strong southern accent and it made some of his words difficult to understand.

'Quite,' said Blanche coolly. She paused, then addressed Madame Vallon. 'Is my son at home?'

'I believe he went on the bus to Albi this morning, Madame Randal. He will be back this evening.'

'I see. Very well. And the Count? How is he?'

The cook smiled. 'Oh, he is much better, Madame

Randal. He is even speaking quite clearly. The doctor said his recovery has been remarkable. We believe that's because he has had a new heart put into him, knowing of Mademoiselle's arrival.'

'He is waiting for you in the library,' said the house-keeper. 'The nurse is with him.'

'Excellent.' The Snow Queen's eyes flicked over their heads, towards the door. 'Then you will have to excuse us. Good day to you all.'

I followed her in through the French doors, with their eyes on my back. I thought, dazedly, my grandfather must indeed have heaps of money, if he can afford to pay the wages of all these people! It wasn't like the old days, either, when you could pay people peanuts and house them in grotty attics. Nowadays you had to do things properly. It must cost a packet to look after a place like this.

Inside, the castle was just as lovely as out. The rooms were big and airy, the walls partly panelled in light-coloured wood and partly plastered. The ceilings were painted with decorations of flowers and birds, there were beautiful rugs on the polished wooden floors and paint-ings everywhere. The furniture was also very elegant, mostly antiques. The windows were open and there were flowers on some of the tables and a nice smell everywhere, like the beginning of spring. There was a welcoming air to the whole place that made my spirits rise. Whatever happened, I'd always remember this. The castle itself didn't reject me. In fact, it drew me to it.

Aunt Jenny is fond of saying that all houses have a spirit. Some of them are harsh and unpleasant, others soft and welcoming. Some make you feel like an interloper, others fold you into their embrace at once, others still are indifferent or hostile. Some are like evil enchanters, others like good fairies. Blackbird Castle, as I called it in my mind, was a good-fairy house . . . one that made you feel happy, just by being in it.

We turned down a passage and stopped in front of a heavy oak door. Blanche looked at me. 'It is good that Monsieur le Comte is better,' she said, 'and I am sure he will be delighted to see you. But you must understand he is likely to get tired rather quickly. Do not be offended if you are dismissed sooner than you might expect.'

'I . . . I understand,' I faltered.

'Very well.' She knocked. Loudly, she said, 'Monsieur le Comte, it is Blanche Randal, bringing you Mademoiselle Rose.'

There was silence for an instant – an instant that seemed to go on forever, as my heart bumped madly against my ribs – and then the door opened. A middle-aged woman in nurse's uniform stood on the threshold. She looked at us, unsmiling. 'The Count is expecting you. Come in.'

At first, all I saw was the room. It was exactly the sort of castle library you read about in books, or see in films. It was large but somehow cosy, lined with ceiling-high shelves and enormous bookcases, and all of them filled with books. Books old and new, books of all shapes and sizes, in all kinds of glowing bindings. There were comfortable-looking armchairs, a big desk, a low table covered with magazines, a big Persian rug in the middle of the floor, floor-length velvet curtains, and a fireplace. But though it looked all so very traditional, there were signs of modern times, too: the fireplace held a smart glass-doored wood-heater and in the centre of the desk was a laptop computer.

I took all this in at a glance. But then I saw *him*. He was sitting in an armchair with his back to the door, almost hidden by the chair's large frame. I gulped. Now was the moment of truth . . . He'd take one look at me and tell me to get lost, say it had all been a mistake, that I was to have nothing to do with him, with his family, with this place.

He spoke. His voice was deep and pleasant. 'Nurse, you may leave us. Blanche, bring the child where I can see her.'

No sooner said than done.

'Monsieur le Comte, this is your granddaughter, Rose.'

I stared at him. I had imagined him as some sort of fallen giant but in fact he was small, smaller than my father had been. His hands were delicate, his frame rather thin. He was dressed in a soft shirt and trousers with a dark-green velvet dressing-gown over them, and green leather slippers on his feet. But his vigorous white hair, the determined set of his jaw and the hard stare of his hazel eyes belied any suggestion of weakness. He held my gaze. 'Are you satisfied with what you see, child?' His intonation was crisp and clear. You'd never have known he'd suffered a stroke less than a month ago.

'I'm . . . I'm sorry,' I stammered. 'I didn't mean to stare.'

'And why shouldn't you stare? You've never seen me before. I intend to stare at you too,' he retorted, with a little twitching of the lips. 'Hmm. You look a little like Philippe, but also like your mother, I'd imagine. And a little like me, too. And you have my mother's name. Philippe always was very fond of his grandmother . . .' A pause. 'Well, child, I am pleased you are here. I hope your voyage was not too tiring.'

'Oh, no, thank you, it was –' I began, but he cut me off.

'I have never been to Australia, myself, never could

stand the idea of all that time on the plane. And there was no reason to. He had made that quite clear, your father. He wanted nothing more to do with me. What do you think of that, eh, child?'

I shot an anguished glance at Blanche Randal, who looked back expressionlessly. There would be no help there. I said, 'I – I don't know, Monsieur le –'

His eyes flashed. 'What's this Monsieur business? I am your grandfather. You will call me Grand-père.'

'Yes, Grand-père,' I murmured.

'You seem to speak and understand French very well,' he remarked. 'I am glad. I speak reasonable English but I don't like to do so. English is a blunt instrument. It does not have the subtleties of French.'

'Oh, but I don't –' I began, but he cut me off again. 'I am a writer. Language to me is the breath of life.'

'I – I've heard about your books,' I said, timidly. 'I should very much like to read them.'

He waved a hand around the bookshelves. 'You will find them here and there. Read them if you wish. Though I doubt Napoleon is to the taste of your generation.'

'Oh, no, I think it's really interesting, with the battles and the Empress Josephine and all that,' I floundered, catching the Snow Queen's amused eye at that moment and knowing that she was remembering my earlier smart-arse comment about Napoleon. No prizes for knowing I wouldn't repeat that here, in front of the formidable small man who was my grandfather! I longed to tell him I wanted to be a writer myself, but was too shy to do so just yet. Or too scared.

He smiled for the first time. 'Did you know that one of our ancestors was an officer in Napoleon's army? That was why I became interested in the first place. But I soon got beyond him. What a time! What men! I should have liked to have been alive then, instead of our dull, safe times.' He sighed, and went on in a different tone, 'But we have met each other, and that is enough for now. Blanche, kindly take my granddaughter to her room.'

'Very well, Monsieur le Comte.'

'And then come back to see me please, Blanche. There is urgent business to attend too, if you are not too tired.'

'No, Monsieur le Comte. I mean, yes.'

The Snow Queen was flustered, I thought, amused. I hadn't thought anyone could fluster that icy poise. But there you go, she'd proved she was human once more. 'Grand-père,' I said, as she turned to go, 'I – I am most glad to have met you. And I hope we can talk further another time?'

'I certainly intend it, Rose,' he said, closing his eyes. And as I went out behind the Snow Queen, I thought, that's the first time he actually said my name, and not just 'you' or 'child' or 'granddaughter'. Did that mean anything? I had no real idea, but I thought it might.

Be bold, be bold,
but not too bold

My room was gorgeous. It was a sunny room on the first floor, with a tall double window opening onto a view over a beautiful walled garden full of early spring flowers: crocuses and tulips of all colours. The walls were papered in a pretty yellow, white and blue flowery pattern, and the curtains were pale blue. The bed was a great big four-poster, its blue curtains drawn back. There were lots of comfortable-looking pillows on the bed, and a big fluffy pale yellow quilt, and a soft bedside rug. There was also a bedside table, and a beautiful old desk on which were piled two or three large books. I went over to look at them, and saw they were leather-bound photograph albums. There was a note on the top one. It was written in a rather shaky hand. 'I thought you might like to look at these to know your family a little better. V. D. M. L. T.'

'Valentin du Merle de la Tour,' said Blanche, seeing my puzzlement. 'Your grandfather.'

'Oh.'

'The wardrobe's this way,' said the Snow Queen, going to a door at the end of the room and opening it. I followed obediently. Beyond was a passageway lined on either side with hanging space, drawers and shelves. My suitcase was already there. 'You can put all your clothes in here,' she went on. 'There's a small dressing-room just beyond the wardrobe. You can dress in there if you like, or in your room. The dressing-room is not heated in the spring and summer, however, so it may be a little cold in there right now.'

'Oh,' I said, gobsmacked by the idea of having a dressing-room of my own.

'You will have all the afternoon to rest,' she said. 'Dinner will be at seven. When you hear the bell, come down at once. The Count does not like to be kept waiting.'

'And of course everyone obeys him,' I said. 'He's quite a guy, isn't he?'

Two red spots appeared on her porcelain cheeks. Her eyes glittered icily. 'The Count is a man such as they no longer make,' she snapped. 'You are fortunate to have him as a grandfather, just as I am fortunate to have him as an employer.'

'I didn't mean anything against him,' I cried. 'It's just that obviously he's used to being obeyed and I thought it's funny that –'

'There is nothing funny in it,' she hissed. 'You don't understand, Rose. It's not a question of obeying. It's a question of respect.'

'But I don't not respect him, it's just that I . . .'

She ignored my feeble attempt to defend myself, and changed the subject abruptly. 'Now, you may wish to explore the castle. You are welcome, of course, to do so. I would especially recommend the portrait gallery to you. It is on this floor, just two doors down from this room. But please be aware that though the Count has had much of the castle restored these last few years, not all the rooms are safe, especially on the next floor and in the attics. Floors giving way but also some faulty old-fashioned wiring. We've had to close some of them, so don't try to get in. They are locked for a good, practical reason.'

'Oh,' I said, not knowing what else to say.

She gave a wintry smile. 'Also, there's one more thing you must understand. The grounds are perfectly safe and very pleasant to wander in. I am sure you will enjoy them. But not far from the back garden are the woods. They are safe if you know what you're doing. But not if you don't. They're much denser and more difficult than they look, and many people have got lost there. So, if you wish to go for a walk in the woods, please inform me, and I will arrange for Louis to go with you. He knows the woods very well. I hope you understand.'

'It's okay,' I said, lightly, 'I doubt I'll want to do that. I've never liked bushwalking.' But my skin was prickling with unease. I suddenly remembered a line in a rather spooky old story called *Mr Fox*, which is like a version of *Blue-beard*: 'Be bold, be bold, but not too bold', it goes. It was both a challenge and a warning. What was the Snow Queen up to, telling me these things? Hopefully there was nothing sinister in it. She was just being the Snow Queen, freezing me out, warning me I was an interloper she didn't approve of, flustering me with her much greater knowledge of this place. What a fool I'd been, thinking she was warming towards me, thinking I could be more friendly with her, thinking she was becoming more human. Would she tell my grandfather what I'd said? I didn't think so. She seemed to treat him like some sort of god whose word was law. But she wouldn't forget it, either. She'd make me feel ashamed I'd spoken like that. Well, stuff her. I'd do what I like. And I'd make up my own mind about things, including my grandfather.

'If you don't mind,' I said, in a voice that tried to be haughty but only ended up sounding squeaky, 'I think I'd like to be alone for a bit.'

She gave me another of her looks. 'Very well. I understand. Is there anything else I can do? Would you like some refreshment sent up, for instance?'

'It's okay,' I said. 'I'll – I think I might go down to the kitchen, later, have a look. And I'd like to call Aunt Jenny, later, when it'll be morning in Australia. Is that okay?'

'But of course,' she said, raising her eyebrows. 'This is your family home. Do as you wish.'

'Thank you,' I said, rather ironically. But she either didn't get the irony, or ignored it.

'I will leave you now. I will be busy with the Count's business for some time. But if you need me, I shall –'

'Thanks, I'm sure I'll be fine,' I said hurriedly. I heaved an angry sigh of relief when at last she left, closing the door softly behind her. I raged to myself for a bit. Who did she think she was, the queen of the castle, or something? She was only my grandfather's secretary, after all. What gave her the right to make me feel two millimetres tall? And those stupid warnings of hers, she must know they would spook me. She'd done it on purpose. What a cow. What a truly nasty cow.

Still smarting, I gazed out of the window at the garden below. Little by little, its quiet beauty calmed me. Why was I letting myself get all steamed up over a person like that? She wasn't worth it. She didn't have anything to do with me, not really. She wasn't a part of the family. Thank goodness for that. And my grandfather – well, he might be treated like some sort of god or king or whatever by her and maybe the others, but he wouldn't be by me. I'd be myself with him and that was that. He could like it or lump it.

I had an idea, though, that he might not be like her. He might not think he was such a legend as she made out. After all, he'd been quite modest about those books of his, hadn't he? I'd decided that I would at least have a look inside them. See what his style was like and all that. Napoleon didn't interest me, not really, but it could have been worse. He could have written about scientific subjects, or politics, or economics or messages and meanings in literature or something like that. And then I'd have had to struggle through pages of gobbledegook, in French what's more, and pretend I liked it. At least with Napoleon you had a bit of a story. Then after I'd read a bit of his stuff, I might be able to tell him what I dreamed of doing. Maybe it would make a bond between us that was more than just this family tie I hadn't even known existed till a few days ago.

I glanced over at the albums. I should have a look at those. It was nice of him to have thought of it. There would be a whole lot of people in there who I didn't know, but maybe there'd be photos of Dad when he was little. And of his mother. I hadn't heard any mention of her at all. Not even from Dad himself. The only person he'd mentioned was his father. Grand-père. The Count. And then only in a negative sort of way. But what about Grand-père's wife, Dad's mother?

I opened the first album. It had thick black pages, each separated by a filmy sheet, with the photographs mounted on the black pages. But the first page was cream, and on it was painted a coat of arms featuring a blackbird against a silver tower, with a motto above and below it: *Preux chasseur, grand honneur*. I puzzled over that for a moment. *Chasseur* was a hunter. *Honneur* was honour, of course, and *grand* was big, or great. And *preux*? I'd only seen that word once. It was an old-fashioned word. I thought it meant something like 'brave' or 'bold'. I'd look it up in the dictionary to be sure, but I thought that perhaps our family motto said something like, 'Only a bold hunter can earn great honour.' In other words, no gain without risk. It made me laugh aloud. Be bold, be bold, and always bold! And never take no for an answer! I rather liked it, I thought, as I turned the page.

I'd been afraid that I wouldn't know who everyone was. But I need not have worried. Everything was clearly labelled and dated, in neat silver script. I soon realised that I was looking at an album that started in 1966, the year before my father's birth.

The very first photograph was of a wedding party outside a church. I didn't even have to read the neat silver label underneath to know it was the wedding of my grandparents. *Valentin du Merle de la Tour d'Argent et Caroline de la Motte, le 4 aout, 1966, Eglise Saint Martin du Merle.* So they'd married on the 4th of August 1966 in the church of Saint Martin du Merle. That must be the village church. I recognised its distinctive open belltower. Saint Martin du Merle was also the name of the village. I peered at the bridal couple. You could easily tell it was him, he hadn't changed a great deal. He was slim rather than thin, and his hair was jet black instead of snowy white. But the gaze at the camera was the same, and the elegance was the same. He was not tall, but there was a power and a wiry strength to him that made him seem a much bigger man than he really was. The young woman beside him – Caroline de la

Motte, my grandmother – was quite different. She was also quite small but fair rather than dark, and with that kind of soft prettiness that looks to me like it's been moulded of plasticine. The sort that doesn't have much character to it. She wasn't gazing at the camera, but at him, in an adoring sort of way. But he wasn't looking at her at all, just straight ahead.

Poor thing, I thought. You're in love with him, but he isn't with you. Silly, I know – I mean, what did I know about it, really? But that was just the feeling it gave me. I looked at the parents of the couple, standing on either side of them. My grandfather's father had the same build as his son, and his mother had similar eyes, but a different look in them – warm and laughing. This was Rose, too, I reminded myself. My namesake, my great-grandmother. I would have liked her, I thought. But my grandmother's parents I wasn't so sure of. They looked stiff, stern, unbending, and not particularly happy. Poor Caroline!

I turned the page. More wedding photographs. Several were of the reception, which had obviously been held outside. In the castle grounds, most likely. There were lots of people sitting at long tables, roses in bloom everywhere, and a good time being had by all, except, notably, Caroline's parents, who never seemed to be caught smiling. I lingered over one photo, of Valentin dancing with one of the guests, a gorgeous-looking girl with a dark gypsy sort of beauty. She was dressed in an off-the shoulder frilly blouse with a full red skirt and high-heeled sandals. It was a beautiful picture – the photographer had really caught the moment, and the couple's faces – but there was something unsettling about it. I looked at the unusually terse label underneath, *V et R*. I thought, Well, if it was me, I wouldn't have wanted to stick in a picture of my new husband dancing with some other woman at my wedding! But she didn't write her name down so she must not have liked her too much. I looked through the next lot of wedding photos, but there was no more R, whoever she was. And I soon forgot about her as I turned the next page and discovered the first photos of my father as a baby.

He'd been born only six months after their wedding, I discovered. So Caroline had been three months pregnant when they married. In those days that probably meant he *had* to marry her. The whole thing might be the explanation for Caroline's parents' sour faces.

But then there was Dad. And there were the two of them, smiling over the top of his little blond head. Real smiles. In one of the pictures, they were holding each other close, the baby between them, the cheerful label reading, *Notre petite famille*, Our little family. Whatever had happened before, they were happy then. They had found something to really unite them. And perhaps her parents had even stopped being sour too. After all, they were grandparents now. And everything was all right. No more scandal.

The pages went on. There was Dad as a toddler, and as a bright little boy, playing with bucket and spade at the seaside. There was his grandmother Rose, holding him up high for the camera, both of them laughing. There was his mother Caroline, holding his hand for his first day at school, the caption underneath reading, *Philippe va à l'école*, Philippe goes to school. And there was his father, Valentin, swinging him round and round, both of them looking as though they were having a great time. Tears pricked at my eyes. He'd been a loved child. You could see that so easily. It was so good to see. And yet so puzzling. What had happened?

I took up the next album, hoping there'd be more photos of Dad and his parents that might give me a clue. But it was from older times. Valentin as a baby, Valentin as a child, Valentin as a young man. Each photo or group of photos was clearly labelled in the same neat hand. I was sure it was Caroline's. It was odd. The albums seemed to express something of her personality and her feelings. I was beginning to feel that she was there, somehow, that her spirit was rising up from those black pages. Not in a spooky kind of way, you understand, but rather real. Like reading people's letters, or their diaries. You got a sense of what she was like, and what she loved.

Valentin, above all. All those photos, lovingly captioned. The stiff baby photos, the solemn child ones, the dashing young man ones. At one stage, he must have been in the Army, for there he was, in a very smart uniform. He was too young to have fought in the Second World War, perhaps it had been in another one, like in Algeria or Vietnam, where French forces had fought in the 1950s and '60s. Or perhaps he'd just been in the Army, not in a war at all. Anyway, he looked good in his uniform. Then there were ones of him out on the town, dressed up in '50s outfits, or posing next to cars in front of the castle. There were often girls posing beside him. They were conscientiously remembered, each not with a first name but a 'Mlle' – a 'Miss' – and a family name. Valentin et Mlle L'Heritier, Valentin et Mlle de Galtier, Valentin et Mlle Marinetti, Valentin et Mlle St Jean-Dessaix, and so on and on. Seemed like Grand-père had been quite a playboy. I remembered the 'R' in the other album, and looked for her, but she was nowhere to be found. Instead, almost at the end of the album, Caroline appeared, looking rather beautiful, in a posed photo of her in a ball gown. It must have been a fancy dress ball because she was holding a mask in one hand, and the dress was a kind of foamy, lacy thing, with a big crinoline skirt. Her hair was done up in golden ringlets too, decorated with blue ribbons. The old-fashioned look suited her, made her look much more at ease than the bold clothes of the 1950s.

Perhaps it was at that ball she had met him? I couldn't be sure because she hadn't written her usual caption underneath, but because the next one showed them together, I assumed it must be so. She looked happy in those first few photos, happy and pretty and laughing. Poor thing, I thought, and my heart felt heavy though I wasn't sure quite why it should. After all, I had no real idea what had happened in their lives, had I? I didn't even know when she'd died, in fact, or how, or why Dad had never mentioned her.

I turned to the third, and last, album. That was even older: sepia photographs of my great-grandparents as children. One I especially liked, of my great-grandmother Rose as a little girl. There were photos too of my great-great-grandparents, back in the nineteenth century, posing in that stiff old-fashioned way. I'd read once that those old cameras took ages to set up and you had to sit there like a statue staring at it so that hardly anyone ended up smiling. There were one or two photos even further back, back to about the 1860s, and then nothing more.

The other ancestors must be in the portrait gallery the Snow Queen had 'recommended' to me, I thought, closing the album. Well, I might as well go and have a look at them, seeing as I was on a family history roll. And I could explore at the same time.

It was a long, narrow wood-panelled room, rather dim, because it had only one small window, high up on the wall. I had to turn the light on to see anything much at all. A strange place to stick your ancestors in, I thought, especially when you came from a proud noble family like Grand-père's. Still, perhaps there was no space anywhere else for such large paintings, or maybe he thought they would overwhelm any other room. I walked up and down the lines of paintings – one on either wall – checking out these people who had contributed to my genes. Some of them looked like the kind of people you might want to meet, others like the sort you'd want to avoid. That guy in the velvet cap with the laughing eyes, for instance, he wasn't half-bad. And that girl in the red dress with the determined chin, she looked like someone with spirit. But I'd have run a mile from that man in the ridiculous eighteenth-century wig and the superior sneer on his face. And that awful-looking woman with the turned-down mouth – she looked like a dragon.

It wasn't only distant ancestors who were there, however. There were also oil paintings of people I'd seen in the photos. There were the great-greats. And there, the great-grandparents, my namesake looking very pretty in a caramel-coloured velvet dress. I gave an exclamation, and peered closer. Yes! I thought it was! She was wearing my blackbird brooch – the one Dad had given me – pinned on the shoulder of the dress. It must have been hers originally.

I found the painting of my grandparents in the darkest corner. It was different to the others. It was a family portrait – my grandmother, in a rather ugly beige suit, sitting on one of those carved chairs I'd seen downstairs, holding my father, a solemn toddler in a sailor suit, on her lap. My grandfather stood behind them, dressed up in his uniform, looking rather stuffy. None of them, in fact, looked relaxed. Perhaps the painter had made them hang around for too long. Or maybe they did not like his style. He had painted it thickly, with crusts of paint and whirly things and everything a bit exaggerated, the colours a bit loud. Unlike the other paintings, this one was signed with a flourish: Ricardo Orazio.

Italian? Spanish? I wasn't sure. I could see why the painting had been stuck in the darkest corner. It was ugly compared to the others. I'd looked at those lovely photos in the album of the three of them, and I knew his painting hadn't done them justice. Perhaps Ricardo Orazio, whoever he was, hadn't liked them. Maybe he was one of those sorts of guys who think aristocrats are all bastards just because they're aristocrats, or maybe he hated having to paint portraits for money and would far rather have been doing his own thing. Who knew? Anyway, it was intriguing. Lots of things were intriguing here. There were so many stories you could see in those faces . . .

I went slowly out of the portrait gallery, my head full of exciting ideas. I'd only ever written short stories and poetry before. I mean, properly. I'd tried writing a novel once but though it started well, I couldn't work out how to keep it going. I got bored with the characters and I just couldn't finish it. But maybe that was because they were all made up so they bored me. If I used real people – but not living people – if I used ghosts, I mean, my ancestors, and just found out stuff about them, asked questions, and then imagined other things around them, then maybe it would work. They'd feel real – living – and I'd change their names and stuff. I just knew that many of those people in the portrait gallery had had adventurous lives. Especially the older ones. They'd lived in dangerous times. They had probably done amazing things. I had to find out if there were good family stories that I could weave into a novel. A really big family saga, a big fat book that would be really thrilling with lots of excitement and adventure and danger and love affairs – it would definitely become a huge bestseller. The sort of thing that people love to take to the beach, or that gets made into a fantastic film or TV series. The more I thought of it, the more excited I became. Where should I start? In stories you often had to go and talk to the servants if you wanted to find out secrets and things. Servants always knew stuff they weren't supposed to know. Well, I'd been going to go down to the kitchen anyway to get something to eat, so I could start there.

I raced back to my room to get my notebook and my little pencil. I'd make notes but tell Madame Vallon that I just wanted to try to remember things so I wouldn't be embarrassed in front of my grandfather. She'd understand that. I slipped downstairs and quickly found the kitchen. I knocked. Samantha Vallon's voice called, 'Come in.'

I went in. To my dismay, she was alone. I'd picked her mother as being more likely to gossip. I said, 'I hope I'm not disturbing you.'

She looked a little confused until I realised I'd been speaking in English. Blushing a little, I repeated it in French. She relaxed, and smiled. 'No, you're not disturbing me at all,' she said. She'd been sitting at the table, having a cup of coffee. 'You fancy one?' she said, pointing at the coffeepot. 'It's still hot.'

'Please.'

'A biscuit, too, perhaps? We made them this morning.' She pulled out a box which proved to be full of almond macaroons, the most delicious ones I'd ever tasted, because there was none of that horrible almond essence in them. I couldn't stop eating them. I was discovering I was actually rather hungry. 'They're wonderful,' I said at last.

'Yes, they're not bad.' She smiled at me. 'You look very fresh, considering that long trip of yours.'

'I feel great,' I said. 'Not really tired at all.'

'It's the excitement, I suppose.' She took a sip of her coffee. 'It must have been quite a shock.'

'What, finding out about Grand-père?' I shrugged casually, as if such a thing happened every day. 'It was quite surprising, I suppose.' It was easy to talk to her, she was so friendly.

'Didn't your father ever tell you anything about the family?' She was considering me, and I realised she was pumping me for information, not the other way round.

I flushed. 'I was very young when my dad died. He – he and Grand-père didn't get on.'

'Oh, I know that. I've heard enough about it.'

'Have you?' I said, cautiously.

'They had a huge quarrel the day your father left,' she said. 'Of course, I wasn't there. I was only a little schoolgirl, but Maman told me all about it. It was the talk of the village for months. She said your grandfather was very upset. You know that he'd had to bring Philippe up practically by himself since a rather young age.'

'What?' I said, blankly.

'Your grandmother – Caroline – she ran off with some painter when Philippe was only five or six,' she said. 'Didn't you know? She never came back or wrote.'

'No, I didn't know,' I said, my mind jumping to Ricardo Orazio. Was it him? And those photograph albums, that finished when Dad was about five or six – was that the reason? 'Dad never . . . mentioned his mother. Maybe that was why.'

'I'd say so,' she said, with a sideways glance. 'You wouldn't be too keen on her in the circumstances, would you? Pity he had to quarrel with his father as well, though. That made him practically an orphan. Oh, sorry,' she said, flushing, 'I didn't mean to . . .'

'It's all right. I'm used to being an orphan. I've been one for eight years. But Samantha, tell me. What did Dad quarrel with Grand-père about? A love affair or something?'

She laughed. 'Oh no, nothing romantic like that. It was over a stupid thing. He had his heart set on your father becoming a writer, or a journalist, or a diplomat, or failing that a man of politics or a great businessman. But your father said he just wanted a job to earn his living but that he wasn't going to throw himself into any major work like that because it gobbled up too much of your time and your family never saw you. Apparently your grandfather took that as an insult. He yelled at your dad, told him he had no ambition, that he would end up wasting his life and that he wouldn't help him. Good, said your father. He said he didn't want his father interfering in his life all the time and watching over him like a hawk. Then your grandfather got really angry and shouted about how sorry he was that he had sacrificed so much for his ungrateful, stupid, useless son who was turning out just as weak and unreliable as his mother was. And then, this is the worst part, your father just looked at him and said, "Now I know why my mother left." And then he packed his bag, left the castle and never came back.' She paused, sighed deeply and took a last sip of coffee. 'So there you have it.'

'Oh,' I said, weakly. I was amazed at the amount of detail she remembered from what her mother had told her. It was as if she had been there herself. It must have really struck her.

What a silly, silly fight. But how awful. How ridiculous and sad that they hadn't been able to make it up before Dad died. 'Didn't Grand-père . . . didn't he try to find out where Dad had gone?'

She sighed. 'He's a proud man. He hates to admit he might be in the wrong. Not that he was, altogether. Both of them, I suppose, just as stubborn as each other.'

'Hmmm . . .' I remembered my father, gentle and cheerful most of the time, but when he didn't want to do something, as immovable as a rock. Maybe his attitude to his father would have changed, in time. But he hadn't had the chance. And neither had Grand-père.

There was a lump in my throat. I said, 'It must have been sad for him when he found out Dad was dead.'

'Yes,' she said. 'I think it was.' Then she smiled at me. 'But he's very glad he found you, and that you're here. We all are.' She paused. 'Except for . . .'

At that moment, the door opened, and Madame Vallon came in. She smiled when she saw me. 'Ah, You found us. I was going to bring a tray up to you.'

'It's all right. Thank you. Samantha gave me macaroons and coffee. They were great.' I felt uneasy under her curious scrutiny, for some reason.

'I was telling Rose about what happened, when her father left,' said Samantha, lightly. 'She was most interested.'

'But of course,' said Madame Vallon, nodding. 'I don't suppose you knew, did you, my poor child. That one – the Randal woman – I don't suppose she'd have told you.'

'No,' I said.

Mother and daughter exchanged a glance. 'Well, that's not surprising,' said Madame Vallon. 'She's not what you'd call very – sympathetic, that one. One feels sorry for the son.'

'Maman,' said Samantha, warningly.

She shrugged. 'Well, it's true. You wonder sometimes if it's her coldness that has . . . Well, never mind. Is everything all right? Do you require anything else?'

'No,' I said, hastily. I got up. 'I'm – I'm thinking of going for a walk. I mean, in the garden.'

'A very good idea,' said Madame Vallon, heartily. 'It's beginning to look very nice now that all the flowers are coming back. I have to say this for Pierre Daudy, he knows his job, even if he has no other virtues.'

'Maman,' said Samantha, again, with a humorously raised eyebrow at me. I took my leave and fled, eager now to get away from the malicious backbiting that I sensed was at the very heart of Madame Vallon's character. It was just as well I'd talked to Samantha instead of her, I thought. She was nice. Then I remembered what Samantha had said, or been about to say, before she was cut off by her mother's entrance. Who wasn't glad to see me here? Was it her mother? Or Blanche Randal? Of the two, the Snow Queen seemed the most likely. I knew already that she probably didn't approve of me. But did it go any deeper than that? Why should it matter to her, really, whether I was here or not? After all, she had no claim on the property, did she? Or had she? Had she been left something in my grandfather's original will, perhaps – something he might not leave her, now he had found me? But that was ridiculous. He might leave her a bit of money but he certainly wouldn't leave her the castle or the land or the bulk of the fortune. Hadn't she said something about him planning before to leave that to the 'nation, or an institution'? So there was no reason for her to actually hate my presence here, was there? But the unwelcome thought lodged in me like a burr and I couldn't brush it away.

Black knight,
white knight

I spoke to Aunt Jenny briefly on the phone that evening before dinner. It was strange because the line was so clear. It sounded as if she was just next door. And yet I felt so far away from her. Not only in distance either. I found it really hard to explain what I felt, so I didn't say much except that I'd arrived safely, that everything was fine, that I'd met Grand-père and talked to him a bit, that the castle was cool and that I thought I'd have a good time here.

She said that was wonderful and that I must write her a letter and tell her more. She doesn't like emails, you see, reckons they can't be kept and pored over like letters. She said too that she'd seen my friends in the street and that they'd sent me emails. But I could hear that there was excitement in her voice and it wasn't about my trip so I asked her if anything had happened. She said she'd been given a fun new commission out of the blue, to make costumes for a local amateur production of a play set in the 1930s. She was full of that and so I let her talk, grateful I didn't have to say much. When I got off the phone, I felt a bit weird. I suppose I expected Aunt Jenny to have been hanging on the phone waiting for my call, but it didn't feel like that. Her life had gone on without me. I felt a bit cheated, in a way. And yet when I thought about it, that was stupid. I should be happy for her.

I was too tired to check my emails that night, though my grandfather told me I could use his computer if I wanted to. Unlike Aunt Jenny, he was a great if late convert to the internet, and as we went into dinner together, he chatted to me about the websites he liked to visit and the email correspondence he'd had with readers and other writers on the internet. 'It been quite a revelation to me, Rose,' he said. 'I have to admit there's a good deal I don't like about modern life, but this is one of the things I do like, and wholeheartedly. Do you know, I'm thinking of starting up my own website on Napoleon and his times, featuring my books, of course. What do you think?'

'Oh, I think that would be great! I think all writers should have their own site. So many more people get to hear about your work that way.'

'I'm glad you think so, child,' he said, patting my hand. 'I'm afraid Blanche thinks it's a "waste of my valuable time". Perhaps you and I might plot out something together, eh?'

'Yes, if you'd like, Grand-père,' I said, feeling a sudden rush of affection for him. I was about to tell him about my blog, but something made me hesitate. I wasn't sure if I was ready yet for him to see it. It was quite personal, in many ways, and besides, I wanted the freedom of being able to post up stuff for my friends without having to worry about what he or anyone else in the castle might think. No, I thought, I'll keep it to myself for the moment. Later, maybe . . . or maybe not. We'll see.

We went into the dining room. It wasn't the big formal dining room with the great long table that I'd glimpsed earlier. This was a much smaller, cosier one with a round table, set for four. The first course was already laid out: a collection of cold things, tomatoes, salad, smoked salmon, prosciutto-like ham, and a peppery, tasty salami I learned later was called *saucisson sec*.

There were two people already in the room: Blanche Randal, and a young man who I knew at once must be the son I'd heard about.

It might not surprise you to learn that Charlie Randal was one of the most handsome young men I had ever seen. Correction: he *was* the handsomest young man I had ever seen. Tall and broad-shouldered, he had a face that was like a masculine version of his mother's, and his eyes were blue, though a deeper shade than hers. And his hair was not dark. It was a rich tawny brown that fell to his shoulders, or would have done if he'd not tied it back with a velvet ribbon. He was wearing pale-coloured trousers, and a light-blue shirt with a soft collar, and over that a kind of brocade cream waistcoat, and tan leather boots on his feet. He looked astonishing, as if he'd stepped down from one of those paintings in the gallery. Or out of the pages of a Gothic romance. But despite the ribbon, and the romantic clothes, there was nothing at all girly about him. In fact, he seemed to give off a disturbing, brooding kind of masculinity.

My grandfather waved a hand. 'Rose, this is Blanche's son. Charles-Louis. Known as Charlie to all and sundry. Sit down, sit down, all of you.'

We sat. I was opposite Charlie. I said, stammering a little, 'I'm – I'm pleased to meet you.'

He looked at me, and nodded, but said nothing, and bent to his first course.

'Did you have a good afternoon, Rose?' asked Blanche. Her voice was a little high, I thought, a little forced.

'Yes, thank you,' I said. 'I looked at photos, and at the portrait gallery, and then I had a walk around the garden and a bit around the Chateau.'

'Oh, good,' she said. 'Then you did not get bored.'

'Not at all,' I said. I picked at my food. It was all absolutely excellent, but I felt like I could hardly taste it with Charlie just across the table from me.

'Blanche, by the way, Rose thinks the website would be a good idea,' said my grandfather.

Blanche put down her fork. 'The website, Monsieur le Comte?'

'Oh come, come, Blanche. The one I've been trying to persuade you about for weeks. Rose likes the idea.'

'Does she, now?' said the Snow Queen, in her most icy voice.

My grandfather laughed. 'Don't worry, my dear. It won't mean more work for you. Rose and I will work on it together.' He glanced at Charlie. 'And perhaps you might think of helping us, Charlie?'

Charlie lifted his eyes from his plate. He stared at my grandfather, and shook his head.

'Charlie!' said Blanche Randal, sharply.

'Don't worry, Blanche,' said my grandfather. He sighed. 'Really, Charlie, you have to get over this ridiculous aversion to computers. How will you ever get a job if you won't go near them?'

'It's what I try to tell him,' said Blanche Randal. 'You know that, Monsieur le Comte.' She sounded a little breathless, and for an instant I wondered if she was on the verge of tears. It was embarrassing, I can tell you. Not knowing where to look, I busied myself with stuffing my face.

Fortunately, then Samantha arrived with the second course on a trolley. It was roast chicken and vegetables, and tasted as good as it smelt. To my relief, the subject of Charlie was dropped, with my grandfather and Blanche instead taking it in turns to tell me about the history of the castle, from the building of the first one way back in the early Middle Ages. I listened with half an ear, both because I was beginning to feel that jet-lag weariness leadening my limbs again, and because I couldn't help but be aware of Charlie's presence.

He didn't speak a word. He just ate, and looked into the distance, most of the time, as if he wasn't there, or at least wished he wasn't. Once or twice, though, he caught my eye. It seemed to me there was a mysterious sadness, almost a plea, in his glance. I could feel my skin prickling again, with a sense of foreboding.

And then, just as the second course was being cleared away and the desserts appeared, I caught a glance between him and his mother. There was no mistaking the cold anger in her eyes or the fear in his, and with a little shiver that rippled down my spine, I knew that there was something very wrong here. Charlie was afraid of his mother. She had some sort of hold over him. Some sort, I thought, with a thrill of horror, some sort of a spell.

The mad thought made me feel panicked. I got up suddenly. 'I'm sorry. I – I feel rather ill.' And indeed, I did feel ill. Dizzy. Nauseous. As if I was going to faint.

'My dear child!' My grandfather looked shocked. 'Whatever's the matter?'

'She's tired, I suppose.' Blanche Randal pushed back her

76

chair. 'It's all that travelling. And a sudden change of climate. I'll help her to her room, Monsieur le Comte.' Her eyes as they rested on me were expressionless. But I had a horrible feeling that she could see right into my soul. I shuddered.

'It's all right, I'll find my own way up.'

Grand-père nodded at Charlie. 'Maybe you can take her up.'

I saw Charlie's quick glance at his mother. She said, flatly, 'I need Charlie to help me.'

'Really, Blanche,' said Grand-père, looking rather cross, 'Rose isn't used to the place and she –'

But I cut him off. 'It's okay,' I said hastily, just wanting to get away from the table and the strange heavy atmosphere. 'I know my way about already.'

Grand-père smiled, 'That's good. Off you go then, Rose. You need a good night's rest. I'll see you in the morning.'

'Yes, Grand-père. Thank you for being so understanding.' I hesitated, wanting to kiss him on the cheek but not quite daring to, just yet.

'Pah,' he said. 'Stop talking and get yourself up to bed.'

As I left the room, I suddenly caught Charlie's eye. There was no doubt about it – he looked haunted, his gaze fixed. Spellbound . . . Stop it, I told myself as I hurried away. You're imagining far too many silly things. He's just a sulky young man and she's just a bossy mother and that's all. Stop thinking you're living in a fairytale or whatever. This is real life and wicked spells and things don't happen in real life. But then, said my treacherous brain, neither does the granting of three wishes. And yet yours came true. All three of them came true. So why couldn't there be bad stuff in this strangely magical other world in which I'd so suddenly found myself? Why couldn't there be fear – danger – nightmare – as well as the good things?

Why didn't Charlie Randal speak? What was wrong with him? I remembered Madame Vallon's interrupted comment, about how maybe it was his mother's coldness that had done something to him. Was that it? Or something more sinister?

Later that night, I got up to go to the bathroom. The house was very quiet. But as I came out of the bathroom, a door down the corridor opened. There stood Charlie. I stopped dead.

'Er – hello,' I said, nervously drawing my old dressing-gown tighter around me, wishing I was dressed in something nicer.

He said nothing, just nodded.

'Have you – er – have you lived here long?' I said a little wildly, not knowing what else to say.

He nodded, and came closer. Oh my God, he really was so incredibly handsome!

'Do you – do you like it here?' I squeaked.

He smiled. It wasn't a very amused smile.

I longed to yell at him to speak. I wanted to shake him, to say, for God's sake, wake up! You're not really under a magic spell of silence, it's all rubbish, things like that don't happen! But then I looked at him again and thought I saw another expression in those beautiful eyes of his: that plea, again, that mysterious sadness I thought I'd seen at dinner. It gripped at my heart.

He came very close. I said, hastily, 'Well, I'd better be going I suppose and –'

And then I was the one struck dumb, because he

suddenly took me by the shoulders, bent down to me, and kissed me, very quickly and softly, on the left cheek. He whispered, 'Rose.' Then he turned and was gone down the passage before I could do anything more than stare stupidly after him, my heart hammering, my cheek flaming from the imprint of his lips.

I lay awake for what seemed like ages, going over and over that little scene. So obviously he could speak. And the first thing he'd said had been my name. Rose, I told myself, stop it, you idiot. He's absolutely gorgeous but that's the trouble. A guy like him will already have a girlfriend, for a start. And then there's the Snow Queen. She might not be a witch after all – but there was something odd going on there, anyway. Why had he looked scared of her?

She'd said he was two and a half years older than me. He would've left school. But he didn't seem to have a job either or be going to university. Maybe she thought he was just bumming around. Maybe she was angry with him about that. Maybe he was scared of her because, well, because she was scary. And if she didn't like me, she probably wouldn't like me being around Charlie either. But hadn't she said something about him needing friends? It was very confusing.

Well, I don't care what she thinks, one way or the other, I thought defiantly. She can't rule my life. My mind kept turning back to him. Maybe he felt the same way I did . . . Oh, Rose, stop it. Stop it. Stop it. One kiss on the cheek – for God's sake! – and one whisper of your name, and you're gone. You're acting as though you've never been near a boy before, as if you've never been kissed by anyone. Well, I had, but it felt nothing like this – this thrilling, this *amazing*

79

feeling. I'd never met anyone like him before. Don't be an idiot, Rose. He's just a flirt. A French flirt. And they're world champion flirts, everyone knows that. Anyway, a guy like him, he's probably got like a million girls running after him. Bet you that's what he was doing today, when he was out: visiting his girlfriends. I pictured them lined up in a row, blondes, brunettes, redheads, all French beauties, so chic and classy, going, 'Ooh la la, Charlie!'

Portia, Alice and Maddy would laugh like drains if they knew. No they bloody wouldn't. They'd fall for him as well. Or at least Portia and Alice would. Maddy would say he was too handsome to be true and that you shouldn't trust very handsome men. They were vain and the only people they loved were themselves. 'Beauty is skin deep,' was one of her favourite proverbs. I thought that was untrue. Sometimes beauty went all the way through, sometimes it didn't. Ugliness did that too. You just couldn't tell . . .

I fell asleep without even knowing it, and straight into a mass of wild and agitated dreams. At some point in the night, I woke with the strange feeling that someone was in my room, standing over my bed, and that I could hear soft breathing. It panicked me for an instant, but there was no-one there, and then I realised I was hearing myself breathe, and promptly fell asleep again, into a heavy sleep this time. I woke up again after what seemed like only a short time but was in fact hours and hours later. The curtains were drawn. The sun was streaming into the room, and my grandfather was sitting in an armchair by the window.

'Good morning, Rose. I thought we could have break-fast together here this morning,' he said, smiling. He took a mobile phone from his dressing-gown pocket. 'I'll call the kitchen and tell them we're ready. Do you feel better?'

'Oh yes,' I said, sitting up in bed and drawing up my knees under the cover.

'Good, good,' he said. 'Now I hope you don't mind, but I've ordered already. Orange juice, coffee, croissants and fresh bread. The baker delivered just half an hour ago. Does that suit you?'

'Oh, yes,' I breathed.

He flipped open the phone and dialled. 'Samantha, she's awake. Yes. Now, please.' He closed the phone and put it in his pocket. 'They'll bring a trolley. We can have it here by the window. Come on, get up. It's a lovely day.'

I scrambled out of bed and put on my dressing-gown over my flannel nightie, and stuck my feet in my slippers. I wished I'd thought of buying some new nightclothes when I'd gone on my shopping spree. Mine looked old and tatty, beside Grand-père's elegance.

But he didn't seem to notice. He smiled at me as I pulled over a chair and sat beside him. 'Well, Rose, what do you think of us, then, eh?'

Taken by surprise, I could only stammer, 'Oh, you're – er – you're all fine.'

'Don't be shy.' The hazel eyes, so like my own, regarded me with amusement. 'We're a pretty strange lot, wouldn't you say?'

'Most people are strange in some way,' I said solemnly, and he laughed.

'True enough. Rose, my dear, I wanted to have breakfast with you alone this morning because I want to talk to you. About your father, and what happened.'

'Oh,' I said, flushing a little, because I suddenly felt sorry that I had jumped the gun by asking Samantha about it. He misread my flush.

'Don't worry. There's nothing particularly unpleasant about it. It's just foolishness that parted us.' And he proceeded to tell me much the same story as Samantha had told me, including the fact that his wife had run off with another man. He finished by saying, 'You see, Rose, I was angry then because it felt to me that Philippe had chosen the path of mediocrity. And that I couldn't forgive him at the time. It felt to me like giving in to the small things, to the petty part of life I wanted nothing to do with – neither me nor mine. I thought that if you couldn't be the best at something, then life wasn't worth living.'

'But Dad *was* the best,' I said, with a catch in my throat. 'He was just the best father. Ever. Him and Mum, they were the best parents . . .'

'Yes. You must miss them very much,' he said gently.

I nodded. I couldn't trust myself to speak.

At that moment, Samantha came in with the trolley. 'Good morning,' she said, cheerfully, then saw our faces. Her smile faded. She busied herself with arranging the trolley between us, poured some coffee, and then left.

'I should like you to tell me about Philippe. And your mother,' said my grandfather. 'Tell me a little of how they were, with you, in that faraway country. Will you do that, Rose?'

'Yes,' I said, my throat thickening again.

He gently reached a hand across the trolley to me. I took it. It was cool, light, bony in mine. 'I was a fool to wait so long. Forgive me, Rose.'

'You're . . . you're forgiven,' I said in a strangled voice.

The hazel eyes filled with his smile. 'Good. Come then, before we start on our trip down the years, let's dispose of this excellent breakfast, or Samantha and her mother will be angry with us.'

It was an excellent breakfast, in more ways than one. In between devouring the delicious, buttery croissants and the crunchy bread, I found myself telling Grand-père all sorts of things about my life with my parents, and the funny thing was, it didn't make me feel sad but happy, remembering them. I told him about all the things they used to do, and how they were two of a kind, and how they loved having fun, and the sorts of things we did together. I told him about visits to the zoo and the beach and the joy-flights and the fairy party they'd thrown for me one year. I told him too how much they loved each other and me. I talked and talked, and he listened without interrupting, his eyes bright.

When I finished at last, he said, quietly, 'You are quite right. Of course he was the best father you could have had. And he was happy. Then I am glad. I only wish I . . .' He broke off, then resumed, in a stronger tone, 'But regrets are futile. I was a stubborn old fool back then and he was a stubborn young one and, well – there you are. Don't let that happen to you, Rose. Don't ever let stupid things come between you and those you love.'

'No, Grand-père,' I said. 'I won't.'

'Your Aunt Jenny,' he said. 'Blanche said she was a good, honest woman and clearly cared for you, though things have not been easy financially for her. We must do something for her.'

'Madame Randal said that?' I said, surprised.

He laughed. 'Blanche can out-royal the king, that's true, but she's a perceptive woman, and there's warm blood flows in those veins of hers, not ice water, as you might think. I've known her a long time, Rose, and she's a surprising woman. And a courageous one. Her life hasn't been easy, what with that absconding husband of hers, and having to bring up Charlie herself. And you've seen yourself he's not an easy child.'

He isn't a child, he's a man, and a gorgeous one at that, I thought, feeling my cheeks flaming again and hoping Grand-père wouldn't notice. If he did, then he made no mention of it.

'Anyway, never mind Blanche for the moment. It's your aunt I want to speak of.'

'Oh yes,' I said, quickly. 'Well, she has always dreamed of having a little design studio, but she needs a proper shop, you see, and she doesn't have the money to buy or lease one . . .'

'Excellent idea,' he said. 'We will see what we can do. And we must certainly have her over here as soon as possible. I should like to meet the lady who has taken such good care of my granddaughter, and thank her from the bottom of my heart.'

'Oh, she'd like that,' I said. 'But she's busy right now, I think. She said she had been commissioned to make costumes for a play or something . . .' I don't know why I said that, really. I knew Aunt Jenny would find time to come over if she was invited. But somehow I felt a little reluctant. I wanted to feel my own way around here a bit more before she came over. I needed a little more time to get used to things. To know whether, despite my grandfather's apparent warmth and affection, I really fitted in here. Perhaps it was also because of Charlie. I don't know. It made me feel a bit mean, but there you go, I couldn't help it.

'Very well,' said my grandfather, giving me a sharp glance. He didn't miss much. But he said nothing about it, just as he'd said nothing about my blush when Charlie's name was mentioned. We finished our breakfast in companionable silence, doing justice to the last of the bread and butter and beautiful homemade jam.

After breakfast, Grand-père went off to get dressed. He said he often did a little work in the morning, catching up on letters and emails with Blanche, but that if I wanted, I could use the computer after that, and when I was finished, he could show me his books, if I was interested. Of course I was, and we parted on the best of terms. I sang as I showered and dressed in my new off-the-shoulder blouse, and green and silver skirt, and after only a moment's hesitation, the silver shoes. As I did so, I remembered the old woman's words, back in that weird junk shop: 'There's magic and magic, dearie. May the silver shoes bring true love to you . . .'

Charlie wasn't anywhere to be seen on this floor, or downstairs. But as I stood looking out of the French windows onto the terrace, I saw him, in the distance, just going out of the gates. Well, I thought, he's heading out to the village, and so will I, what can be more normal, after all, than to go exploring on your first full day? So I clattered down the cobbled driveway, opened the gates, and stepped out into the street.

It was not as quiet as when we'd arrived. I soon saw why. The fishmonger's van had arrived. I learned later that there was no shop in the village any more and vans bringing various things came round every few days so people could buy stuff. The baker came every day, but other shopkeepers

– a butcher, a grocer, a greengrocer and the fishmonger –
came every three or four days. It surprised me because
there were big supermarkets in Albi and other towns and it
wasn't that far to drive there. But Samantha told me that
the old people and families with little kids liked the vans,
and also that the travelling shopkeepers went to a lot of
different places, so it was worth their while.

Anyway, there was the fishmonger's van, with the side
of it open to reveal a counter, and half a dozen or so people
lined up. Charlie was waiting in line too, behind a fat lady
in a headscarf and a thin old man in a beret. I hesitated,
but too late. The people in the queue had seen me. They all
turned as one to stare at me. I still had to learn that about
French country people. *They stared*. They weren't at all
embarrassed about doing it quite openly if they found you
interesting. And they certainly found me so!

Charlie saw me too, of course. He smiled, and waved
me over. So I had to go, didn't I? I couldn't just stand there
blushing like a complete idiot in the street while the whole
village looked me over. I trotted over to the van, trying to
maintain my dignity and pretend I didn't notice the stares.
But I just knew I was scarlet by the time I reached Charlie.

'*Bonjour, messieurs, mesdames*,' I said awkwardly, feeling
their eyes surveying me from head to foot. I caught more
than one sardonic glance at my silver shoes.

But Charlie smiled at me, the warmth of his gaze
sweeping over me from head to toe. I could see he
approved, and that was all that mattered. Looking at the
villagers' clothes, anyway, you'd hardly take them for
fashion gurus!

'I got sent to buy the fish,' he whispered to me. 'I'll
break the ice for you. Ladies and gentlemen,' he said

loudly, turning to address the others, 'this is Rose, the Count's granddaughter.' So that was when I heard his voice properly for the first time. It was light, rather toneless, but still nice. But then, I'd have thought it was nice even if it had turned out to be high and squeaky. And his introduction broke the ice all right.

'Welcome to Saint Martin du Merle, Mademoiselle,' said the fat lady in the headscarf. Her beady black eyes were bright with curiosity, her voice was shrill. 'Quite a change after Australia, I should think, yes?'

'Oh yes,' I began, but the old man in the beret chimed in, saying, 'She won't be missing those crocodiles and sharks and all those wild beasts I saw in that documentary the other night, I'll be bound. Not many wild beasties here, Mademoiselle.'

'Of the four-legged variety, you mean,' laughed someone else in the queue. 'Plenty of the other sort in France.'

'Ah, she'll be keeping away from that sort, won't she?' cackled the old man, his accent so thick it was all I could do to decipher his words.

'The Count must be pleased,' said the fat lady, 'he's ever so –' Then she fell silent and stared, and so did the others. I turned around to see this new source of interest.

Someone was coming up the road on a motorbike. It was a black motorbike, and its rider was dressed all in black leathers with a black motorcycle helmet on his head. For an instant, it looked a bit weird, like a black knight in his black armour riding up to the castle on his black steed, ready to challenge the white knight.

The motorbike pulled up beside the van, and the rider got off. He took off his helmet and I saw it was a young man, about my age or a bit older. He had a head of short, curly fairish hair, intelligent brown eyes and a big nose. It was a strong face, rather striking, but not what you'd call handsome. Aunt Jenny would have called it a face full of character. '*Messieurs, mesdames*,' he said, as he joined the line.

'Paul,' said the headscarfed woman, eagerly, 'guess who the young lady is!'

Paul looked at me, briefly, then at Charlie. I thought I could see the immediate conclusion he'd leapt to, and coloured. But all he said was, 'I'm sure I don't know, Madame Perlet.'

'She's the Count's granddaughter, Paul. The long-lost one, come from Australia.'

Was it my imagination, or was everyone stilled, watching us – me and Paul – while the fat lady talked about me as though I wasn't there? I couldn't help myself. I said, sharply, my head high, 'My name is Rose. Rose du Merle.'

'De la Tour d'Argent,' said Paul, softly. His eyes flicked over me. 'Yes, we know the full catastrophe, Mademoiselle.' He gave me a stiff little nod. 'Good morning to you. I am Paul Fontaine.' He looked as though the name should mean something to me, but of course it didn't. I just gave him a stiff little nod back, my stomach churning a little with the feeling that something had happened here that I didn't understand.

As the line settled back into the important business of selecting and buying fish – the fishmonger had been as interested an observer as the others – Charlie whispered to me, 'Don't worry, Rose. It's just a village feud. I'll tell you all about it later. '

The curse and the tomb

'The feud started in the Emperor Napoleon's time,' said Charlie, as we walked back to the castle with the fish. 'Back at the beginning of the nineteenth century.'

'You're kidding me!' I exclaimed. 'Do feuds really last that long?'

'This one has. Anyway, the then Count was an important officer in the Emperor's army. He had gone off to Russia to fight. He was away for ages. His wife got bored with being on her own. She had an affair with a local farmer. His name was Martin Fontaine.'

I gaped. 'You mean . . .?'

'Yes. He was Paul's ancestor. And apparently a very handsome man. Well, the affair didn't last long, but the Countess got pregnant. Fortunately for her, her husband had come back around that time. So when her son was born, the Count thought it was his. Perhaps he was. No-one knows. But, anyway, she didn't feel safe while her ex-lover was still around.'

I was drawn into the story now. 'What about *him*? What did he think?'

'Oh, he had a good reason to keep quiet too. He was married as well, you see, with a couple of other children.

89

And he was scared of his wife, she was the local *bonne dame.*'

'What's that?'

'The sort of person who makes herbal remedies and cures warts and makes love potions and stuff like that.' His blue eyes glittered with amusement. 'People who want to use her services call her *bonne dame*, the good lady, because it pays to be polite with people like that. But unsympathetic people call them witches. Anyway, it appears that the Countess decided that Martin had to leave the village. She prevailed on her husband to get him a position in the Army, and when the Count next went off to fight, so did Martin.'

'But did he want to?'

'I think he was glad to get away. He was restless, you see. Well, he never came back. He was killed in battle. And that's when Martin's wife cursed the family.'

'What?' We had reached the terrace. I stopped dead, staring at him.

Charlie laughed. 'Yes, isn't it great? Like something out of the Middle Ages. Your family has an authentic witch's curse hanging over it. '

A sliver of ice crept down my back. But I shrugged. 'I don't believe in curses, or witches. Silly superstitious stuff.'

'A defiant attitude. But people hereabouts would not share your opinion.'

'Even now, these days? That's absurd!'

'You'd be surprised. Old beliefs die hard. Besides, it's true that unpleasant things have happened in your family, particularly to the women. That's who the curse was directed against, because of what the Countess had done. That Countess died in childbirth two years later, as did her daughter-in-law, twenty years later.'

'People died all the time in childbirth then,' I said crossly.

'Wait, let me tell you the rest. The next Countess had a riding accident and was paralysed. The next one was all right, but it was her daughter who died, of scarlet fever. Then we come to your great-grandmother, who was also called Rose, did you know?'

'Yes.'

'You look so grim. Can it be you believe in the curse after all?'

'Don't be silly. It's all coincidence. But go on.'

'Your great-grandmother Rose – she didn't get ill or die suddenly or anything. But she had an accident in her car while she was driving along the little roads near here. It didn't hurt her, but it killed someone. A young boy on a bicycle. And he was a relative of the Fontaines.'

'Oh my God,' I whispered.

'She was acquitted of dangerous driving. But the village, and especially the Fontaines, were convinced she was guilty and had been let off because of her social position. She never lived it down. And I don't think she ever got over it. They say she was never the same again and was prone to fits of depression. Then, after that, your grandmother Caroline –'

'Please,' I said, 'I don't think I want to hear any more.'

But I couldn't help thinking – grandmother Caroline, well, she ran away with that painter and never came back, and my mother . . . I didn't want to finish the thought. I whispered, 'I don't believe in the curse. But if there was bad blood between those families, well, it all happened such a very long time ago. Surely Paul Fontaine – or the village – can't blame *me* for those old events!'

'I don't suppose they do, rationally speaking,' said Charlie, with a faint smile. 'But you're from the castle family, and that's enough for some people. They just think of you as rich and unfairly lucky. Besides, people don't always behave rationally, you know. And not everyone takes the Fontaines' side. Some are on your side.' He took my hand, briefly squeezed it, and released it. 'Anyway, that's the history of the feud between the du Merles and the Fontaines. Quite a colourful thing, isn't it? Something to tell your Australian friends about.'

I swallowed. 'I don't think so. It's horrible. What does my grandfather think of all this?'

'He's like you. He thinks it's all nonsense. He doesn't even like people mentioning it, so you'd better not tell him I told you.'

'I won't,' I said. It was the last thing I wanted to do. 'You know so much about the family, Charlie.'

He shrugged. 'I'm interested in the old days and the old ways,' he said. 'And I've lived here for years. It's only normal to be interested. Besides, I –' He broke off, his expression changing. 'I'd better take this fish to Madame Vallon. She's waiting for it.' And without another word, he disappeared into the house.

Astonished by this behaviour, I turned around. Blanche Randal was coming towards me.

'Your grandfather wants to see you in the library,' she said, her eyes on her son's disappearing back.

'Oh,' I said, feebly, and was about to go, when she said, quickly, 'So he's talking to you.'

For a moment, I didn't know who she meant. Then I nodded.

'Good. He needs a friend, I think.'

'Mmm,' I muttered, uneasily. She was talking about him as if he were some sort of little kid. And the expression in her eyes was odd – something I couldn't put a name to.

'However, I have to warn you, Rose. Take what he says with a grain of salt. He's inherited a streak of fabulism from his father.'

'Fabulism?' I said.

'He tends to gild the lily,' she said, crisply. 'He can't help it, I suppose, but there it is. Do you understand?'

I coloured. She was as good as telling me her son was a liar. It made me feel even more uneasy. I said, 'I'd better go and see my grandfather if he's asked for me,' and I fled, leaving her behind.

It was a relief to be back in the library, with Grand-père smiling at me. 'Hello, Rose. Well, you do look very nice this morning! Just like a fairytale princess with those silver shoes and that lovely skirt.'

'Oh, thank you, Grand-père,' I said, blushing. 'I'm glad you think so. The village people – I mean, I think maybe they thought I was too dressed up.'

'Oh, you met some of them, did you?' he laughed. 'They aren't bad types, just a bit challenging at first. You have to prove your mettle, you see. But they'll get used to you, don't worry. Now, then. I thought you might like the tour through the books. And not just mine, either, but all the things I've collected – and look, here, there's a shelf with your father's books, the ones he used to love reading as a child.'

We spent a lovely hour or so like that, taking down volumes from the shelves, with him talking about them. His own books were solidly impressive, in several editions:

paperbacks, hardbacks, and special, beautiful Académie Française editions in red leather with gold writing. ✎➳

I read the first paragraph of a book called *Le Jeune Napoleon*, The Young Napoleon. I could read it quite easily. It was nicely written, making you imagine just what it was like, being a child in that big, lively, ambitious Corsican family. We looked also at books in his collection, from very old ones to the latest thing, and then he showed me my father's childhood books.

Dad had liked adventure stories and mysteries, just like me. In one of the books, a fat paperback of *The Three Musketeers*, I found his childish scrawl, laboriously going through his full name and address: '*Philippe Auguste du Merle de la Tour d'Argent, Chateau du Merle de la Tour d'Argent, Saint Martin du Merle, Departement du Tarn, France, Europe, Hemisphere Nord, Le Monde, l'Univers.*' I had written things like that myself, when I was a little kid, going through the whole deal, street, suburb, state, country, hemisphere, world, universe. It made me feel suddenly very close to my father. I felt as though I could see him sitting in that chair over there, swinging his legs and writing that down in one of his favourite books, making it his, forever. It didn't make me feel sad, to think that. Instead, it felt good, because I thought that he had been happy here as a child. You don't write that kind of thing when you're unhappy. You do it when you're feeling good about yourself and your place in the world. Things might have changed later, but at least then, he was happy, living here with his father. Curse or no curse.

I didn't know what to think about Charlie's story, now, after what the Snow Queen had said. I didn't believe that Charlie was deliberately lying but maybe he was just embellishing things. After all, in the warm golden light of the library, curses that doomed every female member of the family sounded very far-fetched. But there must have been *something* to begin with, because that Fontaine boy definitely didn't seem to like me. And as I didn't know him from a bar of soap, it must be because of my family. Maybe there had been a bit of weird stuff happening, but maybe also Charlie had strung it together to make it sound more like a story. After all, I thought, I like to create stories too, even if I write them down, not tell people. Hadn't I thought before that I could write a novel based on family stories?

A sudden thought struck me then. What if he's like me – if he wants to become a writer? I mean, I know basically nothing about him. And I have no idea what the problem between him and his mother is. He looks scared of her, he won't talk to her and she says he makes stuff up and that he's difficult. Anyway, the thing is, he's being very friendly to *me*, and maybe he told me all that stuff because he wants to impress me or something. And if he wants to impress me, that must mean ... A lovely warm feeling went all the way through me as I thought about just what it might mean. I didn't really care if he made stuff up, everybody did that sometimes. He was so gorgeous you could forgive him a small thing like that. And besides, I was hardly going to take his mother's word for it, when I'd not liked her from the start. What sort of mother, I thought indignantly, says those sorts of things about her own child, anyway? She had mentioned about him inheriting 'fabulism' from his father. And Grand-père had said something about her husband 'absconding'. Perhaps that was the trouble. Charlie reminded her of his unsatisfactory father, and she was taking it out on him.

Later, Grand-père left the library, leaving me to answer my emails. Alice, Portia and Maddy had all written. It was funny, reading what they said, like getting communications from another world. They were all so excited about what I was doing, and wanting to know stuff, and not much happening at their end. Maddy also told me that Koschei character had posted another comment on my blog. She seemed to think he was a real weirdo. But I can't say I paid much attention. There was too much going on right here. I answered with one email to my three friends, because I didn't feel like answering each one separately. Then I thought of posting up something on the blog but before I could, I was called in to lunch.

Charlie wasn't at the table. Nobody said why, and I didn't ask. I just supposed he didn't feel like facing his mother. She sat there listening to Grand-père and me talking about books without saying anything very much. She seemed preoccupied. But after lunch, she went off to post some letters, Grand-père went to have a nap and Charlie came looking for me.

I was out on the terrace, sitting in the sun, reading my father's copy of *The Three Musketeers*. *Les Trois Mousquetaires*, as it was in French. I'd seen the film, ages ago, and I'd read an abridged English version of it, but never the real thing, in French. Despite my fluent spoken French, I found it a bit of a struggle, because it was written in that high-flown nineteenth-century style. Like reading Dickens or Jane Austen would be for a French person in the same position as me.

'Am I disturbing you?' he asked, sitting beside me.

'No. Oh, no.' I hurriedly put the book down. 'I was just – it's just that it was one of my father's favourites.'

His glance flicked over the book, then at me. He smiled. 'Which character do you think he saw himself as?'

I was startled. 'I don't know.'

'I'd say d'Artagnan,' said Charlie. 'That's who most people identify with. Or maybe Porthos.'

'Athos is too brutal,' I agreed. 'And Aramis is cold.'

'No, he's intelligent,' said Charlie. 'He hides his game.'

'He's too religious for me,' I said.

He laughed. 'Oh, Rose, I love the way you speak. That perfect French, and that lovely Australian accent, and those determined opinions . . .'

I went bright red. His eyes twinkled mischievously. 'Talking of religion, would you like to go and see the church, Rose?'

'What? Oh, I suppose that would be interesting,' I faltered, trying to sound as if I could keep up with his train of thought.

'I think you'll find it *very* interesting. Come on.'

We walked out of the grounds, down the little steps that led to the other side of the village street, and down the slope to the church. The village was very quiet. Perhaps they were all having a nap like Grand-père.

The church of Saint Martin du Merle was small and simple. Its single distinguishing feature was its open bell-tower, which I thought looked a bit Russian or something. There was a kind of onion-dome shape on top, with a bell hanging in an archway. Then under that a kind of stepped shape, with more bells in two archways.

'I haven't heard them yet,' I said, looking up at the bells. 'I thought church bells rang often.'

'Not these days. We don't have a priest living here any more. The priest from Castelnau – that's the market town

97

– comes every couple of weeks to say Mass. The church is closed the rest of the time.'

'Then why are we –'

'You'll see,' he said, and walked straight past the church door to a gate set in the high wall just beyond it. He opened it and stood waiting for me.

It was the churchyard, of course. The cemetery, attached to the church. Surrounded by that high wall, planted here and there with trees, it was a quiet, peaceful, sunny place. Rather like the walled garden at the castle. Unlike that, though, it was planted not with flowers but with tombs – lots and lots of them, some merely marked with gravestones and crosses, others with big monuments above ground, with statues of angels and stuff. There were jars of flowers placed on many of the graves, and framed photographs of the dead people. When they were alive, I mean, of course. Their faces smiled at me as I walked along the path through the graves, following Charlie, who was purposefully leading the way to the back. Full of life, those smiling faces looked, in those photos, while down below . . . I shuddered. I didn't really want to think of what lay below. Why had he brought me here?

'Here we are.' Charlie was standing in front of what looked a bit like a mini Greek temple, but with thick walls, a locked door and steps leading up to it. There was a little gated fence around it. He said, 'This is your family vault. It was built in the eighteenth century. The older ones are in the church.' He pushed open the gate. 'Come, Rose. Let me introduce you to your ancestors.'

'No,' I said, taking a step back.

'You're not afraid, are you? Don't be silly. The dead are dead. Besides, they're more likely to haunt you if they think you don't care about them.' He took a key from his pocket. 'I've got the key to the vault. We can go right in.'

'In there?' I squeaked.

'Yes. Don't worry, you won't see any skeletons or anything like that. The coffins are all walled in, you won't even see them. The vault's really interesting, you know. You must come and have a look.' He grinned. 'Don't tell me this is the same girl who was so splendidly scornful of the curse! You disappoint me, Rose, you really do.'

That did it, of course. I tossed my head and said, 'Oh, okay. Lead on.'

He inserted his key into the lock. The door opened, not with a creak and a groan, as I'd half-expected, but smoothly. 'Come on. There's nothing to be scared of.' And he disappeared inside.

Reluctantly, I went up. In the doorway, I paused, and peered in. It was dim in there, the only light coming from the open door. But I could see it was a square room, quite empty except for a stone bench in the middle and a sort of curtained alcove at the back. Charlie was standing by that, with the expression of a magician about to pull a rabbit out of a hat. I said, nervously, 'What are you doing?'

He waved at the bench. 'Come in and sit down.'

'But what if I don't want –'

'For heaven's sake, Rose.' He was beginning to look sulky. 'Don't be such a wet hen. Can't you see the plaques?'

Now I looked, I could. There were brass plaques inserted into the walls, with names and dates inscribed on them. I recognised some names from the portrait gallery, including, yes, my namesake. There she was: *Rose Marie du Merle de la Tour d'Argent, née Desplin, 6/4/1909 – 6/4/1969.* She was only 60 when she died, I thought, thirteen years younger than my grandfather is now. Dad must only have been three when she died.

Charlie said, 'Did you notice, she died on the same day – April 6 – as she was born? I wonder what the odds are of that. Quite high, wouldn't you say?'

'I suppose so,' I said, uncomfortably.

'She wasn't an aristocrat, either, you know. Did you notice her maiden name? It was just plain Desplin. She must have been quite something to have been chosen by a du Merle, in those days, don't you think?'

'Hmmm, I don't know,' I said. 'Is this all there is to this, Charlie? Because I'd like to go now if that's it.'

'No,' he said. 'You are so impatient! Lovely Rose, with her thorns out!' He smiled at me then, and I felt myself flaming all over, my legs turning to jelly. I went over to the bench and sat down. I said, harshly, 'Well, what is it, then?'

'Here,' he said, and in a swift movement, drew back the curtain over the alcove. I gasped. Behind the curtain was a table, and on that table was a beautiful miniature model of the Chateau, each detail perfectly replicated. The walls were made of the same brick, only much smaller, the roofs of the same silver slate, only in miniature. 'Look,' said Charlie, and pressed a lever on the side of the model, and the whole thing slid open. Inside was a completely unexpected, eerie but strangely beautiful sight – a crowd of miniature portraits about the size of small plates, each made of wood, and framed in gold.

'They're all here,' said Charlie, waving at the miniature castle and the portraits. 'It's quite a sight, isn't it? I think it must be unique. Craftsmen made it for the du Merle who built this place – and look, here's his son, the one who was in Napoleon's Army. Here's that one's wife – yes, the one who dallied with Martin Fontaine. Here's their son – or is it Fontaine's son? You and Paul might be distant cousins, you know, Rose. Isn't that strange? And here's the girl who died of scarlet fever – and here, of course, is Rose. The first Rose.' He looked at the portrait, then at me. 'You know, you do have a similar look to her. The same eyes.'

'They're Grand-père's too,' I said, uneasily. At first, the model and the miniatures seemed amazing to me. I'd never seen anything like them before. Now I was beginning to feel they were rather morbid. The du Merle dead couldn't just rest in peace, they had to stay in possession of the castle, even if it was just a model. They were anchored to this place by their ancestor's pride.

Charlie gave a soft cry. 'What on earth . . .?'

'What's the matter?'

He showed me. On the wooden back of the portrait of my great-grandmother someone had written a word, in thick black, block letters. It read *Assassin*. 'Murderer', in French. Next to it, there was a crude drawing of a skull and crossbones. Those thick black lines spoke of hatred, a rage that seemed inexplicable to me. I looked at Charlie, my heart pounding.

'That was never there before,' he said. He had suddenly gone pale. 'I know, I've looked at this place often enough, and this portrait too. Somebody's been in here and done this, Rose. Recently.'

'But why? Why would anyone do such a thing?' I stared at the ugly word, the ugly drawing, and my skin crept.

'I don't know,' he said. 'It's quite horrible.' He hesitated. 'We should take the portrait to your grandfather and show him. But I'm afraid . . .'

'Of what?'

'He's just had a stroke. Oh, I know he recovered well but if he gets a shock, it might be really bad for him. And he loved his mother, you know. Loved her a lot. People say he was much more grief-stricken when she died than when his wife left him. I think that was a kind of relief for him.'

'You're right,' I said, shakily interrupting him. 'I don't think we should tell him. But oh, Charlie, can we clean that horrible stuff off? Don't let's leave it like this.'

'Yes. We must,' he said. He put the portrait in his pocket, and closed up the castle. 'Madame Collot has some powerful cleaning fluids in her cupboards. I'll get the writing off and then put the portrait back, and no-one will be any the wiser.'

'But how did anyone get in here, Charlie? The door was locked.'

'There are three keys,' he said. 'This one I've got, that belongs to a bunch that's kept in one of the drawers of the kitchen table. Another key that's kept in the church. And the third one, that your grandfather has in his library. Anyone could have access to this key, I suppose. It'd be the easiest to get of the three keys. Anyone in the house, and even people from outside it, if they have reason to come into the kitchen.'

'Do you think Paul Fontaine might have got it? Or someone in his family?'

A strange expression flitted into his eyes. He said, too heartily, 'Now that would be carrying the feud a bit far, don't you think? Still, it's true that –' He broke off.

'True that what?'

'He has been around at the kitchen once or twice, to give Samantha a lift to Castelnau.'

'Samantha? But she's years older than him!'

'They're not going out. Her father's a cousin of his mother's, or something. Everyone's related, in this place.'

'Oh. But he'd have access to the key, then.'

'Yes. But I can't believe . . .' He broke off, again. 'The other key, of course, is inaccessible to anyone except your grandfather. Oh, and my mother, of course.'

I looked quickly at him. 'Surely you can't imagine she –'

'I would not put anything past my mother, if it served her purpose,' he said, bitingly. 'You have no idea what she can be like, Rose.'

I wasn't sure how to respond to this.

'But in this case there would be no advantage to her,' he went on. 'So it's unlikely.'

'Let's go, Charlie,' I pleaded. 'Please, let's go.'

'My poor Rose,' he said, 'how you must hate all this.' Then his arm was around me, and he was kissing my hair, and I could feel myself melting towards him.

I said, breathlessly, 'Please, not in here, not in here,' and he released me.

He was laughing, softly. He whispered, 'What is it one of your English poets said?' And he went on, in a richly accented English that somehow made the words seem really sexy: '"The grave's a fine and private place, but none I think do there embrace." We can prove him wrong, Rose,' he went on, reverting to French.

'Oh no,' I said, heading for the steps. 'Not here.' As he locked the door behind him and followed me down the steps, I said, more to hide my turmoil than anything else, 'I didn't know you spoke English, Charlie.'

'I'm a man of many hidden talents, my dear Rose,' he said, and laughed as I blushed violently. But once we were outside, he didn't try to kiss, embrace, or even touch me

103

again. He walked beside me out of the churchyard and into the street, talking to me quite normally about the village. I was sick with disappointment, and furious with myself at having blown it. Although, I have to admit, I was kind of relieved. Was I really ready for something like this? Something big? I just knew that if I got involved with Charlie, it would be complicated. There would be problems. It would be exciting, but it would also be scary. He wasn't like other people, that was clear. And there was that mother of his. Talk about feuds. There was a monster one going on between those two, and I was pretty sure I didn't want to be caught in the middle of it.

In Blackbird Wood

Charlie disappeared for the rest of the day. I wasn't altogether sorry. It gave me time to think. Or at least, to shut myself in my room and lie on my bed going over and over things without coming to any conclusion.

I wished I could talk with someone about it all, especially about Charlie. But there was no-one I could really speak to. Not here, and not in Australia. I shrank from the idea of emailing my friends, though they were dying to know whether I'd met anyone, as Alice had put it in capital letters, MALE. By which of course she meant YOUNG MALE. GORGEOUS YOUNG SINGLE MALE. Which was definitely Charlie. But I couldn't bring myself to write about him to them. He disturbed me too much. And as to that bit with the portrait in the tomb, and the curse, I couldn't really tell them either. It would be all over the whole school if I did. They wouldn't be able to help themselves.

So in the end I did what I've always done when I've felt tongue-tied and helpless but desperate to talk. I wrote. I took up the fat notebook I kept as an on-off sort of diary, and I wrote. And wrote. And wrote, about everything that had happened since that fateful day Blanche Randal turned up at Aunt Jenny's flat. And as I wrote, I could feel myself becoming calmer. By the end of it, my hand was aching like mad, but my head felt clear. I'd written myself into a decision. I would cool it. I would make Charlie cool it. I couldn't handle a relationship with him, not a full-on one, anyway, right now. But I wanted to be his friend. I felt sure I could handle that. I really wanted to.

But I was nervous when I went down to dinner. It's one thing to feel sure of yourself when you're looking at a piece of paper covered in your own writing, and rehearsing the words you're going to say in the mirror. But it's another to face the object of your resolve, not as a shadow on the page but a flesh and blood person. However, I need not have worried. Charlie wasn't at the table again, and neither was his mother.

'She's driven him to the station to catch the train to Toulouse,' said Grand-père, catching my questioning glance. 'Something came up, some job, I believe. Let's hope this time it meets with his lordship's approval.'

I wasn't sure what to say to that. Grand-père's tone held in it a mixture of exasperation and affection. Perhaps, I thought, like me, he can't quite work Charlie out, but likes him, nevertheless.

'Charlie and his mother don't seem to get on very well,' I said cautiously.

He looked at me. 'It's not always easy for an outsider to know what's really going on between two people, especially in a family, my child. Blanche is devoted to her son. And I'm sure he is to his mother, despite appearances.'

It was on the tip of my tongue to tell him what Charlie had said about her, in the tomb. But that would have been to tell him about that episode, and I couldn't. Just couldn't. So instead I said, 'But he never seems to talk to her.'

'Charlie can be childish, sometimes,' said Grand-père. 'It's all about punishing his mother for some imagined or real slight, I suppose. The sooner that boy grows up, the better. I've told and told Blanche that for his own sake she must cut him loose and let him cope in the world on his own, but she won't hear of it.'

I couldn't help thinking rebelliously that was what he had done with his son, and that hadn't exactly worked brilliantly, had it? But I said nothing, just nodded.

'It's a pity that young people these days don't have the opportunity to prove themselves as early as we had to,' he went on. 'Their parents are too nervous, too protective. They think the world is much worse and more dangerous now than it ever was, and that's not true. Let me tell you, Rose, it's just not true.'

'Yes, Grand-père,' I said, a little uncertainly.

'People have always been a mixture of good and bad. Some are much more bad than good, some much more good than bad. The rest of us, though, are between the two. Nothing in modern life changes that.' He twinkled at me. 'But let's stop talking about such serious subjects, and talk about something much more fun. Like the fact it's my granddaughter's seventeenth birthday in just a couple of weeks' time and I'd like her to have a wonderful party. I want to open up the old ballroom and hire a band, just like the old days. What do you think, Rose, my dear?'

'Oh, Grand-père! That's just – just so marvellous. I don't know what to say.'

'You've said it, my dear,' he said, smiling. 'I was afraid you might think I was an interfering old badger who wants his own way all the time.'

'No, Grand-père!'

He laughed. 'Actually, it's quite true. I *am* an interfering and imperious old badger, but perhaps that's because I've spent too much of my life writing about Napoleon and his ways have rubbed off on me. No, don't protest, my dear, I know my faults. So, you think about what sort of party you want, and we'll put it on for you.'

'Thank you, Grand-père!'

He smiled. 'You sound excited. I hope it hasn't been too dull for you, the last few days.'

'Oh, *no*!'

He laughed again. 'There's a world of fervent meaning in that little no.' His tone changed. 'I'm so very glad you came here, Rose.'

A big lump came up in my throat. 'And I am so very glad, too, Grand-père.'

He reached over to pat my hand. There was a little silence, then he said, lightly, 'And now we had better concentrate on Madame Vallon's excellent *canard à l'orange*, or she will be most upset. Will you pass me a slice of breast, my dear?'

So we set to demolishing the delicious duck and its crisp golden skin and tangy orange sauce with great gusto and lots of laughter. It was a great night. And when at last we finished eating, Grand-père declared himself to be so tired he had to go up to bed immediately. I was still so buoyed up by it all that I went off to the library and put up my long-promised blog post about the castle, with the photo I'd taken the very first time I saw it. Then I went to bed, tired at last but feeling light and free, without any of the confusion that had dogged me earlier.

I woke later that night from a horrible nightmare. I'd dreamed I was shut in a dark place, a place where I could not see a thing but where I could feel presences, waiting for me. They were waiting for me to panic, and then they'd pounce. There was nowhere I could hide from them. I was blind and they were creatures of the night. They could see me but I couldn't see them. I was frozen and unable to move, every limb was heavy. I opened my mouth to scream but it felt like it was made of lead. Then I felt a cold finger touching my face. Colder it got, colder . . .

I woke then with my heart pounding. Gradually, as I calmed down, moving in spirit from that nightmare place to my moonlit bedroom, I realised the cold wasn't in my imagination. The room felt chilly. I turned my head and saw why. One of the windows had come unfastened and had blown open.

I was sure I had closed it before I went to bed. Of course I had. I lay there for an instant, the nightmare helplessness overwhelming me again. Then I shook myself. Don't be an idiot, Rose, I told myself, sternly. No-one's climbed into your room through the window. You just didn't fasten it properly. It had those old-fashioned kinds of fastenings, where you have to twist the window-knob so that it pushes down a rod into a hole down the bottom, and closes the window. Easy not to twist it far enough.

I got up and went to the window. I was about to close it when my eye caught a flicker of movement in the walled garden. My heart stilled. Someone was down there. Someone who had been in my room, and had climbed down again before I woke up.

Oddly enough now I felt anger welling in me. And it trumped my fear. I opened the window wide, and looked out. I was just in time to see the door in the wall, the door that went from the walled garden to the grounds outside it, close. But I only caught a glimpse, a tiny glimpse, of the figure slipping out. It was a shadowy suggestion only, a flicker of black, nothing more.

I stood there for what seemed like ages. I didn't know what to do. It was the middle of the night. I couldn't go and wake people up. After all, nothing had really happened to me. I mean, I wasn't even sure that open window and the figure in the garden were connected. It might just be a coincidence. I leaned out of the window and looked down. The window was quite high up, as the room was on the first floor, and you couldn't climb up the brick wall. What about the drain or the gutter? I looked to the left and the right of the window, but though there was a piece of guttering some distance away, it was too far for anyone to climb from it on to the windowsill. No-one could have got in that way. And the other windows, to my left and right, were also too far away to make a good launch pad up to my window.

I looked up. There was a room with a small balcony on the left, above me. I had a sudden vision of someone leaping down from that onto my windowsill like Spider-man or something. Don't be stupid, I told myself. Who'd do a thing like that? You'd have to get up onto the balcony for a start, and then you'd have to aim pretty carefully. One slip, one false move, and you'd miss the sill and break your leg, or your neck, or both. And why would you take such a dumb risk – just to look at me as I slept? Or to leave my window open and spook me? No, that was stupid. The two things must be unconnected. There had been someone in the garden, but I'd only seen them because I'd got up to close my window – which had just blown open as I'd not twisted the knob properly. It wasn't anything to do with me – it was someone slipping into the castle

110

unobserved for some reason of their own. Or maybe slipping out. I mean, it could be any of the staff, going off on some secret visit to someone in the village, or some villager returning from a secret visit to someone in the castle. Maybe someone had a secret lover they didn't want anyone else to know about. That glimpse of the figure had been too slight. You couldn't even tell if it was male or female.

Yes, that must be it. Someone was carrying on a secret affair. I wondered who it might be. Samantha? She might be carrying on with someone in the village, maybe even a married man. Or Paul Fontaine? Charlie had said he came round sometimes to give her a lift on his motorbike. He'd said they weren't going out but maybe that wasn't true. Maybe Paul's family disapproved of the relationship, or Samantha's parents, or something. But it might not be Samantha. It couldn't be Charlie, thank goodness, because he was away in Toulouse. His mother had come back about 10 pm and said he was staying in the city the whole weekend. But it could be any of the others, really, if you discounted the fact they were middle-aged and not all that attractive. Except for Blanche Randal, of course. She was beautiful and she was without a bloke, or appeared to be, and she might well have some secret assignation somewhere.

The more I thought about it, the more likely it seemed to me that it was her. It was right up her street, I thought, this kind of midnight secrecy, pretending she's the frigid Snow Queen in front of everyone, and sneaking off to her lover while the whole house is asleep and her son is away. But maybe Charlie knew all about it. Maybe that's why he'd frozen her out. He didn't like what she was doing.

111

Maybe he even knew the guy. Maybe the man's married, with dozens of kids, or a crippled wife, or something like that, and he's seduced by the cold beauty of that woman into neglecting them all.

And maybe you're imagining things, Rose du Merle, I told myself severely as I closed the window and got back into bed. But at least imagining things had wiped all the fear from me, and I slept like a baby till nearly ten the following morning.

Unlike the previous day, Grand-père wasn't in my bedroom to greet me when I woke. I had a shower, got dressed in a pair of jeans, a shirt and my cashmere jumper and went downstairs. The house was quiet and there was no-one in the dining room, or the library. So I went along to the kitchen and found Samantha and her mother there. Madame Vallon told me her husband had taken Grand-père off in the Mercedes, for what she believed was an appointment with his lawyer in Albi. Her beady little eyes twinkled at me meaningfully as she spoke, but I didn't understand what she was trying to say.

It was only because Samantha said, 'Oh, Maman, stop it, Rose doesn't want to think about such things, after all, she'll only get it if the Count dies.' Then I understood he was going in to see his lawyer to change his will, and I felt sick at the thought of losing him.

'I hope he never dies,' I said, fiercely. 'I've only just got to know him.'

'Everyone has to die,' began Madame Vallon, with an offended look, but again her daughter interrupted.

'We all hope your grandfather has many, many years to enjoy,' she said. 'And that you can enjoy them with him.'

She smiled. 'Now, you haven't had any breakfast, have you? Would you like a cup of coffee and a slice of brioche?'

'Yes, please,' I said, glad to be here in the warm and cosy kitchen with them, even if Madame Vallon was an old gossip with a nasty tongue. But there was no denying she was a great cook, and to placate her – she still looked a little miffed – I told her how much Grand-père and I had enjoyed her duck the night before. Her expression changed at once, and she beamed and said it was a pleasure, and perhaps I might like to know what she was planning to serve up today? I said of course I would, and so we spent a few cheerful moments talking about the quiches they were making for lunch, and the steak, sautéed potatoes and chocolate and orange mousse we would have for dinner. Flushed with pleasure at my genuine interest, she mentioned that on Monday she and Samantha would go to the market in Castelnau and perhaps I'd like to come with them, as the market was quite a sight for someone who'd never seen such things.

I said I'd be delighted, and they both looked pleased. A little later, I finished my breakfast and went out into the gardens, not sure what I was going to do now neither Charlie nor Grand-père was around.

It was a nice morning. The gardens were at their best. There were birds singing. I wandered from the flower gardens through the herb garden into the vegetable garden, and saw someone working there. It didn't look like Daudy, the regular gardener. I was about to continue on when the person straightened up, turned around and looked at me. It was Paul Fontaine.

I couldn't just scuttle past and pretend I hadn't

seen him. So I said, in as steady a voice as I could manage, 'Good morning.'

'Good morning,' he said. He didn't look quite as unfriendly as the other day, so I said, 'What are you doing?'

'What does it look like?' he returned. Then he relented. 'I usually come in on Saturday mornings to do a bit of work.'

I remembered now that right at the beginning something had been said about 'village lads' coming in to help Daudy sometimes. I said, 'Oh. Is it interesting?' Idiot, I thought, straight after. He probably just does it for a bit of pocket money. But he surprised me.

'Yes, actually it *is* interesting,' he said, with a brief, crooked smile. 'I like working with plants.'

'Really?' I had no interest whatsoever in plants or gardening, but I did enjoy walking in gardens, and enjoying the pretty or yummy things that came out of them. 'Is that what you're planning to do, later?'

'I started at a horticultural college last year,' he said. 'I'm planning to have my own nursery one day.'

'Oh.'

'I think this conversation is about to run out of steam, and I've got to finish this bed,' he said, and bent down over his spade again. I stood there for an instant, not sure how to take his abrupt dismissal, and then decided I'd just leave with as much dignity as I could muster.

What an annoying and rude person he was, I thought, hotly, as I walked away. He's got a chip on his shoulder, that's for sure. I fumed for a few more minutes then forgot Paul as I caught sight of a blackbird hopping around on the grass. What a cute little thing it was, so busy and cheerful-looking! It seemed to catch sight of me in the same moment. It cocked its head and looked at me with its bright eyes. Then as I sneaked closer, thinking maybe I could get it to come and sit on my hand, it flew up onto a branch of a big tree, opened its yellow beak and began to sing.

Its plump little body filled with a clear, bright, melodious song. I stood there listening to it, enchanted. I had never heard a blackbird's song before, for the one I'd seen the day I first arrived had only whistled. I wondered if it was the same one.

The blackbird stopped singing. It sat on a branch looking at me, then it flew off and I followed it. It landed on a tree further along, then flew off again almost immediately. I followed. On and on it flew, landing every little while, till at last it halted on the top of the wall at the very back of the gardens, right above a rather battered door.

Daudy was there, too. He was pushing along a wheelbarrow full of sticks and stuff. He looked at me inquiringly, and said, in his thick accent, 'Good morning, Mademoiselle. Anything I can do for you?'

'No,' I said, a little flustered, 'It's just that bird. I was . . . er, I was following it. I thought it might be the same one as I saw the other day, when I first arrived.'

He looked up at the blackbird, and raised his eyebrows. 'Quite common they are around here, you know, Mademoiselle.' He jerked a thumb towards the wall, at the trees waving outside it. 'It's not just the castle and your family named after 'em, either: the wood also goes by his name.'

'Whose?' I said, foolishly, not sure I'd understood him properly.

'*Le Bois du Merle*,' he said. Blackbird Wood. 'That's what

it's called. On account of them blackbirds nesting there. It's a very old wood, Mademoiselle. They say it's been there since the time of the Gauls and maybe before. It was here long before your castle was thought of, anyhow.'

'Is it a safe place to walk in?' I asked, remembering Blanche Randal's warning.

He laughed. 'Is any wood altogether safe?' he said. 'Some say that one's enchanted, but I say, if you keep to the path, you'll be fine. No-one's ever got lost keeping to the path. It's only those who stray off it who come to grief.'

'Are there any, er, wild beasts in there?'

He laughed uproariously. 'And you coming from Australia, where there are sharks and crocodiles and huge spiders and deadly snakes! I would have thought you'd be eager to wrestle some of our own wild fauna to the ground!' Then he saw my expression, and sobered. 'Don't worry, Mademoiselle. There are a few boars and deer in there, but they're pretty shy. I doubt they'll harm you. In the summer, there're vipers, too, but they won't be around yet. Otherwise, it's mostly birds and rabbits and foxes and things like that. You'll be safe enough.'

At that moment, the blackbird flew to a tree outside the garden wall. It whistled twice. Daudy looked at me, a sardonic expression on his weatherbeaten face. 'I think your little friend is calling you, Mademoiselle.'

'If you think it's all right . . .' I said, my hand on the door handle. He shrugged.

'Why shouldn't it be? It's broad daylight. And it's a nice wood. You'll like it.'

I looked at my watch. It was eleven o'clock. 'I'll be back by 1 pm, Monsieur Daudy,' I said. 'If anyone asks.'

'And if you're not, we'll call out a search party, eh?' he

said, jovially, as I walked out through the doorway and into the wood beyond.

Daudy was right. It *was* a lovely wood. A short distance from our wall the path began, a little dirt road that snaked in and out of the trees and bushes. Because the winter had been quite mild and the spring was already warming up, everything was a haze of green. The air was scented with woodland smells – wet leaves left over from last autumn, springtime blossom beginning, dew-dropped grass, and occasionally, ranker, wilder smells. I remembered what Daudy had said about the animals living here, and wondered what I would do if a wild boar suddenly emerged from the undergrowth. He'd seemed confident they were shy and wouldn't attack, but I'd heard they could be rather dangerous if they felt cornered.

The blackbird was still hopping about in front of me, flying from tree to tree as though it was really leading me in. It felt a bit odd. But it was an easy walk, the sun was shining and the wood was quiet and green and lovely. I didn't mind following.

After a little while, I looked back and saw that the silver towers of the castle had vanished behind the veil of trees. I felt momentarily uneasy but remembered what Daudy had said. Keep to the path, and you'll be right. There was no way I was going to stray off it, that's for sure.

Further along, I stopped and sat on a fallen tree, listening to the sounds of the wood around me. When you sat quietly like this, you could hear sounds you couldn't when you were walking along. Scratchings, rustlings, the occasional crack of a twig. Not scary at all. I kept imagining the busy little animal and bird lives that were going on in that wood. They had been going on forever, generations and generations of them, since the world began. Animals lived in a weird kind of time, I thought, a sort of always-and-forever-time that was like fairytale time.

I got up. The blackbird flitted above me. 'Okay, little fellow,' I said, aloud, 'where are you taking me? Hope it's not to the gingerbread house, eh? Though come to think of it, a little bit of gingerbread wouldn't go astray . . .'

I stopped. I'd heard the cracking of a twig. Not just a little crack, like I'd heard before. This was a much bigger noise, something heavier than a rabbit or a fox. I tensed, immediately imagining some huge great boar with ginormous tusks and wicked red eyes about to burst in on me. I looked around wildly for a tree to climb . . .

And was startled by a sudden yell. 'Ow!' So it was a person, there in the undergrowth off the path. I tensed again, thinking at once, for no apparent reason, of the shadowy figure I'd seen slipping out of the walled garden. Then I rallied. Someone sneaking after me, meaning me no good, would hardly yell 'Ow' at the top of their voice. It was just someone else walking in the wood, like me. Except they hadn't kept to the path. Naughty them!

The twigs creaked and cracked. I could hear whoever it was lumbering through the undergrowth towards the path. They were breathing hard.

In the next instant, I saw them. Or rather, her. She was a rather large old lady, wearing a shapeless black dress over a shabby coat. Her white hair was in an untidy bun, her face was red, her eyes small and brown and suspicious. Her bare legs were heavily scratched, and her shoes were muddy. She was carrying a battered little case in one hand, and a walking-stick in another.

I stared at her. She stared at me. She was the first to recover.

'Who are you, and what are you doing in my wood?' Her voice was harsh and peremptory.

'Your wood? I – I'm sorry, I didn't know . . .'

'Not good enough, not good enough,' she said, and took a step towards me. But she tripped over a tree root and would have fallen if I hadn't rushed forward to steady her.

'All right, all right, girl, stop fussing.' But she didn't let go of my arm. Instead, she pointed imperiously to the fallen log. 'Help me to sit. I'm hot and thirsty and need a rest.'

I helped her down. She sat there, breathing heavily, then picked up her case and opened it. Out of it she drew a clear bottle filled with what looked to me like a kind of tea, with leaves and things floating in it. She uncorked it and took a swig. She breathed deeply. Then she held up the bottle towards me. 'Have a drink, girl.'

'Er . . . no . . . thanks, it's all right, I'm really not thirsty,' I replied hurriedly.

'It's good stuff,' she said. 'I make it myself. A great tonic. I had the recipe from my grandmother.' She looked at me, her little eyes twinkling. 'It's not hooch, if that's what you're thinking. There's not a drop of alcohol in this, girl. It's all herbs. Come on, have a go.'

'Ummm, it's just that I –'

'Drink,' she said, fiercely, and so I took the bottle from her, and took a swig. Oddly enough, it was one of the nicest things I'd tasted, refreshing and tangy, with a hint of lemon and a touch of spice. I drank more than I meant to, because it was so nice.

'Well, girl, not so bad, is it?' The old woman grinned at me. Her two top teeth were missing. It made her look exactly like a witch.

'It's very nice,' I agreed, still a little uncertain.

'Told you it was,' She waggled her head at me. 'Come on, don't stand there like a ninny. What's your name, girl?'

'Rose,' I stammered. 'Rose . . . du Merle. I live in the Chateau.'

'You do?' She stared at me, her eyes glittering with an expression I couldn't quite fathom. 'Why, I never thought to meet a ghost this day, wandering through the wood . . .'

'I'm not a ghost,' I said. 'I'm alive. I'm a real person. Oh,' I went on, suddenly thinking that maybe she'd known my great-grandmother once, 'I'm not who you think I am. I mean, I'm the Count's granddaughter, and I've just come from Australia, and I've only been here a few days —'

'Enough,' said the old lady, with a wave of her hand. 'You chatter like a sparrow, child. Right. Now I can place you. You're Valentin's granddaughter. Philippe's daughter, the one we never knew he had.'

'And Annie's,' I said, suddenly feeling I needed to say my mother's name. 'My mother, she was called Annie.'

'As you say,' she said, and gave a deep, booming sort of sigh, like a walrus or something. I suddenly wanted to laugh, but didn't dare to, not with those eyes peering at me. Fortunately the blackbird distracted us both then, for it jumped down from its branch and fluttered onto the path, where it cocked its head at us and whistled.

The old woman looked at it. Then she put two fingers to her mouth and whistled back. It was uncanny. It sounded exactly like the bird. The bird whistled again. And she whistled back. I stood watching in astonishment as the two of them kept it up for a little while. Then the blackbird seemed to grow tired of it, fluttered up into a tree, whistled one more note, then flew away, soon disappearing from view.

'Oh,' I said impulsively, 'now I won't be able to follow him any more.'

'You don't need to,' she said. 'You can find your way home easily enough, if you keep on the path.'

'But it isn't time to . . .' I began, then looked at my watch. To my surprise, it read 12.15. I hadn't noticed the time passing at all. 'Yes, I suppose I'd better go,' I said. 'It'll take me a while to get back and they'll be waiting for me, for lunch.' Then I paused. 'But you – Madame, will you be all right? I mean, perhaps I should help you –'

'Don't be absurd, girl,' she snapped. 'I told you this is my wood. My home. Why shouldn't I be all right at home?'

'But . . .' I looked around for signs of a house, but saw none. She noticed my glance.

'Never you mind about me, I'm fine. Help me up, there's a good girl, and then be on your way.'

I was going to protest again, but the look on her face stopped me. So I helped to heave her off the log, and set her on her feet. I said, 'If you're sure you'll be all right, Madame.'

'My name's not Madame,' she said. 'It's Renée. Tati Renée. That's what everyone calls me, anyhow. Auntie Renée. Even those whose auntie I'm not. You can call me that if you like. Or not, if you don't like.'

'Yes, er . . . Tati Renée,' I said, feeling like a fool.

'Goodbye then, Rose du Merle,' she said, and held out a hand for me to shake, which I did. She gave a little start.

'Your hand,' she said. 'Let me look.'

She opened my hand, though I was mightily embarrassed and keen to get away by now. What was this, some kind of hokey fortune-telling? She looked into my palm and said, 'Take care. There's danger awaits you, and it's very close. Someone wishes you ill, Rose du Merle, and it'll take more than a blackbird to guide you to safety.'

I dropped my hand as though I'd been scalded. 'I don't believe in that sort of rubbish – fortunes and curses and all that rot,' and without thinking at all of my dignity this time, I turned away from her and ran up the path, not once looking behind me.

Death's bells

I ran nearly all the way back and burst into the castle grounds hot, red and breathless. It was just after one o'clock. Daudy was nowhere to be seen as I hurried back up the garden path. But when I got to the terrace, there was Blanche Randal, waiting for me with a thunderous face.

'Where on earth have you been? I've been looking everywhere for you.'

'But . . . I told Monsieur Daudy where I –'

'He went home more than an hour ago,' she said. 'And he said nothing to anyone. Where have you been?'

I swallowed, then said, defiantly, 'I just went for a walk in the wood.'

'I thought I told you not to go there on your own!' she snapped.

'It was perfectly safe. I kept to the path.'

She looked me up and down. 'Then why are you looking as if all the demons of hell were after you?'

'I don't. They aren't. I just met an old woman.'

'Tati Renée, I'll bet. That crazy old biddy. Should have been locked up years ago.'

'She didn't seem crazy to me,' I said. I don't know why I was defending the old lady, who *had* freaked me out. But

123

I suppose it might just have been the Snow Queen putting my back up.

Her eyes flashed. 'Here two minutes and you think you know everything,' she said scathingly. 'Must be nice to be born so all-knowing.'

'It must,' I said bitterly.

She ignored that. 'That woman is a menace, I tell you. A troublemaker. And she has it in for this family. '

'It didn't sound like it –' I began, but she cut me off.

'Hatreds run very deep here. She isn't a picturesque character, but a disturbed, wicked woman with a talent for manipulation and an illusion of power – an illusion all too many of the villagers seem to share.' She stared at me. 'If you're wise, you'll keep well clear of her.'

But I'd had quite enough. 'I don't see why it's any of your business,' I said, coldly. 'And I think you're being awfully vehement against someone you say is just a crazy old biddy. I don't believe in witchcraft and all that rot. But *you* must if you're so afraid of her.'

She went even whiter than normal, if that was possible. Her eyes were like two points of ice. 'How dare you!' she hissed. 'You stupid little Australian girl, you have no concept at all of what you've blundered into.'

'Maybe I don't,' I said defiantly, 'but I understand now why your own son won't even speak to you.'

She raised her hand as if to strike me, then checked herself with an effort. Her eyes went quite blank. 'Your grandfather is waiting for you,' she said, in a dead sort of voice. 'You are late for lunch.' And she turned on her heel and stalked away from me.

Still trembling from the encounter, I made my way to the dining room, where I found Grand-père in good spirits and not at all angry with me for having made him late for lunch. 'It doesn't matter at all,' he said, indicating the quiches and salad. 'It's all cold, anyhow.'

I sat down. He said, 'Where's Blanche?'

'I – I don't know,' I said, then thought, no, damn it, why shouldn't I tell him? 'She and I have just had a bit of a fight, Grand-père. I'm sorry, I didn't mean to, but she was so overbearing.' I told him the whole story, and he listened without interrupting, calmly eating. Then he laid down his fork and knife, sighed and said, 'Oh dear. That was uncalled for, on her part, but she does get so anxious. Things are getting too much for her, I think. Perhaps she needs a holiday. That son of hers . . .'

'I think *she's* actually the trouble,' I said, getting worked up, 'not him at all. She probably tries to order him around and run his life for him all the time. And she's cold. She's –'

'Hush, Rose,' said Grand-père, gently. 'She's not really who you think she is. It might seem black and white to you, because you're young. But try and be charitable. Hers has not been an easy life. Her husband . . .' He broke off. 'But I shouldn't gossip about her private business, even to you. Take it from me, though, Rose. She's had a good deal to put up with.' He paused. 'I have a lot of time for her. I've known her for years, you see, even before she was married. She was different then.' He smiled at me. 'But eat your food, come on.' After I had swallowed a few mouthfuls, he said, 'So you went for a walk in the wood, then, and you met Renée? What did you think of her?'

'A bit scary,' I said, frankly, 'but not awful. Quite interesting, in many ways.' I didn't tell him about the fortune-telling. It seemed absurd that I'd got upset over something like that. I mean, I laugh at Alice who takes her stars seriously and goes on about zodiac signs and stuff and yet I was spooked by that!

'Oh yes, Renée is certainly that,' he said, smiling. 'She always was a character. And she was quite a beauty as a young woman, you know. That gypsy sort of beauty. Half the male population of the village was after her. I must admit there was even a time when I was quite taken with her.'

'Oh,' I said, slowly, as a picture flashed into my mind. 'I think I've seen a photo of her in the albums you left out for me.'

'Yes, that's right, the pair of us dancing at my wedding,' he said, with a little smile. 'Caroline was rather jealous, I remember. There was nothing to be jealous about, not by then, anyway – but I'm surprised she left that photo in. Ah, well. She was a complicated woman too, I suppose. My whole life, I've been surrounded by complicated women.' He looked mischievously at me. 'Perhaps that's carried on to the new generation too.'

'Oh, no, I'm not complicated at all,' I said lightly. 'I'm pretty straightforward, actually.'

'I hardly think so, you're a du Merle,' he replied cheerfully. 'Still, there's complicated and complicated, the kind that enriches life and the kind that twists it, and I have a feeling you're in the first category.'

'Grand-père,' I said, not really paying much attention to this philosophy, 'it's not true, then, is it, that the old lady – I mean, Tati Renée – that she has it in for this family? The Snow Qu– . . . I mean, Madame Randal said she did, but she didn't seem like that.'

'Oh well, she's a Fontaine, isn't she – I mean, Renée is,' said my grandfather.

'She's related to Paul Fontaine?'

'Oh, so you've met him? Yes. A nice boy, although a bit prickly. Not sure of himself yet, you see. But he'll grow out of it once he finds his feet. Yes, Renée is his great-aunt: his grandfather's sister. I think he's inherited some of her skill with plants.' He looked at me, his eyebrows raised. 'I see by your stricken expression that someone's already hastened to tell you about the curse that a Fontaine witch was supposed to have called down on us. All nonsense, of course, but in a village such things are held as gospel truth. Even Blanche isn't immune to that. And I don't suppose Renée is averse to a bit of mischief-making of her own. It might well amuse her to pretend to be carrying on the ancient grudge in front of gullible people.'

'Grand-père,' I said cautiously, 'is it – I mean, I was told all sorts of strange things had happened in our family, bad things, especially to the women, and that this was the curse working. Is it true?'

'You mean, is the story of the curse true, or does it work? Well, as far as I've been able to find out, there was some trouble back in the days of our Napoleonic ancestor, some rumour connected with his wife and one of the local farmers, who may or may not have been a Fontaine. Nobody's quite sure, there was nothing official, you see. But it makes a good story, especially as several of the Fontaine women have been associated with herbalism and things of that nature over the generations. My personal opinion is that the story's grown as time's gone by. The village has always been obsessed with the castle, both in a good and bad way.' He smiled. 'It helps to relieve bad feeling if you think those high and mighty ones in the Chateau are groaning under a curse, doesn't it?'

'I suppose so.' I'd never thought about it like that.

'And as to whether the curse works, well, if that's so, it must be a very hit and miss kind of hoodoo, because it only seems to strike some people. And all those things can be explained rationally. It's true there are some families to whom a lot of things appear to happen – but you know, if you scratch the surface of most families and go back far enough, you find all kinds of bizarre happenings. That's life for you. Full of tricks and traps. You could say the whole of the human race is cursed, back to Adam and Eve. A knowledge of death is the price we pay for being aware we're alive.'

So he knew all about these things, and he took them in his stride. I found it immensely comforting. 'Oh, Grand-père, I'm so glad I spoke to you about it. I feel a lot better.'

He beamed. 'Good, good. But you really mustn't worry about all these stories and superstitions. They're fascinating, I grant you, but you must not let them rule your life. We are the masters of our destinies, Rose. Under God, of course, but we have free will and may choose our life's course. Our faults lie in ourselves, not in curses or dooms or being born under evil stars. And now, Rose, there's something I want to tell you. You know I went to Albi this morning.'

'Yes.'

'I saw my lawyer there, and have instructed him to draw up a new will. Under this new will, everything I own, except for a few legacies to Blanche and the other staff, will go to you when I die.'

I could feel the colour draining from my face. 'Grand-père, I don't want –'

'My dear child, just because we mention my death

doesn't mean I'm going to die. In fact, I intend to live for a good long while yet, being an interfering old badger in my granddaughter's life! Now then, the lawyer will be coming here next week to have the will signed and witnessed, and then it will be all set, and your future will be taken care of.'

'But . . . but I don't want to think about it,' I cried. 'It makes me feel scared, Grand-père.'

'There's nothing to be scared of,' he said, gently. 'Nothing at all.'

But though I tried to smile, I couldn't shake off the feeling of dread that washed over me. It wasn't as if this was an unexpected development. These were the things I had wished for – wealth and excitement. But now I felt burdened. Yes, my future would be taken care of because it would anchor me firmly in the past. I would become a du Merle de la Tour d'Argent, with all that meant. I would never be just plain Rose Dumerle again. And though I was growing to love my grandfather and this place, I suddenly felt a great longing for what I had left behind. It seemed so very far away now, Aunt Jenny's, school, my friends, Australia . . . so far away, in a much simpler world. A world I yearned for, but was afraid I might never see again.

The rest of the day passed without incident. Grand-père went off to have his customary nap and I spent the time trying to distract myself by reading *The Three Musketeers*. But I felt weary and sad and unable to concentrate, and in the end went to my room, lay on my bed, took up my diary, and wrote. I wrote about what had happened, and about Renée Fontaine, and how strange life was, that it should turn a lovely laughing young woman into a weird old 'biddy' crashing around in the woods. Physically, it had not changed Grand-père as much, but perhaps its blows had changed him more on the inside . . .

I must have been more tired than I had realised. I woke up to find the diary fallen out of my hands, and a cramp starting in my legs. I looked at my watch. It was nearly six-thirty. I got up and went to throw some water over my face. I looked at myself in the mirror, and saw a stranger looking back at me, a haughty girl who carried an ancient name and lived in a castle and never had to worry about money, not ever again. No, I told my reflection, angrily, you're not me, not yet. Not yet!

I went down to dinner. Blanche Randal was there this time. She was quite polite to me, but without even the slightest trace of warmth. I noticed Grand-père looking from me to her once and twice, and I knew he was a little dismayed. But he didn't say anything about it. Instead, he talked about taking me to Toulouse on a shopping trip next week, so I could have a look around for what I wanted for my birthday. And he talked to the Snow Queen about matters to do with his publishers. I tried to respond with enthusiasm, but it must have been obvious to him that my mind was elsewhere. I excused myself soon after dessert, and he looked a little concerned, but let me go without a murmur.

It wasn't just that I felt weighed down with a sense of my destiny. It was also that just at the moment I couldn't bear to be in the same room as that woman. There was something about her that repelled me instinctively, something I'd felt from the very start. I couldn't understand Grand-père's defence of her. I certainly couldn't see the struggling, suffering Blanche he'd described. I thought he was discounting Charlie's feelings, too, just because Charlie was young and hadn't made his way in the world yet like Grand-père thought you should. A little tremor went over me as I thought that was perhaps what he expected of me; he'd failed to mould his son into the shape he wanted and now he had a chance to try again with his granddaughter. Stop it, I told myself bitterly. You're such an ungrateful sod. You've got what you asked for, you've got your three wishes in your hand, and now you say you don't want them.

As I got into bed, I thought of what that idiot troll of a Koschei had written in his last comment on my blog. 'I hope you enjoy it. It won't last long. There's always a price to be paid.' Was this the price, I thought, that I could never again be what I had been? That I had to change, to be moulded into a shape I didn't recognise?

I was dropping off into an uneasy sleep when I heard them. The bells, I mean. The sound came insistently through the closed window. I'd heard bells before, of course – rung for Christmas and Easter and when there was a wedding on. But those had been joyful peals, and this was quite different. Long, deep notes, with a mournful, frightening sort of sound. I'd never heard anything like it before.

Then I heard voices outside, people talking loudly. They sounded surprised, dismayed, even a little anxious. I went out of the room, and down the stairs. There was a little clump of people in the hall. Blanche Randal, the Vallons, Madame Collot.

'What's happening?' I said.

They all looked at each other. It was Madame Vallon who said, 'It's the bells, Mademoiselle. They're ringing the death knell.'

'The death knell?' I repeated, stupidly.

'It's the toll that's rung when someone's died,' said Samantha. 'The one that's rung for a funeral.'

'But who's died? No-one's told us. And what are they doing, having a funeral at this time of night?' said Madame Collot, fretfully.

'There *is* no funeral,' said my grandfather's voice. He was coming down the stairs, in his pyjamas and dressing-gown. 'We would have known about it. Someone's playing a practical joke of very dubious taste. Louis, come with me. We will sort out these hooligans.'

He took his coat off the rack and put it on, then he and the chauffeur left by the front door. There was a silence when they left, then Madame Vallon crossed herself and said, 'I hope it's not the . . .' She broke off, shooting a sideways glance at me.

Blanche Randal said in a voice as cold as ice, 'If you were going to say what I thought you were, Eloise Vallon, I am glad you did not finish your sentence. There is nothing supernatural in a death knell, nor in hooligans' practical jokes.'

I stared at her. A shiver ran over me. I hadn't even thought of a supernatural cause until then. Now, my over-active imagination was making me see some ghostly bellringer ringing the toll for someone whose death would soon follow. Someone who had already been warned. Someone for whom danger was very close . . . Someone whose face I'd seen staring back at me from the mirror. Not plain Rose Dumerle, Australian schoolgirl of uncer-tain prospects, but the future Countess du Merle de la Tour d'Argent, whose good fortune could not protect her from the inexplicable malevolence of a hidden enemy. A line from something I'd read once – I think it was by John

Donne – suddenly leapt into my head. 'Do not seek to ask for whom the bell tolls – it tolls for thee.'

Suddenly I felt very cold. I pulled my dressing-gown around me and tried not to shiver, trying to act like I didn't understand the looks on their faces. I said, 'I thought the church was all locked up, anyhow. So how could anyone get into the belltower?'

'Oh, it *is* locked,' said Madame Collot. 'But there's a key kept in the village.' She exchanged a glance with Madame Vallon.

Samantha said, hotly, 'But that's absurd. Paul's family wouldn't –' She stopped midsentence.

'It's that crazy old witch,' said Blanche Randal. Her hands were clenching. 'Ten to one, it's that madwoman. Well, now they'll have to act against her.'

'I'm sure that –' Samantha began, but hushed when the door opened and Grand-père and Louis Vallon came in. Grand-père was breathing heavily.

'We were too late,' he said. 'They got away.'

'Did you see them?'

'No. Damn and blast it,' said my grandfather, 'what a foolish thing to do. And for what? For what?'

'A mad person needs no sane reason,' said Blanche Randal heavily.

'A mad person? No, this was mischief. Sheer mischief. A practical joker. '

'Monsieur le Comte, there is only one other key to the church, besides the one the priest has,' she went on. 'And you know who holds it.'

'Anyone could have taken it,' Grand-père responded. He was rather flushed. 'I've seen where they keep the key. It's on a nail in the porch. Anyone could take it.'

'But you must also know how to ring the knell,' added Louis Vallon reluctantly. 'And not just anyone can do that.'

'No, but there are several people in this village who could do it, not just the Fontaines. Me, for example. I got Renée's brother to teach me, long ago.'

There was a little silence. Then Louis Vallon said, carefully, 'Monsieur le Comte, I think you can be discounted. You were here when the bells started ringing, and you came with me while the bells were still ringing.'

'I might have been operating them by remote control,' said Grand-père lightly. Then he sighed. 'You're not in a mood to appreciate my jokes, I can see. But really I do think there are other people in the village who could have done it. Or even from outside it. And in any case, there's no harm done. They're just bells, after all.'

'Death's bells,' said Madame Vallon in a deep tone.

My grandfather drew himself up. 'For goodness sake, Madame Vallon, can't you see you're spooking my granddaughter? And all for nothing.'

'I don't think it's nothing,' said Blanche Randal. 'Monsieur le Comte, you must see that this is intolerable. You must find out who is behind it.' Her face clearly expressed that she had made up her mind as to who the guilty party was.

He looked quickly at her, then at the others. Their set faces showed they agreed with her. He sighed. 'Oh, really, it's all a storm in a teacup. But to satisfy you, I will make enquiries tomorrow. I'm sure we'll find out they're plain and simple hoaxers. Young fools, I'd say. This is a spry young person's trick, not that of an old one with bad legs. They got away pretty quickly, anyway. Well, never mind. We'll find out tomorrow.'

I had a sudden picture of Paul Fontaine, running away from the scene of the crime in his black leathers, exulting that he'd made the haughty castle people shake in their shoes. I remembered, too, what Charlie had said, about there being one key to the vault kept in the church. So Paul wouldn't even have had to sneak around and get the kitchen key. But really, why would he do this kind of thing? Did people really act like that in this day and age? Could he really hate me so much just because of who I was descended from? I thought of the defaced back of my great-grandmother's portrait and shuddered. I wished now that we had shown it to Grand-père. After all, the death knell being rung like that must have been a shock, too, and yet he had coped well. Maybe, when Charlie came back, I should talk to him about it and we'd tell Grand-père together.

By the pricking of
my thumbs...

The next day was Sunday. I awoke rather earlier than I wanted to and couldn't get back to sleep. So I got up, looked at the bleak grey day starting outside, and slipped down to the kitchen, thinking I'd just make myself a hot drink and go back up to bed. I hoped no-one would be there. But to my dismay Madame Vallon was already up and bustling about. She looked delighted to see me.

'Sit down, sit down, Mademoiselle Rose,' she said. 'I'll make us both a nice hot chocolate.'

It was plain she wanted to talk. Her beady little eyes kept darting to me as she expertly made the chocolate and set it down before us in big blue cups.

'Quite a to-do last night,' she said, when she saw I wasn't going to open the conversation. 'Louis and I were talking about it for quite a time afterwards.'

'Oh,' I said, wishing I had the guts to just get up and walk off with my cup of chocolate, ignoring the staff like an old-time Countess might have done.

But Madame Vallon knew I wouldn't dare do such a thing. Leaning towards me, she whispered, 'I don't believe Renée Fontaine had anything to do with this, whatever Madame "High and Mighty" Randal says. She's always hated her since –' She broke off, giving me a significant look.

'Since what, Madame?' I said, rising to her bait.

'Twenty-two years ago or so, when Blanche Randal – or rather Planchon, as she was then – first came to work for Monsieur le Comte, she was a most striking young woman. There was a time when we thought Monsieur le Comte might . . . well, that he might consider marrying again. Blanche might well have fancied she was the chosen one.'

I stared at her. 'But she's years and years younger than Grand-père!'

'So what? Old men – particularly rich old men – marry much younger women every day of the week, Mademoiselle. Besides, he wasn't so old then, only in his fifties, and vigorous, too. A fine man, and a good catch for anyone like that woman who, despite her airs and graces, has come up from nothing.' She smiled, thinly. 'We all remember old man Planchon, and so do half the bistros in Castelnau.'

I was struck by the venom in her voice. I said, rather feebly, 'It's not her fault if her father was a drunk.'

'No, it's not, you're right,' said Madame Vallon, with a quick glance at me, 'but it *is* her fault if she sets herself up above everyone and pretends she's much better than all of us. Anyway, she holds a grudge against Renée Fontaine because she believes that Renée advised Monsieur le Comte not to marry Blanche.'

'But why would she do that? And why would he listen?'

'Renée has a gift,' said Madame Vallon. 'She sees things others can't. And Monsieur le Comte respects her a good deal. Mind you, there's no saying it really happened. There's not even any proof there was any thought of marriage or anything like that in Monsieur le Comte's mind at the time. It's just what Blanche Randal believes.

And her son too, I shouldn't wonder. That woman's a good hater. I mean, just look at what she did with her husband.'

'What?' I said, fascinated now, though part of me was also repelled by this gossip.

'Cut him off without a word, without a centime,' said Madame Vallon, shaking her head, sadly. 'I mean, even if the man was a useless no-hoper and a petty crook, you don't just turn your back on your child's father. But, you see, she hated him because he'd pretended to be what he wasn't. He'd told her he was wealthy and that he had a mansion and all the works. He was a good liar, and he was handsome, and he spent money freely – money that wasn't his, of course. He had all kinds of scams going, and she never saw through him till it was too late. She'd have been stinging from not being made Madame la Comtesse, too, I suppose, and so easily led up the garden path. But it didn't last long. Charlie was barely three when she left his father. And she refused to see him, ever again. Oh, he used to turn up here, years ago, trying to reconcile with her – most likely touch her for a loan, I suppose – and she wouldn't see him or allow him to see Charlie. He gave up, in the end.'

'Did she come here then when her marriage broke up?'

'Well, your grandfather saw she was in a mess, and asked her if she'd like her old job back.' Her little eyes sparkled maliciously. 'Your grandfather's a good man. Especially where women in distress are concerned.'

I didn't like the way she said that, but I didn't know how to tell her off. So I finished the last of my chocolate, stood up and said, quickly, 'I'd better be going.' She smiled faintly, but didn't try to stop me, so I left, hurriedly, not remembering that she hadn't told me who she suspected of ringing the bells last night. And once I did remember, there was no way I was going to go back and ask her. I felt uncomfortable and a little unclean.

Later that morning, I went to church with Grand-père. 'It's the week when the priest comes from Castelnau to celebrate Mass,' he'd said. 'Come with me, Rose. It'll be an occasion for us to give thanks we've found each other, and for me to introduce you to the rest of the village, quite naturally.'

He did not say anything about the death knell and so I took my cue from him and didn't mention it either.

Inside, the church was quite lovely, though small. It had an arched ceiling, a few fine statues and paintings and a very beautiful stained-glass window that Grand-père told me had been donated to the church by one of our ancestors. There were a fair few people there, though most of those were old or middle-aged. To my surprise, Blanche Randal wasn't amongst them. But the Vallons were, including Samantha, and Paul was there at first, accompanying Renée and a younger woman whom Grand-père said was his mother.

'Paul's father won't set foot in the church,' Grand-père whispered to me. 'He's a Communist, you see, as many of the Fontaine men have been. But the Fontaine women are often very pious indeed.' He smiled at my expression. 'It's often like that in French villages,' he said. 'Some of us love the priests, others hate them.'

It was hard to imagine anyone hating Father Richard, the Castelnau priest. He was a wispy, thin man with a harried expression and a rather distracted way of talking. Grand-père introduced me to him after Mass and though he smiled kindly and wished me well, it was clear he wasn't all that interested in me. Which suited me very well, I have to say. I'm not sure how to make small talk with a priest.

People stood in little knots in the church porch, complaining about the weather and how it had suddenly turned cold. Grand-père introduced me to everyone, though I remembered a couple of them from the fishmonger's queue. Madame Perlet, for instance. Unlike the priest, they *were* interested, I could see that. It wasn't easy for me, being the focus of all that attention. I kept thinking I'd say the wrong thing or trip over my feet or do something stupid.

At last, we came to the Fontaines. Somewhat to my relief, Paul had vanished before the end of the service, and so it was just Renée and Paul's mother, Geneviève, who we chatted with.

Grand-père seemed quite at ease with them, though I noticed Geneviève Fontaine looked a little uneasy. That unease deepened when Grand-père started talking about the death knell episode and how he wanted to get to the bottom of it.

'We didn't hear it, Monsieur le Comte,' she said, with a quick glance at the impassive Renée. 'You know the farm's too far from the village for that.'

'Oh, I know,' he said, 'I just wondered if your key had gone? Someone got into the church to do it, you see, and Father Richard has the only other key.'

'So you think we did it,' said Renée calmly. She had obviously made an effort to look a bit respectable this morning, for her shoes were clean and the blue dress she wore was not as shabby as the one I'd last seen her in. But the whole effect was still quite odd. She wore a large flowery jacket over her dress and a black hat with a feather in it perched on her bird's-nest hair. At least she'd left her battered old case behind, though she still had the walking-stick.

Grand-père didn't even look embarrassed. I suppose he'd known her a long time and didn't take exception to her blunt pronouncements. 'Of course I don't,' he said. 'But I wondered if we might come and have a word, to see if we can find the key, and so on. Perhaps Paul or his father or brothers might have seen something. I'd thought I might be able to speak to Paul after Mass, but he seems to have gone home early.'

'He wanted to finish making Sunday lunch, so it would be ready when we got home. Anyway, neither he nor my husband had anything to do with this,' said Geneviève anxiously.

'Of course,' soothed Grand-père. 'It's just that, you know, it did rather scare my granddaughter.'

Renée looked at me. 'Did it, now? Perhaps it's better that way.'

'What do you mean?' he asked.

She didn't answer.

He sighed. 'Very well. Make pointless mysteries if you must. Madame Fontaine,' he went on, turning back to Geneviève, 'will it be all right if Rose and I come to see you this afternoon? We are not accusing anybody of anything – far from it – we just need to know if the key left your house. Anyone could have taken it, I know that. We just need to know.'

'The one who rang the bells needed no key,' said Renée, with a strange little smile. 'You know that, Valentin. It is a warning, and your Rose should do well to heed it. As should you.'

I shuddered. But Grand-père said harshly, 'That is nonsense, Renée. It was human hands rang those bells, and I'm going to find out who, and why.'

'Very well,' said Renée, with a shrug. 'Ask away, Valentin. You'll learn nothing from any of us.'

He ignored her. 'Madame Fontaine? Do I have your permission to visit this afternoon?'

'Of course, Monsieur le Comte,' she said, a little fretfully. 'But please, remember my husband –'

'Has no great love of my family,' said Grand-père, with a wry look. 'I know that, Madame Fontaine. Do not concern yourself. I shall be the soul of discretion.' He smiled. 'And do not be afraid that I have any notion that your son or your husband or indeed any of your family is involved. I know you are not at all the sort of people to play malicious tricks of this sort.'

She smiled back, her anxious expression fading. 'We will look forward to seeing you this afternoon.'

As we walked back to the castle, Grand-père said to me, 'I do wish Renée wouldn't try to live up to her reputation as village witch quite so much. She's an intelligent woman.'

'Perhaps that's why she does it,' I said.

He laughed. 'Perhaps you're right. It's a standing of some sort. I'm sure that's what happened with witches throughout the ages. If you're just some poor old woman living alone, people pity or despise you. But if you're a witch, they respect and fear you. Yes. But it's a dangerous game to play.'

'Not these days,' I said. 'No-one burns witches any more.'

'No. But they can still make make enemies.' He sighed, and I knew he was thinking of Blanche.

'Grand-père,' I said, cautiously, 'do you really think there's no way Paul Fontaine can be involved?'

'Yes. Well, no. I'm not sure, to tell you the truth, my dear,' he said. 'He does have a wild streak, it's true. But he's bright, too. You know he topped the region in English and Spanish at his *baccalauréat* – his leaving exams – a year ago? His parents were all set on his trying for a really good university and maybe going into the diplomatic corps. Instead, he went to that horticultural college. It was what he'd always wanted but they were still pretty annoyed about it.' He paused. 'Going back to our problem – I can't see why Paul would do a thing like that. It seems so pointless.'

'Not if he *does* want to scare me,' I said.

'Now why would he want to do that?' Grand-père said. 'I'd think it more likely he'd want to impress you, pretty young girl like you.'

'He was rude to me. He doesn't like me, it's quite clear,' I cried, flushing.

Grand-père laughed and took my arm. 'Perhaps he's just not used to girls, my dear Rose – he only has two older brothers. He might just be shy, that's all.'

I didn't think so. But I wasn't going to argue the toss with Grand-père. After all, what did I care about Paul Fontaine?

It began to rain quite heavily after lunch, so instead of walking to the Fontaine farm, as Grand-père planned, we went in the car. Just out of the village, we turned down a road whose signpost read, 'Lac St Jean, 10 kilometres.'

'There's a lake here?' I asked Grand-père, and he nodded.

'Well, in a manner of speaking. Not a natural lake, you understand, just a filled-in quarry, really. But it's a bit of a picnic spot in summer. Too cold, at present, though.'

The farm was about a kilometre down the Lac St Jean road. It was set on a small hill, with views all around. Grand-père said the Fontaines were good farmers and had bought up two or three neighbouring farms in recent years, so they produced quite a lot and were quite comfortably off. 'In fact, I wouldn't be surprised if their fortune doesn't match mine, in the long run,' he said. 'They're canny people, these Fontaines.'

He said the two older brothers, Jacques and Simon, ran the farm with their father Marcel. Their mother meanwhile raised ducks and chickens. 'That one we had the other day, that was one of hers,' said Grand-père. 'She knows her business. They're always excellent birds. She makes a tidy sum out of them.' He said that Paul was different though. 'He's bright, but no business sense and no interest in making money, unlike the rest of his family. He reminds me most of my dear old pig-headed Renée. I only hope his tongue and his temper don't get him into as much trouble as it has her.'

We drove up the stone drive to the farmhouse. It was a long, low stone building with a roof of the local tiles. Around it were barns and outbuildings filled with tractors, harvesters and farm machinery of all sorts. A couple of dogs came barking towards the car as it pulled up, and someone, alerted by the noise, came out of the house as we opened the car doors.

He was a tall, large man with Paul's brown eyes and his big nose, though his hair was quite dark, not fair like his son's. This was obviously Paul's father, Marcel.

'Geneviève said you'd be coming,' he said as we hurried towards him, trying to beat the rain. 'Come in.'

He stood aside to let us pass. I was aware of his unblinking scrutiny. But he said nothing more as we stepped from the covered porch into a big, warm kitchen.

Geneviève came over, wiping her hands on her apron. She looked nervous. She bustled around, pulling out chairs. 'Oh, please, sit down. I'll make some coffee. Thank you for coming to see us –'

'Stop it, girl, with your airs and graces. You know he's come here to quiz us about those bells. Well, let me tell you, Monsieur, no-one in this family had anything to do with it.' Marcel Fontaine's voice rang out defiantly, his face was hard and set.

'I know that, Monsieur Fontaine,' said Grand-père comfortably. 'As I explained to Madame, your wife.'

And he proceeded to tell Marcel what he'd said earlier while I sat there, looking curiously around me. It was a rather bare room, even if it was warm. There were some framed photographs on the walls, a big tall grandfather clock and a dresser full of patterned china. Apart from the table, chairs and kitchen stuff, there was nothing else. I thought of how Grand-père had said the Fontaines were now well off. They must not spend any of their money on such things.

I was jerked back to the conversation by Marcel's voice. Or rather, by what he was saying. 'If it was me,' he said, 'I'd put my money on that boy of Blanche's. It's just the sort of thing he'd do.'

'Charlie is a bit of a problem, I agree,' Grand-père said. 'But in this case, he's quite innocent. He's been away in Toulouse all weekend. And we can vouch for that.'

'Yes, we can,' I said, warmly, before I could stop myself. 'And I don't know why you should think it's the sort of thing he would do. He's a very kind and considerate person.'

Marcel's eyebrows raised. He gave a sardonic smile. 'I'm sure,' was all he said, but I could plainly read in his eyes what he thought. I flushed.

'It's not fair,' I began, but Grand-père held up a hand to hush me.

'We're not here to discuss the merits or otherwise of Charlie Randal,' he said, sharply. 'We're here to find out how this joker, whoever it is, got into the church last night in order to ring those bells.'

'The key's still on the nail,' said Marcel, shrugging. He got up and went out of the room and into the porch, returning a few seconds later with a big heavy brass key dangling from his hand. He put it on the table. 'Here it is.'

'Did you see it there last night?'

Marcel sat at the table and folded his arms. 'Can't say I looked.'

Grand-père looked at Geneviève, who was making coffee. 'What about you, Madame?'

She shook her head. 'I don't know. I didn't notice. Tati Renée didn't either – she wasn't here last night but in that hideout of hers, in the wood.'

'I see. Are any of the boys here?' Grand-père asked. 'Perhaps they might have noticed.'

'Jacques and Simon have gone to visit their girlfriends, and Paul is working upstairs,' said Geneviève, glancing at her husband. 'Shall I ask him to come down?'

'If you wouldn't mind, Madame,' said Grand-père firmly.

She left. We three were left there looking at each other. It wasn't the easiest atmosphere in the world. Then Grand-père cleared his throat and said, 'I see they're bringing in some new rules about cropping, Monsieur Fontaine. More rules to make life harder.'

'That's for sure,' said Marcel. 'Those damned bureaucrats have no idea what it takes to run a farm. Do you know, I heard the other day they were even sending in aeroplanes to check up on our fields and what we're growing in them? It's becoming a real burden, these spies and rules, Monsieur, I don't mind saying.' His tone was animated. Grand-père had obviously touched on a sore spot.

'Sometimes I wonder if it's all worthwhile,' Grand-père said, shaking his head. 'For farmers like you.' He continued on, talking to Marcel Fontaine about farming matters of which I knew nothing and cared less. I listened with half an ear for a moment or two, then rapidly grew bored. And Geneviève was still not coming down. Paul was probably refusing to come.

Suddenly I had an intense desire to see more of this place. This family was, if you believed the stories, my family's ancestral enemy. It was always good to know your enemy's camp. And there was only one way to do that. I said, 'Excuse me, but may I please – I mean, is it possible . . . I would like to . . .' I coloured, as if I was too embarassed to say what I wanted, but Marcel understood. For the first time, he looked uncertain of himself.

'You want *le petit coin*, Mademoiselle?' he said. The little corner, that meant. A funny nickname for a toilet, but as good a euphemism as any, I suppose. I nodded, my eyes downcast.

'There's one downstairs, near the back door. And one upstairs, first door on your right. Go to the one upstairs. It's, er . . . more decent. My wife uses that one.'

'Thank you, Monsieur,' I said, and fled.

I went through into the next room, which was a living room, sparsely furnished like the kitchen, except for a huge TV that sat in a corner, and a wedding photo on top of it, which was obviously of Marcel and Geneviève. I walked through a corridor and climbed the stairs. As I opened the toilet door, I could hear raised voices coming from a room further along. Then I heard a door opening, and quickly slipped into the loo. I didn't want to see Paul.

I waited until I heard footsteps going downstairs. Two sets of footsteps. I was sure of that. Then, quietly, I slipped out of the loo and went along the corridor, trying each door in turn. The parents' room. Another bedroom. I looked in. It was messy. There was a bed, a chair on which clothes were piled, a table on which sat a pile of CDs and a stack of farming journals. Beside the bed was a photo of a young woman with an engaging grin. I thought, this must be the room of one of the older brothers. I closed the door and looked in the next room. This time, the room was very neat, the bed made, the clothes put away. There was a desk with a neat pile of books on it and a laptop computer. It was still on, but had gone into screen saver mode. Something – a fizzing in my veins, a pricking in my thumbs – told me I should go into that room and have a look at the computer, but I hesitated. What if Paul came back up? I listened hard. I could hear raised voices downstairs. They were all down there. I swallowed, then slipped into the room. I went over to the desk, and touched one of the keys of the computer, bringing back the screen Paul had been on when he was interrupted by his mother.

I gasped. It was a Google search page, and the search was on my name. My heart thumping, I stared at the page, scanning the things the search engine had brought up. It was all pretty random, stuff about camping grounds called something *merle*, and vineyards called *chateau du merle*, and all kinds of odd things like that. But nothing actually on me appeared, at least not on that first page. I was about to go for the next, when I heard Paul's voice behind me.

'What do you think you're doing?'

I whirled around. He was standing in the doorway staring at me. I faltered, 'Nothing. I . . . I thought I . . .'

He entered the room. His eyes were full of cold fury, the base of his nostrils were pinched and white. 'You thought you'd come up and snoop around. Is that it?'

I suddenly felt very frightened. And when I'm really frightened, as I think I've told you before, it makes me angry. I hissed, 'How dare you accuse me of snooping, when you're doing the exact same thing, only on the internet!'

He gave me a baleful glance, strode to the desk, and slammed down the lid of the computer. He turned to me. 'I think you'd better go.'

'I think so too,' I said, icily, my hands shaking. 'And if you think you're going to find something out about me on the web that will help you scare me away from my grandfather's house, or whatever it is you're trying to do, you've got another think coming!'

He laughed. There was no amusement in the sound. 'You little fool.'

'I'll tell my grandfather what you were doing.'

'Tell away,' he said carelessly. 'What will it prove?'

'It will prove you're interested in me and are looking for . . .' I stopped, my cheeks flaming, as I realised what I'd said.

He smiled, and once again there was no amusement on his face. He said harshly, 'Ah, that makes the dear little Countess-in-waiting hesitate, does it not? One of the local peasants perving on her over the internet, that's really too shameful for words, isn't it?'

'Shut up,' I said, furiously. 'You know very well that's not what I meant.' I stood there breathing heavily, hating him, wanting somehow to wipe that smile off his face.

'Grand-père thinks you're nice, but if he knew you not only rang that death knell but also vandalised his mother's portrait, he'd –'

He stared. 'What do you mean?'

'Don't act the innocent. The portrait in the family vault. My great-grandmother. My namesake, Rose. The one who . . . who ran over that boy from your family. There was a word written on the back – assassin – and a drawing of a skull and crossbones. In black ink. It was horrible.' Terror raced through me, and it made me speak even more harshly. 'What's wrong with you, Paul Fontaine? What are you trying to do?'

He shook his head. In a very quiet voice, he said, 'I don't know.' Then his voice sharpened again. He said, 'What happened to the portrait?'

'Charlie took it away to be cleaned.'

'Charlie!' he said sardonically.

'Yes. Charlie. Charlie, who's been helping me and looking after me.' I was horrified to find tears pricking my eyes. I thought suddenly of just how much I missed

Charlie, and how much I wanted to see him again. I said, 'You need not worry. I'm not going to tell Grand-père because I don't want to hurt him. But I'm going to tell Charlie. And you'd better not think you can do anything more against me, Paul. Or I'll tell not only Grand-père, but the police. Stay away from me, do you hear?'

He made a sudden movement towards me. I thought he was about to hit me. With a little squeak, I ducked out of the way, ran to the door and flew downstairs. At the bottom of the stairs, I stopped to draw my breath. He hadn't attempted to follow me. I stood there for an instant, trying to compose myself. There was no need to come bursting back into the kitchen and have everyone start asking questions. Obviously the Fontaines had no idea their son had done anything. And I'd dealt with it. I'd warned him off. And that would be enough. Or so I thought . . .

Something wicked this way comes

Charlie didn't get back home till Monday evening. That morning, I went with Madame Vallon and Samantha to the local market town, Castelnau. Grand-père didn't come with us. He said he felt a little tired and would spend the morning resting in bed.

I was a little tired too. I hadn't slept well the night before, because I'd lain awake thinking about everything. Had I done the right thing, speaking to Paul in that way? I was half-expecting he'd pull some trick on me that night and had made sure all the windows were firmly closed and my door locked, with a chair pushed up against it, for good measure. Nothing happened, but I kept imagining I would wake up to find the doorhandle turning. Once, I was startled out of an uneasy doze by an owl hooting somewhere outside the window. Another time, I was sure I heard footsteps just above my head, and sat bolt upright for a few seconds before deciding the quick pitter-patter was rodent, not human. None of it made for a peaceful night. But when morning came, I didn't want to stay in bed. I wanted to get out. I felt like I'd been in a kind of cell all night and needed to escape. So I was glad when the Vallons reminded me they were going to the market in Castelnau, and did I want to come with them?

It was raining again. Madame Vallon drove her Renault rather slowly, which wasn't surprising as the roads around the village are quite narrow and winding. The windscreen wipers were working full-time and there was a kind of mist rising from the fields, tending to pretty much blot out most of the way ahead. Anyway, we reached Castelnau without incident and parked the car near the market square. The markets were held under cover in an arched pavilion, open on all sides, which had served as a market-place since the late Middle Ages. Madame Vallon said that the stalls usually spilled out onto the square outside as well. Today there would be less stalls, and all of them crammed into the pavilion.

It was very busy in there, and very colourful, with stalls piled high with fruit and vegetables and cheeses and *saucisson* and olives and fish and all sorts of things. I walked around with the Vallon women for a little while, watching and listening as they bargained and bantered with the stallholders, filling their baskets with stuff. Madame Vallon insisted on introducing me to a couple of the stallholders, and gossiped shamelessly about how exciting it was to have the du Merle heiress back at the castle, while I stood on one leg, blushing and trying to look blasé. I managed to extricate myself and went off wandering through the market with my camera, taking pictures. I thought that would be something good to write about on the blog, something neutral that the girls back home would like. Food's always good for that. And everyone knows France is famous for its food. I certainly wasn't going to say anything much about what had happened. I might tell my friends later, by email or letter. Certainly not in a place where just anyone could read it. Certainly not now that I knew Paul had a computer and was looking up stuff about me. Not that he could do much, even if he did find my blog, except write rude comments on it or maybe try to hack it, if he was good at that sort of stuff.

After the marketing was finished, we went off to have a cup of coffee in one of the local cafés, and then Samantha and Madame Vallon went to do some other things while I wandered around under my umbrella, peering in at shop windows and taking random pictures. Castelnau is a compact little town, and practically all the shops were in streets that branched off the market square, so I covered the place pretty quickly. I browsed in a couple of clothes shops and in a music shop. In one pastry-shop window, I stared entranced at the most beautiful display of cakes I'd ever seen in my life. I met up with the Vallons again, and we went in and bought some fantastic cakes to take back with us. Then Madame Vallon declared we needed a nice hot lunch and so off we went to a little restaurant just off the market square. It was a popular place, noisy and crowded, filled with stallholders who had shut up shop for the day. We had big bowls of a yummy leek and potato soup, with thick crusty bread and a coil of the tastiest sausages ever, really meaty and peppery, with a hint of garlic and herbs. Madame Vallon said this sort of sausage was a speciality of Toulouse, and that she thought they were the best in the world.

I found myself relaxing and enjoying the Vallons' company very much. Well, I'd liked Samantha from the start. But even Madame Vallon seemed nicer away from the castle. She didn't even seize the opportunity to nosy-parker, as I half-thought she might. Instead of grilling me about my life, she talked about food, and recipes, and then about how she had met her husband – in a cheese shop, of all places! We all laughed at that, and she laughed loudest of all, and said that everyone knew that the way to a man's heart was through his stomach and she'd proved that with her Louis, that was for sure. Then she looked sideways at Samantha. 'You know that too, darling, don't you?'

Samantha shrugged. 'It's a bit more complicated than that with Simon.'

Her mother laughed. 'Oh no, dear, men are never complicated, it's just us who would like them to be so. You haven't given him enough yet to entice him.' The conversation continued on but I zoned out.

Simon. So it wasn't Paul she was interested in, just as Charlie had said. But though it was the first time I'd heard her boyfriend's name, it seemed to me there was something familiar about the name. Something I'd heard, and recently, too. In a moment, I got it and sat there feeling dismayed, all the cosiness disappearing. Simon was the name of one of Paul's older brothers. Of course it might not be him, there might be other Simons around, but it fitted with Paul giving her lifts – probably to the farm – and all that sort of thing. I'd begun thinking I might perhaps trust Samantha with some of what had happened, but now I was glad I hadn't. If she was in love with Simon Fontaine, she'd hardly want to hear things against his brother. Oh dear. It had been a nice morning, and I'd forgotten about the Fontaines, and now here I was again, plunged back into it.

We went home after lunch and I went straight into Grand-père's library and sat down at the computer and wrote up my posts. I did one about food, as I'd planned, and a little one about the wood, too, because I had taken a rather nice picture of it. ✧ I read them back afterwards and thought how it would be hard to guess what was really going on in my life, if you just went from that.

It's funny, people often seem to think that just because blogs are supposed to be about self-expression and all that, that a blogger is actually going to be honest, to tell the truth about themselves and what's going on. It's as if they think that just because it looks like printed words on a page, it's sort of official and true and all that. They act like they think the blog is wired into your brain or something and all the thoughts pouring down into it are really what's there. They don't think that maybe it's a way of hiding from things. A sort of mask. You put up this virtual person on the internet, and it's sort of you, but sort of not, too. Even if you're mostly honest, you can pick and choose what you reveal. And if you're not honest, you can pretend all kinds of stuff, because no-one can see you. You could even pretend to be a totally different person if you wanted. You heard of nasty types who hung around in chat rooms and pretended to be thirteen-year-old girls when in fact they were really forty-year-old perverts trying to snare kids. But it didn't even have to be quite as horrible and extreme as that. It could be just a matter of living out some kind of other identity, some sort of other life, on the web.

After blogging, I emailed the girls and told them a bit, but only a bit, about what was going on. Well, I told them a bit about Charlie and how cool he was. But I didn't talk about Paul, because to do so made me feel sick. I couldn't understand a guy like that. I mean, why would you do the things he did? Did he really believe that he was, indeed, my ancestral enemy and that he had to make the curse work on me? Surely that was mad-person stuff. Only someone with mental problems would seriously think that was an okay way to run your life. And what had he been hoping to find out about me on the web? I just didn't get it. But I knew I wanted it to stop.

Grand-père came down a little later. He was looking pale, I thought, but said he felt a lot better for having had a very quiet day in bed.

'I've been thinking about your birthday presents,' he said, 'and an idea came to me. Instead of going to Toulouse, Rose, why don't we go to Paris?'

'To *Paris*?' I repeated, astonished.

'Yes, for a few days. We can go shopping, I can show you around. I haven't been there for a long time. It would be a pleasure for me too, Rose. A real holiday.'

I gave him a hug. 'Oh, Grand-père, that would be fantastic! I would just love to see Paris!'

'I thought we might perhaps take Blanche with us,' he said, with a quick glance at me. 'If I do get tired, there'll be someone to show you around.'

'Oh, no, Grand-père, *please*. I'm sure I can find my way around Paris, if I have to. There are maps, after all, and I can ask people.' I had only seen Blanche Randal again briefly that day, after we got back from Castelnau, and she'd gone off to the station now to meet Charlie's train. She had treated me with a cold courtesy verging on disdain. I could not bear the thought of going to Paris with her. She would spoil everything. 'But perhaps Charlie?' I hazarded.

Grand-père shot me a quizzical look. 'I don't think that would be quite suitable, Rose.' A pause, then he went on, 'He's a very handsome boy, I know. But –'

'But he's also very nice,' I said. 'And he thinks a lot of you, Grand-père. He really does! He thinks a lot of all our family. He knows so much!'

'Does he?' said Grand-père, gently. 'Poor Charlie. He doesn't have much of a real family, I suppose, so that's why he's so interested in us. Ah, well. Sorry, Rose, but I still think it won't do. We'll go on our own then. We'll leave tomorrow. The lawyer was going to come on Wednesday, but I'll put him off. That can wait. Now then, I'll book some plane tickets right now, and we'll stay at the hotel I usually stay at when I'm there. You'll see, it's a lovely place. So, Rose, what do you say?'

'Oh, Grand-père, I think it's just wonderful!'

We had dinner with Charlie and his mother that night. To my surprise – and relief – Charlie seemed to have given up on giving his mother the silent treatment. In fact, he seemed animated and even happy. And Blanche kept smiling at her son. It was soon clear why. Charlie had got the job.

'I start on Wednesday,' he said. 'They said I was just the sort of person they were looking for. And they said that if I did well, there would be very good opportunities for promotion.'

'Marvellous! This calls for a glass of champagne,' said Grand-père heartily, and we all raised our glasses and toasted Charlie and his success. I was a bit hazy on just what the job was that he'd gone for – it sounded like it was in an office or something – but everyone else seemed to know, and I thought I'd look stupid if I asked. It was odd to think of Charlie working in an office like an ordinary person. But of course I didn't know what kind of office, did I? There were all sorts.

Grand-père said, 'So I suppose now you're going to have to learn to use a computer, Charlie. No more excuses.'

'Oh, I can learn on the job if I have to,' said Charlie, airily. 'I don't suppose it'll take long.'

'No,' said Grand-père, 'if even an old man like me can learn, it should be easy for you. Well, Charlie. Does this mean you'll be leaving us and getting a flat in Toulouse?'

I shot an anguished glance at Charlie. I couldn't help it. He met my glance with a warm look that made my heart beat faster. He said, 'I don't think so. I'll go on the train every day. Maman has said she'll drive me to Castelnau station, but once I get a bit of money, I'll buy a moped and use it to get to the station myself. Later, maybe I'll get a car and go down the motorway to Toulouse. I was told that after the first week or two, I can do some of the work from home.' He looked at Grand-père. 'If you don't mind my staying here, of course, Monsieur le Comte.'

'Of course not, my boy. This is your home. I just thought . . . well, you're a young man and you might prefer to be in Toulouse, where things are happening, than being buried here in the countryside.'

'I'm a country boy, not a city one,' said Charlie softly. 'And I love it here.'

'So I see,' said Grand-père, rather sardonically, glancing at me. 'Well, Charlie, you must do as you think fit. But you might well get tired of the constant toing and froing. Still, that's your business, and Blanche's, if she's willing to be the taxi for a while.'

'Oh yes, Monsieur le Comte,' said the Snow Queen. She was looking positively thawed out, her eyes sparkling, her movements quick and bright. She even seemed to look on me kindly tonight. She wasn't a fool. She must have seen

159

Charlie's expression as he looked at me, and decoded Grand-père's glance. But even though she'd warned me off her son before, tonight, things seemed different. Perhaps it was just that she was so relieved. Grand-père had told me that Charlie had been unemployed ever since he'd left school, nearly three years ago, and that she'd despaired he'd ever find a niche. Now it appeared he had, and she was thrilled.

I didn't get a chance to talk to Charlie alone till well after dinner. I'd already gone up to bed when there was a soft knock on my door. I went to open it. There stood Charlie.

'Can I come in?'

I was glad I'd just been writing my diary at the desk and hadn't yet got into my seriously uncool nightclothes. (Memo to self: Get some good PJs in Paris!) 'Sure. Come in.'

I was trying to seem relaxed. I had made the decision that we should just be friends, remember? But hell, it wasn't easy. He was just so gorgeous, and he smiled at me so warmly that my insides began to melt.

He sat on the chair. I sat on the bed. He glanced over to the desk. 'You writing something?'

'Just my journal,' I said uncomfortably.

'Oh. Good practice for a future author,' he said. 'Look, Rose, I wanted to tell you – I got that portrait cleaned up. It'll be fine to return now. So what's been happening here? My mother told me about the death knell being rung. Who did it? Do they know yet?'

'Well, I think – I'm nearly sure – it was Paul Fontaine,' I said, and I told him what had happened. Charlie listened with a darkening expression. When I'd finished, he said,

'Good God. I always thought there was something up with that guy but now I'm sure. He's loopy. What do you think we should do, Rose?'

'I was hoping you would think of something. I don't want to tell Grand-père. Not right now, anyway. I don't want to worry him before we go away.'

'Yes, you're going to Paris, aren't you? Well, I think that's a good thing. I mean, you won't be here, so Paul won't be able to do anything against you, and you'll be safe.'

'But why, Charlie? I don't understand. I mean, why would he want to scare me? Is it just because of the curse? That seems crazy.'

'It does,' he said. 'But I'm tempted to think that even if Paul *has* lost his marbles mentally, there's method to his madness. The curse is maybe just an excuse. There is another reason. Something not mad, but bad.'

'But what?' I almost wailed.

'I don't know. But while you're away in Paris, I'll do some poking around on my own, see what I can come up with.' He got up and came to sit beside me. He put an arm around me. 'You look pale. Did he really frighten you that much?'

'It's hard to think that someone can hate you like that,' I said, swallowing. Paul's hate wasn't the only thing making me tremble, though. Much more potent was Charlie's closeness. To master myself, I started telling him about the other stuff, the prowler in the garden, the walk in the wood, Renée Fontaine and what she'd said.

'Well, my poor little Rose, you've had quite a time of it, haven't you?' he said, softly. 'I wish I'd been there.'

'I do, too, Charlie,' I said, 'except that then you'd not have got your job.'

'That's true. But it's a pity it had to be that weekend. Anyway, now things will be different. I'm going to unmask that creep Fontaine. It wouldn't surprise me if that lunatic aunt of his is also involved. She's always had a grudge against the family. She had her hooks into your grandfather before he met your grandmother.'

'Oh,' I said cautiously. He must have got that story from his mother. I remembered what Madame Vallon had said, but of course I wasn't going to let on. Charlie might not get on with his mother most of the time but what you can say yourself about your parents, you're hardly likely to accept from an outsider. Besides, it was plain Madame Vallon didn't like the Snow Queen, and it was possible she had twisted the truth. As to Renée Fontaine, I wasn't sure about her at all. Grand-père seemed to like her, but then Grand-père, I thought, seemed to think the best of everyone.

'In fact,' Charlie went on, not noticing my reserve, 'I think it was your grandfather's mother – the first Rose – who put her foot down about him seeing her any more. Oh, my God, Rose, I've just thought. The damage to the portrait – that might well be her doing.'

'Yes,' I said, slowly. 'It could. Or them, together. Oh, Charlie, do you think – that thing she told me, in the wood – maybe it wasn't just a bit of fortune telling, or even a warning. Maybe it was a threat.'

'Yes,' he said, soberly. 'I think it was.'

'Charlie, I don't know what to do.'

'You don't need to do anything,' he said, and turned me around to face him. 'I will do it, Rose. I will do it for you.' And he bent his face down to mine and kissed me. A proper kiss, and not at all the kind of kiss I'd had from any other boy before. Charlie Randal knew how to do it. There was no clashing of teeth or sucking of lips and no fumbling or anything awkward or embarrassing. It wasn't like his earlier kisses, either. This was a real kiss, and I was gasping and shaking when it finished.

'Charlie, I –'

'Don't say anything,' he said, gently putting a finger to my lips. 'We've got lots of time to say lots of things, you and I. We don't have to rush. Just remember, I'll always be here for you, and when you come back from Paris, everything will be all right. Everything.' He got up, and stood there looking down at me, and smiling.

'Charlie,' I began in a strangled sort of tone, 'you don't have to go yet . . .'

'Yes, I do,' he said. 'Now, you go to bed and get your beauty sleep, and I'll go to bed and dream of you.'

'Okay,' I said, twisting my hands together. I wasn't sure whether to be sad or glad.

'You're beautiful,' he said, 'Goodnight, sweet Rose'. He took my hand and touched it with his lips, softly, just as if we were back in the old days, when the castle had first been built. Giving me an ironic little smile, he bowed and left the room, and I was left sitting there staring into blank space.

After a moment, I got up. I didn't feel at all sleepy. I paced around for a bit, trying to calm myself down, then I sat myself at the desk and re-read what I'd written in the diary, up till now. It seemed curiously far away. Even reading about what Paul Fontaine had done didn't touch me. I just kept thinking, Charlie said I was beautiful. No-one's ever said anything like that to me before. I picked up the pen and drew a heart. I wrote, 'Rose loves Charlie.

Charlie loves Rose,' and then sat looking at it, my heart thumping, my brain racing, trying to tell myself I was joking, just trying it out, but knowing I wasn't, not really, that I was falling for Charlie big time, and that it wasn't like anything I'd ever felt before . . .

At that very moment, I looked up and saw my door handle turning. But I wasn't scared. I knew who it would be. 'Charlie?'

No answer. I said, a little more loudly, 'It's all right, you can come in, I haven't locked the door.'

No answer. I got up and went to the door. The handle slipped in my hand, and it was a few seconds by the time I got it open and flung open the door.

There was no Charlie standing there smiling at me. No-one was there at all. Frowning, I looked down the corridor. There was no-one. Everything was very quiet. Very normal.

Should I go to Charlie's room and tell him? But tell him what? What had really happened after all. I had seen a doorhandle turning. *Or I thought I had seen a doorhandle turning.* Now I really came to think about it, did I really, really remember that? Confused, I went back to my room and shut the door. After a moment's thought, I locked it, and put the key under my pillow. I sat there for a little while, watching the doorhandle, but it didn't turn again. I began to think I must have imagined it, went to bed and fell asleep.

I awoke in the dark of the night, pulled out of sleep by a sound. Footsteps sounded overhead. And it was definitely not the pitter-patter of rats or mice. Someone was walking just above my head. I lay there, listening, thinking I didn't need to worry, that it was someone's room on the second floor. But deep inside me I knew there was no-one up there. I mean, no-one who *should* be there. There were locked rooms up there, Blanche Randal had told me. Rooms that were out of bounds because they were unsafe. I thought, I've got to get Charlie. I've got to tell him Paul's got into the house, somehow, and he's walking around up there and God knows what he's going to do.

I didn't stop to think. I flung on my dressing-gown, unlocked my door and padded along the corridor to Charlie's door. I knocked, softly. No answer. I knocked again. Still no answer. I tried the handle. It was locked. I smiled to myself. Did he think he'd save me from myself, by locking me out or something? I put my mouth to the keyhole, and hissed, 'Charlie! Charlie!'

At last, he answered. He sounded rather breathy and shaky, as if I'd awakened him from a bad dream. He whispered, 'Rose? Is that you?'

'Yes. Unlock the door.'

In a second, there he was, his hair out on his shoulders, rubbing the sleep from his eyes. He looked pale. 'What's up?'

'I heard footsteps – up above me. I think it's in one of the locked rooms on the second floor.'

'What? But how –' He ran a hand through his hair, and seemed to wake up properly. 'I'll go up and see.'

'I'll come with you.'

'No, it might not be safe.'

'Don't be silly. We'll scream the place down if he tries anything. We need the keys. Where are they?'

'In the kitchen drawer, along with the others. Quick, you go down and get them. I'll go up there, see what I can see.'

So I hared down the stairs, as quickly and quietly as I could, found the bunch of keys, and raced back up the stairs with them. The stairs to the second floor were at the far end of the corridor, beyond a door, and they were narrower than those leading up to the first floor. They were also creaky. I went carefully, not wanting to wake up everyone. Strangely, my earlier fear had given way to a strange excitement. It was sort of thrilling, chasing down intruders in the dead of night with the one you loved! I felt like I was capable of just about anything, I was brave enough to try anything at all. Paul wouldn't know what hit him, I thought proudly as I reached the top of the stairs and opened the landing door.

Charlie was in the corridor. He had a torch in his hand. Its thin pencil of light made a spot on the floor. He beckoned me forward. 'I've had a look in the unlocked rooms,' he whispered. 'There's no-one there. It's all mostly storerooms and so on. You got the keys?'

'Here they are.' I handed them to him. He peered at the labels printed on them. 'Let's try this one.' He unlocked the door, flung it open and shone the torch in. Dust and mould greeted us, nothing more. He tried the next one, and still nothing. Then he opened the third door. 'I think this one's just about directly above your room.' He shone the torch in, and I peered over his shoulder.

It was a large room, nearly as large as my bedroom, but quite empty. It had a pair of French doors opening on to what must be a balcony. One of these was partly ajar. I suddenly thought of looking up the other night, and seeing that balcony. A little prickle of cold crisped over my skin.

'Look at that floor,' said Charlie, shining the torch on it.

The floor was very dusty. In it you could plainly see the mark of a shoe. Charlie said, 'Someone's been in here.' He shone the torch over the room. As he did so, I saw a pile of rags in a corner. I took little notice of it. There was nothing particularly sinister about it.

Charlie said, 'I should go in and take a proper look.'

'There's no point. You can see it's empty. He's not here. Look at that door. It's a bit open. He must have got out when he heard us coming.'

'Yes, I suppose he must have,' said Charlie. He frowned. 'I don't like it. Why should he take a risk like this?' He moved a little into the room, testing the floor with one foot. 'Just checking it's not going to crash down in a shower of wood and plaster on to your bed,' he said, lightly. But the floor held firm, though it creaked a bit. He reached the doors, opened them fully, and stepped onto the balcony. 'There's nothing out here,' he declared, as I walked in my turn, cautiously, over the floor towards him.

The rain had eased a little but it was still a fairly dark night. You had to peer for quite a while before you could see anything. But it was true that there seemed to be nothing and no-one out there. However Paul had got in, unnoticed, he'd left the same way. We left the balcony, closed the French doors and went back into the room.

'That idiot chose a nasty night to be out on his tricks,' said Charlie. 'He'll be drenched, if he doesn't break his leg first.'

'I wish he would,' I said, savagely. 'I wish he'd break his neck and leave us alone.'

'Now, now, Rose,' said Charlie, with a laugh in his voice, 'that's not a very nice thing to say.'

'I don't care! I still think it!'

'Yes, well, it's not going to happen. We have to catch him another way. Rose, can you go and get a piece of paper and a pencil? I think we should make a drawing of these footprints. Somehow I can try and check if they match one of Paul's shoes.'

'I'll go and get them,' I said, and flew downstairs to my room. Someone wicked had tried to scare me and make me feel like I was in danger. But it was no good. I was not scared any more. With Charlie by my side, there was no way Paul or anyone else could get the better of us two working together.

Interlude in Paris

The rest of the night passed without incident. I went back to my bed, Charlie went back to his. I fell asleep not on thoughts of the footprints in the dust or the open door in the abandoned room, but of Charlie's voice as he said that I was beautiful. I slept deeply and well and woke up feeling rested and full of energy.

I packed my bag quickly – I didn't take too much, because Grand-père had said not to, and that we'd go shopping – got dressed in my orange trousers, green shirt and jumper, and went down for breakfast. Charlie and Blanche were there too. We had quite a companionable breakfast. Charlie behaved normally to me, not as if we were together, and so, conscious of his mother's and my grandfather's presence, I took my cue from him.

I sensed I could see relief in Blanche's eyes as she talked about how I'd have such a good time in Paris. She would be glad to see the back of me for a week and have her precious son to herself, I thought. But I didn't care. Charlie was a free spirit. He would do his own thing, no matter what she wanted. He'd made that very clear already. Yes, I thought, I would miss him, while we were in Paris. But there was a deep golden glow in my heart which made me feel I could wait like he wanted. Still, I wanted to keep in touch. Under the cover of the other two making arrangements for mail and so on, I leaned over to Charlie and whispered, 'I wish you had an email address. I could send you emails while I'm away.'

'Sorry, Rose,' he said, 'but I've never liked the internet. All that instant communication without thought. I don't think it's very healthy.'

I smiled. 'You just say that because you've never tried it,' I said. 'I bet you you'll be hooked once you do!'

'Maybe you're right,' he said, smiling back.

'You don't have a mobile phone, either, do you?'

'No,' he grinned. 'I'm terribly old-fashioned, I'm afraid. Ring me here at night, if you want. Or send me a postcard, or a letter. Or both.'

'That I will,' I said fervently.

Not long after breakfast, Louis Vallon came round with the Mercedes and we left. My last sight of Charlie for a week was of him standing there, waving goodbye. I hugged the image to me, and then turned my mind to enjoyment of the week that was to come.

By eleven, we were in Toulouse. Our plane was not leaving till nearly two, so we all three went for a delicious lunch in a rather nice restaurant not far from Place du Capitole, Toulouse's grand main square. It was my first sight of the city. Though it wasn't the best weather to see it in, I liked the look of it and resolved to explore it one day. Grand-père told me that in the Middle Ages it was one of the richest cities in Europe, because of its involvement in the production of the blue dye known as pastel. Most of the city's grand buildings and beautiful houses dated from then. Later, the city had fallen on hard times, but now it was well known again, because it was where the giant European aviation company Airbus was based. It was here that the supersonic jet Concorde had been tested, Grand-père said, with a regretful sigh. 'Do you know, Rose, I took the Concorde once for a trip to New York? It was marvellous. What a shame it all ended so badly with that horrible accident. It was a good plane, but maybe ahead of its time. Still, at least I can say I did travel in it, at least once.'

He'd lived such a glamorous life. How little I knew about it all, about all the things he'd done before I even knew he existed, all the people he'd known! I was sure he must have wonderful stories to tell. I thought this week would be the time to find out. I was filled with happiness. Never mind the doomsayers and the frighteners, things *were* turning out for the best. All my wishes had come true, and no terrible price had been exacted from me for having had my wishes granted. I was living a real-life fairytale. I'd become like a princess in a castle, with the king being a loving grandfather who was taking his granddaughter to the most beautiful city in the world for a week of wish-granting, and I'd even met Prince Charming. What more could a girl ask for?

The plane ride was a bit bumpy because of all the heavy clouds, but I found it quite fun. And it was over quickly too. By three-fifteen we were taxiing into Orly airport. Half an hour later we were on our way through the Paris traffic, heading for our hotel. It was teeming with rain but that didn't stop my enjoyment sticky-beaking at Paris through the window. Grand-père pointed out things to me as we went along. 'Look, there's the Closerie des Lilas – it's one of the most famous cafés in Paris, all sorts of famous people used to go there, like Hemingway, and Lenin, and Trotsky, and Verlaine. Any day of the week you can still find celebrities there. Did you know, an aristocrat bought the place as a present for his mistress, at the beginning of the twentieth century – that's the kind of place it is. Oh, and there, look, there's the Luxembourg Palace, beautiful gardens there, we'll go for a walk there if this weather ever clears up – and over there, you can glimpse the Halles, that's where the big Paris markets used to be. Nowadays it's all chic shops and artists and so on – and look, there, Rose, Notre Dame! And the Seine, of course . . . We'll have to go for a trip on it. What do you say?'

He was as excited as a child. As excited as me. By the time we pulled up to the hotel, he had already started planning a dozen trips, a hundred trips, all the stuff we could do in Paris, all the things we would see. If we'd been in Paris a month, we couldn't have done a third of it. But it didn't matter. It didn't matter at all. We were in Paris, the most romantic city in the whole wide world, and we were going to enjoy ourselves!

Our hotel was called Hôtel Pavillon de la Reine, or Hotel of the Queen's Pavilion, and it was housed in a beautiful eighteenth-century mansion in the heart of the Place des Vosges, in the Marais district of Paris, very central to everything. Grand-père had stayed there before. He said in his opinion it was the best hotel in Paris, with the best location in Paris too. It was easy to see why. The Place des Vosges was a beautiful, atmospheric sort of square, lined with arcaded shops and gorgeous old buildings that once formed part of a royal palace. Because you came into it through a kind of portal, it felt cut off from the traffic outside, set in its own serenity and beauty. I liked it at once.

And I liked the hotel too. If I'd gone there straight after arriving from Australia, I'd have felt completely overawed because it was really grand and beautiful, with its antique furniture, oak beams, huge stone fireplaces and flagged entrance room. But I'd come from the Chateau. The hotel felt familiar, almost like home, and the staff were not snobby at all. And that was another thing – for the first time I realised, from the staff's attitude toward him, just how my grandfather was regarded outside our small world back in St Martin du Merle. It wasn't as the Count, or as my grandfather, but as the writer Valentin de la Tour. And that name meant a great deal to many people. And it wasn't only the staff who admired him. More than once people approached him in the lobby, wanting to tell him how much they'd enjoyed his latest book. It was strange but nice, watching it happen.

Grand-père had booked us a suite on one of the top floors. It was fantastic, huge, with beautiful paintings on the walls and a view onto the hotel's interior courtyard, which must be gorgeous when it was sunny – even now it looked nice. My room was almost as good as my bedroom at the Chateau, and everything seemed just right. Grand-père looked pleased when I told him I thought it was perfect. 'I'm glad it wasn't just an old man's loyal eyes,' he said.

We had a bit of a rest, and spent the rest of the afternoon just enjoying the hotel. Then we went out for a short walk under the arcades, looking into the windows of antique shops and art shops and rather chic boutiques. We had a wonderful dinner at the hotel, and went to bed early, so the next day we could begin our exploration of Paris nice and early.

*

Days passed. They were wonderful days, filled with sight-seeing and talking and walking and exploring and laughing. We went to all the spots you must go to, when you're first in Paris – the Eiffel Tower, Notre Dame, the Luxembourg, the Champs Élysées, the Left Bank, Mont-martre, the Opera and much, much more. We traipsed through a small bit of the Louvre – I had no idea the place was so huge – and dutifully peered at the Mona Lisa and many other famous paintings and sculptures. (I was a little surprised by how small the painting of the Mona Lisa was, and disappointed because it was difficult to see it properly through the reinforced glass that protected it, and over the heads of dozens of tourists with flashing cameras. But at least I'd seen it!)

We went for a ride in one of those glass-covered tourist boats down the Seine, which was really cool, because it was the first time Grand-père had gone on one so it was a new experience for us both. We went to the Invalides, where Napoleon's tomb was, and talked about the Emperor in low voices, but not so low that one of the staff didn't hear us, recognise Grand-père and insist on hauling him in to see his superiors. Grand-père had to sign some books and talk shop, which he did with a little wry wink at me. We caught taxis and the Metro but generally tried to walk as much as we could, dodging the rain under our large umbrellas. We had lunch in cosy little cafés and dinner in swish restaurants. We went to a concert and to the cinema and called into bookshops and boutiques. We window-shopped along the Avenue Montaigne and Rue du Faubourg Saint-Honoré, with their high-fashion houses, like Dior, Yves Saint Laurent, Versace, Louis Vuitton and Hermes. But we didn't go in or buy anything there. Grand-père said that for a young girl it might be more fun to buy clothes in what he called *'les grands magasins'*, the big shops or department stores.

So one blissful day, after a good breakfast at the hotel, we set off to Boulevard Haussmann, where most of the department stores are, and I was let loose to rummage through them to my heart's content. Grand-père said big shops tired him so he sat in a café, read books and wrote letters while I kept popping back and forth, excitedly reporting the things I'd seen. My favourite *grand magasin* was Les Galeries Lafayette, with its gorgeous glass and steel dome, and my feet and brain ached by the time I had explored just some of its ten floors. But I'd found things I wanted there – some fabulous nightclothes, two new pairs of trousers, three shirts, a dress, a skirt and three jumpers – so Grand-père came back with me, and bought them. He also encouraged me to buy a lovely silver evening dress to wear at my birthday party, which he had decided would be held at the castle the following weekend. (We'd talked about it and decided that we could have a fancy dress party another time, maybe for my eighteenth. This year would be quieter.) Later that same day, we went to a very posh jewellery shop and I chose my actual birthday present – a necklace of silver, moonstones and jade that was absolutely stunning and definitely the most valuable and beautiful thing I'd ever owned in my life.

Don't think, though, that Paris was just about buying things, gaping at monuments and tourist sites. It wasn't, though of course that was all heaps of fun. It was also about being with Grand-père and getting to know more about him, about the stories he told me over our meals together. He told me about the places he'd been to, the people he'd met, but most of all he told me more about himself and his family. About his rather wild youth, and his parents, and the courtship of his wife.

'Caroline reminded me of the Mona Lisa,' he said. 'She had a face like that – calm, a little smile, never giving anything away. I was a little awed by that calm and serenity, because I was nothing like that at that age.'

I thought of what I'd imagined, when I'd looked at those family photos – how I'd thought Caroline looked so anxious and uncertain and Grand-père so calm and collected. I'd obviously been quite wrong. I would never have picked her as the Mona Lisa. Wrong colouring, for a start. But then, as Grand-père would have said, that was poetic licence.

Grand-père talked about my father too, and that was the sweetest thing of all. It seemed to me that I could see Dad before me as his father told me about all the things he used to get up to: how he learned to drive really early; how he liked to play tricks.

'He could be really naughty, Rose, but he did play quite a good trick once, on a weekend when Caroline's parents had come for a visit. They weren't very nice people, I'm afraid, terribly stuffy and snobby, the sort who give the nobility a bad name – you know, the sort of people who live on the laurels of their ancestors and never do anything for themselves. They were horrified by Caroline running off, of course – they refused to ever see her again. Great ones for condemning people for immorality, they were. But it's fair to say too that they hadn't liked me from the start. I had an impeccable name, yes – but they thought I was a trifle vulgar, because I wrote. A gentleman didn't

176

write, in their opinion, and certainly, if he must, then he should publish slim volumes of poetry and not thumping great popular history that just anybody might read.' He laughed, but I could see that his eyes still held a trace of the irritation he must have felt back then. 'They had never given poor Caroline the affection she needed – that wasn't done, you see – and I think that was the source of many of her problems. Poor Caroline!'

He sighed. 'I wish I'd been more patient with her. When she left me I was angry, but that faded in time, almost to a sense of relief, I'm ashamed to say. She could be very difficult. Anyway, back to my story. When Caroline left, her parents kept their distance for a while, because they were ashamed, but then they started visiting again, saying they wanted to see Philippe. How could I stop them? Besides, I felt rather sorry for them. I thought they might have mellowed. I was wrong. They were just as critical as ever. Nitpick, nitpick, all the time. Philippe couldn't stand them. And one night, he took his revenge. He took a cardboard tube, slipped into their room in the dead of night and stood behind the curtains intoning, "Confess, or your time will come," down the cardboard tube, so it would come out in a spooky kind of way.' He laughed. 'Caroline's father woke up and thought it was the voice of his conscience speaking to him and, in a blind panic, said, "I promise I won't see her again, I promise I won't see her again." His wife heard his confession and there was hell to pay. Turned out he'd been seeing another woman for years, the old humbug.'

'What did they do then?'

'Oh, they just left the next morning, in high dudgeon with each other and us. Philippe and I didn't clap eyes on them again for quite a while, thank God.' His eyes suddenly changed expression. 'Oh, Rose. If only I could wind time back and change things. If only I had remembered how much I loved my son when he was a child and hadn't let my stupid pride and disappointment come in the way of it. I talk of those precious humbugs of the de la Mottes, but am I really any better? No, I'm not. And don't argue, Rose. It's true. I've regretted it for a good while now, but I can't hide from the truth of it. I was a selfish, snobby, inconsiderate beast every bit as bad as Caroline's father.'

'I don't suppose he regretted anything,' I said warmly, trying to comfort him.

He smiled. 'He didn't, but that still doesn't make me better than him. I took too long to come to my senses.'

'Yes, but now you have, Grand-père. Let's not talk of sad things. Let's talk of happy ones. Tell me about the day Dad was born.'

'Ah, that was a day and no mistake,' he said, his expression lightening. 'This is what happened . . .' And he was off on another story, and his face was changing again, filled with the sweetness of the memory.

One night I called Charlie from the hotel, but his mother told me he was out. I was a little put out – I had kind of expected he might be waiting for a phone call from me – but I told myself it didn't matter. I decided nevertheless that I was not going to call him for the rest of my stay. It was better to write to him. Anyway I'm always better at expressing myself on the page. On the phone I stutter and say stupid things because I don't like awkward silences. So I sat down that night after filling in my journal and I wrote him a letter, the first love letter I'd ever written in my life. It made me feel really good, but when I read it back, I became nervous and decided I really couldn't send it. It was too much, too soon. He'd think I was going too fast. So I tore it up into little pieces and instead wrote him a flippant postcard of the 'wish you were here' kind.

On the Friday night, I also went to my blog and wrote up a piece about Paris. ✍ I noticed that Koschei had put another comment on my blog, on the post I'd written the other day. It said something about 'beware the witch in the woods'. That gave me a shock because I couldn't help thinking about Reneé. Who the hell was this Koschei, and why on earth did they keep on popping up like this on my blog? Then I thought, there's often witches in woods in fairytales, and I'd mentioned an old lady who looked like a witch in an earlier blog. I decided Koschei was just trying to psych me out. So I pushed it aside.

Portia, Alice and Maddy had all emailed back, excited about my revelations about Charlie. Alice, bless her, said I had to ask him if he had a younger brother or a cousin or anything, and that I must then get this person's email address and send it to them. They all wanted me to post a photo of him but there was no way I was going to do that. Not only did I not particularly want everyone to perve on him, I was also unsure what Charlie himself would think if I splashed him all over the internet. I was pretty sure he'd hate the idea.

To my surprise there was also an email from Aunt Jenny. She said she'd thought she might hear from me a bit more if she modernised herself and so she'd gone to the library and got herself started on the internet. Her email was full of typos, and some of it was partly in capital letters, a sure sign of hunt and peck computing. It touched me strangely. Partly that was because I felt shame at neglecting her, I suppose.

I wrote back to her saying I was sorry I hadn't been in touch but that I was so busy and blah blah blah . . . and told her about our trip to Paris, and how fantastic Grand-père was, and everything, but nothing about Charlie and certainly nothing about Paul. I also said that she should come over, that I was missing her and that I thought she would love it here and she deserved a holiday. I wrote that on the spur of the moment but when I'd sent off the email, I decided it was all true. I *had* missed her, in a way, and I did think she needed a holiday. I could just see her in some of the chic shops we'd been to, and in those elegant streets where you could just imagine Audrey Hepburn sitting at a café table or walking a little dog. Aunt Jenny would love it. She would just love it.

It was on the second-last day that an extraordinary thing happened. On Sundays in Paris, you can get into the museums for free, and so Grand-père and I decided we'd go back to the Louvre to see some of the art we'd missed. We were wandering around in a lovely little gallery of French paintings from the eighteenth century, looking at portraits of solemn little boys in pigtails and fluttery-eyed girls in flouncy dresses when someone said, 'My God, I don't believe it.'

I saw the colour drain from Grand-père's face at the sound of that voice. Startled, I turned and saw an elderly woman looking at us from just a few steps away. Elderly she might be, but she looked smart. Her white hair was shaped in a fashionable short cut, and her clothes – cream trousers, navy-blue roll-neck jumper, cream trench coat, aquamarine scarf, pointy navy shoes – were pure Paris. Her eyes were a faded blue behind her smart glasses.

I looked at Grand-père. He was standing there like a statue, staring at her. She smiled. 'Come now, Valentin, is it really so dreadful to see me again?' Her curious gaze flicked across to me.

My grandfather finally found his voice. He said, faintly, 'My dear Caroline, of course it's not dreadful. It's –'

'Unexpected,' said the woman. I stared at her too, unable to believe . . .

Grand-père pulled himself together. 'It's been a long time, Caroline.'

'It has. A very long time.'

'You've changed,' he said. 'You look more –'

'More old?' she said, smiling.

'That. But then, so do I. No, I meant, more confident. Poised.'

'Things change,' she said levelly.

'Yes.' He paused, then went on, 'Ricardo . . .?'

'My husband is dead,' broke in Caroline, briskly. 'He died more than ten years ago.'

'I – I see.'

'Aren't you going to introduce me to the young lady? Family of yours, is she?' said Caroline, inquiringly.

'And of yours,' he replied, softly.

Now it was her turn to stare. She searched my face, my eyes, then she looked back to my grandfather. She went a little pale. 'Please, Valentin, tell me.'

'This is Rose,' said my grandfather. 'Your granddaughter. Philippe's daughter.'

She went completely white then. She looked like she was about to faint, so that we both moved towards her to catch her. But she mastered herself. She whispered, 'My God. I can't . . . I can't . . .'

'I know. I couldn't take it in either, at first,' said Grand-père. His voice was steady now. 'I think we all need a cup of coffee, don't you?'

So we went to the Louvre café and tried to talk to each other, and catch up on years of anguish and separation. It was very romantic and very exciting but it was also scary and hard. Most of all for them. Because both of them had, each in their own way, abandoned their child, my father, and now they were here with his daughter, trying to paper over the cracks.

I sat there and thought about what Grand-père had told me about Caroline just a few days earlier, and I looked at her profile and wondered if she too regretted things or not. Then I thought about Grand-père and what it must be like to be suddenly faced with the wife who ran away from you nearly forty years ago. I felt sorry for both of them but I also felt angry about what they'd done. Or not done, too. Why hadn't my grandmother contacted her family again? How could you just leave your little boy and never go back to see him, and only ever write him letters and send presents on his birthday and at Christmas? Perhaps it was because she was ashamed, or thought it was better like that, but it still seemed wrong to me. And why had Grand-père allowed Philippe to just disappear, and not patched things up before it was too late? What dreadful things people did to each other, I thought, and how they hurt each other – it was unbearable to think about. Then I listened a bit more to what they were saying and heard Caroline talking about Ricardo, the painter she'd left everyone for, and how they'd been very happy together, and had three children. And that made me suddenly more angry than anything else.

'If only Dad had known,' I said. 'He would have loved to have had brothers and sisters. He said so, more than once.'

Her face crumpled as she looked at me. 'Oh Rose, my dear, I'm so sorry. Forgive me.' Her hand, with its cargo of beautiful rings, rested on mine for a moment. I pulled it away. She sighed. 'I know how you must feel.'

'No, you don't,' I said, harshly. 'You don't at all.'

There was a little silence. Then she said, quietly, 'You're right. I don't know. And I have no right to intrude at all.'

She got up, pulling on her gloves. I could see tears shining in her eyes and it made me feel a little guilty. But I wasn't sorry for what I'd said. It was no use pretending.

Grand-père got up too. 'Don't just go like that, Caroline. Don't just disappear . . . again.'

They looked at each other. She said, faintly, 'Very well,' and pulled a card out of her handbag. She handed it to Grand-père. She said, 'When you're ready, perhaps?'

'Yes,' Grand-père said. And then she gave us a funny little smile, said goodbye and walked away, her back very straight, her heels clicking on the floor. I sat there looking after her, thinking that I'd been very cruel but that she deserved it, while Grand-père sat staring at the card in his hand.

He was the first to break the silence. 'What a thing. What a thing.' He flicked an uncertain glance at me. 'Odd to see each other again after so many years. I felt –' He stopped abruptly.

'What did you feel, Grand-père? It must have been so hard.'

'It wasn't. That's the odd thing. She was – it was like a different person standing there. A person I could talk to more easily than I could the old Caroline. A stranger, and yet not an unwelcome stranger.'

I said nothing. He looked at the card in his hand and said, 'Madame Caroline Orazio. She must be on holidays in Paris too, because her card says Bordeaux. Well. I don't know . . .' He stood up. 'We'll see about contacting her. If you really don't want to see her, Rose, we won't.'

'You should,' I said. 'It's important to you, Grand-père.'

'No, it isn't. Time has passed. Too much time. But for you, Rose . . . come what may, she is your grandmother.'

'I don't think I'd want to, not just yet, anyway,' I said honestly. 'Maybe later. Can we please go and have a look at some more paintings, and not talk about this, for the moment?'

'Of course, my darling girl,' he said, and taking my arm, he led me through the maze of galleries to the beautiful paintings of the Renaissance masters. But although we talked about everything but Caroline that afternoon and evening, her shadow hovered between us.

Grandma's footsteps

We didn't get back to the Chateau till late that Monday afternoon. To my disappointment, Charlie wasn't there. His mother said he had told her he was staying in town till the following evening as he had a lot of work to finish. And no, he hadn't left a message for me. She looked at me with a faint smile of triumph as she said this, and I felt like slapping her.

But when I got back to my room, I found a note slipped under a book on my bedside table. It said, 'Meet me Tuesday at 6.30, in the churchyard. Don't say anything to anyone. C.'

I sat looking at that note for quite a while. While we'd been in Paris, I'd almost been able to forget all the stuff that had been happening here. Now here I was, plunged back into it. What had Charlie found out? Why didn't he tell me? Why did he want to meet me in the churchyard? And – almost as important – what did he feel about me? There was no 'love', no 'kisses', not even that homely French version called *bisous* that you send out to friends and family. Very brief, very to the point and a little scary.

It nagged at me that night as we had a light and early dinner and again as I went up to bed. I looked at that note I don't know how many times, but I still didn't come to any firm conclusions. It made me feel uneasy. I wished I had Charlie's number so I could ask him what he meant by it. But I didn't have it, and I had no intention of asking his mother.

It was the middle of the night when I awoke from a nightmare. It was rather like that nightmare I'd had a few nights ago, when I dreamed I was stuck in a dark place, with unseen, hostile presences around me. This time, though, it was even worse. In the dream, I was playing that game known as 'Grandma's footsteps', you know, when you creep up on someone who's got their back to you, and you have to try and reach them before they turn around and see you. If they do turn around and catch you moving, you have to go back to the beginning. I used to love and hate that game when I was a little kid. It scared me silly, especially if I was 'It', with all those people trying to creep up on me. But I loved it too because it was exciting.

Well, anyway, in the dream, I was 'It', except I was in that same dark place and there was someone, or maybe several someones, creeping up on me. It was like I was blind in the dark and I knew someone was out to get me but though they could see me, I couldn't see them. I could only hear them, hear their footsteps getting closer, step by small step, and I was too scared to turn around and catch them.

I lay there, my eyes open on the dark, still in the dream hearing those footsteps shuffling closer and closer and closer. With a jolt of my heart I realised it wasn't just happening in my dream. The footsteps were real. Shuffle, shuffle they went – no, not in my room, I knew after a moment of throat-tightening terror. They were above my head.

Above my head again. I sat up in bed, remembering the last time I'd heard them, and how Charlie and I had found the footprint in the dust of that disused room. This time, as I got up and put on my dressing-gown and socks, I'd catch them. Catch him, at whatever he was doing . . .

Then just as I was about to open my door and go out into the corridor, I heard more footsteps. Light ones, this time, approaching my door. I held my breath, expecting someone to try the handle. But nobody did. Instead, the footsteps hurried past my door and away.

I didn't hesitate. I slipped out of the room, just in time to see the edge of a dressing-gown disappear round the corner of the door at the end of the passage, the door that led to the stairs going up. Something was going to investigate the footsteps upstairs, I thought. But who? My heart in my mouth, every sense alert for I know not what, I crept up the stairs to the second floor. I heard a door open and close, and then, as I hurried along the passage towards the door of the disused room, a murmur of voices.

I put my hand on the doorhandle and tried to turn it. It didn't move. It was locked from the inside. I put my eye to the keyhole. Of course I saw nothing – the key blocked my view. But I could hear. At first it was just a low murmur, where words could not be clearly distinguished. That, and the constant shuffle, shuffle of footsteps, like the pacing, I thought, of an animal in a cage. Then quite suddenly, I heard, quite clearly, a word that made the hair stand up on the back of my neck. It wasn't just the word but who said it, for I recognised the speaker quite clearly. 'Paul,' said the voice, in the sharp, cold, precise tones of Blanche Randal. 'I've told you. You must be quiet. She'll hear you. She'll find you.'

A rumble from her companion. I could not distinguish any of his words. She said impatiently, 'He suspects, Paul. And he's back tomorrow. If he finds you here . . .' Her voice dropped and I couldn't follow the rest of what she said. But it was enough.

She was in it with him! She was part of this – this persecution, this campaign of fear that Paul Fontaine was running against me. And she didn't want Charlie to know either.

A pulse beat in my throat. My hands felt clammy. But anger burnt fiercely in my chest. I almost hammered on the door then, demanding that they open it, demanding that they stop and explain themselves. But something stopped me. Truth is, I didn't know just what those two might do. And also at this end of the castle I didn't know if anyone would hear me scream. I thought of that balcony door and shivered a little. It was a long way to the ground below. I could imagine my body lying on the gravel below, my neck broken, my eyes staring, unseeing.

I couldn't help giving a tiny gasp as the image flooded my brain. It was a mistake. I heard Blanche say sharply, 'What's that?' and I fled, not waiting to hear the rattle of the handle as she hastily unlocked the door.

I've never moved as fast or as quietly in my life as I did at that moment. I was back in my room, the door locked, the covers drawn up over my head, in less time than it takes to write it down. I heard footsteps coming close to my door. I fancied I could hear her breathing as she stood there outside my door, listening. I nearly gave a loud snore to convince her I was asleep before realising that would be rather an obvious thing to do. Instead, I turned over and gave a little sigh, like you sometimes do when you're asleep. I could sense her standing there, and then, suddenly, she was gone.

The relief was so enormous I nearly fainted. I lay there covered in a cold sweat. But my mind was strangely calm. I knew now I had two enemies, not just one. I knew the who, but not the why.

I had thought Renée Fontaine was in this with her great-nephew. Blanche hated Renée. Surely they couldn't both . . . But no, perhaps it was all a facade and they were just pretending. Or perhaps, more simply, Renée really wasn't involved. After all, I had real, hard evidence now of Blanche's and Paul's collusion, but not of Renée and Paul. Just because they were family didn't mean they were plotting together. I didn't think his brothers or parents were, so why his great-aunt? Whereas tonight I'd heard the damning words straight from Blanche's mouth. There could be no mistake.

But, why, why, why? This was the dreadful thing. Why did they want to scare me, or even harm me? The Snow Queen wouldn't care about the curse, even if Paul did. I remembered Charlie said that there must be something bad, rather than mad, behind all this, but for the life of me I couldn't work out what. I knew she didn't like me, hadn't approved of me from the moment she'd set eyes on me, but surely that wasn't enough? What could she hope to gain from it?

I woke late with a dull headache and gritty eyes. I could barely drag myself into my clothes and go down to break-fast. What would I do when I set eyes on the Snow Queen again? Would I be able to control my reactions? I must pretend to act normally, but I wasn't sure if I could.

To my relief, though, she didn't put in an appearance that morning. Grand-père was in a cheerful mood, but I only half-listened to what he was saying. I just couldn't wait till I saw Charlie again and told him what had happened. The knowledge of it sat in my stomach like a lead weight, and the sense of being stalked grew ever more unbearable.

'Rose,' said Grand-père, suddenly, 'you look rather pale. You're not ill, are you?'

'No, no, I'm fine,' I stammered. 'Just – just a little tired.'

'I can understand that,' he said, gently. 'We did rather a lot in Paris, didn't we?' He looked sideways at me. 'I'd hoped today we might make a start on that Napoleon website, but you look as if you need a rest instead.'

'Oh no,' I said, quickly, all at once desperately wanting to do something that would stop me from brooding about what was going on. Anything to do with computers takes time and effort, I find, so it would make the time fly by till I could meet Charlie. I didn't care any more about having to meet him in the churchyard. The dead could hold no terrors against the malevolence of the living. 'I'd love to make a start on it, Grand-père. I really would.'

'Excellent,' he said, smiling.

And so I spent all the rest of that morning with him in the library. For starters, we had a look around the internet at a few websites about Napoleon. And there are quite a few, let me tell you, in French and English and other languages too! The guy's still a big, big celebrity, nearly two hundred years after his death. Reading the websites almost made Grand-père abandon his idea of starting one himself.

'What's the point,' he said, 'when everyone's doing it?' We talked a fair bit then about what Grand-père actually wanted to do with the site. I nearly told him about my blog, but something still held me back – shyness, perhaps.

We hadn't set anything up yet by lunchtime, and after lunch Grand-père went off for his nap. I went back on the internet, though, and had a look at my blog. My friends had commented on my latest entries, but so had that annoying Koschei. He had included his blog address on his comment, but I was damned if I was going to give him the pleasure of having a look. An idiot try-hard like that didn't deserve any attention. It was better to ignore him completely. Portia, Alice and Maddy all thought I should ban him but what was the point? He'd just get himself another email address and come lobbing back. That kind do.

I put up a small post about helping Grand-père to do his website, checked my email – there was nothing there – and logged off, because I was getting tired of crouching over a computer.

It was drizzling outside. I sat in the library for another couple of hours, curled up on the sofa, reading an old Agatha Christie paperback. It was *Endless Night*, and in English. I'd read it before, and it had always given me the creeps. It's about a campaign of fear that leads to a death that gets written off as an accident but is really murder, of course. And the criminals almost get away with it.

In the past, though, the creeps were pleasantly mixed with excitement. Now I read it with new eyes and I couldn't help shivering. In the book, the criminals do end up paying for it but you see the girl's dead anyway and nothing can change that. It felt awfully close to me. But I didn't have time to brood on it for Grand-père came back down to the library.

'I don't feel like fussing around with the computer just now,' he said. 'Let's go and have a look at the ballroom and see what needs to be done for your party next weekend.'

The ballroom was huge. It was mostly kept closed, because it was hardly ever used these days. But unlike the rooms on the top floor, it was kept in perfect condition. The marble floor shone, the heavy gold brocade curtains gleamed.

'We can have long tables along the sides of the room,' said Grand-père, gesturing, 'with all the food on it, and a big space in the middle so everyone can dance. Now, I suppose you'd like to get some modern band or other or one of these disc jockey persons, but I was wondering if you'd mind making a compromise with your old grand-father and choosing something not too noisy. I'm inviting the whole village, so there'll be all sorts, you see.'

'I'll leave the music up to you, Grand-père,' I said, linking my arm in his. 'I don't listen to that much music anyway, so I don't mind. And do we have to invite the *whole* village? I thought this was going to be a quiet party!'

He gave me a shrewd glance. 'Tell me later just who you want and don't want. Now, do you want a decorating theme?'

'A theme?' I said looking around the big, airy room. 'I don't know. Can I leave that up to you, too, Grand-père?'

'Of course, my dear, I'm delighted. I promise I won't make it Napoleonic,' he went on, grinning.

We both laughed. It was good, standing there and talking of silly, fun things, thinking of lovely dresses and jewellery and how I was going to do my hair, and who I would dance with, and whether Charlie would be a good dancer. And whether people would bring me presents, and what they'd be like. So busy were we with our plans that I scarcely noticed the time passing and when I next looked at my watch it was edging on for 6.20.

My heart bumped against my ribs. I had to go and meet Charlie. I made an excuse to Grand-père, that I needed to go and freshen up before dinner, and hurried off.

I went up to my room and grabbed my coat. Looking out of the window, I noticed it was starting to get dark. I opened up all my drawers, looking for a torch, but found none. There'd probably be one in the kitchen, but the Vallons would be bound to be there, they'd ask questions. Charlie had said to tell no-one.

Then I remembered I'd seen a box of matches on the desk in the library. I slipped downstairs, went carefully into the library – no-one was there – and pocketed it. On impulse, I also looked in the drawer of the desk and found a little pencil torch. I pocketed it too. I was just about to leave the library when all of a sudden the door opened and Blanche Randal walked in.

She stopped dead when she saw me. 'What are you doing?'

'Nothing,' I said. 'I was just looking for something I left here.' I was trying hard to sound defiant and strong but my voice came out all squeaky and stupid.

'Why are you in your coat?' she said, sharply.

'Um – nothing – I'm just . . . I just need a breath of fresh air before dinner, I've been inside all day.'

'I see,' she said, raising an eyebrow. 'You know dinner's in less than an hour.'

'I'll be back long before that,' I said, and edged past her, smiling in a placating sort of way and hating myself for it. I was afraid of her, I thought. I just hoped she couldn't see that, couldn't see, in her Snow Queen laser-eyed way, that I'd overheard her talking to Paul. I had a mad impulse to say to her, 'So, where is he now? Where are you hiding him now?' I hadn't heard any more footsteps and thought he had most likely gone home. Or maybe he was prowling around, waiting to catch me unawares . . .

I shivered. She saw me. Her pale eyes fixed me. 'You shouldn't be going out. You don't look well.'

'I'm fine,' I faltered. 'I just need some fresh air.'

'Very well,' she said, and let me go, standing there watching me as I raced up the hall away from her. I could feel the cold eyes on my back long after I'd slipped out of the house and headed down the hill towards the church. But she made no attempt to follow me.

The gate creaked as I went into the churchyard. It had stopped raining, and the temperature had gone down, so in this low-lying place, a kind of ragged mist had gathered, lending a kind of horror-movie atmosphere. So eerie did it look, in fact, that Charlie or no Charlie, I almost turned back. But I mastered myself. I was sure he wouldn't have asked me to be here if there wasn't a really good reason. I turned on the torch. The light was pretty feeble, but it was better than nothing, and made me feel a little more in control. I looked around. The cemetery was quite deserted. I was the only living soul there – as far as I could see, anyway.

'Charlie?' I called. 'Charlie, are you there?'

No answer. I walked along the first row of tombs, calling his name. Then down the second row. Then suddenly, I thought I heard an answer, faintly, 'Rose! Over here!'

His voice was strangely distorted by the mist – flattened, deadened. But I was sure it was his voice. I called, 'Charlie, is that you?' and began walking in the direction the voice had come from. Soon I was standing in front of the du Merle family vault. The door was slightly ajar, and I thought I could see a faint light in there. Of course, where else would he be? I opened the gate and approached the door. 'Charlie?' I said. No answer. I walked up the steps to the door. I pushed it open, and shone my torch in. I couldn't see Charlie. And the light, if it had been there in the first place, certainly was not on now. But the curtain at the back, the one that hid the alcove containing the model of the Chateau and the portraits, was slightly open. He must be there. But why wasn't he answering me?

I took a step towards it, then another. Horrifyingly, I thought this was like a game of Grandma's footsteps. I pushed down the stupid thought, took another step towards the curtain, reached out a hand, pulled it across, and saw – nobody. The model of the castle sat there mutely, and when I opened it, I saw all the portraits, neatly arranged. I shone my torch in and picked up the portrait of my great-grandmother Rose. I turned it over. The back was quite clean now, the writing gone.

Then I saw there was another picture in there. It wasn't like the others. It was just a photo stuck to a bit of cardboard. I couldn't help staring at it. It was a picture of me, a blurry picture, taken against a background of trees. Somebody took it while I was in the woods the other day. My skin crawled. Someone was spying on me . . . I turned it over. On the back it said, 'Fee fi fo fum.'

That's all, but I dropped the picture as though it had scalded my fingers. I turned. In that same moment, the door slammed. I lunged forward, desperately fighting to reach the handle. Too late. I heard the click as the key locked. I beat against the heavy door with my fists, yelling and screaming to be let out. But the door didn't budge one millimetre, and no-one came to help. I was shut inside the tomb.

Fee fi fo fum

I flung myself at the door again and again, banging on it till my fists felt red and raw. I shouted, I yelled. But no-one came. The door remained shut.

But worse was to come. The torchlight, which had been feeble to begin with, began to flicker and fade. I shook the torch. For an instant, the light grew brighter, then it faded again. I shook the torch once more. This time, the light did not brighten. The battery was running out. Soon, I'd be in the dark.

No, no, no, it must not happen. With trembling fingers, I dug into my pocket for the box of matches. Yes, it was still there. It was an almost full box. I'd just light the matches, one by one, when the torch gave out. Someone would find me long before the matches were exhausted, I told myself. They'd be sure to. They'd miss me when I didn't turn up for dinner. They'd go looking for me.

I sat on the floor near the door, the dimming torch clutched in one hand, trying to stop myself from totally panicking. I must not let myself think too much about where I was, shut in the dark, like in my dream, with unseen presences all around me – the presences of the dead, of my ancestors. I didn't believe in ghosts, did I? And even if they were true, why would they want to hurt me?

I was their descendant. They'd want me to survive, to carry on their name. Stop it, Rose, I told myself, as the hysteria escalated, stop it. Don't worry about ghosts, you've got more to worry about than that. Far more. Yes. Like being walled up alive in a tomb. Like being shut in the heavy darkness of the dead, without any fresh air. You'll suffocate, you'll die, slowly . . . Stop it, stop it! You fool, you've been caught in a trap, you let yourself be lured here by your enemy.

It wasn't Charlie who had written that note. That much was clear. That was why it had seemed strange to me, so brief, so curt. It must have been Paul. Or the Snow Queen. They tricked me because I didn't know what Charlie's handwriting was like. They'd lured me here, and left me to die. No, no. Not to die, surely not. They just want to scare me, to terrify me, not kill me. Why would they want to kill me? Don't be an idiot. Don't. Don't.

But my breath was coming fast and short and ragged. My head was filling up with fog. There was no air in this place, no air, the door fitted too tightly and there were no windows, no vents, nothing . . . The panic bubbled up in my throat, unstoppable. And at that moment, the torch went out. I was plunged into total darkness.

Sobbing, I pulled out the box of matches. My hands were shaking so badly I could hardly light a match. At last I managed it. The tiny point of friendly golden light flared up in my hand. I held the match tight, knowing that soon it would go out, soon it would be gone . . .

I lit another match. And another. And another. If I kept going at this rate, the whole box would be gone within a matter of minutes. I tried to get a grip on myself. I must try and ration out the matches. But I couldn't just sit in the dark. I rummaged through my pockets. There were scraps of paper in there, stuff from our Paris trip, Metro tickets, receipts from somewhere, even a brochure from some Paris museum, folded flat. I'd burn those things. But I had to try and make them last. I twisted the papers together, made a little pile of them and set a match to it. A blue flame flickered along the edge of the pile, turned golden, rose higher. The little fire was well alight.

And suddenly, I could see more. The light threw shadows into the corners of the tomb, but at least within its circle I felt a little safer. My breathing began to slow down, my heart rate to quieten. My mind began to clear a little.

They would come and find me. Charlie would be back at the castle soon, he'd know something was wrong. He'd find the note in my room. He'd know what they'd done. He'd come and get me. But no, that wouldn't happen. *Because his mother knew, of course.* She'd know that I had fallen for the trick, she had seen me going out 'for a walk'. She would dispose of that note long before anyone else found it. She wouldn't tell anyone I'd gone out. Or maybe she would, and tell them a lie. Maybe she'd say I'd told her I was going for a walk in the woods or something. They'd go looking there, not here. No-one would come here. I'd be left here. Left here to . . . to . . .

No, no. I wouldn't. I wouldn't. I'd be rescued. Charlie would think. Charlie would know. He'd think about it, because we had been here together before. Oh my God, I thought, then, I told Paul that we'd been to the vault. I told him what we'd seen there. That was how he knew I'd be likely to fall for that lure of his. I'd made the trap myself, like the blind, complete idiot that I was.

The fire was burning brightly now. In its light, I suddenly caught sight of something lying over near the curtained alcove. A square of coloured paper. I crawled over to it. It was the photo of me in the woods, that I'd dropped when the door had slammed. I stared at it. The terror cruised like a shark in my mind, ready to devour all sanity, all common sense. This malevolent little thing, this nasty object, was like hatred made visible. A visible curse. The threat, made tangible.

Fee fi fo fum, read the black script on the back. I remembered that verse from one of the stories Mum had read to me when I was a little kid. It was what the ogre said, in *Jack and the Beanstalk*. 'Fee fi fo fum/ I smell the blood of an Englishman/ be he alive or be he dead/ I'll grind his bones to make my bread.' It had scared me as a little kid. It scared me now, much more. Yes, I thought, yes. They do want me to die. They want me to *die*. Walled up alive in the tomb, I'd never get out. I'd never see the daylight again. I'd never see Grand-père again, or Charlie, or Aunt Jenny, or my friends, or anyone. I was quite alone, cut off from everyone I loved. I'd die but even before that, I'd go mad. It was no good fighting the truth. That was what would happen, and I might as well accept it.

The fire was dying down. I sat beside it for ages, clutching the photo, the dreadful thoughts swamping me like a bitter, unstoppable king tide. I could feel my mind already beginning to slip away.

And then – I hardly know how to describe it – I heard, no, I felt, no, I saw a whisper, that seemed to be both inside me and outside of me. Faint words came to me, words I strained to catch. *Rose – Rose? Is that you?*

My heart leapt. I said, 'Who . . . who is it?'

Silence. The silence of the grave. I said, more loudly, 'Is anyone there?'

Nothing and no-one answered me. My pulse raced. I got up, slowly. At my feet, the fire was dying out. I thought, I'm going mad already. I'm hearing things.

Rose? Hold on. We're coming.

I jumped. I had definitely heard it. But not . . . not in the usual way. It was like a voice in a dream. It was a little distorted, but I was sure it was a woman's voice.

I said, 'Please . . . please come quickly. Whoever you are, please.'

The voice didn't answer. I sat down again by the dying fire, trembling all over, not sure if I'd really heard anything or if I was going mad. But the terror that had threatened to gobble me alive seemed to be moving further away.

I still had the photo in my hand. On a sudden impulse, I threw it on the fire. It flared up brightly, the edges of the picture crumpling and disappearing. It didn't take long to burn away, and when it had, I felt, all at once, a sudden lightening of the spirit, as if the thing had been some horrible bit of black magic that had cast a spell of fear over me.

And in that moment, as the fire died down again after its brief shining, I heard the doorhandle rattle. I heard the click and shake as a key was turned in the lock. I threw myself up as the door creaked open, but for a moment, dazzled by the bright torchlight coming in, I couldn't see who it was. And when I did, my heart nearly stopped beating.

For it was Renée Fontaine who stood there, framed in the doorway. And behind her, tall and looming darkly in the dazzling light, was Paul!

I gave a gasping sob and fell back. 'No – no . . . no . . .'

They advanced on me. They were quite unsmiling, their

faces set in some dreadful stillness. I knew then that they'd come only to finish me off. And then quite suddenly, the last of the terror left me, and I was furiously, wildly, recklessly angry. I rushed at them, screaming like a banshee, and they fell back. I raced for the opening, but before I could get there, Paul stepped across it. He grabbed me by the arm. I clawed up at his face with my other hand, and managed to give him a good scratch across the cheek. He yelled, and grabbed at my other arm. I kicked him, hard. He yelped. He shouted, 'You little fool, stop it! Stop it! You don't know what you're doing!'

'Yes, I do,' I yelled, and kicked him again. But before I could do it once more, Renée spoke. She said, 'Rose, you don't understand. We've come to take you home.'

'Liars!' I screamed. 'Dirty rotten wicked liars!' In my terror and anger, I'd spoken English. Then I stopped abruptly. The whisper was in my head, that strange dream-whisper returned, only louder now, clearer. *It's us, Rose. We've come to help you.*

I stared at Renée. 'That was you,' I faltered. '*You?*'

'Yes, of course,' she said, briskly, quite as if it wasn't the weirdest thing in the world to whisper in people's heads. 'It's something I do, very occasionally, when there's no other way. Usually doesn't work. But on the right person, it might. Do you understand?'

My shoulders slumped. I could feel all the fight ebbing out of me. I looked at Renée's calm features, and then up at Paul's face, set and grim, his brown eyes unreadable, and I could feel something happening deep inside me, something I couldn't put a name to. I whispered, in English, my French deserting me, 'No, I don't understand,' and then fainted dead away.

I came to a short time later, as something cold touched my face, my neck. My eyes flickered open and I saw Paul bending over me, a damp piece of cloth in his hand. He said, very gently, 'Don't try to get up too quickly, you'll get dizzy. Do you feel any better?'

'Yes,' I said. I looked up at him. His eyes were soft, full of some emotion I could not bring myself to place. I said, quickly, the French returning to me in bursts, 'Why did you do it?'

'What do you mean?'

'Why did you rescue me, if you . . .'

'If I what?' The softness was leaving his eyes now, the grimness returning.

'If you lured me here in the first place . . . the note.'

'What note? I didn't lure you here,' he said, biting off his words. 'I don't know why you came here, but I suspect it's because Charlie told you to meet him here. Am I right?'

I nodded, swallowing.

'Well, then, why do you think it was me?' His voice was hard, accusing.

'Because I . . .'

'Because I'm a much more likely culprit than him? Because he's so handsome, and he's already got you wrapped around his little finger. Is that it? Because you look at him and see only what you want to see, and believe everything he tells you? What do you know, what do you *really* know, about Charlie Randal?' His eyes were blazing, his whole body as taut as a bowstring.

I looked away. To my horror, a tear welled up. Then another, and another, and the stupid tears were rushing down my face, and I couldn't stop them. I wanted them to stop, I was so angry with myself, so ashamed, so sickened, so confused. I whispered, 'I'm sorry . . . I – I can't think . . . I don't know what to think any more. Please, I just want to go home . . . to Grand-père.'

Somewhere deep down there, the terror hadn't quite gone. I felt as though I were in a dream, or rather a nightmare, I didn't know any more who was friend and who was foe. Was Paul telling the truth, or lying? Like a bolt of livid lightning, the memory of Blanche Randal talking to Paul, up in that disused room, flashed across my mind. All the rest might have been circumstantial, maybe, things I'd connected together without real evidence, but that one was real, real, I'd heard it with my own ears. My own ears.

And yet, there it was. They'd come for me. He had looked at me not with hatred but with tenderness. He seemed genuinely concerned for me. No, I didn't understand. I didn't understand any of it.

Behind us, Renée said, gently, 'Help her up, Paul.'

'It's okay,' I said hastily, but I swayed a little as I got up, and he caught me. For an instant, his arms were tight around me, and I could feel the warmth of him flowing into me. A strange, bewildering feeling came over me. I wanted to stay there, in his arms, to hide, not to think, not to know. Not to let daylight into the dark confusion in my mind, because I didn't think I could bear it. I couldn't bear it.

What an idiot you are, Rose. You can't trust him, or her. You can't trust anyone, not any more. You don't understand, and maybe you never can. You're a naïve and ignorant stranger adrift in a world of dark secrets, you're out of your depth, out of your place, you don't belong here, with any of them, not even your grandfather. You were much better off before in your own safe little world.

'Rose,' began Paul, but I shook my head, not wanting him to say any more, not wanting to look at his face or see what I might read there. I saw Renée look at him and shake her head gently. Then she took my arm, led me down the steps and out of the tomb.

The lights in the castle were blazing. There were people everywhere, and exclamations, and shouts. But I only saw Grand-père in that crowd – Grand-père, looking old and frail and pale. I'll never forget the look in his eyes as I staggered in, flanked by Renée and Paul. I went straight to him, and didn't move for quite a while, with his arms about me. Vaguely, I heard him speaking to the Fontaines. Vaguely, I heard them replying, explaining that they'd found me locked in the vault, and that they'd gone there because Renée had 'had one of her flashes', that they'd unlocked the vault with the extra key that was kept in the church. But I couldn't bring myself to speak, couldn't bring myself to think clearly at all.

Then I heard something that made my heart race. 'Louis and Charlie are still out in the woods looking for her. Blanche thought that's where she might have gone.'

With a lurch of the heart, I thought, Charlie's looking for me in the woods. That must mean Charlie doesn't know where I was. Or that Charlie's *pretending* not to know where I was. And his mother – she had sent them off there, just as I'd thought. Oh God, how can I bear this? All I know now is that the Snow Queen's definitely involved. Charlie maybe. Paul too. But it couldn't be both, could it? It couldn't. What kind of mad conspiracy was this?

I started shaking in Grand-père's arms, and he felt it and said, 'My darling Rose. My poor little girl.' He was shaking too. He said, 'I don't know what happened, but I'm going to find out. And whoever is responsible for this extremely tasteless practical joke is going to pay very dearly for it.'

'It's not a joke, Grand-père,' I whispered, but he didn't hear me. Or perhaps he didn't want to.

His arm tightened around me. 'It's all over,' he said. 'It's all fine, thanks to Paul and Renée.'

I didn't answer. I looked beyond the circle of his protective arm and saw Paul looking at me. Our eyes met, for an instant, then he turned away and said, 'There is nothing to thank us for, Monsieur. We did what we had to do.'

'Exactly,' said Renée.' She gave a faint smile. 'And you'll have to do better than that, Valentin. This was no joke. Your granddaughter is in real danger.'

'Don't be absurd, Renée,' said my grandfather, with a flash of his old fierceness. 'Why should she be in danger?'

'Change brings danger,' said Renée levelly, 'especially if that change suddenly robs someone of something they felt entitled to.'

A heartbeat of silence, then my grandfather said shakily, 'Absurd. There is no-one here in that category. No-one, do you hear?'

'If you say so,' said Renée. 'But I'm afraid you're blind, my dear Valentin. Take good care of your Rose, or next time, the joke, as you call it, will have a deadly earnest result.'

He said nothing, but his grip tightened on me. I wanted to say something to Renée and Paul, to thank them, but the words wouldn't come.

A moment after Paul and Renée left, I heard Blanche's voice. 'Monsieur le Comte, Louis and Charlie are coming back. I saw them. They did not appear to have found . . . Oh!' She stopped abruptly as she caught sight of me. 'You're back then,' was all she said, but it was enough. Without quite knowing what I was doing, I tried to launch myself out of Grand-père's arms at her. But he held me back. 'Rose, what on earth are you doing?'

'I hate her,' I yelled. 'She's the one who's behind all this. She's the one who arranged to lock me in the vault. She's hated me from the start. She never wanted me here!'

'Rose,' said my grandfather, 'Rose, my dear girl, whatever are you saying? Blanche, what does she mean?'

'I have no idea. I'm afraid she is overwrought and in great shock, Monsieur le Comte,' said Blanche, and her voice was cold as the grave. I could see her eyes shining like twin points of deadly ice and her lips were drawn back in a snarl.

All around us people were staring, half-appalled, half-delighted. Grand-père saw it and he waved a hand. 'Please leave us alone,' he said, and his voice rang with such command that no-one uttered a word in protest, but melted away.

'Now then,' said Grand-père, in the same commanding tone of voice, 'Blanche, you will have to tell me if there is any truth in Rose's accusation.'

'Monsieur le Comte,' she said, in a strange, jagged sort of voice, 'you have known me a long time. Do you think I am capable of such things?'

'Of hatred, Blanche? Yes. You have a passionate nature. Of deliberately trying to frighten Rose? I don't think so.'

'Why would I do it?' she cried. 'Why?'

He looked away. 'You have lived here a long time. You may have thought –'

'That I had expectations?' She laughed. It was an unpleasant sound. 'I gave up on those, if I ever had them, a long time ago, Monsieur le Comte. I was well aware you still held a candle for your disloyal wife, despite what she had done to you.'

I felt Grand-père's start at that. But he said, quite calmly, 'I suppose I meant other expectations.'

'You mean, what you might leave me? I assumed that one day your son would return. They do, when their need of money gets greater than their supposed feelings.' Her voice was very bitter as she said that. 'And even if he didn't, I assumed you'd leave the bulk of your money in a manner befitting a man like yourself. Gifts to the grateful nation, perhaps. Charities. I have never expected anything from you, Monsieur le Comte, except for what my job has meant for my self-respect. For that I will always be grateful.'

'Blanche,' he said, and his voice shook a little. 'I'm very sorry. But perhaps Charlie might have assumed –'

'Charlie was away, as well you know,' she said, sharply, and her eyes were bleak. 'He did not get back here till after 7.30.' I looked at the hall clock. It was nearly a quarter to nine. I'd lost all track of time in the vault, but I must have been in there at least two and a half hours, maybe more.

Blanche was still speaking. 'Charlie was on the bus from Castelnau till then, and after that he joined in the search for Rose. So how could he have locked her in the vault? Why do you accuse us?' She looked terrible. The fine bones of her face stood out under her skin, her cheeks looked hollow, her eyes burnt with a feverish light. It suddenly came to me that it wasn't only fury that marked her face. It was also fear. Blanche Randal was frightened of something. Something, or perhaps someone.

'I don't accuse you, Blanche,' said Grand-père gently.

'What about other people? What about that crazy old Fontaine witch, or her delinquent great-nephew? Someone like that, tearing around the roads on that dangerous machine of his, with his rough manners, and the history of his family, someone like that is much more likely to play such a wicked trick. Why haven't you accused him?'

'Because,' he said, even more gently, 'because they were the ones who found Rose, and brought her safely home.'

She gave a little faint cry. Two red spots appeared in her waxy cheeks. Then she rallied and said, 'But they were most likely pretending. How did they know she was there if they hadn't set it up in the first place?'

He looked at her, troubled. 'I'm sure they didn't. I'd trust Renée with –'

'With what, Monsieur le Comte? Your granddaughter's life? You must be blind, begging your pardon. She's got a grudge against you and yours. Are you the only one in the village who doesn't see it, plain as a pikestaff?'

It was at that very moment that Charlie came in. As soon as he saw me, his eyes lit up. 'Oh, thank God, Rose, you're safe!' he said. He strode towards me and took my hand. 'I was so worried, wondering what had happened . . .'

'Were you?' I said, bleakly.

He stared at me. 'Of course I was.'

'You left me a note,' I said.

'What?'

'A note, which asked me to meet you at the vault. That's why I went.'

'What? I never wrote a note. And why on earth would I

ask you to meet me there? Why wouldn't I talk to you first about it?'

'I – I don't know,' I said.

'I swear to you, Rose, I sent or left no note,' said Charlie, earnestly. 'It was obviously a trick designed to lure you out there.' His face was quite open, devoid of any guile. I couldn't believe he was lying. I just couldn't. He'd have to be too good an actor for it.

'I – I did think afterwards it must have been a trick,' I admitted.

'I told you to be careful, Rose,' he said. 'I told you I'd try to find out what had been going on.'

'I thought this was part of it,' I said. I could feel the unbearable tension slowly relaxing in me. How could I believe Charlie would ever try to harm me?

Grand-père broke in. 'Whoa. What's been going on? What are all these mysteries?'

I shot a glance at Blanche. Grand-père said, quietly, 'Blanche, would you mind leaving us?'

'No, Monsieur le Comte,' she said, icily. She threw a look at her son, a hopeless, pleading glance – but he turned away from her, deliberately. I saw her swallow, then she turned without another word, and left the room.

'Now then,' said Grand-père, 'first things first. This note, Rose. Do you still have it?'

'It should still be in my room,' I said. 'That is, if no-one's disposed of it in the meantime.'

'Let's go and have a look. And yes, Charlie, my boy, you're to come with us too. Mind you, I want to hear every word of what's been going on. Do you hear? Every word! Don't leave anything out.'

The man in the mask

We didn't find the note. Just as I'd thought, it had vanished from my room. But I remembered exactly what it said, word for word, for I'd stared at it long enough. I told them both, and as I spoke, I watched Charlie's face closely. So, too, did Grand-père. Charlie knew it, of course, but it didn't seem to worry him. He just said, 'Quite a curt sort of note, then. Didn't give much away, did it?'

'No,' I said. 'that's why I thought it was odd.'

'Yet you still went there. Oh, Rose!' said Grand-père, reproachfully. 'Why didn't you come and tell me?'

'She didn't want to worry you, sir,' said Charlie earnestly, before I could reply. 'That might have been my fault, I'm afraid. When things started happening, I thought perhaps that as you'd been ill, well –' He broke off, embarrassed.

Grand-père raised his eyebrows. 'You thought I would have another stroke if I found out what was going on? My dear Charlie, that's thoughtful of you, but I'm tougher than you think. I'd rather know danger was there and face it squarely than not know and have the shock of some-thing happening to Rose. That's much more likely to cause a stroke, don't you think?'

'Yes, Monsieur le Comte, I'm sorry.'

'You meant well, I'm sure,' said Grand-père a little dismissively.

I saw Charlie's colour rise and said, hastily, 'It was my fault too, Grand-père. I did want to tell you but then I was scared to. Anyway, we want to tell you all of it, now, don't we, Charlie?'

'Of course,' said Charlie.

It was such a relief to tell him everything. Well, almost everything. I didn't mention hearing Blanche last night with Paul, because for some unknown reason I felt as if I needed to speak to Paul about that first. Give him a chance to explain, or something. I felt as though I owed him that at least.

Charlie told some of the story too, the bits he'd been involved in with me. Of course, the times he was away, I described those. Grand-père listened to it all very carefully, the expression on his face going from neutral to bewilderment to anger to a dark grimness that suddenly reminded me of the expression on Paul's face, in the tomb, when I'd questioned him.

When we'd finished, he was silent a moment. Then he said, with explosive force, 'This is a diabolical business. And it has gone on far enough. We will have to put it in the hands of the police.' He looked at me. 'It's a pity you burnt that photo, Rose. It could have been useful evidence.'

'I'm sorry,' I cried. 'But I couldn't bear it. That thing . . . was evil, Grand-père.'

He nodded. 'I understand. But we have nothing concrete now to go on. The note's gone, the photo, too, and you cleaned the back of the portrait, Charlie, so that's also gone.' He thumped his fist into his palm in a frustrated, violent gesture. 'Damn them, whoever they are, to defile the

212

memory of my poor mother! She never got over that poor child's death, you know, never. It poisoned the rest of her life. She tried to make amends, she paid for the other children to go to good schools and university, but she never ever forgot it. She never felt forgiven, though the parents told her they had forgiven her. She saw that poor child's face in her dreams every night. It shortened her life, that's for sure. And then for this creature, whoever he is, to use such a thing to frighten you, Rose . . . Sometimes I wish we were living in another age. In another age, if I'd found that creature, I would have killed him, without hesitation.'

He saw our expressions. 'Don't worry. Sadly or not sadly, I am a modern man and live in a modern age. I know I can't take the law into my own hands. And I have no wish to go to prison for a creature with no conscience and no humanity.'

'I have no wish for you to do that either, Grand-père,' I cried. 'I need you here with me.'

'I know that, my dearest girl,' he said, and smiled, and touched me gently on the shoulder.

'I'm here too,' said Charlie. He was very pale. 'Whenever you need me.'

Our eyes met. I was the first to look away. 'Thank you,' I whispered.

Grand-père looked from one to the other of us. But all he said was, 'Here's what we'll do. Tomorrow morning, we will go over to the Fontaines' place and go with them to the police in Castelnau.'

'But sir,' began Charlie, 'we thought that possibly it was Paul who . . .'

'Stuff and nonsense,' said Grand-père, 'I've known that boy even longer than I've known you, Charlie, and I know he'd never do a wicked, underhanded thing like this.

Violence, maybe – he's got a stiff neck and a hot temper, like all Fontaines – but not this kind of mean, sneaky psychological warfare. It just isn't Paul. Or Renée either,' he went on, fiercely.

'Then who do you think . . .?' said Charlie, biting down on his lip.

'Not you either, boy, don't worry,' said Grand-père, a shade too brightly. 'I'm convinced that we're dealing with a stranger. Not a complete stranger – someone who knows something of us, of our history, but has it garbled. Someone with no scruples. Someone who hasn't shown himself yet.'

'Or herself,' I put in.

'What? Oh, you mean, a woman? It's possible, I suppose. But I think it's most likely a man.'

'A hidden enemy, then,' said Charlie, quietly. 'A hidden enemy, in the dark. The man in the mask.' His blue eyes were full of horror. I shivered.

'Don't say things like that, Charlie. Can't you see it scares her?' said Grand-père crossly. 'Now, I think that's quite enough of this. We all need a good night's rest.' He looked at me. 'Are you feeling all right now, Rose? Would you like me to sit here with you till you go to sleep?'

'Monsieur le Comte, I could –' began Charlie, but Grand-père shushed him with a wave of the hand.

'Not at all appropriate, my dear boy. Sorry, Rose, but that's the way it is.'

'Yes,' I said, rather embarrassed. In truth I didn't want Charlie there. I wanted Grand-père. I felt safe with him. But I didn't want him to sit up all night there with me. He was old, after all. It would tire him too much. 'Couldn't I just come and sleep in your room? I can just bring a mattress in.'

'No need,' said Grand-père, 'I've got one of those sofa beds in my room as well as my own bed, so you can sleep on that. I think it's reasonably comfortable, though I can't say I've ever tried it out myself. Charlie, run and fetch some sheets, a quilt and a pillow from the linen room, will you? And bring them to my room. I don't want to wake up Madame Collot just for that.'

'Of course, Monsieur le Comte,' said Charlie. I thought he sounded rather put out. No wonder, I suppose, with Grand-père ordering him around like that. But he went willingly enough, while Grand-père and I went off to his room, which was just a few doors away from mine.

It was a nice room. Bigger than mine, full of rich, deep colours. Heavy dark green velvet curtains hung at the windows, the four-poster bed was large and high, with hangings of the same green velvet as the curtains. The fold-out sofa looked big and comfortable too, and not just your standard pull-out job. There was a large Persian rug on the polished floor, and rows of paperbacks in a bookshelf on one wall, and several paintings, a couple of landscapes, and some portraits. I recognised a couple of the people – his mother, Rose, and his ex-wife, Caroline. Grand-père saw me looking at that one, and he said, with a sigh, 'Blanche is right, you know. I never really looked at anyone else after Caroline. I threw myself into my work. But I couldn't forget her. Yet it seems she was not thinking of me, she had a whole other family we knew nothing about. Well, that's life. Some love, some are loved.'

'Oh, but surely, Grand-père, you can have both!'

'It does happen,' he conceded. 'Was it like that for your parents?'

'It was,' I said. 'I'm sure of that, Grand-père.'

'Well, my son was a luckier man than I,' said my grandfather.

I said, in a rush, 'Grand-père, Renée, in the tomb . . . I heard her voice in my head. Can that be . . . do you think that's possible?'

'I don't know,' said Grand-père. He looked a little uncomfortable. 'Sometimes terror can make us imagine things. But I've known Renée a long time and there are things about her that are – well, not quite like other people . . . Anyway, darling, the main thing is that she and Paul found you.'

At that moment, there was a knock on the door. Grand-père said, 'Come in.'

It was Charlie, carrying a pile of bedclothes. Under Grand-père's instructions, he pulled out the sofa bed and would have made the bed, too, if I'd not stopped him. 'It's okay, Charlie,' I said, awkwardly. 'I can make a bed by myself. I'm not a princess, you know.'

'Aren't you?' said Charlie with a quizzical smile, and a glance at Grand-père, who laughed.

'I suppose I might think she is, at that,' my grandfather said, 'but even a princess might need to know how to make her own bed, sometimes, so thanks, Charlie. And good night.'

'Good night,' he said, and taking my hand, he kissed it gently, and made me that funny little bow, while Grand-père watched with his eyebrows raised. But he said nothing, for which I was grateful. I could still feel the cool imprint of Charlie's lips on my skin as he left the room.

'Oh la la,' said Grand-père, as the door closed softly behind Charlie. 'I do believe that young man has feelings for you, Rose, and no mistake. Are these feelings shared?'

'I – I don't know,' I said, going scarlet. It was strange. I'd been meaning to say yes, but somehow that didn't come out.

He looked at me, shrewdly. 'He's a charming boy. A romantic. Another refugee from the modern age, I think, at heart. But . . .'

'But what, Grand-père?'

'I don't think he's quite steady. You know, steadfast. True.' He shot me another disconcerting glance. 'Not like Paul.'

'Paul?' I said, going even redder, if that was possible. 'I'm not interested in Paul.'

'He is in you,' said my infuriating grandfather with a grin. 'Ah well! You're shaping up to be a true du Merle woman. The flame around which the moths congregate.' His expression changed. 'But you're only sixteen, Rose.'

'Nearly seventeen,' I countered, pertly.

'Yes, but still young. Now, it's lovely to have a romance at your age, but nothing too serious, you understand? Or your old grandfather will have to take out his hunting rifle and chase them off, eh?'

'Grand-père!'

'Don't worry, I was joking,' he said. 'Now then, Rose, how about making this bed of yours? I'm just about dead on my feet, even if you're not.'

So I made the bed, and went into the bathroom to change into my nightclothes. When I got back, Grand-père was already in bed. I turned off the lights, and hopped into the sofa bed with a delicious sense of security. Things had been taken out of my hands now, and everything would be all right.

Heart of ice

It was well past ten in the morning when I woke. I'd slept for more than twelve hours! It felt wonderful! I opened my eyes to weak sunlight streaming into the room. I was alone. Grand-père's bed was neatly made, his dressing-gown hanging on the bedrail.

It was funny. Last night, I'd had one of the worst experiences of my life – second only to that terrible day when I'd heard of my parents' deaths – but this morning, I felt as if I could take on the world. I felt free of the burden of suspicion and fear that had lain so heavily on my shoulders – I hadn't realised before just how heavily. I felt sure Grand-père was right. My enemy, 'the man in the mask', as Charlie had called him, was a stranger. A wicked stranger with a heart of ice. We'd put the matter in the hands of the police. They'd find him, this mysterious spy who had intruded into our lives, who had stalked and harassed and terrorised me, but who would now be on the run, because it was out in the open now, all that he'd done.

There was still the matter of Paul and Blanche – their conversation, I mean – but I was going to clear that up. As to the Snow Queen herself, I shied away from thinking about her. I remembered the things I'd blurted out to her and felt, well, not exactly sorry, because I was sure she disliked me and didn't want me here, but a little touch of embarrassment. After all, Grand-père didn't seem to take seriously the notion that she'd be involved, and he'd know, wouldn't he? He'd known her a long time, far longer than I had. Perhaps what she'd been talking about to Paul was something completely unconnected to any of this. They might be smuggling things in, for instance. Or out.

And perhaps the 'she' she'd referred to wasn't me, but someone else in the household. It might be Madame Vallon, or Samantha, or Madame Collot . . . Samantha, perhaps, most likely. But the 'he' she'd referred to must be Charlie, because she'd said 'he's away'. I thought again of the tone of it, and thought, with a jolt, Could it be that they're having an affair? I mean, yuck, she must be decades older than him, but I guessed it happened, and it wasn't like Paul was at school or anything, he was an adult and it was true she was very beautiful if you liked that Snow Queen style. That would explain her not wanting Charlie to find him there, or Samantha to know, because she'd disapprove. She didn't like Blanche, and neither did her mother.

But I found I didn't like to think about it much. It wasn't just the yuck thing, either. It made me feel bad. Angry, to think of him and her. Did I actually care for Paul Fontaine? I mean, I'd thought he was trying to kill me or even just scare me silly just a day or two ago and here I was defending him in my own mind and feeling angry because I imagined he might be sleeping with that ghastly Snow Queen. I'm a mess, I thought furiously, I don't even know what I think or feel any more. But clear as clear came the tender look he gave me when I had come to in the tomb and it made me feel unsteady all over again. But then I thought about Charlie and the feel of his lips on my hand and my feelings shifted yet again.

I'm torn between two men, I thought, and it felt both thrillingly sweet and sickeningly scary all at the same time. It had never happened to me before. I'd had boyfriends before but nothing serious, just to go out with casually. Maybe boys in France were different. Of course they were.

Imagine if Alice, Portia and Maddy knew. They'd think it was so cool. But they'd be scared too. They'd tell me I had to be careful. It might sound romantic but it could be weird too. And imagine if the boys wanted to fight each other? I knew that people didn't fight duels any more over a girl but there was no love lost between Paul and Charlie . . .

Which one would I choose, in the end? I didn't know. Maybe neither. But it was just fun to think about it, even while it was also a bit sick-making.

And what about that strange stuff with Renée? In the daylight, now, I wondered whether I had indeed imagined it, that voice in my head. But no, she'd said she'd done it, in that matter-of-fact way.

Before I went downstairs, I rang Aunt Jenny. She answered after the first couple of rings. She sounded rather sleepy (I'd forgotten to think about the time difference!) but when I asked her if I'd woken her up, she said very quickly that it was quite all right, she'd been watching the late, late movie on TV. She sounded really pleased to hear from me and when I said that we really wanted her to come over, she sounded so delighted that I suddenly felt ashamed. Ashamed because I should have done this ages ago. She chatted on a bit about what airline she'd take, and how long she could afford to come for, and then talked about what was going on at home, about the play she'd made the costumes for. I listened and made comments now and then. It was kind of nice to be speaking and hearing English, for a change. Relaxing.

'Oh, and before I forget,' Aunt Jenny said, 'Portia rang this morning. She said that she'd sent you an email but you hadn't answered so she gave me a message to give to you in case I spoke to you before you got a chance to go online again. She said to say you should have a look at some website, I think she said it was called Posh, or Kosh, or something like that?'

I couldn't work out what it was, at first. Then it hit me. 'Oh, you mean Koschei.'

'That's the one. She sounded insistent, Rose. Seemed to think it was important.'

'Did she?' I sighed. Portia didn't usually get worked up about things – Alice and Maddy were more likely to – so it did surprise me a little. 'Don't worry about it, Aunt Jenny. It's just some idiot geek who's been annoying me a bit – on the blog, I mean. The girls are a bit worked up about it, that's all.'

'Oh dear,' said Aunt Jenny, 'I hope it's all right.'

'It's fine, Aunt Jenny. Nothing to worry about. I'll have a look later, anyway.' I thought, if you knew what's really been going on here, you'd soon understand why I don't give that troll Koschei much thought. It was totally insignificant compared to what I'd had to put up with here. But of course I didn't tell her. I just chatted to her a bit about the castle and Grand-père and how I liked it here and was meeting lots of people. She seemed interested by it all, but at the end she said, 'What are you going to do, Rose?'

'What do you mean?'

'I mean, are you coming back here, or are you staying?'

'I'm coming back, of course.'

But even as I said it, I wasn't sure. And she knew I wasn't. I could tell by the way she said, briskly, 'Well, anyway, these things have to work themselves out naturally. And I'll see you soon. So there's that to look forward to.'

I agreed heartily. 'It'll be just great to have you here, Aunt Jenny. Make sure you come quickly! Maybe you could be here for my birthday. We're going to have a party.'

'That's a bit close, Rosie,' said Aunt Jenny, with a smile in her voice. 'But maybe not too long after that.'

'We'll wait to have the party till you come,' I said, impulsively, and she laughed.

'Well, that'd be nice, but maybe speak to your grand-father first.'

'He won't mind,' I said, 'and anyway, he does what I say!'

'Like that, is it,' she said, and laughed again. 'Oh, Rosie, you can't imagine how good it is to hear your voice and to know that everything's going so well! Now, this must be costing your grandfather a fortune, so we'd better say goodbye. I'll let you know as soon as I get my ticket, and what time I arrive, and all that. Okay?'

'Okay,' I said, smiling. 'I look forward to that, Aunt Jenny.'

'So do I,' she said. 'Goodbye, sweetheart, and take care. I'll speak to you soon.' And she hung up.

I told Grand-père about the call when I found him in the dining room a little later, reading the newspaper over the last of his coffee. He was pleased, and readily agreed with my idea of having the party once Aunt Jenny had arrived. 'That gives us more time to organise it,' he said. 'We'll do something really fine. A proper ball, Rose! How would your aunt like that?'

'She'd love it,' I said. 'She loves all that old-world glamour. She's into all those old films, you know, with Audrey Hepburn and Cary Grant and Marilyn Monroe and all them.'

'Old films,' sighed Grand-père. 'Oh dear. That's the era of my young manhood, Rose! No, don't look embarrassed, it's quite okay, they *are* old films now, aren't they? Just like I'm an old man. Ah well, I think your Aunt Jenny has good taste. How about we make old-style film glamour the theme of your ball?'

'That's a lovely idea. Aunt Jenny would love that.'

'Would *you*?'

'Definitely. I could wear my hair like they did, and I could still wear my silver dress, and those silver shoes, but maybe I could find a really nice shawl or stole from that period, too, and a beaded bag or something . . .'

'You might find some of that up in the attic,' said my grandfather. 'Things belonging to my mother, and one or two things of Caroline's. There's a trunk or two up there that might be worth rummaging through.'

'Oh, yes!' I had visions of finding all kinds of treasures. I hadn't realised there was an attic. At least, no-one had told me about it before. The stairs to it must be down the other end of the second floor.

The second floor. It jolted me back to our problem. 'Grand-père, have you been to the Fontaines' place yet?'

'Of course not, Rose. I was waiting for you. We'll go just

as soon as you've had breakfast. I rang them earlier and told them we might be there around eleven. Does that give you enough time?'

'I'm not very hungry. I'll just have a cup of coffee,' I said. 'I really want to get this over and done with.'

'Poor Rose,' he said, and touched my hand. 'I can quite understand.'

'Where's Charlie? Is he coming?'

'He had to go to work. Said he couldn't take the time off so soon after he'd started. I can understand that. He said he'd make a statement to the police too, though, if we waited till tomorrow to do that. He said he might be able to get the afternoon off if he asked them today. I think that's a sensible plan. Don't you?'

I nodded.

'And tonight you can sleep in my room again. You can do that till we catch this creature,' he said. 'If you want to, of course. If I don't snore too much.'

'Oh, no, Grand-père, I didn't hear you at all. I didn't hear anything, in fact.'

'Good. I saw you were sleeping like an angel,' he said, gently. 'It's the best cure for many things. Ah, Madame Collot,' he said, as the housekeeper came in, feather duster in hand, 'I'm glad you're here. Just wanted to tell you Mademoiselle Rose is sleeping in my room till further notice.'

'That will account for the sofa bed, sir,' said the housekeeper, smiling. 'Would you perhaps prefer that a better bed be moved in there, a more comfortable one?'

'This one was perfectly all right,' I said.

'As you wish, Mademoiselle. Monsieur le Comte, Madame Vallon asks if you'll be here for lunch.'

'Hmm, more likely wanting to know what we're up to,' said Grand-père, his eyes twinkling. 'Tell her that we will most likely eat out today. We are going to the Fontaines' and after that we might go to Castelnau or to one of the villages round about that has a decent restaurant. All right?'

'Yes, Monsieur le Comte. Er . . . we were wondering . . . whether Madame Randal – whether she would, er, need lunch.'

'You mean, you want to know whether she's packed her bags and gone, after last night's little outburst?' His voice was suddenly cold and hard. The housekeeper flushed.

'Well, sir, we were just . . .'

'Of course. You have a right to know. You live in this house. No, Madame Collot. Blanche has not packed her bags and gone. I persuaded her not to.' He saw our expressions. 'She is a proud woman, and not an easy one, I know. But she is a good woman and honest, I am sure of that. She needs this job – and not just for herself. It gives Charlie a home and security.'

'And God knows he needed that, after the dance his father led them,' said Madame Collot, nodding her head wisely. 'Charm the birds off the trees, that one, and swear to you black was white and you'd believe it, but a thoroughly bad lot. Naturally crooked, you see. Lucky she left him when she did. Still turned up here to pester them from time to time. We all couldn't stand him here. But thank God he can't do that any longer.'

'Why not? Is he dead?' I asked.

Madame Collot shot a look at Grand-père. He nodded, slightly. 'He's in prison, Mademoiselle. For fraud.'

'Oh, no,' I said. Poor Charlie. Why hadn't he told me

225

about all this? And was that what Paul had meant when he said I didn't know everything about Charlie Randal? But if it was that, it wasn't fair. Charlie wasn't responsible for what his father had done.

'Will you please ask Louis to bring the car round to the front in ten minutes? And ask Samantha, or Madame Vallon, to bring Rose a cup of coffee and a brioche here?' said my grandfather to Madame Collot, changing the subject. She nodded, and left.

Grand-père said, 'Well, we've given them a bit of food for thought, all of them, eh? The kitchen must be a hotbed of gossip right now.'

A thought had suddenly struck me. 'Grand-père, could it be possible that the person who's doing all this – this man in the mask person – could it be someone connected with one of the staff? I mean, someone's who's been here and knows something of what happened to the family?'

'It is possible,' said Grand-père. 'We'll have to look into it.'

Samantha Vallon came in then with a tray. She smiled brightly at us as she put the tray down, with its steaming pot of coffee and glazed brioche, on the desk in front of me.

'Do you feel better, Rose?'

'Much better, thank you.'

'You look well.'

'A good night's sleep,' I said.

'Yes. It works wonders. Oh, Rose, I just can't understand it. Paul told me all that happened. Who could be so wicked as to shut you in that place?'

'We don't know, Samantha,' said Grand-père heavily. 'But we intend to find out.' There was a short pause. 'Did Paul tell you if he had any idea as to who it might be?'

She shot me a quick glance. 'He did. But he's not sure.'

'If he means by that that it's Charlie,' said Grand-père wearily, 'I'll have to tell him that he's letting his feelings run away with his reason. Charlie has a job in Toulouse. He can't be in two places at once. He didn't get back to the castle till 7.30, and that's a fact.'

'I know,' said Samantha surprisingly. 'I saw him arrive. Saw him step off the Castelnau bus, as a matter of fact. That's what I told Paul. But he –'

'Well, he'll have to listen to sense,' said my grandfather firmly. 'We're convinced the culprit is a stranger, Samantha. I mean, a stranger to this house.'

'Oh, Monsieur le Comte, is that so?' Samantha's expression lightened. 'That would make things so much easier, wouldn't it?'

'And so it would,' said my grandfather as she left. 'But sometimes the easier explanation is not only convenient but also true. So let's hope it proves to be so.'

'Oh yes,' I said fervently. I'd much rather the man in the mask than anything else, even if it spooked me a little. It was easier on the heart than the other notion – that someone was lying and pretending to be my friend when in fact they were my foe.

Kingdom of shadows

We drew up to the Fontaines' house with what Grand-père said was 'a bit of an unnecessary flourish', with the pebbles spitting and skidding under the tyres of the Mercedes. 'Sorry,' said Louis Vallon, with a grin, 'but the brakes seem a bit soft today, Monsieur.'

'I'll bet they do,' said Grand-père coolly, 'or perhaps it might be that my chauffeur has a hard foot, eh?'

'I'm not admitting anything,' said Louis, cheerfully, and jumping out, he opened the car doors to let us out.

Paul's parents had come out of the house at our approach. Geneviève had an anxious look on her face; Marcel's, though, was set and impassive. But he was welcoming enough. 'Good morning,' he said as he came forward to greet us. 'Come in. Paul will be along in just a minute, he's finishing off a job for me outside.'

They ushered us in, Louis included. We sat around their kitchen table and drank coffee and ate biscuits and talked of anything except what we'd come for. Then the door opened and Paul came in, accompanied by one of his brothers, who was introduced to us as Simon. This was Samantha's boyfriend, I remembered. He was tall, heavy and quiet, but with the odd flash of humour.

After a few pleasantries, we got down to business. Or

rather, Grand-père did. He filled everyone in on what had been happening up to yesterday, and then said, 'Paul, you know we're trying to sort out the sequence of events before we all go down to the police station tomorrow to make our statements. Can you explain to me exactly what happened yesterday evening?'

'I was here studying,' said Paul. 'Alone in the house. Maman and Papa had gone out to the cinema in Castelnau, and Jacques and Simon were out too. Tati Renée called in on her bicycle. She told me that Rose – that Mademoiselle du Merle – had disappeared and that there was a search party out looking for her. She said she'd seen something – you know, Monsieur le Comte, in the way she does. She'd seen Rose – Mademoiselle – in a dark place. Well, then I remembered Rose saying something about being at the vault one day, and I said, "Do you think it might be that?" And Tati said we might as well go and see. So we opened up the church, got the spare key to the vault and, well, that's all.'

'I see,' said Grand-père thoughtfully. 'So really, though Renée had one of her flashes, it was you, Paul, who had the hunch where Rose might be.'

'I suppose so,' said Paul, shrugging. I met his eyes. He looked down.

'It's all for the good,' said Grand-père. 'I don't fancy telling the police about Renée's flashes.'

'They're real enough, Monsieur le Comte,' said Paul.

'Maybe, my boy, but very erratic, eh? I think we might leave them out of it, don't you think, to avoid misunderstandings? Don't want to confuse the police. Now, Paul, you found the vault key to be where it should have been?'

'Yes.'

'So it's likely the vault was locked by one of the other

keys. The ones we have at the castle,' said Grand-père. His eyes narrowed. 'Although there was also that incident of the *glas* – the death knell. Someone had got into the church that day, after all.'

'Ah, but we moved the key after that incident,' broke in Marcel Fontaine. 'Now we keep it in a place only we know about.'

'I took it from there,' said Paul. 'I'm sure no-one outside our family knows about it. No, Monsieur le Comte, the vault must have been locked by someone who had access to one of your own keys.'

'Yes,' said Grand-père heavily. He was silent a moment, then asked, 'Have any of you seen any strangers around the village?'

They exchanged glances. 'No,' said Paul. And 'No,' said Simon, and 'No,' said Marcel. But Geneviève looked more anxious than ever.

'Not really,' she said.

Grand-père pounced on that. 'What do you mean, not really?'

'No-one who had no business to be here, anyway.'

'What do you mean by that?'

'Well, the postman had someone with him the other day – a passenger – I saw him in the van but I thought nothing of it. Except that I happened to be looking down the road after they drove off, and I saw the postman let the man out.'

'Where did he let him out?

'At the crossroads. I didn't see where he went after that. But it seemed an odd place to ask to be dropped off. I mean – why not in the village? The postman was going right in, after all.'

'Why not indeed, Madame?' said Grand-père, eagerly. 'What did this person look like?'

'I hardly saw him. He didn't look at me. I just had the impression of someone rather thin – wiry – grey hair – dark-coloured jumper – that's all.'

'How long ago was this?'

'About ten days ago – two weeks, perhaps?'

'Not long before Rose arrived,' said Grand-père. His eyes were bright. I saw the Fontaine men exchange glances again and knew what they were thinking. He was clutching at straws. 'I'll speak to the postman today,' he went on, 'see if we can find out who this person was, and what happened to them or who they were coming to see.'

'If they were coming to see anyone,' said Marcel coolly.

'Yes,' said Grand-père. 'Well,' he said, getting up, 'I must thank you for all your help. We must –'

I broke in, quickly, 'Grand-père, before we go, there's something – could I please talk with Paul in private?'

I hadn't even planned it. It just came out. I'm not sure how I got the courage to say it, really. But it might have been the way Paul was carefully not looking at me, the way my heart was beating like mad, or the sudden feeling that if I didn't speak now, it would be too late.

'I don't think it's me you need to ask, Rose,' said Grand-père, after a heartbeat of silence.

He motioned to Paul, who flushed, got awkwardly to his feet, met his family's curious stares and said, 'Of course. I'd be glad to, Ro – Mademoiselle.'

We walked out of the room with all their eyes on our backs. I was clutching the rags of my recklessness to me, trying to think what on earth I'd do next, and what I'd say to Paul. But he took it out of my hands. He said, 'I'm glad you did that, Mademoiselle. I wanted to explain properly but I was too –'

'Please don't call me Mademoiselle, it makes me feel weird,' I said, the words catching in my throat and coming out with a bit of a squeak.

'Sorry,' he said, smiling. It transformed his hard, watchful face into something almost handsome. 'I don't want you to feel weird.'

'You're doing a pretty good job of it so far,' I said, trying to sound cool and in control.

'What do you think you're doing to me?' he said, quietly. 'What do you think you've been doing to my peace of mind, ever since I first saw you, standing in that queue, in your beautiful, impractical clothes, and those silver fairy shoes?'

My whole body felt hot. I said, feebly, 'I . . . I had no idea. You spoke to me as though you . . . you . . . disliked me – on sight.'

He winced. 'I'm sorry, Rose. My God, I'm so clumsy. I was angry with myself, not you. I could hardly believe what I was feeling. Like a bolt out of the blue. I didn't mean for you to think . . .' He paused, then continued, 'Do you remember when you caught me that time, looking you up on the internet?'

I nodded, not looking at him.

'I wanted to see if there was a photo of you anywhere,' he said quietly. 'I thought perhaps you might be on one of those sites like MySpace or Bebo. I thought perhaps I could pretend to be someone else, start again, start up a conversation – see if in another world, another life, we might perhaps be friends. Or more. Stupid, wasn't it?'

My heart was beating so fast it made me feel sick. 'No,' I faltered. 'But I'm not on anything like that . . .'

'That's what I found out,' he said gently. A pause, then he went on, 'Well, Rose, what is it? What did you want to ask me in private?'

'I – I . .' I stared at him. I thought, I can't ask him about Blanche right now. I don't want that look to go from his face, I don't want him to go all cold on me. But I had to ask him something. I had to. My mind whirled. Then I suddenly thought of something.

'Talking of the internet – there's something I need to check out. It's something I didn't have a chance to do before we left and I think I should,' I gabbled, talking utter nonsense.

'Now?'

'Yes, now, if you don't mind.'

He smiled and said simply, 'Of course. Anything you want.'

'Oh,' I said, going scarlet. He laughed but said nothing more, and we went up to his room. He sat down at his desk and opened up his laptop. 'So, what are we looking for? Information on our suspects, is it? The mystery man in the postman's van, Charlie Randal – or Paul Fontaine?'

'Paul,' I said, 'I don't –'

'Yes you do,' he said, without rancour. 'A part of you still suspects, even after last night. Even now. After all, I fit the bill rather better than the handsome Charles-Louis, don't I?'

'You don't,' I said wildly, 'any more than he does.'

He looked at me and sighed. 'I can see I'm not going to convince you.'

'I think you're jealous,' I said pertly.

He laughed. 'Of course.' His expression darkened. 'But it's more than that. Rose, I've known Charlie a lot longer than you have. I went to school with him. He's . . . He can

233

be very charming, but he's not always – well, I don't think he's altogether truthful.'

'I don't suppose anyone tells the truth all the time,' I said hotly. 'And things haven't been easy for him, with that father and his mother, well, he's not had an easy time of it.'

'That may well be true,' said Paul surprisingly, 'and I always thought his mother was like the Snow Queen with those eyes of hers that could send a barb of ice through your heart. But still –'

'Oh! I see her just like that, too!' I said. 'I even call her the Snow Queen, in my mind.'

'Great minds think alike,' he said, laughing. He caught me around the waist and pulled me down onto his lap, and then, just like that, we were kissing.

He didn't kiss like Charlie. He was awkward, even a little clumsy, not so much in control, but he was hot, he was passionate and his arms were tight and warm around me. Delight as sweet as warm caramel raced through me. My limbs felt loose. I could feel his heart racing as fast as mine.

After a short time, we drew apart, shakily. I got up. I said, 'Oh, Paul, I don't know if that should have happened.'

'Ssh,' he said, putting a finger to my lips. 'There's no need to say anything. You're not bound to anything. Just take it that I've been wanting to do that for a long time. And I'm glad you don't find me repulsive after all.' He smiled, and his face flooded with sunshine. I thought, how could I ever have thought he wasn't handsome? How could I ever have thought he hated me? Was it really possible to fall in love with two people, and each of them so different? I hadn't meant for any of this. I was confused and scared. I knew it was dangerous. But I couldn't pretend to myself that I didn't find it exciting too.

Just then, there was a soft knock on the door and Geneviève's voice calling out, 'Paul? Mademoiselle Rose?'

Paul shot a humorous look at me and went to open the door. His mother said, 'I'm sorry to disturb you – but Monsieur le Comte has left for Castelnau. He said you should meet him there, Mademoiselle. At the restaurant of the Trois Ecus.' She looked everywhere but at me. I realised that she knew what had been going on and she didn't like it much. She went on, the words tumbling over one another, 'Paul, he asked if you could take Mademoiselle. He's invited you to lunch too. He said he was sorry he had to go, but Louis Vallon thinks the car might need a check-up – Simon thinks there might be something wrong with it, he fiddled a bit but couldn't see what the problem was – and Monsieur le Comte thinks the sooner it's in Castelnau, the better. The mechanics can fix it while you're having lunch.'

Grand-père was playing matchmaker too, I thought. He'd removed himself discreetly from the scene so Paul and I could come to an understanding, or something. It was clear which of my two suitors he preferred! Suitors – what the hell was I talking about?

'That's all fine,' said Paul. 'Isn't it, Rose?'

'Sure,' I said, and I saw her blink. She shot a look at me, then back to Paul. Her anxious expression sharpened. She said, 'Please don't take her on the motorbike, Paul. I don't think her grandfather would like it. Not even in the sidecar.'

I was tired of being spoken about as 'her'. What was I, the cat's mother, as Aunt Jenny would have said? I said defiantly, 'I'm not scared of motorbikes. And Grand-père won't mind.' I thought, how cool would it be, the wind in

235

my hair, my arms around Paul's waist, roaring off through the countryside.

'Nevertheless,' said Geneviève Fontaine. 'Do it for me. Take my car, Paul.'

'All right, Maman,' he said, capitulating rather swiftly, I thought. But as she went out, closing the door softly behind her, he said, 'Poor Maman. She's never liked my bike. I think she expects at any moment to hear that I'm splattered all over the road.'

'I don't think she likes me much,' I said.

'Nonsense,' said Paul. 'She hardly knows you.'

'Neither do you!'

'That's different,' he said, laughing at me. 'And you know it.'

'Do I?'

'I think you do,' he said, and kissed me again. I emerged from his grasp saying, very shakily, 'We have to stop this.'

'Why?'

'Because, because, I don't know! I'm confused! I don't know what to think about all this.'

'So it's still a toss-up between me and Randal then?'

I went scarlet. 'Oh, Paul, stop it!'

'Okay,' he said, smiling at me. 'I don't want you to get angry with me, or you might choose wrongly. And we'll go and meet your grandfather. But before we go, Rose, let's look up that thing you wanted.'

I had almost forgotten about it. 'Oh, it doesn't really matter. I can look later. Grand-père will be waiting.'

'It won't take a minute,' he said.

'It's just someone's website that one of my friends said I should look at . . . It's someone who's been commenting on my blog, and –'

'You have a blog?'

'It's not a real blog,' I said, 'I mean, it is, but I started it because it was an assignment we had to do at school.'

'What's the URL?' he asked and I told him. His fingers flew over the keyboard, and in a trice, there was my blog, popping up onto the screen.

'Three wishes?' he said, and I could see his eyes scanning over my posts. I was glad I hadn't written anything about him or Charlie in any of them.

I went a little red. 'Yes – well, I made three wishes. That was the theme of my blog. You can have a look down there.' I showed him the archived post, the 'three wishes' one. He read it quickly and said, 'So they all came true, Rose.' He looked up at me and grinned. 'This . . . exciting thing you wanted to happen to you – is that me, do you think?'

'Paul Fontaine!' I said, mock-scandalised. 'You're the vainest man I ever met!'

'Is that so, Miss?' he said, in a rather sweet Frenchy sort of English, with the 'th' in 'that' coming out rather more like a 'z'.

I laughed. 'I do think that is so.'

'Then you have clearly not met my rival, Charles-Louis,' he said, lightly, back into French.

I cried, 'Stop it, Paul. Stop talking about him. I don't want to think of him just now.'

'That will suit me fine,' he said. 'Now, what are we looking for?'

'This.' I scrolled down to the places where Koschei had made comments. 'My friends think I should do something about him.'

'He sounds like a nuisance,' agreed Paul, reading the

comments, a bit of a frown on his face. 'Your friends are right. You should always do something about creeps like this or they can completely destroy your blog. That name – it's familiar to me. I've heard it somewhere before . . .'

'Oh, it won't be his real name,' I said. 'It's just his internet handle. It might even be a girl, I suppose, though it sounds like a boy to me. Anyway, he's probably –' and then I stopped, because Paul's quick fingers had brought up http://Koscheithedread.blogspot.com and I was struck dumb.

Black it was, that blog, with green writing, and sinister black and white pictures I hardly took in. 'Koschei the Dread', it was called, and its subheading was 'Into the kingdom of shadows'. But that wasn't why I stared, why my skin prickled all over with cold, my eyes watered, my hands shook. It was because of the very first post that met my eyes.

Fee fi fo fum, it said.

Fee fi fo fum

I smell the blood of an Australian

Now she's alive, but will she soon be dead?

It all depends if she use her head.

'Nasty stuff,' said Paul, scrolling down to the next post, the first one called 'Who am I?' which went something like, 'I am your worst nightmare, I am the haunter of your dreams,' and more in the same ugly, sinister, gloating, stupid way. I hardly took it in. I could only stare at that first post, the sudden terror making my veins turn to ice. 'In fact more than nasty,' he went on, 'I think this is at the verge of stalking, of harassment – we'll have to see if we can shut him down and –' He looked up at me. 'What's the matter, Rose? You look like you've seen a ghost! He's just an internet crazy prowling around the –'

'Paul,' I said, blankly, 'that's what it said, on that photo in the tomb.'

'What do you mean?'

'On the back of that photo of me, the one that I burnt. It said, fee fi fo fum.'

'Like that?' he said, gesturing at the screen. I nodded, unable to speak. He said, 'Are you sure?'

I nodded.

'What is it, this "fee fi fo fum"?'

'It's from a fairytale called *Jack and the Beanstalk*,' I said stiffly. 'An ogre says it. It's part of a rhyme – like . . . like that one. Except it says blood of an Englishman, not an Australian – and the rest is different too. But it's based on the same thing.'

'It could be a coincidence,' he said, but he didn't sound as if he convinced even himself. He took my hand. 'Sit down next to me, *chérie*.'

I sat close to him. His presence and the touch of his hand were infinitely reassuring to me. Looking into the screen at that blog was like looking through a window into a dark and evil realm, ruled over by God knows what ugly passions and shadowy motives.

Paul clicked on the 'view my complete profile' bit of the Koschei blog. Not surprisingly, there was nothing at all listed there. In a calm, unemotional voice, he said, 'The bastard is hiding in the shadows like a mangy wolf. But we'll trap him – we'll hunt him down and trap him.'

'But how?' I couldn't stop staring at that sinister page, with a mixture of horror and terror.

Paul clicked back on to my blog, and onto the comments Koschei had left. 'There's a Google email address attached to this, but it won't show us anything.

Anyone can create a webmail address, simplest thing in the world. I'll have to dig a bit deeper later. I've got a friend who's a real computer geek, he can help. I think maybe it's something to do with IP address tracing.'

He opened another window, onto Google. He entered the name 'Koschei'. Several references popped up. The first was a Wikipedia entry. Paul clicked on it. 'Ha. I thought I'd heard the name. It's the name of an evil wizard from a Russian fairytale,' he said, scanning the entry. 'Listen to this – he's "an evil person of ugly appearance, menacing principally young women". And it says here Koschei couldn't be killed by conventional means, because he's got his soul well hidden, away from his body. Listen to this: "inside a needle in an egg in a hare in an iron chest buried under a green oak tree on the island of Buyan in the ocean".'

I shivered. 'It's the same person,' I whispered, 'the same one, Paul. He's my hidden enemy. He's stalking me on the internet. And he's stalking me out here in real life. He knows who I am. Oh, Paul, I'm so scared . . .'

Paul squeezed my hand. 'He's a knife-in-the-back coward who dares not show his face. But we'll make him. You'll see, we'll make him!'

He clicked back on to my blog. He scrolled through the comments till he found Koschei's first. It was on March 3, on a small post of mine called 'Dreams and wishes.' ❧
I remembered that I'd taken very little notice back then. Paul read it, then clicked on to the other posts. After a short time, he said, 'His first comment came even before you knew about your family here. But he must have known. Which means –'

'He's not likely to be from Australia,' I said. 'I mean, the solicitor who came with Blanche Randal – he knew before we did but no-one else did, and why would a solicitor do anything like this? Then there's that "fee fi fo fum" stuff. Koschei is here. I'm sure he is, Paul.'

'Someone who knows your grandfather or has heard the story,' agreed Paul. 'Word gets around quickly in villages, you know. Your grandfather didn't exactly broadcast the fact he'd found his long-lost heiress, but people found out. For instance, my family heard about it a couple of weeks before you arrived. Samantha told us. She'd heard about it from her mother, who overheard a conversation between your grandfather and Madame Randal.'

'But it's got to be someone who can write English well,' I said. 'Look at those posts. They're in good English. He only made one small mistake, saying "use" instead of "uses". How many people here can write English like that?'

'I can,' said Paul steadily. A pause. 'And Charlie can too.'

I suddenly remembered Charlie reciting the bit from that poem, the first time I was in the tomb. Icy fingers crawled down my spine.

Paul saw my expression. He said gently, 'But there are several other candidates for that, as well – the local teacher, for instance, and two or three other people I know.'

'It can't be Charlie, anyway,' I said, relieved, 'because he doesn't know how to use computers. At least, he's only just started, when he got this job. He doesn't even have an email address. He didn't know I had a blog, either. I haven't said anything to him about it.'

Paul gave a faint smile. 'Lucky for him he's got you to defend him, Rose. Well, what about me? I can use computers, and I can write English.' He gestured at the screen. 'Is it my black heart displayed there for all to see, Rose?'

I held his gaze. I swallowed and said, 'No, Paul. I don't think it's you.'

'I am glad,' he said, simply, but I felt a wave of warmth wash over me.

'Maybe I should send him an email,' I said quickly. 'To Koschei, I mean,' I added, as I saw his quizzical look.

'Whatever for?'

'Just to tell him what I think of him.'

Paul shook his head. 'And what do you think that will do? Do you think he'll be frightened, if you email him?'

'No, of course not. But I can tell him what I think, and it will make me feel better. And if he realises we know that he is the same person who's been –'

'He obviously wanted you to know that,' said Paul, quietly. 'Or else why would he write that phrase on the photo – and on his blog? He wanted you to make those connections. He's been wanting you to see how clever he is, he wants to taunt you. He thinks he's a magician, the king of shadows. He thinks he's invincible, that he can play with you like a cat with a mouse. He *wants* you to be frightened, to be paralysed with fear as he creeps up behind you. Don't you see?'

'But why . . . I don't understand –'

'Money,' said Paul, succinctly. 'Or power. Or obsession with some grievance. Or all three. That's what I'd say.' He looked at his watch. 'We're late. Your grandfather will be thinking I've kidnapped you.'

I started, but he didn't see it. He shut down the computer, closed it, and ushered me out of the room. As we went downstairs, he said, 'Don't worry, Rose. I'll ring

242

my geek friend as soon as I get home, and set him on the trail. He loves that sort of thing. You'll see. We'll know soon what computer the guy's been using and where. And then we can find out who he is. Okay?'

Okay,' I said.

'Good,' he said. 'You trust me then, Rose?'

'Of course,' I said, a little too hurriedly.

He sighed. 'I wish you would, completely, but I understand why you don't.'

'Paul,' I said, going for broke now, thinking that if I didn't ask it now, I never would, and it would gnaw away at me. 'Paul, I must ask you a question. It's an embarrassing question, but I must – I must really ask. You must promise not to get angry.'

'I promise,' he said quietly.

'Was it . . . did you come to the castle, the night before last, and speak with Blanche Randal?'

Whatever he'd been expecting, it clearly wasn't this. He stared at me in absolute astonishment. 'What would I have to say to Blanche Randal? There's hardly any love lost between us.'

'It's just that I heard –'

'What did you hear, Rose? I assure you I was never anywhere near the castle that night. In fact, I was in Toulouse. I went to a nightclub called Etoile and stayed overnight at a friend's.'

'I – I don't mean to accuse you,' I said miserably. 'It's just that I heard Blanche say your name.'

'Paul Fontaine? Is that what you heard?'

'No, just Paul.'

He laughed. 'Paul isn't such an uncommon name! I can assure you, my beautiful little goose, that this particular

Paul is not guilty of trysting with the Snow Queen. Ugh! I'd rather hug a refrigerator. Some other Paul must have had the honour.'

A great weight lifted from me. Of course! I hadn't even thought of the obvious explanation. 'Maybe this Paul is the man who got off at the crossroads that day,' I said. 'Maybe he's Koschei as well.'

'Maybe and maybe not,' said Paul, solemn again. 'What did this Paul say to Blanche, anyway?'

'I didn't hear what he said,' I said. I then told Paul what I heard Blanche say.

'Well, Rose, I understand why it made you uneasy. But it doesn't have to have anything to do with your problem, you know. There could be an innocent explanation for it – much as I dislike the Snow Queen. Perhaps she's just having an affair she wants to keep from the ears and eyes of the rest of the household, especially her son.'

'Why should she care about that?'

'Well, people can be terrible gossips, and Madame Randal is a very private sort. Besides, Charlie's not exactly welcomed any boyfriends she's had in the past. He's a jealous one, that one, thinks the world revolves around him.'

'Paul!' I said, sharply.

He grinned, unrepentant. 'You're not going to get me to praise or pity my rival.'

'Paul, stop it!'

'Okay,' he said. 'I will. But only if you give me another kiss.'

'But, Paul,' I cried, 'your family might come in at any moment! They'll see us!'

'I don't care,' said Paul and bent down to kiss me again, stopping my protests very effectively indeed.

Darkness at noon

This is the hardest part of all to write. I find myself facing the blank page with a feeling of such reluctance I almost feel physically sick. To protect myself, I imagine a scenario. I can see myself getting into the car with Paul, feeling safe with him, yet a little uneasy, dimly aware somewhere deep inside me that just a few minutes away lay an event of such shattering and horrifying effect that – no, I can't write it like that. Despite all that had happened before, despite the edge of terror I'd been on for so long, I can't say I had any idea, any real idea, of what lay ahead of me, and how it would change everything . . .

So I get into the car with Paul. We drive away from the farm, talking first a little about how we're going to proceed next, and then we talk about other things, about each other, just talking and talking about what we like, and the books we read, and the music we listen to, the films we like watching, and what we planned to do in the future. It was funny, because though we had such different plans, he with his plant nursery, me with my writing, we discovered that, despite having lived in separate countries, we shared quite a lot of things, similar tastes in stuff, similar ways of looking at the world.

So there we were, chatting away, Paul gesticulating quite

a bit and driving rather slowly along the road to Castelnau, when suddenly he braked, and stopped. A cop was standing in the middle of the road, holding up a hand. 'Damn,' said Paul, 'hope I didn't forget to bring my licence with me,' and he rummaged in his jeans pocket for it. 'Ah, here it is.'

The cop came to the window. He looked in at us. He had a thin, pale, narrow face with expressionless green eyes. He didn't even glance at Paul's proffered licence. 'I'm sorry, Monsieur,' he said. 'The road's blocked. You can't proceed.'

'What? Why?'

'The road's blocked,' repeated the policeman. 'There's been an accident, Monsieur. A bad one. We've had to close the road. You should find another way of getting to your destination. Where are you going?'

'Castelnau,' said Paul, mechanically. 'What happened?'

'A bad accident,' repeated the cop. 'Very bad. There is another way to Castelnau, Monsieur. If you go via –'

'Thank you, Monsieur, we know where to go. I'm a local,' said Paul, and he reversed the car and then did a U-turn in the middle of the road. Fortunately no-one else was coming.

We went along for a bit in silence. I felt chilled, and Paul was pale. Driving is such an ordinary activity. Even me, whose parents had been killed in a car crash – even I didn't think very much of what might happen. You don't, unless you're a worry-wart like Paul's mother. And so it gives you a shock to come across an accident. Even if you haven't seen it.

Paul said, 'It's a good road, and the middle of the day. I wonder what happened. The police never tell you anything.'

'No. But I'm not sure I really want to know. It must have been bad, or they wouldn't have blocked the road.' I shivered, my imagination conjuring up ghastly scenes of mangled bodies and twisted wrecks of cars, blood everywhere.

'Yes.' Paul didn't speak again till we were on the outskirts of Castelnau, and then he said, 'Look, Rose, this might sound stupid, but I want to ring Maman. Just in case she hears about the accident, and thinks it's us. She worries a lot. I've left my mobile behind, though, so we're going to have to stop at a phone booth. I'll just be a second, okay?'

'Sure,' I said, a little surprised but touched by his concern for his mother.

So we pulled up at a glassed-in booth on the side of the road and Paul went in, dialled the number and began to speak. I saw his shoulders suddenly stiffen, heard his exclamation, 'What?' and saw his expression change as he listened. Then he put the phone down, and returned to me. He looked terrible – quite white, his eyes hollow.

Filled with sudden panic, I cried, 'For God's sake, Paul, what's the matter?' and jumped out of the car. Then he grabbed me and held me and said, 'Rose . . . Rose, my God, Rose.'

'What? What?'

'Maman was in a terrible state . . .' he said, blankly. 'She's just heard from a neighbour.' He held me even tighter. 'Rose, I'm so sorry.'

Ice shot into my spine, my veins, my throat. I said, through lips that felt frozen and hard, 'What is it? What's happened?'

'Your grandfather . . .' He swallowed. 'Louis. There's been a terrible accident.'

I would have fallen if he hadn't been holding me. My ears were buzzing, my teeth were chattering so loudly I was sure he could hear them. My voice sounded high and far away and hideously precise as I said, 'Is he dead?'

He whispered, and I could feel him shaking as he spoke. 'He's unconscious. They don't know yet how bad he . . . And Louis, too, he –'

I broke in. 'Where are they?' That high, precise voice asking the questions didn't belong to me.

'Hospital. Albi.'

'I want you to take me there at once.'

'Rose, they'll be operating on them. I don't know if . . .'

'Take me there at once.' I detached myself from his arms, walked stiffly to the car, opened the passenger door, got in, put on my seatbelt, closed the car door, every action robotic. Or at least that's what Paul told me later. I had no recollection of doing all this. Time had ground to a halt. I was numb. Everything was ordinary around me, people going about their business, cafés starting to bustle for lunch, the sun was even shining weakly, and yet I felt as though I was in a never-ending darkness, a vacuum, a nothingness.

Paul got in and started the car. He looked over at me. His face was full of tenderness and grief and horror. He said, 'If you'd gone with them in that car, Rose, you might be . . .'

But I turned away from him. I said, 'Please, get us there quickly. I must get there quickly.'

He touched my hand gently. When I didn't respond, he withdrew it. 'Yes, my poor Rose,' he whispered, and drew away from the kerb while I stared straight ahead of me.

How we got to Albi I don't know. The numbness left me

a few short minutes into the drive and then I felt as sick as a dog and Paul had to stop the car so I could throw up on the side of the road. Weakly I got back in and then found I couldn't stop shaking, my mind filling over and over with those horrible pictures I'd conjured up earlier, and then with images of that day when they'd interrupted my classes to tell me about my parents. Paul tried to help me, he really did, but I hardly noticed, I was lost in a wilderness of pain and grief and terror so great it blotted out everything else. I shivered and shook and whimpered. And I prayed. I tell you I prayed on that terrible journey to Albi, I just kept saying over and over again, 'Please, please, God, if you save him, I'll do anything . . . anything. I'll give up anything . . . please, please, please don't let him die . . . don't let him die.'

I was thinking of Grand-père, of course. To my later shame, poor Louis Vallon hardly figured in my thoughts. I couldn't bear the thought of losing Grand-père. He was the most important person in the whole world to me, I thought, the most important. And what had I been doing while Grand-père was lying bleeding and helpless on the road? If I'd been in the car with them, I might have been hurt too, as Paul had implied – but equally I might not. Perhaps I'd have been all right. Perhaps I'd have been thrown clear and I could have gone for help at once. I could have . . .

Well, I hadn't been in the car, so I would never know. Instead, I'd been hugging and kissing Paul and looking up that stupid, stupid blog . . .

As if I cared about that now. What did the motiveless, useless malevolence of a creep like Koschei mean to me beside a terrible thing like this? A ghastly accident. I remembered, painfully, how Louis had said this morning that the brakes felt a bit odd. They must have been worse than he thought. If only he'd noticed it earlier! If only they'd got a mechanic to come out and look at it, and not driven the car! Wild thoughts surged through me. If only Renée had seen it coming. What was the use of a gift like that if it didn't warn you, if you couldn't rely on it?

We were nearly at Albi when I said, 'Did she tell you how it happened?'

Paul seemed to start at the tone in my voice. And no wonder, for it was cold, so cold. I knew it but it didn't matter. Nothing mattered except that Grand-père should not die. What Paul and I had said, what we'd done, was tainted now by the thought of what had been happening on that road to Castelnau.

'You don't really –' he began, but I cut him off.

'I want to know, Paul!'

He said sadly, 'No-one's quite sure. The person who found them came on the scene at least twenty minutes after it happened. The car appeared to have swerved and crashed against one of the roadside trees. It looks to have been a single-car accident.' He looked like he was about to say something more, something anxious and tender, but I didn't want to hear it. I nodded and turned away from him, staring blindly out of the window at the passing landscape.

The reception clerk at the hospital was blunt. After putting through the call to emergency, she said, 'You can't go in to see them. It isn't possible.'

'I'm his granddaughter,' I gabbled. 'I'm his only grand-daughter.'

'I don't care if you're the President of France,' snapped the woman. 'You can't go in, and that's that.'

Paul saw I was about to explode. 'Can we wait, Madame?' he said politely.

She shrugged. 'If you like. But you might have to wait a long time.' And for nothing, her glance at me said. I hated her guts for not being touched by what was happening to us. I wanted to tell her so, but Paul took me by the elbow and led me to a chair. He made me sit down while he went to get us cups of coffee from the machine. I sat there like a rock, the hospital bustle all around me, remembering . . .

Mum and Dad had been dead on arrival at the hospital after their crash. I hadn't been taken there. People thought it would be too dreadful for me. I hadn't seen them till two days later at the funeral parlour. They lay in the coffins, side by side, dressed in their favourite clothes. Their eyes were closed, their hair was neatly combed, and they looked quite unreal. They didn't look like the Mum and Dad I'd known. They hardly even looked human. They were like pretend people, like dummies, like waxworks. There was even a strange fixed smile on their faces, like you see on shop dummies. I'd thought I'd be scared, but I wasn't. I was just sure these mannequins weren't them, that some mistake had been made, that any moment now the real Mum and Dad would walk in through the door.

I started as Paul touched my shoulder. Silently, he handed me a paper cup full of hot coffee. I took it but didn't drink it. It got cold sitting in my hand. Paul tried to speak to me but I didn't answer and after a while he gave up.

We sat there and sat there. People came and went. Time ticked on. At last, Paul got up and went back to the desk. I heard him asking the clerk if there was anyone who could help us, who might be able to tell us what was happening. She raised her eyebrows, but picked up her phone and dialled. I didn't hear what she said, because she spoke in an undertone. She put down the phone and said something to Paul. He nodded and came back to me.

'Someone's coming to see us,' he said. 'One of the doctors.'

I didn't say anything. I knew what that meant. Someone was coming to give us the bad news. Someone had been delegated to be the messenger of death.

'Rose,' Paul said, and took my hand. I didn't pull it away but I didn't respond either. It just lay there limp and cold and small in his big warm hand.

I don't know how long it was. But after a while a woman in a white coat came towards us. She was carrying a clipboard. She said, 'You are the relatives of Monsieur du Merle? I am Docteur Dufour.'

'Mademoiselle is –' began Paul, but I interrupted him.

'He's dead, isn't he? Oh my God, he's dead.'

'Calm yourself, Mademoiselle,' she said, quite kindly. 'Your grandfather is not dead. He does not even appear to have internal injuries. However, he has lost a good deal of blood where a flying piece of glass pierced his arm, and he is still unconscious. He is in intensive care, and will remain there for a good while. I'm afraid you can't see him just yet. Probably not today at all. His body is in shock. Mademoiselle,' she went on, looking anxious. 'Are you all right? Do you hear me?'

I heard her all right. I heard her loud and clear, each word edged with gilt, as if picked out by sunlight. A fierce joy surged through me. He was not dead! He was not even badly injured! He was in intensive care – but he would recover. He would. He must. I would not think that he was old and had already had a stroke and that a shock like this might very well kill him. He was strong. His spirit was strong and he was safe in hospital. He would wake up, tomorrow, maybe, and we would –

Then I heard Paul's voice asking, 'And the other person? Monsieur Vallon? Is he – is he okay?'

There was a short silence, then, 'I'm sorry, Monsieur. I'm truly sorry. The driver, Monsieur Vallon, he was very badly hurt. He took the full brunt of the crash. He – he didn't make it. He died on the way here, in the ambulance, despite the best efforts of the paramedics. I'm really, really sorry.'

We stared at her. She repeated, 'I'm truly sorry. Does he have a family? We need to contact his next of kin. Do you perhaps know . . .?'

Paul was the first to speak. In a strange, hollow voice, he said, 'He has a wife and daughter. I'll give you the number.' She handed him the clipboard and he wrote it down. His hands were shaking. 'We know them well. They will want to –' He broke off, and wiped his forehead, vaguely. It was glistening with sweat. I could see tears in his eyes. He murmured, 'We will stay here. Till they come. They will need us.'

'That is not a good idea. You should go home, Monsieur. And take the young lady with you,' said the doctor firmly. 'There is nothing you can do here.' She looked at me. 'We will call you if there is any change in the condition of your grandfather tomorrow, Mademoiselle. Go home, now, both of you. That is for the best.' And she nodded at us and turned away, her heels clicking briskly as she walked off up the corridor.

The house of mourning

I don't remember much of the drive back. We didn't talk. Each of us was lost in our own thoughts. Paul drove me right into the castle grounds and escorted me inside, though I tried to tell him I would be all right.

It was lucky he ignored me, for the castle seemed deserted. Samantha's car was gone, of course, but so was Madame Collot's. There was no Daudy in the garden and apparently no-one else around at all. The place echoed with emptiness. But an emptiness that seemed sudden, like a spell, or a doom. Doors and windows were open. In the kitchen, vegetables lay half-peeled on the table. It was eerie, like stepping into Sleeping Beauty's castle. Or the wreck of the *Mary Celeste*. It was a house of fear, a house of mourning.

'I can't leave you here on your own,' said Paul.

'I'll be okay.' But I said it half-heartedly and he knew it.

'I'll stay, Rose.' He made as if to take my hand, but I evaded him. His face set but he said, 'What are you going to do?'

I looked at him. I said, with a flash of temper, 'Wait for the hospital to ring, I suppose. What else is there to do?'

He winced but made no reply to that. Instead he said, 'Do you mind if I call home?'

I shrugged. 'Why should I mind? You know where the phone is.' I knew I was behaving badly, abominably even, but I couldn't help it. Superstitiously, I felt as though I couldn't allow myself to feel anything for Paul, or Charlie, or anyone else, not till Grand-père was out of danger, at least. Certainly there could be no return to the joyful flirtation of just a few hours ago. It was like I'd made a bargain with God, or fate, or whatever.

'Rose,' he began, 'I . . .' Then he thought better of what he'd been about to say and walked off to the phone in the hall. I wasn't going to stand there and listen to him talking to his family, so I made for the stairs, and slowly began to climb up.

Just as I reached the top of the stairs, I saw the door down the end of the corridor, the door that led to the second-floor stairs, open. Blanche Randal came out. She looked terrible – grey, her cheekbones hollow, her eyes red-rimmed. She stopped dead when she saw me.

'Rose,' she said. 'You're back.'

'Yes.'

'We thought at first you too had . . .' Her voice trailed off.

'As you see, I haven't. I was with Paul Fontaine.'

'So I see. How is he?'

For a moment, I thought she meant Paul. Then I understood. 'Grand-père is unconscious and in intensive care, but they think he'll be all right. He wasn't badly hurt.'

'Thank God,' she said, and colour flooded her pale cheeks. 'Thank God. Thank God.' She came closer to me. 'I'm the only one here. The others have all gone to help the Vallons. Eloise . . . she collapsed, she was in the most dreadful state, and poor Samantha . . .' She bit down on her lip so hard that I saw a bead of blood break the surface. She said, 'It's terrible . . . so terrible. I don't know what to do.'

I stared at her. 'There is nothing we can do, Madame Randal,' I said, and I did not know my voice could sound so cold and haughty. 'We can only hope and wait.'

'But there is no hope for them, is there?' she cried. 'None at all. He's dead, and that's an end to it. An end to it. Oh, God.' Her voice broke, and to my surprise and horror, she began to weep. I stood there like a dummy for an instant, then I took a step towards her, thinking I'd touch her on the shoulder, or do something, try to somehow comfort her. There was just something so terrible about seeing the Snow Queen cry like this, about seeing that icy reserve crack in that horrifying way. I had no idea she had been so close to the Vallons, that she'd be so racked with sorrow at Louis' death. Of course, they'd all worked together for a few years and so it would be a shock. But surely there'd been no love lost between them. My grand-father, now that was a different matter.

But before I could reach her, she took a step back. She said, 'Don't come near me. Don't touch me.'

I stood stock-still. Her sobs were dying away, the pale eyes flashing with an odd light. I said, 'Madame Randal, I –'

'It's your fault,' she hissed. 'Yours!'

I felt as though she'd punched me. I gasped, 'What . . . what . . .'

'You are bad luck,' she said. 'Bad luck from the very first day you set foot here.'

It was my turn to take a step back. My hands were shaking.

'Madame, please.'

'You've blighted everything and brought death in your wake. It wouldn't have happened if you hadn't come.'

Nausea rose in me. I said, 'You're mad. You don't know what you're saying.'

She gave a horrid little laugh. 'Mad, am I? At least I'm not bad. Bad to the bone. It's bred in the bone, the blood. Some are born cursed. Born to destroy.'

She was no longer beautiful but repulsive, her features twisted, her eyes full of a terrifying, cold, deep hatred. She took another step towards me. I don't know what would have happened next if Paul hadn't come up the stairs at that moment. He took in the situation in a glance, and moved swiftly between me and Blanche Randal. He shot me a quick glance and motioned me to move back, which I did at once. Then he took her arm. 'Madame, you are unwell. Let me escort you to your room.'

She stared at him, the hatred leaching from her eyes, replaced by a quick fear. 'You are doomed, do you know that? She –'

'Hush, Madame,' he said, very gently. 'Hush.'

She clutched at his arm. 'Charlie, my Charlie.'

'I'll call him, Madame. You can give me his number. Come.' And gently, soothingly, he drew her away from me and down the corridor towards her room. Once, he looked back over his shoulder at me, and I saw, clear as day, the love and anxiety and reassurance he meant to convey. It was the final straw. I felt my legs shaking and before they could crumple beneath me, fumbled desperately for the door to my grandfather's room. Throwing open the door I went as fast as my tottering legs could carry me, and flung myself on the bed.

All this time, I hadn't been able to cry. All this time, I'd been feeling as though I was separate from my body, floating in a kind of ghastly dark space. But now the tears came, wrenched out of me like acid, gripping cramps that made me gasp. They tore at my throat and my chest and my belly until I thought I would die with the pain of it. Everything was mixed in those tears, not only the terrible events of the last few hours, but all that had come before. Not only everything here, but everything back home in Australia. My parents' deaths, my neglect of Aunt Jenny, the loss of my friends and the ordinary life I used to have. She was right, I thought deep in the darkness of grief, the Snow Queen was right. I had wished my three wishes and they had brought nothing but fear and pain and grief, mostly to others. Born cursed, born to destroy. Was that me? I blighted everything I touched. That's what she'd said. Was it true? Could it be true? I had never intended any harm. I'd been so excited to find out my three wishes had come true.

Careful what you wish for . . . That's what I'd told everyone. But I hadn't taken my own advice. Not at all. I'd just wished blithely, like an idiot, and look what had happened. I had attracted evil and sorrow and death.

Yes, I know. I was becoming completely hysterical. Superstitious. As bonkers as the Snow Queen. Somewhere far down, I knew that. Somewhere, deep down inside me, a cold, clear voice was trying to tell me that there was something deeply wrong with Blanche Randal. And I don't just mean in her mad attack on me. Something had made that icy calm snap. Something had made her mask slip. As my sobs began to die away, the conviction grew stronger, the cold, clear voice louder. The something that had made her crack – it wasn't a newly discovered love for the Vallons or relief at my grandfather's escaping serious injury. It was to do with the accident, but more than that.

I remembered her reaction, too, when the death knell was rung, and then when I'd been rescued from the tomb. She'd acted strangely then, not as you might expect at all – she'd been extreme, odd, on edge. I cast my mind back, trying to remember even further back, how she'd been with me right from the start. She'd alternated between being cold and quite nice, as if she was swinging between fear and hope. Fear and hope – that was the key, somehow. She'd been afraid, really afraid, as if by coming I might set off something dreadful. But she'd hoped, too. She'd hoped that nothing would go badly. But then that meant . . . that meant –

'Rose. Rose, I'm so sorry. I meant to come back sooner.' Paul was at the door, hesitating. He had a phone in his hand – the portable, from Blanche's room – and he looked both worried and wary. He was not sure of his welcome, and no wonder. I suddenly felt a squirm of shame.

I sat up. 'Come in, Paul.' I wanted to hold out my arms to him, but couldn't quite. I tried to smile at him, though I knew my face must look a real sight, all blotchy and creased and puffy with tears. 'I'm sorry, Paul. I've been really quite revolting to you, and –'

'Don't,' he said, sitting on the bed, and smiling a little sadly at me. But he didn't try to touch me. 'I quite understand. It's been a terrible shock.'

I saw his expression, and knew that now was not the time to try to explain myself. I said, quietly, 'Did you get on to Charlie?'

'No. The phone rang and rang, but no-one picked up. It's a bit odd, as you'd think an office would always have someone there to man the phones. But they're probably all out at a long lunch. And he doesn't have a mobile, either, so we can't reach him that way. He does have a friend in Toulouse whose number his mother had, so I rang him. It was a mobile, and not switched on, so I left a voicemail message. Hopefully he'll hear it soon and go round to Charlie's work for us. If not, well, I suppose he'll be back this evening.'

'How . . . how is she?'

'Much calmer. Well, she's asleep, actually. I wanted to call her doctor, but she refused. Said she had some sleeping pills, and would take those. I gave her a couple from a bottle I found in her drawer. She's just fallen asleep. That's why I couldn't come till now. She wouldn't let me go. I hope she might sleep till Charlie gets back. That's why I brought the phone with me, so that if he rings, or the hospital does, I can answer without disturbing her. He hesitated. 'I took the bottle of pills away with me too, just in case.'

I stared at him. 'You think she would try to take them all?'

'I wouldn't put anything past her in that state.' He paused. 'Shock affects people in different ways, Rose. You must not think that –'

'That I'm a jinx, and I bring death and destruction?' I said, trying to sound light. 'Why should I take any notice of what a hysterical Snow Queen says?'

'Oh, my poor Rose,' was all he said, but it was said with such a depth of feeling. I put my hand out to him, timidly, and he took it and held it and we said nothing else for a few heartbeats of time. Then he said, 'I'm going to stay here, till the others get back, at least those who are coming back.'

I didn't say that I didn't need him to stay, or that I would be all right, or anything stupid and meaningless like that. I just said, 'I'm glad, Paul,' and then I did hold out my arms to him, and we stayed like that, hugging tightly, for a few moments. Then he pulled me gently from him, looked at me and said, 'You look so tired. You need to rest.'

It was true. I felt suddenly, utterly exhausted. My eyes were aching and my whole body felt bruised, shattered. I felt like I could sleep for a hundred years. But I was afraid too. 'I don't want you to go,' I said.

'I won't.' He looked at me and read my expression. 'I locked her door,' he said, softly. 'I thought that would be for the best. I have the key right here in my pocket.'

All my body relaxed. I could feel the tension leaving me like poison from a wound. I said, softly, 'You think of everything. You're . . . you're wonderful.'

'Don't swell my head now, will you,' he said lightly, smiling at me.

'Wake me if the hospital rings, won't you, Paul? Even if I'm fast asleep. Promise!'

'All right, I promise,' he said. Through eyes that were already half-closing, I saw him pull over an armchair to the bedside and sit down, the phone on his lap. I thought, I'm safe here, safe with him, and her under lock and key, and my enemy unable to get to me, and I can just let go and sleep.

I woke suddenly a couple of hours later. For a moment I didn't know where I was. Then memory came flooding back. I turned my head. The armchair was still by the bed, but Paul wasn't in it.

I sat up, cautiously, because my head ached. The room

was quite empty. I was alone. I felt a tiny fluttering begin in my chest and told myself not to be so stupid. Paul wouldn't have gone far. I would get up and go and find him.

I got up. Damn, my head hurt. And my eyes felt really swollen too. I'd slept heavily, but not all that restfully. I went to the bathroom to splash some water over my face. I looked at my face in the mirror. I still looked pretty awful but at least I felt a little better, though my head still hurt. I found some paracetamol in the cabinet and took a couple of tablets. Then I set out to look for Paul, softly calling his name.

I stopped in front of Blanche's door. Silence. I looked through the keyhole. I could see her lying on the bed. She appeared to be asleep. I tried the handle. Yes, the door was locked. Thank heavens. I took a deep breath and walked along the corridor, opening doors. My room. Nobody. Another bedroom, unused, but clean and dust-free. Nobody. A linen cupboard. Innocent of anything but sheets and towels. Charlie's room. Locked. Charlie must have taken the key with him. He must not trust his mother not to go snooping about, I thought. Or other people, come to that.

I was about to move away from that door when I heard a faint sound in there. A rustle, followed an instant later by a muffled cry. I stood rigid. I whispered, 'Charlie? Paul?'

No-one answered. But then perhaps they hadn't heard. I hadn't exactly spoken loudly. I was about to speak again, more loudly, when I suddenly thought better of it. I don't know why – maybe it was just an uneasy feeling that whoever was in there was taking great care to be quiet. And that locked door . . . I mean, if it had been Charlie in there, wouldn't he have come to see me first? And why would Paul be in there with the door locked?

So I put my eye to the keyhole and peered through. At first I could see nothing but an outline of part of Charlie's room. I could see the window, open. A chair. A table. Then someone moved into my range of vision, and I knew at once it wasn't Charlie. And it wasn't Paul. It wasn't anyone I knew, in fact. This was a complete stranger.

The man had thick grey hair, but I couldn't see his face clearly. He was quite short, wiry, thin. He had on dark-coloured, cheap-looking clothes – a jumper, trousers. He moved restlessly about, searching. There was an intensity about what he was doing that suggested to me he was looking for something quite specific, and not finding it.

I thought, I've got to do something. I've got to stop this man and whatever he's doing, in Charlie's room. But I can't tackle him on my own. Paul. Where was Paul?

All at once, a door slammed downstairs. I jumped. So did the man in Charlie's room. As he turned, I had a glimpse of his face. He dived for the window just as I shrieked, 'Paul!' and for an instant, what looked like a shocked, appalled instant, he checked. But just for an instant. In the next moment, he was out of the window and vanished from sight.

Paul came thundering up the stairs. 'What on earth is going on?' He saw my face and said, more calmly, 'I thought you were asleep. I didn't want to wake you. I was on the phone downstairs and –'

'Paul, there was someone in Charlie's room. I saw him, just now.'

'What do you mean? Is he back?' Paul tried the door. 'It's locked.'

'He got in through the window,' I gabbled. 'He got out

again that way too. No, it wasn't Charlie, Paul,' I said as I saw the question about to form on his lips, about why Charlie should choose to break into his own room. 'It was that man. That other Paul.'

For a moment Paul looked bewildered. Then his expression cleared as he remembered what I'd told him, earlier. He said, 'Charlie's room looks out over the back near the terrace, doesn't it? That man's probably long gone by now, but we'd better go and see if we can find him.'

Of course, by the time we got down to the terrace, the man was nowhere to be seen. He could have gone anywhere. Into the village? Into the woods? Down to the church? Or he might still be hiding out somewhere in the garden. I said as much to Paul, who nodded grimly. We raced off to the walled garden, but here, too, there was nobody. Up and down the alleys of the other gardens. Still nobody.

At last, we had to admit defeat.

'And you're sure this was the man Blanche Randal was with the other day?' said Paul.

'I'm not a hundred per cent certain, but who else could it be? I think I know who he might be.'

'Who?'

'I think he's Charlie's father.'

He stared at me. '*What?*'

'It was just something about his expression, I don't know, something about the shape of his face, it suddenly reminded me of Charlie, and that would explain it, wouldn't it? I mean his name's most likely Paul, Paul Randal, nobody said what his first name was, but why not that? And Madame Collot said the other day that Charlie's father was in prison for fraud but what if he escaped and he's been hiding out here, he's been forcing his wife to hide him ... that's why she's so stressed and nearly bonkers.'

'Wait, wait, wait,' Paul said, looking overwhelmed by my flow of words. 'If he had escaped from prison, surely the police would have come looking for him long since? It's the first place they'd think of, don't you think, the place where his wife or ex-wife or whatever she is to him and her son live.'

'Oh. That's true,' I said, crestfallen.

'But that doesn't mean it's *not* him,' said Paul. 'I mean, he might have been let out early. Maybe Madame Collot didn't know his prison term had ended.'

'Oh, yes! That could fit. And his wife probably hated having him around here, but maybe she had no choice. Maybe he threatened her or something.'

'Or played the pathetic victim with nowhere to go,' he said.

'Yes, maybe. She didn't sound that scared when she was speaking to him that night, only annoyed and impatient, and nervous, but only about other people seeing him.' I paused. 'What the hell was he looking for in Charlie's room?'

'God knows,' said Paul. 'But you said it sounded like Blanche Randal didn't want her husband to cross paths with her son.'

'That might just be self-preservation,' I said. I was amazed by how calm and lucid I could be about the Snow Queen, despite her ranting and raving against me. Maybe it was because she was locked in, asleep and helpless against me. Or maybe it was because I was beginning to feel pity for her. 'I mean, it's obvious she and Charlie don't have a good relationship. He probably despises his father thoroughly as well. Poor woman, she probably just doesn't want more trouble.'

Paul shook his head in mock astonishment. 'Well, Rose,' he said, 'I'll never stop being surprised by you. The woman calls you all kinds of names and you can still be kind about her.'

'Not kind,' I said. 'I don't like her. I dislike her very much, in fact. But I don't hate her. Not really. She didn't mean all that stuff. It's rubbish anyway. It doesn't mean anything. It was – what'd you call it? Displacement, or something. She doesn't dare to say what she really feels, so she just says all that stupid stuff against me. She was probably annoyed too that I was back and hubby was still hanging around putting her in danger of being found out.'

'Brave Rose,' said Paul, and put an arm around me. He drew me to him and we kissed, gently this time, and oh, so sweetly. Then I looked up at him and said softly, 'Did – who were you speaking to on the phone? Was it the hospital?'

'No,' he said. 'It was Simon. My brother, you know. He was with Samantha, and he said it had all been quite dreadful, and that Madame Vallon had had to be sedated but that Samantha was holding up . . . well, better than might be expected, and she was the one trying to make practical arrangements for the body to be moved and the funeral and all that.'

'Oh, poor Samantha,' I said, and the tears rose to my eyes. 'Poor thing.'

'Yes,' he said sombrely. 'He also said that the police had told them that the skid-marks on the road showed clearly that Louis had swerved violently to avoid something and

266

lost control of the car. There were no other tyre marks, so there wasn't another car involved. But there's the possibility of an animal – a deer or boar, say. They come out of the woods and cross the road sometimes, there have been accidents involving that sort of thing before. They don't know yet, anyway. Perhaps your grandfather might be able to tell them when he recovers consciousness.'

'I don't think the brakes were working properly either,' I said quietly. 'I remember Louis saying . . .'

'Yes,' he said. 'Yes. They'll be checking it all out. They're very thorough. Don't worry, Rose, *chérie*.'

Just then I heard a small sound behind us and turned. Charlie Randal was coming up the drive towards us. He stopped stock-still and stared at us both. He looked very pale, his eyes brilliant, a little wild. I felt the sudden sting of his stare, suddenly as cold as his mother's.

'What are you doing here?' he whispered.

I looked nervously at Paul, who answered, 'I'm looking after Rose, Charlie.'

'Why?'

'We've been trying to get on to you,' said Paul. 'We rang your work and your friends . . .'

'Yes?' Charlie was very still. I could see a muscle working in his cheek. I thought, helplessly, he must have heard us, seen us. He's angry. Furious. Jealous.

'We needed you to come back early. Your mother needed you. Did you get the bus? I didn't hear it,' said Paul.

'Not that it's any business of yours,' said Charlie, icily, 'but we had a late lunch and someone offered me a lift home. That's why I got here earlier. I didn't get any messages.'

'Well, at least you're here,' said Paul, curtly. 'Your mother will be glad of that. Though why, I can't imagine.'

The two young men stared at each other, the hostility between them almost tangible. It made me angry, and I lost my temper. 'Stop it, both of you! Stop it!' Taking a deep breath, I went on in a calmer voice, 'Charlie, there's been a terrible accident and Louis Vallon has been killed and my grandfather's unconscious and . . .' I couldn't finish my sentence through the lump that rose to my throat.

Charlie went even paler, if that was possible. He whispered, 'What?'

'Just as Rose said, there was a terrible accident on the Castelnau road,' said Paul quietly. 'That's why I'm here. We've been to the hospital.'

'Monsieur le Comte?' questioned Charlie. He looked as if he was going to be sick.

'They think he'll be all right,' I said, very softly. 'He wasn't badly hurt.'

'Oh, thank God,' said Charlie, his voice changing, thawing. 'And thank God, Rose, that you weren't in the car when it happened. Where were you?'

'She was with me,' said Paul briefly.

Their eyes met. I said quickly, 'We were doing something – I mean, looking up something on the computer and –'

Charlie raised his eyebrows. 'You don't need to explain to me,' he said, and the coldness was back in his voice. 'You are a free agent, are you not?'

'That she is,' said Paul, sharply, and once again I saw that enmity flash between them.

I said hotly, 'Anyway, Charlie, we wanted to get in touch with you because of your mother. She's been taken rather bad, the shock, I expect, and then your father –'

'Rose!' Paul said warningly, but it was too late.

Charlie's eyes narrowed. His hands clenched together. 'What about my father?'

I sighed. I thought he needed to know the truth. 'He's been here, Charlie.'

He took a step towards me. His face looked about as friendly as a glacier. 'What do you mean?'

'She means just what she says,' said Paul with a set face, moving closer to me. 'Your father's been here.' He paused. 'Is his first name Paul?'

Charlie smiled faintly. It was not an amused smile. 'Yes. Rather a common and boring name, don't you think?'

'Charlie,' I said swiftly, before Paul could say anything, 'please, this is not the time to play stupid games. Your mother's been hiding him here, Charlie, and that's why she's been so jumpy, why she cracked, and . . .' I touched him on the sleeve, timidly. 'It might even have been him, playing those stupid tricks against me.'

He stared at me. When he spoke, his voice had changed again. It sounded more like the old Charlie, the attractive one I knew. He said, 'Oh, Rose. That would explain a lot, wouldn't it?'

'Yes,' I said, biting my lip. 'It would.'

'He always was a nasty piece of work,' said Charlie gently, looking into my eyes. 'I never really told you about him, did I?'

I shook my head, a swirl of emotions churning in me. Poor Charlie! He looked so lost, bereft. He said quietly, 'My mother left him but she never really got rid of him. I think she clung to her memories of him, you know. He could be very charming. Or maybe she was just scared of him. I don't know. I grew up hating him. I imagined killing him, even. Can you imagine what that's like? To hate your own father so much you want to kill him . . . Well, then he went to prison and I thought we were safe from him for a while. But now – he must have been let out, I suppose, and he's come to wreak havoc in our lives again.'

'Oh, my God, Charlie, I'm so sorry.' I touched his sleeve again and this time he took my hand and held on to it. He looked into my face. 'Where is he, Rose?'

'He ran away,' said Paul, grimly, his expression like thunder. 'Don't know where.'

'He was in your room, Charlie,' I said, gently disengaging my hand, and not looking at either of them. 'I saw him. He was ferreting through your things.'

Charlie's face hardened. 'That dirty rotten sneak-thief! And my stupid, stupid mother!' Without another word he ran up to the terrace and disappeared into the house.

'We'd better go after him,' I said, with a sideways glance at Paul. 'He's in a real state.'

'Yes,' said Paul, a sardonic expression I didn't much like on his face. 'Better run after the poor little boy, Rose, before he does himself an injury, eh?'

A wild anger surged through me. 'Oh, you're hopeless. Hopeless, the pair of you!' I shouted. 'Can't you understand, if he sees his mother right now, he might go crazy. Oh!' I yelled, beside myself with fury, 'see it just the way you like, Paul Fontaine, I don't care!' I turned and walked quickly away and up to the terrace, trembling with anger and other things I couldn't quite figure out.

270

Who can you trust?

I caught up with Charlie at the top of the stairs. 'Please, don't do it, Charlie,' I gasped. 'It's not her fault, I'm sure it's not.'

'What are you talking about?' he said coldly.

'Leave her alone, she's sleeping, there'll be time later for –'

'You think I'm going to confront my mother?' His voice was without inflection.

'I thought . . .' I faltered.

'No. You *don't* think. That's your trouble, Rose,' he said, scornfully, and began walking away from me, down the corridor towards his room. Stung, I went after him.

'I'm sorry, Charlie. I didn't mean –'

'No? What *did* you mean, Rose?'

'I don't know,' I said, miserably. 'I was just . . . just concerned for you, Charlie.'

'I suppose I should feel flattered that you still think of me at all,' he said, biting off the words. 'I rather felt you'd found another focus for your thoughts.'

I went scarlet. 'Charlie, I – I'm sorry.'

'I thought we'd made a promise to each other,' he said quietly. 'I thought you'd be true. I thought I could trust you. But you have betrayed me.'

I swallowed. I felt hot and cold in turns. My stomach churned. 'Charlie, no. Please don't do this. It wasn't like that. We never promised anything.'

'You might not have,' he said, and his eyes flashed blue fire at me. 'I did. Maybe not in words, for I thought you'd understand.' He thumped at his chest. 'In here. In my heart, my soul.'

'But Charlie . . . please, I don't –'

'And with him,' he went on, relentlessly. 'Him! You have taken the enemy's side! You trust him after all that's happened. After that campaign of fear against you, the way he's stalked you.'

'It wasn't him behind all that stuff,' I said, not looking at him. 'It wasn't. I think it was your father. That fits much better.'

'Only because you want it so. There's just as much evidence pointing to Fontaine. Maybe more. Isn't there?'

Despite myself, I couldn't help thinking of Koschei's blog. As Paul himself had admitted, he had the skills both in computer and in English. Had Charlie's father? I said, weakly, 'Does your father use a computer?'

'A computer?' said Charlie, looking puzzled. 'I doubt it.'

'But you don't know?'

'I don't.' He looked hard at me. 'What is it?'

Of course, he didn't know about it. I said, 'Just . . . just something we found out today. That's all.'

'Tell me, Rose?'

I shook my head. I didn't want to talk about it. He said, sharply, 'Obviously something to do with computers. An email you got? Something on the internet? What is it? Are you afraid to tell me, because you know it incriminates him?'

Tears sprang to my eyes. 'Stop it, Charlie. It doesn't. It really doesn't.'

'My poor Rose,' he said, and then he was beside me, sweeping me up into his arms. Before I knew what was what, he was kissing me, whispering, 'I'm so sorry, Rose. I should have been here with you. I should have been the one to rescue you from that tomb. I blame myself.'

'No. You must not think that. You were at work,' I faltered, my senses reeling, my legs shaking. It wasn't the kiss or his words either. It was something I understood in that moment. Something I had to say.

But too late, for there was Paul, coming up the stairs. He saw us in each other's arms, of course. His face went quite blank. It was like a shutter descending over a window, completely blocking the view of what lay behind. He said to Charlie, 'I just came to tell you I think I saw him again. Your father. In the garden.'

'Paul,' I said, but he ignored me.

'Will you come with me, Randal? If we're to try and get him, best if there's two of us.'

Their eyes met. I felt sick. I said, 'I'll come too.'

'No,' said Paul, curtly.

'No, Rose,' said Charlie, gently. 'It's not safe. '

'But Charlie, I –'

Charlie smiled at me. 'Don't worry, Rose. We'll be back soon. Everything's all right. You'll see. It'll be fine. Don't be afraid of him.' His glance had layers in it, layers of meaning for me.

'I'm not,' I said. 'I'm really not afraid.'

But they had started off down the stairs already. I was left there by myself, my stomach churning, the headache returning and a burning pain in my chest. I had no idea what to do. No idea at all. What had seemed such a thrilling thing – to have two boys in love with me at the same time – seemed now like a nightmare. A nightmare I'd sleepwalked into, like a complete fool. Now I knew what I really felt. And it was too late. I'd blown it completely. And I only had myself to blame.

I went back to Grand-père's room and sat on the bed and forced my mind onto the problem of Paul Randal. I didn't know yet if it was him who'd been terrorising me, but it did make sense. I tried not to think that it was just as Charlie said, that I *wanted* it to make sense. It really did. Just the fact that he was still prowling around here proved he was up to something. He was a chancer, a crook. Perhaps he'd got the impression that his wife would inherit something substantial under Grand-père's old will and he'd tried to frighten me away before a new will could be signed. After all, we hadn't done that yet, despite it all. There had been too many things happening for Grand-père to remember it. All sorts of things had happened to delay it, and to destabilise me, Grand-père and the household. And now, after the accident, we wouldn't be able to do it for quite a while. If things had gone differently, Grand-père might be dead, too, and not just poor Louis.

A frightening thought burst into my mind. What if the accident was no accident at all? I'd read crime stories in which people tampered with brakes and then there was an accident as the driver lost control and couldn't brake – what if that had happened here? Paul Randal could easily have got into the garage and fiddled with the Mercedes. It was an older model, not one of the computer-controlled ones that are supposed to be tamper-proof. You didn't need to be anywhere near the scene of the crime when it happened. Anything could happen. As they'd said, maybe a boar or a deer or a hare or something ran across the road, it's instinct to brake, to swerve, but if the brakes fail you, then . . .

It could be Paul Randal, my mind nagged coldly at me. Or Paul Fontaine. Both had the opportunity and the motive. Motive? What's my Paul's – I mean, Paul Fontaine's – motive? Why would he want to do such a ghastly thing? No. No. Of course it's not him. But there's the Koschei angle, too, my desperate thoughts continued. Paul Randal will be in his late forties, at the very least. And he's recently been in prison. Surely a blog is more a young person's thing. I mean, yes, my English teacher had been keen on the idea but she hadn't got one herself, as far as I knew. And that whole thing of commenting on my blog, too. It sounded more like an internet-savvy kind of person. He'd have had to find my blog first, for a start, then get himself an email address and all that. Well, he could do that on a blog search. And Grand-père was in his seventies and he loved the internet. He'd taught himself. Paul Randal could easily too, or he might have learned in prison. But then, there was the English. Did Charlie's father write English well enough to pass as Koschei? A memory jagged into my mind like an iceberg above water. A memory of Grand-père saying that Paul Fontaine had done well in his leaving exams. Extremely well, especially in English and Spanish. Charlie – well, Charlie knew English, that was clear. But he didn't know about computers. He knew nothing about blogs.

I went over to the window, rubbing at my throbbing temples. It was getting dark, the garden was getting dim, the shadows gathering. They wouldn't see much out there now.

Slowly I drew the curtains against approaching night, my confused thoughts running round and round like mice on a treadmill. I didn't know what to think. Or who to believe. In Charlie's arms, my instinct had told me one thing. But here, it told me another. I thought of how Grand-père had spoken of 'the man in the mask', and wished with all my heart that it was true. I wanted it so much to be Paul Randal. But I wasn't sure, much as I wanted to be.

I jumped. The phone was ringing downstairs. I raced down and picked up the receiver, my heart thumping. 'Hello?'

'Mademoiselle du Merle?'

'Yes.'

'It's the hospital. Docteur Dufour.'

'Yes?' I said, clutching the phone, all thoughts of my enemy retreating. 'Is Grand-père – he's not . . . not . . .'

'Don't worry, Mademoiselle. He's fine. Or as fine as can be expected, in the circumstances. I just rang to say he's already recovered consciousness.'

'Oh! Oh! That's wonderful! Can I come and see him? I'll get a lift straightaway.'

'No, Mademoiselle. It's too late, and he's asleep again. But asleep this time, not unconscious. He's very, very tired and still in shock, and it's much better if you wait till tomorrow afternoon for a visit. I just thought you'd like to know. He seemed quite lucid. There is no sign of brain damage.'

'Oh, thank God! Oh, thank you so much, Docteur! It's so kind of you to ring.'

'Not at all,' she said, briskly. 'I made a promise and I make a habit of keeping my promises.'

'Did he – did he say anything?'

Her voice changed. 'Yes. He asked if you were all right. And he asked after the cyclist.'

'The *cyclist*?'

'That's what we thought. What cyclist? But of course the car had swerved and the police had said it might be an animal. But it must have been a cyclist. Your grandfather was most insistent they had come round a corner and there was a cyclist bearing down on them and they didn't have time to react properly. He was very worried they might have killed him. We were able to reassure him on that score.' She paused. 'But if it was a cyclist who unwittingly caused the accident, where is he or she now?'

'I – I don't know,' I said, bewildered. 'Does Grand-père know about Louis? I mean, Monsieur Vallon?'

'No. It would be too much of a shock right now. Mademoiselle, I'm afraid I have to get back to work now.'

'Thank you so much for calling me,' I said sincerely. 'I really, really appreciate it. And if my grandfather wakes before tomorrow afternoon, can you please tell him I'm coming to see him? That I can't wait to see him?'

'I will tell the nurses to make sure they do just that. Goodbye, Mademoiselle.' And she hung up.

I stood staring at the receiver for a moment, my thoughts whirling. Then I heard the door open and Charlie and Paul came in from outside.

'What's up, Rose? You look strange,' said Charlie, coming towards me.

'I just got a call from the hospital,' I said.

They both looked at me. 'Is Monsieur le Comte . . .?' began Paul, his eyes alight with worry.

'No,' I said, swallowing. 'He's fine. Or will be. The doctor rang to tell me he'd regained consciousness.'

'Oh, that's excellent news! Oh, Rose, you must be so relieved.' Charlie took my hand. 'Did he say anything?'

'He spoke about a cyclist.'

'A *cyclist*?' Charlie dropped my hand. Both young men stared at me.

'Seems that is why Louis swerved, to try to avoid him or her.'

'But no-one said –' began Paul, looking puzzled.

'No. There's no sign of a cyclist at the scene. No-one hurt, anyway. No twisted bicycle or anything. It appears whoever it was got away scot-free.'

'Is your grandfather sure there was a cyclist?' said Paul. He met my eyes, expressionlessly, as if we were strangers. It made my stomach churn.

I said sharply, 'I'm sure he is.' I looked defiantly at him, my head held high. 'He hasn't lost his marbles, you know. They said there was no brain damage.'

'My God,' said Charlie. We both turned to look at him. His face was full of a dawning horror. 'It's something I've just remembered. That accident – the one where Monsieur le Comte's mother hit the child on the bicycle – that was on the road to Castelnau. Wasn't it, Fontaine?'

Paul's eyes flickered. 'I think so.'

'What an irony,' said Charlie softly. 'What a terrible, tragic irony. I mean, that such an accident should happen again – only the other way around.'

We stared at him. A nameless fear swept through me. 'What do you mean, Charlie?' I cried.

Paul made a movement towards me, quickly repressed. In a hard tone, he said, 'If you mean by that cryptic utterance that a ghost ambushed Rose's grandfather, Randal, you've got serious problems.'

Charlie flushed angrily. 'I'm surprised you deny such things, Fontaine, with your great-aunt being what she is! You of all people should know there are more things in heaven and earth than are dreamt of by rationalists! But no, I meant no such thing. There are other possibilities.'

I should have said something then. I should have said what I suspected about the car. But I hated this situation. I didn't want the two of them there glaring at each other over me. I didn't want to see Paul looking coldly at me or Charlie looking to defend me. I just wanted – oh, I just wanted the whole thing to be over with. It made me more waspish than I realised when I said, 'I suppose the police will find out one way or another. Did you find him?'

They both looked puzzled. Then Paul said, 'No. We didn't. I must have made a mistake. There's no sign of him in the garden.'

'We should maybe call the police then,' I suggested.

'No,' said Charlie quickly. 'Not yet. Anyway, what can we say he's done? We've got no proof of anything.'

'We don't,' said Paul.

'You should go home, Fontaine,' said Charlie. 'I'll take care of things here. After all, he is my father. I know what he's like. And I can deal with my mother, too. Don't worry, Rose will be fine with me.'

'Rose?' said Paul, meeting my eyes. I couldn't read his expression properly, but I thought I could see scorn, anger, but also a kind of pleading. There was a short silence. Part of me wanted to say, no Paul, don't go, I need you, I believe you, I'm sorry . . . I want to explain – but another part thought, no, go, it's best that way, I can't bear this, I can't,

279

I just want to be left alone. That part won. I said, shrugging, 'I'll be fine. I'm going to go up to Grand-père's room and lock myself in.'

'Very well,' said Paul, coolly, turning from me. He looked at Charlie. 'Call me if you need me.'

'I will,' said Charlie. There was a new assurance about him just then, a kind of ease I hadn't seen before. He was in charge.

Paul left without saying goodbye. As I heard his car start up outside, I felt a hollow feeling in the pit of my stomach, and I didn't know if it was relief or regret or an unstable mixture of the two.

Charlie said, 'I wonder if he did see my father out there, or if that was a pretext?'

'What do you mean?'

A strange look came over his face. 'Oh, nothing.'

I was going to ask him more, but thought better of it. I didn't really want to know what he suspected Paul of – I could see the picture all too clearly, of himself being lured out there into the dark, so Paul could hit him over the head. That was ridiculous! If he wanted to hurt me, he'd had the opportunity all day. We'd been alone several times. No, it was impossible. Impossible. Then why did my brain conjure up those outlandish images?

I said, 'I'm tired, Charlie. I'm going to make myself a sandwich and I'm going to go up to bed.'

'I could stay with you,' he said.

'No!' The exclamation came out too quickly, and I tried to soften it. 'I mean, no, thank you, Charlie, but I'd really rather be on my own. If you don't mind.'

'Of course I don't,' he said gently, but I'd not missed the

glint of pain in his eyes. I was the clumsiest fool on earth. I hated myself.

I touched him on the hand. 'I've got to be by myself for a bit and think. Do you understand?'

'Of course I do,' he said, and snatching at my hand, he lightly kissed it. 'Sweet dreams, sweet princess, and may the morning bring better things. I'll stay downstairs and keep watch.'

'You're going to stay up all night?'

'Someone has to watch while there are prowlers about,' he said, with a humorous tilt of the eyebrow, 'and it might as well be me.'

'Take care then, Charlie,' I said quietly, and he nodded.

'I will. Don't worry. If the bogeyman comes, I'll be ready. Go up to bed, Rose. You look exhausted. I'll wait in the darkness and watch while you sleep, don't you worry.'

I made myself a sandwich and a thermos of hot tea and then I went upstairs. I went to listen at Blanche's door but could hear nothing. I looked through the keyhole and saw her form still and quiet on the bed. The effect of the pills had obviously not worn off. I went back to Grand-père's room and locked myself in. I ate the sandwiches and drank the tea and read a history magazine I found in the drawer of the bedside table. I tried to concentrate but I felt uneasy, and my brain kept switching away from the words I was reading to the questions I kept turning over and over in my mind.

Half an hour or so later, I heard a car door slam outside. Then the door opening, and voices. I went out of the room and to the top of the stairs. I looked down into the hall. There was Charlie, talking with Madame Collot. It must have been her car I heard.

'...asked me to stay and watch over her mother... poor child,' I heard the housekeeper say. 'Sorry it took so long. Did Mademoiselle worry?'

'No. It's okay,' said Charlie. 'She's gone up to bed. You look exhausted, Madame Collot.'

'That I am,' said Madame Collot, with a sigh. 'What a day it's been! I won't forget it as long as I live.'

'Neither will any of us, Madame,' said Charlie. 'Cup of coffee, maybe?'

'I don't mind if I do,' said the housekeeper, a surprised note of pleasure in her voice, as if this was something she didn't expect of Charlie. Their voices faded as they walked away from the hall towards the kitchen. As for me, I went to bed, cheered by the thought that the brisk and capable housekeeper was back, bringing a welcome feel of normality with her.

It did the trick. My unease slowly faded. I took the magazine up again and began to read but soon found my eyes closing as drowsiness overcame me. In no time I was fast asleep.

I was on a motorbike. I felt afraid, and didn't know why. My arms were wrapped around someone's waist. The motorbike was hot. I could feel its engine growling under me but it wasn't moving. I couldn't see who I was with, only that he was all in black from head to foot. I tried to speak, to say, 'Let me off, let me off,' but I couldn't. I was struck dumb. I tried to move off the bike, but I couldn't move my hands from my companion's waist, and my legs were glued to the sides of the machine. Then the rider turned his head towards me. And I saw – a fleshless face, a lipless mouth, hollow eye sockets. I saw a skull grinning at me. I tried to scream, but couldn't. The death's head turned back, the engine roared, and the bike began to move. And then, by a superhuman effort, I managed to wrench myself off, and tumbled off the bike and . . .

Thumped on to the floor. The shock woke me up and I discovered I had tumbled off the bed, the sheets wrapped around me, I was covered in sweat and trembling like a leaf. I extricated myself from the bedclothes and got to my feet, still shaking, but so glad, oh so glad it had been just a dream. But what a horrible dream! What was it trying to tell me?

But I knew, all right. I remembered my first sight of Paul, on his motorbike, and how I'd seen him instantly as the black knight who brings death to the gates of the castle. My sleeping mind had returned to that. It was trying to tell me the truth, to warn me. Danger was still very close. Death was still lying in wait for me . . .

Then it struck me. That engine growling. That had been very real. What if – what if Paul *had* come back, but on his bike? What if I'd heard the sound of it in my sleep and had constructed my nightmare around it?

I looked at my watch. It was not long after ten o'clock. Not as late as I'd thought. I went over to the window, and looked out. It was very dark, because there was no moon. I couldn't see anything at all. Anyway, why would he be out there? I had to know. But I couldn't go there on my own. I had to have Charlie with me. I badly needed to have Charlie with me. I shrugged out of my pyjamas and into some clothes and shoes. Then I thought, what if I meet him on the way, and he . . . I looked around wildly for a weapon. What could I take with me? There was nothing remotely useful. Then suddenly I had an idea. I ran to

Grand-père's wardrobe, and flung it open. I looked along the rack of clothes, looking for . . . Ah, there it was! A wire coathanger. Most of the other hangers were wooden and useless for my purpose. But this one would do. I threw off the shirt and pulled at the hook of the hanger till it straightened. It was a weapon of sorts, now, a vicious pointed bit of wire that could double as a dagger. Holding my makeshift weapon tightly, I slipped downstairs.

The house was very quiet, but I could see a light on in the library. I was walking towards it when I suddenly heard a groan. It was a deep groan, and it nailed me to the floor. I whispered, 'Who – who's that?'

The groan came again. It came from the library. I said, 'Charlie? Madame Collot?'

A small silence, then Charlie's voice, faint, broken, but unmistakeable, 'Help, help, Rose.'

I didn't stop to think. My heart thudding so hard it filled my ears, and clutching my wire dagger tightly, I raced along to the library. The door was ajar. I could see that one of the lamps was on, though not the overhead light. I tried to peer in. 'Charlie?'

I thought I heard the groan again, then a thump. A sickening thump.

'I'm coming,' I said. 'I'm coming, Charlie.' Holding the wire hanger out straight before me, ready to jab it at any aggressor, I pushed open the door and went in.

As soon as I did, I saw it. The laptop, open on the desk. It was facing me, its screen brightly lit up. And on the screen, a familiar sight. Green writing on a black background, bright, sharp, taunting me. Koschei's blog. And a new post, very brief, and all in capitals:

I AM HERE. YOU ARE MINE. TURN AROUND.

The lamp clicked off. The wire hanger fell from my shaking hands, useless. Slowly, I turned around. And then, dimly, for an instant only, I saw a figure lying crumpled on the floor behind the door. And then, I saw a shadow, a movement, rise to meet me . . .

I'll huff and I'll puff and I'll blow your house down!

Icouldn't see anything. I couldn't open my mouth. I couldn't move. Yet my body was being bumped and shaken. And I could hear a roaring, rushing noise. But I had no bearings. No idea what was happening or where I was. If my head hadn't been throbbing so much, if my body hadn't felt so bruised, I would have thought I was dead.

My poor brain tried to get a grip on where I was. No, I wasn't dead. I was dreaming. This was another night-mare. I just had to make an effort to wake up. I must force my eyelids to open, my mouth to yell, my limbs to move and roll me out of bed. I tried. I tried very hard. I really did. But nothing happened.

A sharp pain shot through me as my body was flung against something hard. I was pinned down, unable to save myself, to stop whatever it was from hurting me. I had never had such a terrible dream. It felt so real. I could not fight a nightmare that had actually taken shape, a darkness that had taken flesh. I could not remember anything that had happened earlier. Perhaps I was dying and this was just the terrible land in between life and death. The thing you had to get through in order to get to the other side. On one side, life. On the other, death. In between, a nightmare realm, not quite death, not quite life, but harsh and dark and horrible.

An image came crowding into my confused brain. A black-clad figure on a motorbike, a death's head turned to me, a desperate attempt to be free. I had thought it meant one thing. But it had meant quite another. I had been wrong. I had been looking down the wrong end of the telescope.

Somehow the thought cleared the fog in my mind. No, I wasn't in a dream. This was real. That noise I could hear, that rushing – it was the sound of a motorbike racing through the darkness. That bumping, that shaking – it was a road, a bumpy road. My eyes that couldn't open – I was blindfolded. The paralysed limbs – I was bound. My mouth was stopped with a gag. I was being carried like a helpless package, like a dead body.

But how? It was convenient for him, the bike. But he couldn't just have flung me on the back. Not enough room. And I would have felt the heat of the engine. No. I was being carried in something else. A sidecar? Dimly, I half-remembered Geneviève Fontaine mention it. Yes. It must be. That would explain the feeling of being bumped up and down, the jolt as my body hit the sides.

My brain was working like a demon now. Memory was slipping back. I saw the library, the laptop on the desk, the words in capital letters, the certain knowledge that I was looking through the screen into a deranged brain and a black heart. The certain knowledge that here was a turn of phrase, something that clicked in me, some unease, finally full-blown. I didn't know why or how yet. But somewhere deep inside me I knew who. Yet too late. I saw myself turning, the crumpled body behind the door, and the shadow coming for me. Then there was nothing. Till now.

I must think. I must think. I had no idea where he was taking me, but I was sure it was nowhere good. And what about – what about my poor, sweet, brave boy, lying crumpled behind the door? What had happened to him? Was he dying – perhaps already dead? Or only stunned, like I had been? I hoped so. I prayed so.

Oh, God. I had been so sure. I had not listened to the warnings. I had not wanted to believe. I was so sure it wasn't possible. I hadn't understood. And now I would pay the price for my stupidity and blindness and trust.

Suddenly the engine revved hard. The sidecar tilted. We were going uphill. I could hear the skittering of stones under the bike's wheels. Then the jolting and bumping ceased, and soon after, the engine stopped. It was suddenly very quiet. I was still blind, still helpless. But, though riven with terror, I could hear. And do you know what I heard? I heard – I heard him *whistle*. Cheerful, it was, that whistle, as if he didn't have a care in the world. Which maybe he didn't. How was I to know? I didn't understand anything about him any more. Nothing made sense.

The sidecar tipped as he got off the bike. I heard his steps coming round to me. I felt his hand on my head and a spasm of revulsion raced through me. But I stayed quite still. Some instinct told me not to struggle. I felt his hands on mine, and thought I would die from the disgust. But I stayed still. I realised he was untying my hands. He was untying my feet. Why?

I can't tell you how I managed to not move, even then. Was it an instinct born of unbearable terror? Perhaps. I can't explain, but I knew I must not move, not at that moment. I must make him think I was still unconscious. I knew he must think I was, because of that whistle. That was the sound of someone who thought himself unobserved. Safe, home and hosed. He was planning something for me, but it didn't involve killing me whilst I was tied up. It was something else. Something cleverer, something ghastlier, even. Something that wouldn't touch him or involve him. Something that would look like someone else had done it.

I kept my eyes tight shut under the blindfold, knowing that soon he must take that off. But I let my mouth go slack. Now I could feel his hands on the gag. He lifted up my head to untie it, and I let myself go all limp, so that he'd think I was out to it. He pulled off the gag, and I let myself moan, softly, like someone who's still unconscious but maybe going to surface soon. I could feel him check, for an instant, and I let my head loll on my neck, and then go limp again. Then he was ripping at my blindfold and pulling it off. I could smell him – the hot sweat of him – as he bent over me. It made me feel sick. But I managed to keep my eyes shut.

After what seemed like an eternity but must actually have been only a few seconds, I heard him move away. His footsteps were firm, decided. As they died away, it became very quiet, and in that quietness, I heard a new sound. A small, steady, liquid sound. The sound of water lapping gently against stones. I thought, we're by a river – a lake – a pond – something like that. A memory came into my head, a signpost saying 'Lac St Jean – 10 kilometres.' Was that where we were?

How long had I been unconscious? I wasn't at all sure. Maybe an hour, maybe less. And if we were beside water, it must be for a reason. In an instant I had it. He wanted me to drown! He was going to roll me down into the water and . . .

But then, why hadn't he just taken me out of the sidecar, and pushed me in at once? I half-opened an eye. There was no-one looming over me. I opened the other eye. I lifted my head up, very carefully, until I could just about peer over the edge of the tipped-up sidecar. I didn't see him. In fact I couldn't see much at all. I could hear the water, though, and sense its presence, out there in the darkness. Out there – *or down there*. We were at the top of a low, stony slope. Down below was the water. It would probably be deep.

At that moment, I heard him coming back. He was dragging something. It was heavy. I could hear him pant with the exertion. I ducked my head back into the sidecar and kept very still. What was he doing? Was he dragging a boulder over or something – something to tie to me, maybe, so I shouldn't escape, so that even if I recovered consciousness when I hit the water, it would drag me down? My mind whirled, fruitlessly.

The dragging sound continued. He was still some distance away. I put my head up again, very carefully. I could see him now – or his back, anyway. He was wearing a heavy coat, its collar turned up. But more than that, I could see what he was dragging. And it wasn't a boulder. It was a body. I could see the legs, in jeans, the shoes, scuffing along the ground, the parka-clad arms hanging limply in his murderer's hands.

In that instant, I knew what he planned for both of us. He must have brought him here first, dumped him in the bushes, then gone back to get me. We'd die together. An accident. Or a murder–suicide. Two bodies plunged into the water, a death-leap with the bike into the depths. Perhaps somewhere a note, explaining why. And he, far away, innocent of any association, mourning, crying that he wished he'd seen, he wished he'd believed, he wished he'd understood. He'd stand by as they dragged our bodies from the water – if they ever found us, that is – and would weep and say we'd been his friends and how could it have come to this, and how much he blamed himself for not seeing the truth sooner. And inside that black heart of his, that mad brain, he'd exult in the knowledge that he had done it, he had fooled everyone and that his soul, his essential soul, was still hidden. Koschei the dread indeed – unkillable, invincible, unknowable, rejoicing in his secret power over life and death, over terror and joy, over paltry human lives. He would glory in the knowledge.

Perhaps it was that image which did it. That's what they tell me to remember. I must remember that at that instant I went from helpless victim to avenging angel. I must remember I went from being terrified to being angry. That's what they say. But at the time it just seemed to me like I leapt out of the sidecar, howling and yelling like a banshee, because I was sure I was going to die, and I wasn't going to go quietly, and that was the only thing in my control.

Whatever it was, wherever it came from, the effect on him was pure magic. That is what I *do* remember. He dropped his burden, he spun around, he saw me. And his face fell. I'd read in books before about someone's face falling, and I'd never really known precisely what that meant. But there it was, in front of me, the jaw going slack, the eyes popping, going from cold killer to baffled fool in an instant. This wasn't in his script, in the sick bit of cinema he'd devised for himself.

But his dismay didn't last, of course. Before I could take more than a few steps, he was after me. I turned, ran, stumbled, tripped, almost fell. I put out a hand to save myself, saw in the same instant a stone lying there, picked it up, turned, and flung it at him with all my might. To my utter surprise, it hit him on the hand. It stopped him for a second. He yelled. 'You bitch! How could you do that to me?'

I was long past wondering about his motives, his twisted soul. I picked up another stone, a flaky stone edged as sharp as a tool, thinking of him now only as a mad dog, something I must beat back or be destroyed by.

Then something terrible happened. Something that I'll never forget. In front of my eyes, he changed. His voice dropped, became soft, caressing. 'Don't, Rose. What are you doing? It's me. I've come to help you. What are you doing? Drop that stone.'

'No,' I said. 'No.'

He began to walk towards me, his hand held out towards me. He was smiling. His expression spoke of utter confidence. 'I found him lying in the bushes. He must have been flung off when he stopped so suddenly. He had you in the sidecar. My God, such a terrible thing. No-one will believe it.'

'If you come any closer, I'll stab you with this stone,' I said, in a voice I could not recognise. 'I mean it.'

'Oh, Rose.'

'Don't speak to me. I don't know you. I don't want to know you.'

'Rose, you're in shock. You've only just woken up from a blow to the head. You don't mean what you say.'

'Shut up.' He took another step towards me, and I flung the stone. This time, because he was closer, it caught him on the side of the face. Like I said, it was a sharp stone. A stone axe, I think now. A prehistoric weapon. You do find such things lying around, sometimes.

And it drew blood. He screamed. 'You will pay for that, bitch!' But I wasn't waiting for him to come after me. I was running, running towards the shelter of a belt of bushes I could dimly see just a short distance away. I plunged into the bushes, expecting at any moment that he was going to come after me. But instead, I heard a thump, and then the sound of a motorbike engine starting up. Then the machine's headlight came on, the stream of white light flooding the bushes, picking me out from my hiding place. He was going to spotlight me, I thought, hunt me through the bushes like a wild animal.

I pushed through the bushes backward. Beyond was open ground, a parking area, perhaps. I could see one or two picnic benches. At the far end was a little wooden hut. If I can make for that, if I can somehow lock myself in there, I might be safe. I didn't think much beyond that. I sprinted across the open ground, terror lending me wings. As I was nearly across, the motorbike burst into the area. He had unclipped the sidecar, so the bike moved much faster now. I could hear him yelling above the noise of the engine, but I didn't care what he was saying. My breath aching, screaming in my chest, I ran like the wind for the hut, and reached it just as he gunned the engine and came straight for me.

I slammed the door. There was a bolt on the inside. I drew it across. I leaned against the door and tried to stop myself from going completely to pieces. I looked around. The hut was a toilet, with a sink as well. The floor was concrete, the wooden building was snugly, tightly sealed, with no window, only a little skylight in the roof. It would not be easy to get into. So I tried to tell myself, trying not to think of him outside there, prowling, looking for a way to get in.

He didn't knock on the door or anything. He didn't try to talk to me. That was what was really scary. I could hear his rustling footsteps, could imagine him walking round and round and round, like the hungry wolf trying to get into the third little pig's house. Well, you can huff and puff all you like, but you're not going to get into this house, I thought, and couldn't help giggling at the thought, a mad, hysterical sort of giggle that made the terror rush straight back into me, making my legs and hands shake and my skin creep with ghastly cold. Never mind a chimney, he'll try to get into there through that skylight, and I've got no boiling pot to catch him in.

Suddenly, I heard him close by. He was at the door. I could hear his breathing. Then he was shaking the door. It was quite a strong door, but I thought he must be quite strong too. What if he just flung himself at it till it broke? What if he – what if he just got on the bike, and ran it straight at the door . . . I'd be caught like a rat in a trap with no way of escape.

And then, oh my God – oh my God, the miracle happened. Another engine. A big car, by the sound of it. And a voice, carrying loud and clear, sounding angry and puzzled.

'What the hell do you think you're doing?'

It wasn't a voice I knew. But I recognised the authority in it nevertheless. And so did he. I heard him mutter something, and then the other voice again, 'Tell that to someone who believes it. Clear off, you young vandal, before I lose my temper. Do you hear?'

The next instant, I heard the motorbike engine start up again, I heard the skidding of pebbles as he took off, and then the sound fading into the distance. And I had the door unbolted, throwing it open, yelling, 'Please, please, please don't go! Help me! Help me, please!'

I saw an astonished face looking at me from the opened window of a big four-wheel drive, the face of a total stranger, a big, heavy man with black hair and black stubble and the look of a farmer about him, and no-one had ever looked so good to me. I ran towards him, still shouting, stumbling. Thunderstruck for a moment, he'd soon recovered, had his car door open and was striding towards me. He caught me before I fell, and said, 'Was it that young man? Was he trying to hurt you?' and I nodded, the tears coursing down my cheeks.

'I thought he was just a vandal – little bastard, we'll make sure they get him, don't you worry, my dear, don't you worry.' He escorted me to his car, an arm around my shoulders, supporting me. 'I'll take you home. Where do you live, little one?' he said, gently.

His kindness and gentleness made the tears flow afresh. I burst into incoherent speech. 'No, not home yet. Oh, Monsieur – my friend – I'm afraid he might be dead, near the dam. We must go there at once.'

He looked at me, his face grim. 'Did that one . . .?'

'Yes. I think he's killed him. Or badly hurt him. He may try . . . please, Monsieur, let's hurry!'

He said nothing more, but started the engine, and we roared off down the track.

Through a glass darkly

At first, I thought that we were too late. His body wasn't lying where I'd last seen it. For one hideously bitter moment I was sure he'd already been disposed of, and the grief tore through me as I staggered about, calling his name, hopelessly.

But my new friend, who had told me his name was Janvier, Raymond Janvier, was more useful. He was the one who spotted the marks leading away from the site, and he was the one who, torch in hand, tracked those marks all the way.

He was lying in some bushes, so still that at first I thought he was dead. 'No,' said Janvier, bending down to him and feeling for his pulse. 'He's just fainted. Poor beggar – he must have crawled all the way here.' He looked at me. 'What happened? Was he shot?'

Fear somersaulted in me. 'I don't think so. But I . . . I don't know.'

Janvier undid the coat, and pushed up the jumper and shirt. He felt the chest, the neck, the waist. He said, 'There's no wound.' He shone the torch on the legs. The jeans were dirty but whole, there seemed to be no hole, and no blood-stains of any sort. I said, kneeling down in my turn, 'I – I think he was hit. Like me. On the back of the head.'

Janvier gently lifted the young man's head. He felt the back of it, and very gently put it down again. 'There's a big bruise, yes. He's been hit pretty hard. We should get him to hospital at once. An injury like that – it could have serious repercussions.'

We lifted him very gently, and put him on the back seat, which we laid flat. We covered him with a warm blanket Janvier had – he said he was a part-time gamekeeper and in the hunting season often had to spend nights in the car. We wedged him in with what we could – a cushion, a cardboard box, my body – for I would not sit in the front with Janvier, but in the back with him, my hand holding his tightly, watching his face, his dear, dear face.

Janvier drove very carefully. I wished he'd drive faster but knew that it was not wise. Who knew what another jolt, another bump, another shock might do to the young man who lay there so still, his face drained of all colour? I held his hand and desperately wished that all my warmth might flow into him and give him strength.

Neither Janvier nor I spoke, but it seemed to me that the car was filled with noise. The unspoken noise of desperate wishes, hopes, prayers. For the person who had done this, I spared not a thought. I didn't even want to see his name in my head. I wanted him to not exist, to be a non-person, an absence forever cut off from us. I held my darling's hand and I concentrated fiercely on him.

And then, quite suddenly, he opened his eyes. I was the first thing he saw. His eyes widened. He whispered, 'Rose?'

'Yes, it's me, Paul, *chéri*.' Saying his name, I thought my own pulse would jump up through my throat and fly away, it was beating so hard, and my hand was slippery with sudden sweat, the back of my neck crawling with cold and hot, together.

'Oh God, Rose, I – I thought you were . . .' He grimaced, the brown eyes darkening with pain.

'Shh, Paul, shh, sweetheart, it's okay, I'm okay, I'm fine,' I gabbled, 'just rest, we're taking you to the hospital. They'll look after you.'

'That's good. Its feels like I've got the worst hangover ever,' he said, with an attempt at a smile.

I saw him glance at Janvier and I said, 'This is Monsieur Janvier, Paul. He rescued me, and found you. If he hadn't come on the scene, God knows what might have happened.'

'Now then, lass,' said Janvier, 'with ifs and buts we could put Paris in a bottle, eh? It is as it is.' He smiled. 'You'll be right as rain, lad, I'd imagine, from listening to you. You make pretty good sense, and you're not wandering in your wits. Head must be pretty hard, I'd say.'

'That runs in the Fontaine family, I'm told,' said Paul. His eyes were lighting up, his skin slowly losing that clammy greyness that had so frightened me, and his hand moved slightly in mine, gently stroking the inside of my palm. It felt good. No, more than good. It felt like heaven. Joy was coursing through me as swiftly and painfully as the terror had done such a short time ago. He was going to be all right, I thought. He was going to be fine!

'Ah. So you're one of the Fontaines!' said Janvier. 'Related to Renée, by any chance?'

'She's my great-aunt.'

'She did some water-dowsing on my in-laws' farm a few years back. Did it well too. My in-laws still sing her praises. Never had the pleasure of meeting any of the rest of your family in person before, though — my own farm is well over on the other side of Castelnau from you, not far from the Lac St Jean, where I found you.'

The Lac St Jean! So that *was* where we'd been. I dimly remembered, seeing the signpost to it, when we'd gone to Paul's farm that first time.

Janvier looked at me in the driving mirror. 'And you, Mademoiselle? Where's your home?'

'I'm Rose du Merle,' I said. 'My grandfather, he has the –'

'Oh, I know. The castle at St Martin du Merle. Your grandfather's the Count. Well, well,' said Janvier, his bright dark eyes surveying us in the driving mirror. 'I didn't know the Count had such a pretty granddaughter.'

'He didn't know he had a granddaughter at all till recently,' I retorted, feeling absurdly light-headed.

He laughed. 'Well, I'm sure there's a story in that, and I'd like to hear it some time. But here we are. Albi Hospital.'

How strange, I thought, as we drove in. Grand-père is here too. The two men I most care for in all of the world will be together, here, tonight.

We had to wait for an hour or so while they took Paul in and checked him, and gave him a battery of tests to make certain that his injury was nothing worse than concussion. They checked me over briefly too, but I was fine. Monsieur Janvier and I sat together in the waiting room. He asked me about how I'd come to stay at the castle and I found myself telling him, well, not my full story, but just about being in France and how different it was from my other life in Australia. He asked me millions of questions then about

Australia, which he seemed to find fascinating. He had funny ideas about it though, called it 'the last frontier', and the 'modern Wild West', said that a person could be free and wild there in a way you couldn't be in Europe. He'd seen TV shows about it, he said, things about cattle stations in the Outback and Aboriginal artists in the desert and Steve Irwin's crocodile shows, stuff like that. I could see he didn't really believe me when I told him that actually most Australians lived in cities and lived pretty ordinary lives and never went near cattle, deserts or crocodiles. It was nice talking to him. It was relaxing and took my mind off my terrible anxiety. When I'd finished, he said, 'You know, Rose, you tell a good story. You could be a writer one day, I think.'

'Maybe I will.' It was odd, I hadn't thought of writing for ages, or about my ambition to become a novelist. I'd hardly even written in my blog since we'd come back from Paris. Too many things had happened.

'Well, tell me when you write a book,' he said cheerfully. 'I'll certainly buy a copy! And I might well come and visit you in Australia one of these days too. My wife and I have often talked of doing it – a big dream trip around the world, visiting all the wild and exciting places.'

'Then you must come and visit us, though I don't think our place is very wild or exciting,' I said, before it struck me that I was talking as though home was back there, not here. But was it, really? Was it with Aunt Jenny and my friends and school and all the things I'd been used to until just a few weeks ago? Or was it here, with Grand-père and Paul, and the castle?

But then, there was still the shadow of . . . No! I didn't want to think about Charlie. Not yet. Not now. Perhaps my face showed something of my feelings, for Raymond Janvier said, gently, 'Later, I can take you to the *gendarmerie*, the police station, if you like, and you can tell them what happened.'

'I'm not sure,' I said, swallowing.

'This man must be caught and punished,' said Janvier quietly. 'Or he may do it again.'

'Yes,' I said, and for an instant, fear rose in my throat like bile.

A little later, they came to tell us that Paul was okay, that he had nothing major wrong with him, but that he'd have to stay in hospital under observation overnight, just in case. He'd been given painkillers and moved into a ward. I asked if I could go and see him, and they agreed, but said I couldn't stay long because he was exhausted and needed rest.

So leaving a tactful Raymond Janvier in the waiting-room – he said he would wait for me and drive me home whenever I wanted – I went in to see Paul. He was propped up in bed wearing a hospital gown, his head bandaged, his curly hair peeping through at the top. There were two other men in the ward, both of them a fair bit older than Paul, and they looked curiously at me as I came in. I nodded shyly to them, and tried to ignore their intense interest as I came over to Paul's bed and sat down on the chair beside him.

'Oh, Paul, I'm so glad you're okay,' I whispered.

His smile lit up his whole face. 'I must say I share that sentiment, *chérie*.' He took my hand. 'You're sure *you're* all right?'

'Quite sure.' But I couldn't help shivering as images from the last few hours flashed into my mind, and Paul felt it. He said, very low, 'If I had that creature in my sight, I'd tear him limb from limb, for what he did to you.'

I swallowed. 'Why did you come back to the castle, Paul? I heard your bike. But I thought I was dreaming.' I didn't tell him what the dream had been. Some things shouldn't be said, even now.

'I was stupid,' he said. 'I came back because I wanted – well, I wanted to ask Charlie something, and I didn't want to involve you. You see, I thought you and he –' He broke off, then went on more strongly, 'I thought I should give him a chance to answer on his own, without you. I didn't want to hurt you, or make you angry with me.'

'Oh, Paul.' I had a lump in my throat. 'What . . . what did you want to ask him?'

'You remember when we were trying to ring him, before, when his mother – well, you know. I'd left a message on his friend's mobile, and on it I'd given him my own mobile number. Well, when I'd been home a while, Charlie's friend, Thierry, rang me back. He seemed puzzled that I should ask him to go to Charlie's work place, and when I asked him why, he said it was because, as far as he knew, Charlie didn't have a job.'

I stared at him. 'Oh, my God.'

'He said he'd thought he'd gone for an interview recently, but hadn't got the job. He can be a bit difficult, you know, Thierry said. Arrogant. Employers don't like that very much. Well, of course then I thought, if he hasn't been going to work, what has he been doing? To make sure, I asked Thierry if he'd seen him that day, in Toulouse, and he said no. I asked if he'd seen Charlie that week, or the week before, and he said no. He might have been with other friends, though, he said.'

'Or he might have been hiding near home,' I said, slowly. 'There are all sorts of places, even in the grounds of the castle, where you could hide out. Garages, barns, outbuildings.' I shivered. 'Even in that vault. He seemed quite familiar with it.'

Paul nodded. 'Exactly. He could hide most of the time, and pretend to come home on the bus – he could easily have caught it just down the road, if need be. I could see he had the opportunity, all right, if his job alibi collapsed. Well, Thierry seemed to realise from my tone that something was up, because he said, "Look, Charlie's a bit wild, and he's very secretive, and he tells fibs a fair bit, so I don't really know what goes on with him, and I can't vouch for anything."' He paused. 'I said I understood, and rang off, and sat there for a while thinking I should ring you up and then thinking you'd hate me if I told you what I knew.'

'Oh, no, I'd never, ever hate you, Paul!' I cried passionately, and the other patients heard me and grinned.

Paul grinned too. 'I know that now,' he said, 'but then, well, I was not sure of anything at all. I thought that you felt something for Charlie.'

'I did,' I said honestly. 'But it wasn't what I thought. I knew that as soon as he held me, that time when you saw us, you know?' He nodded, and I rushed on, my cheeks flaming, 'It was like he was someone in a dream – not real, somehow – as though there was nothing flowing from him to me, really, if you know what I mean?'

'I do,' he said gravely.

'I'd been feeling a bit guilty, because of – you know, because of us. But then I wasn't, any more. I felt sorry for him, though. Because of his parents . . . and stuff like that. And because he could never, ever be like you. Not ever.'

'And here was me thinking you were in thrall to his handsome face,' he said, lightly. 'What a fool I was, Rose. I put us both in danger because of my stupid blindness, and my pride.'

'I did too,' I said quickly, and he laughed. 'Well, then, we're well-matched, for we're both as silly as each other,' and pulling me down to him, he kissed me gently on the lips, to the great delight of the other two patients.

As we drew away, I faltered, 'So what . . . what happened then?'

'Eventually, I decided I had to go and have it out with him,' Paul went on, his tender gaze on me. 'The place was quiet when I came in. I found him in the library. He was at the laptop. And he was typing away at that blog of his. I was so taken aback that I reacted too slowly. So he had the advantage over me, you see. He just went for me with that heavy paperweight of your grandfather's . . .'

I shivered. 'What lies he told. He always made out he knew nothing about computers or anything like that. I totally believed him. I never thought of questioning it. I was so stupid!'

'No you weren't. Most people take things on trust. You have to. Why would you think someone would lie about something like that?'

'I think he even lied to his mother about it. And Grand-père,' I said.

'Exactly. I think he just enjoyed pulling the wool over everyone's eyes,' said Paul grimly. 'He enjoyed the secret pleasure of it. It was the oddest thing – I knew at once, when I saw him sitting there hunched over his blog, why it had seemed familiar to me. It wasn't just that Koschei name that I remembered. It was like looking into a glass, darkly, and seeing someone there reflected, someone familiar but twisted beyond all recognition.'

'I know just what you mean,' I said. 'I felt the same. That blog gave me the creeps. He must have been using internet cafés to post stuff, when he couldn't use Grand-père's laptop without being caught. He must have stumbled across my blog on the internet, seen my name in the profile and started having a go at me before I even arrived. Even before he met me, he must have decided to do all those things . . .' The thought of that calculated malevolence filled me with horror. 'I can see now that he had the opportunity – and the means. But the motive? I don't understand. Why . . . what had I ever done to him?'

'Nothing, *chérie*, nothing.' Paul's hand gripped mine. 'I don't suppose you really existed for him, as a person. It was all to do with *him*, with things inside him. He's a narcissist. A psychopath. The world revolves around him. Perhaps he was jealous, or envious, or angry at your good fortune. Perhaps he thought he would get your grandfather's money one day, if you were out of the way. Perhaps he just enjoyed his secret power over you. I don't suppose we'll ever know.'

'Do you think he . . . do you think he's gone for good?'

'I don't know. But I'd say that was highly likely. He's hardly going to want to stick around, now he's been unmasked. He might like playing sicko games, but he's very fond of his own skin and is not going to want to face the music, I bet. He's probably halfway to Spain by now, if he's put some petrol in my bike. Damn it! That was a good bike,' said my boyfriend, with a faint smile. 'Bastard probably has no idea how to look after it.'

'I didn't know he could even drive.' There were just so many things I hadn't known about Charlie Randal.

'Oh, I knew he could do that, though he doesn't have a licence, of course. I just thought he was too damn lazy to do it himself, as long as he had his mother to wait on him hand and foot,' said Paul grimly.

'Poor Blanche,' I said softly. 'Do you think she knew what he was doing?'

'Poor Blanche, my foot. She suspected it, I'm sure of it. I'd say she knows pretty well what her son's capable of. And she's always protected him from the consequences of his actions. Even when we were at school, he'd do stuff – steal things, tell lies – and she'd say it wasn't his fault, but someone else's. It was always someone else's fault.'

'Monsieur Janvier thinks I should go to the police station and make a statement. Do you think –'

'I do,' said Paul, with a vigorous nod of the head which then caused him to wince. 'Ouch. Yes, I think you must make a statement, and I'll make one as soon as I can, too. We can't let him get away with it.'

'No,' I said, but I couldn't help trembling a little.

Paul said, 'He still frightens you, doesn't he?'

'Yes. I – I can't help it. It's not just those things he did to me. And you. It's also – the accident. I'm not sure – I'm not sure if he didn't have something to do with it. The brakes didn't work properly. What if he tampered with them? And the cyclist – the cyclist they couldn't find. What if it was him? I mean, what if he deliberately waited for them on that road and went across knowing Louis would have to swerve, and the brakes wouldn't hold?'

'Oh, Rose,' said Paul horrified. 'I hope that isn't true. But Charlie used to have a bike that he rode quite a lot when he was younger.' He was now looking very tired. 'I don't know if it's true, but even the suspicion of it must make you realise you must go to the police. You must tell them everything. Everything.'

'Yes,' I said, 'I will.'

'Promise,' he said.

'I promise.'

'I love you, Rose,' he said, so softly that at first I didn't hear, and then he repeated it, and my whole body filled with such joy that I thought I would faint.

I said, 'I love you too, Paul,' and this time it was my turn to bend down and kiss him on the lips while our audience watched interestedly. And do you know, I wasn't even embarrassed by that.

Some people say you can't really fall in love at our age, but I know they're wrong. It depends on the people involved. This was love, real love, starting to blossom. Love that would develop as we did, that would only grow stronger as we got to know each other more and more. Paul had recognised it before I had, maybe because he was older than me, maybe because he was more perceptive than me. Maybe, in a way, he'd kind of inherited something of his great-aunt's instincts. Well, we had a chance now. It might work and it might not. You couldn't be absolutely sure of that. Nobody ever knew the future for certain. But it was worth trying. He was real, Paul, he was true. What was it Grand-père had said? *Steadfast.* There was a strength to him, a core that was rock-solid.

Turned to stone

I didn't go home to the castle that night. After leaving Paul, I went to check on Grand-père in the intensive care ward. The nurse told me I couldn't see him yet. He was asleep. But I could come back tomorrow morning. So I left with Monsieur Janvier, and went round to the *gendarmerie*, where a kindly desk sergeant took my statement and said that wheels would be set in motion. I didn't ask what wheels. Would they start a hunt for Charlie, arrest him, bring him in for questioning, charge him if it turned out he'd been responsible for the accident as well as all the other things? If they found he was responsible for the accident, then that was the charge they'd lay against him. A charge of murder, because Louis had died. And attempted murder, against Grand-père. Beside the enormity of that, the way he'd stalked me and harassed me seemed less important. And yet he'd been prepared to go right to the end, when he was cornered. Prepared to kill me and Paul, and then to throw the blame on the dead.

How was it possible that that handsome face, that graceful body, those caressing eyes, could hide such a terrible secret, could harbour such vile things? Even now it was baffling. I remembered the feeling of being helpless, in his power, back at the Lac St Jean. It wasn't just my predicament. It was that feeling of being suddenly face-to-face with naked evil. I wondered how I would cope if they caught him and brought him back to face us all. It was not a nice thought. Worse still was the thought they might *not* find him – and that he might decide to come back looking for us. Paul had seemed to think it unlikely. But how could he be sure? How could you be sure of anything with a man like that? What if – what if he had just gone back to the castle? What if he was waiting for me there? My blood ran cold at the thought.

As we went out of the *gendarmerie*, I said to Raymond Janvier, 'I – I don't think I want to go home. I'd rather stay in Albi tonight, so I can be on the spot tomorrow morning to visit Paul and Grand-père.'

'Of course, that's a good idea,' he said, with an insightful look. 'I know a nice little hotel very close by, very secure, where you can stay. I'll take you there now, and settle you in. Then, if you're okay, I'll go to the castle and let people there know what's going on. And I'll come back tomorrow morning, take you to the hospital, and then we can decide what you want to do after that. How does that suit you?'

'Oh, Monsieur Janvier, you're so kind. I don't know how to thank you.'

'Bof,' he said uncomfortably. 'Now, what about your friend? Would you like me to go and see his family too?'

'Paul didn't say he wanted that,' I said, stammering a little, because I have to say it was the first time I'd considered what the Fontaines might be thinking. 'I don't think they know he's missing. They probably just think he went out. I don't know if he'd want to worry them at this stage.'

'Maybe not. Well, tomorrow we'll see, eh? Now, let's get you to your hotel.'

It *was* a nice little hotel. Cosy and warm, with only a few rooms and the nicest woman you can imagine running it, with a Southern accent so thick I had to strain to understand her. Madame Colzac, that was her name. She didn't seem to mind being woken up so late as she said she never went to bed till long past midnight. Monsieur Janvier didn't tell Madame Colzac much, only that I had been in an accident and that though I was okay physically, I had had a bit of a shock, and tomorrow I had to go and visit people in the hospital.

She exclaimed, 'Oh, *mon pauvre petit chou!*' or 'my poor little cabbage'. It's a French endearment, believe it or not. Then she said that good hot food was the best treatment for shock and though it was so late, bustled off to rustle me up the best ham omelette I've ever tasted, and good fresh bread with lashings of butter, and the biggest cup of steaming, creamy hot chocolate you can imagine. I hadn't even realised I was starving until then. But I polished off that meal in double-quick time and sipped on the brandy she gave me as a finish, 'to put you in the mood for sleep,' as she said with a big smile. I'm not used to strong stuff like that, and what with the food and the brandy, when Monsieur Janvier left, a short time later, I was feeling a whole lot better. I was also beginning to feel very sleepy as every aching muscle and every tense nerve in my body slowly relaxed in the warm, secure atmosphere of Madame Colzac's little hotel.

I slept like a baby most of the night but woke up rather early, in the grey dawn. I was a bit disorientated at first.

Then memory returned and I lay there, trying to stop the dark thoughts from filling my mind. I could not let Charlie continue to stalk and frighten me, even in his absence. I couldn't keep dwelling on evil, when love and kindness was all around me. I must stop worrying and be glad that we had come through it.

But not all of us, my dark thoughts reminded me. Not poor Louis Vallon. Not the Vallon women, forever bereft now of husband and father. Not even the Snow Queen, who would have to face now just what her son had become. I had a sudden image of her as I'd last seen her, lunging at me with her nails, her face twisted with hatred. Or was that fear? Fear *for* Charlie, or fear *of* him? Maybe both. How ghastly. Maybe she *had* done the wrong thing with Charlie, as Paul had said. But she wasn't responsible for this. She had been alone, her husband worse than useless. How do you cope, when your kid turns out to be a bad lot, and you find it harder and harder to control him? It would be hard enough for the most together person, and even harder for someone like the Snow Queen.

Had she really hated me? I didn't think so. She'd been quite human to me some of the time, especially that brief time in Australia. But once we were back in France, and things started happening, perhaps she began to suspect he had something to do with it. Then I became, not a person to her, but a bad omen. A threat. A jinx. A catalyst of trouble . . .

I couldn't bear lying here any more. I got out of bed, got dressed and went downstairs. There was a smell of coffee and croissants. Madame Colzac was already up. She came out, saw my face and, ushering me to a table, she fussed over me, bringing me breakfast, chatting about this and that. I was grateful that she didn't ask about what had happened, but seemed content just to talk on and on while I tried to listen in case she asked me anything. Concentrating on that, though, made the dark thoughts fade so that by the time Monsieur Janvier turned up to take me to the hospital, I was in a more positive mood. He was with Madame Collot, who had insisted on coming with him. As we drove to the hospital, she told me what had happened back at the castle the night before.

Blanche Randal had woken up from her drugged sleep a couple of hours or so after what had happened in the library. Finding her door locked, she had hammered and banged on it, yelling with all her might. When nobody came – for Madame Collot slept at the other end of the house and didn't hear her – she flung open her window and shouted for help into the night.

'I woke up with a start,' she said. 'I couldn't figure out what was going on. I jumped out of bed and ran in the direction of the noise – but when I got to Blanche Randal's door and found it locked, I was so confused I couldn't think what to do. Then I remembered my master keys and ran back to fetch one. But when I got back, I found the door had been forced open, and there was Madame Randal, sobbing in the arms of –'

I shrank back. 'Oh my God. Charlie did return.'

'No. Not Charlie. Paul. Paul Randal. Blanche's husband. Seems he'd been prowling about upstairs, and had heard Blanche screaming. Well, I gave him pretty short shrift, demanded to know what he thought he was doing. He said he had been staying there unbeknownst to anyone except Blanche. I gave him a blast, and he just stood there looking hangdog.'

'What did Blanche Randal do?' I breathed.

'She pulled herself together, saying it was none of my business, that it wasn't illegal, as far as she knew, to have a guest. I protested that Monsieur le Comte hadn't been told, but Blanche Randal said it was no business of his either. It was amazing, that woman with her ravaged face looking down her nose at me and giving me lessons.'

'That's her, all right,' I murmured.

'I then asked what all the fuss was about, and why Blanche had locked her room, and she yelled and said she hadn't locked herself in. That someone had taken her key. She asked if Charlie was there, and when I said he was, we went off to his room, but found it empty, the bed not slept in. We went to look for you and found you not there too and then we went to the library and found it a mess ... and the laptop broken on the floor.'

'What did you think had happened?'

'Well, Blanche was certain you had done something to Charlie – or Paul Fontaine had. But Paul Randal and I – well, we assumed the opposite, actually. Blanche insisted on calling the Fontaines. They couldn't find Paul or Charlie, of course. They raced over to the castle to see for themselves. Everyone was in a complete flat-out panic by the time Monsieur Janvier turned up, and told them what had happened.'

'And then?'

Janvier, who had been listening all the while, gave a thin little smile. 'Well, then all hell broke loose, as you can imagine. The mothers just about went mad and tried to attack each other. It took Fontaine and Randal and I the devil of a time to calm them down. Anyway, they did, after a while, and the Fontaines went off to call the hospital to check their son was indeed okay, as I'd assured them – I dissuaded them from turning up there at that time of night – while Randal took his wife back to her room to keep her calm. She had collapsed. All the fight had gone out of her. It was odd, I didn't like the look of that fellow much at first – especially considering he'd been a stowaway in your grandfather's house – but he was very gentle with that witch-woman of his. He told me he'd had a lot of time to think. In prison. And he thought Blanche had done the best she could with Charlie . . .'

I thought about how everyone had spoken of Paul Randal as an unreliable crook. I thought of how he'd made life very difficult for his wife, and been so distant from his son. I thought of what that might do to you. If Paul Randal had been there earlier . . . if he'd been around to help his wife, would things have been any different? Maybe yes, maybe no. Who can tell?

I felt the tragedy of it all, the pointless tragedy. How strange people were, and how sad life could be. Was that why Charlie had done what he did? Had the pain of his childhood gathered and grown in him till he'd become monstrous with it? Paul had said Charlie was a narcissist, a psychopath. Someone who thinks only of themselves and how things affect them. In people like that, emotional pain might become like a kind of cancer which ate away every-thing that was good and left only the bad stuff. I don't know. Maybe that's true and maybe it isn't.

When we got to the hospital, we found Paul's parents already there. They had their backs to us as we came in. But Paul's face lit up when he saw me that they turned around. His mother said, 'Oh, it's you, Mademoiselle du Merle.' Her voice wasn't exactly enthusiastic.

Her husband put a hand on her shoulder and said gently, 'Paul's been telling us how brave you were. Geneviève and I particularly want to thank you, for helping our Paul.'

'Please, it's normal,' I said, trying to sound light. 'Paul and I – we're very important to each other.'

Even now, as I write these words, I can't believe I said that! I mean, that I had the guts to say it. It came out of my mouth, somehow, without my planning anything at all. I went red as soon as I'd said it. But not for anything in the world would I have taken those words back, especially when I saw the look on Paul's face.

'Well, we're glad to hear that,' said Marcel Fontaine softly, and his own hard, wary face was transformed with sweetness. It made him look very like his son. 'Very glad indeed. Your great-aunt Renée will be too, Paul. It's time and more than time that our two families become important to each other in the right kind of way. Isn't that so, Geneviève?'

He spoke softly, but passionately, and I saw Paul looking at his father in faint surprise. But his mother nodded, and tried to look as if she agreed wholeheartedly. That was nice of her. After all, I expect that somewhere deep down she half-blamed me for dragging Paul into trouble, disregarding of course the fact that *no-one* can drag my independent-minded and hard-headed Paul into anything he doesn't want to do.

Later I went to visit Grand-père. He was awake at last. They'd moved him from intensive care to another ward. He looked very frail and tired propped against the pillows, and I suddenly felt a frightened leap of the heart. Please,

God. I want to spend time with Grand-père, lots of time, years and years. He must get better. He must!

Then he saw me, and reached out to me. 'Rose! Oh, my dear little Rose. I'm so happy to see you.'

'Don't try to move, Grand-père.' I sat close by his bed, and took his hand.

He said, 'You haven't been here all night, have you?'

'No, I –' I was about to tell him, then I thought, I can't explain all that right now, not when he's like this. So I said, instead, 'They say you're going to be all right.'

'I am,' he said, 'bar feeling that I ache all over. I'm a tough nut to crack, my dear.' His expression changed, and he said sadly, 'But then I'd always have said that of Louis.'

'They told you?'

He nodded. 'I insisted.' A pause, then he went on, 'He was a good man. And a good driver. I'll miss him. And his poor family – I want everything possible to be done for them. I'll see my lawyer as soon as I'm out of here.' He was silent again, then said, more strongly, 'And I thank God you weren't in that car too, my dearest child.'

I said nothing. He went on, 'I'm glad that we didn't run over that cyclist. He came out of nowhere, you know. Just out of nowhere. Like a jack-in-the-box, popping up.'

'Yes,' I said heavily.

'No-one's come forward, have they?' asked Grand-père. I shook my head.

'I suppose the police are going to want a description of the whole thing,' said Grand-père, with a sigh. 'Not that I can tell them much. It all happened so quickly. I suppose that cyclist, if he wasn't injured, is lying low somewhere.'

I bit down on my lip. 'I suppose so.'

'I'm surprised the brakes failed so badly,' said Grand-père. 'I know Louis looked after the car very well. How could they have got into such a state? I know he was saying they were a bit soft that morning, but still –' He broke off. 'Anyway, it does no good talking about it. Better to leave it to the police and their investigations. Oh, Rose! I can't wait to be out of here, and back home.'

'And I can't wait for you to *be* home,' I said, in a rush. 'I'll look after you till you're quite well, Grand-père.'

'My dear Rose, you don't know what you're letting yourself in for, I'm a very grumpy convalescent,' he said cheerfully, and squeezed my hand. And I was glad he didn't ask me any more questions. There'd be time enough later for him to come to grips with it all.

Time passed. Paul came out of hospital that first afternoon, and I spent a good deal of time with him, at his house and at mine, and also sometimes with his great-aunt Renée in the woods. She hasn't tried again to send thoughts to me, and we never talk about that strange moment in the tomb: I know she doesn't want to, and neither do I. Not really. Some things are better left alone. But we have grown to like each other a lot.

I had been afraid I'd have to face Blanche Randal back at the castle. But both she and her husband were gone when Monsieur Janvier, Madame Collot and I drove back to the castle that first day. She had left a note sealed in an envelope for my grandfather, a note he read after he was back, and after he knew both what had happened to me and to Paul, and about the suspicions about the accident. The investigators had found that there was a possibility the brakes had been tampered with, though the front of the car was too badly damaged to be absolutely sure. No trace had been found of the cyclist, however, though Paul and I found a bicycle in one of the back sheds, a bicycle covered in mud. It was Charlie's bike when he was younger, Paul said, and by rights, if it had not been used since, it should have been dusty and cobwebby, not muddy. It wasn't proof, of course, but it was pretty close to that. But we did not say anything to Grand-père, or the police, because by then, there was no point.

You see, Grand-père did not tell us for quite a while what Blanche Randal's note had said, its words engraved on his memory, though he'd burnt the note itself.

I have brought shame and betrayal to your house, she had written, *and for that I am deeply sorry. Yet I sometimes think that if I'd married you, and not Paul Randal, Charlie would have been born good. I am afraid he thought rather that if I'd married you, he'd be a Count, and the heir to a large fortune. He was angry, Monsieur le Comte. Burning with it. Angry with me, and with you, for not doing what he thinks we should have done. With your granddaughter, for having been born what he wanted to be. He thought it should have been him, in her place, and that if she wasn't there, if he frightened her away, or worse, then you would turn to him, make him your heir, give him the name, the place, the identity. That is all I can think of to explain it. I am deeply sorry. But our fate is our fate, and written for us long ago, don't you think, Monsieur le Comte? And knowing that can turn us to stone.* She had signed it, *Your faithful secretary, Blanche Randal.*

And as to why Grand-père did not tell anyone for so long – well, first because he was shocked and saddened by it, and secondly, because there was one last thing in store for us. It happened just two days after Grand-père came home.

The police turned up at the Fontaine farm. They had just received notification, they said, of an accident on a road in the high Pyrenées, near Roncesvalles in Spain. A motorbike had been involved in a fatal accident, when its rider had failed to negotiate a bend and crashed into a rock wall on the side of the road. The rider had been killed instantly and he and his bike consumed by flames. But part of the machine had been salvaged and from that, police had been able to trace it as a motorbike reported stolen from St Martin du Merle, its registered owner being a Paul Fontaine. In their stolid police language, the officers told us the rider's identity was still being established. Nothing could be confirmed till forensics had been completed. But their eyes told us they knew who it was, and they knew Paul would know, and all of us.

Roncesvalles is famous in French history, because it was there the great knight Roland, nephew of the medieval Emperor Charlemagne, was ambushed and slaughtered with all his men. But it's also one of the traditional crossing places between France and Spain, and a rest stop for pilgrims going on the great walk to Santiago de Compostela. What was Charlie doing there? Was he going into Spain, or going back to France? What was in his heart as he rode along on Paul's motorbike? Revenge, or reconciliation? Hatred, or remorse? We would never know now.

Our fate is our fate, and written for us long ago. And knowing that can turn us to stone.

And they lived happily ever after

A year has passed. I'm sitting here at the table in my room, writing the last words of this account. Soon, I'm going to have to close my notebook and get ready. It's the day before my eighteenth birthday, and in an hour, I'm leaving to go to the airport.

The psychologist said this would help. Writing it all down, I mean. And she was absolutely right. At first, you see, I thought I was okay, because Paul had recovered, Grandpère was a lot better and we were safe from Charlie, for always. That couple of weeks, I was filled with a wild kind of relief and joy that we had survived it, though that joy was tempered with sorrow for the Vallons. Rather to my surprise, though, both the Vallon women chose to continue working at the castle. Samantha told me later that her mother had considered retiring and going to live in Albi, but that in the end she preferred to stay where she and Louis had been happy and where she could still feel his presence.

Aunt Jenny came over from Australia and stayed for a while, and that was great. I even wrote up a last blog post, to tell all my friends in Australia that I was all right, even happy. I was strong, I thought. I'd got through unscathed. When Renée Fontaine tried to tell me things might come back to haunt me, I brushed her off.

Aunt Jenny and Grand-père and I had talked of what might happen next, how maybe I could spend part of the time in Australia, part in France. I could go to school in Australia and come over every holidays or maybe the other way round. Or I could do the International Baccalaureate by correspondence or something like that so then I could choose where I wanted to go to university or if I wanted to go to university. Paul and I saw each other every day and that was wonderful. We talked and laughed and enjoyed being together.

But then, quite without warning, the nightmares returned. I overheard the police talking to Grand-père about how Charlie had written a last post on his blog, before his death. It had been written the day after the events at the Lac St Jean. The policeman said he'd called it *Careful what you wish for*. He said it showed he'd been intending to come back . . . and that he had no remorse at all.

'Post-traumatic stress disorder,' said the psychologist to me when I was brought into her office. 'You have to understand you can't get over anything as traumatic as what you've been through quite as easily as you thought,' she went on, echoing what Renée had said. 'It's normal to be on a roller-coaster of emotions, to fear that even in death he could reach out and hurt you. In time it will pass. You must allow the process to happen, and to be honest about how you feel. But it also needs to be under your control. I could prescribe tranquillisers, but I think I'd like you to try something else first.' It was then she suggested I might like to try to write it all down. She'd spoken to me about the things I liked doing and what I wanted to do later, so she knew I wanted to be a novelist.

I thought at first I'd never be able to do it. Not only would it be painful, but I didn't know where to start.

But it began to bug me. Once the idea was there, I knew I wanted to do it. I really wanted to get going. But I felt blocked. Blocked, me who had always written stuff at the drop of a hat! I tried all kinds of beginnings, but none of them worked. I screwed up and chucked away I don't know how many bits of paper. Then one morning, Paul came over to see me. I talked to him about it, and he said, 'Well, in a way, Rose, it all starts with your blog, doesn't it?'

Something clicked in my mind then, like a key unlocking a door. I knew how I had to begin. As soon as he'd gone, I sat down and opened a new, blank page in my notebook. I looked at it, my heart beating fast. I took up my pen and began to write.

Now, months later, I've just about finished. I filled up one notebook, and then another. They're both fat, full of my messy writing. In there is the story of what happened to me, all of it. I've tried to be as honest as possible. Sometimes it's been hard. Really hard. But as the words have come, as the pages have flowed, I've felt the nightmares receding, the flashbacks getting less and less. Now I no longer needed to go and see the psychologist. On my last visit, she smiled and told me she rather felt she'd done herself out of a job with her suggestion of writing things down. She told me she thought I was a born writer. It was good to hear that.

There's not a lot left to tell now. But all of it's good. I went back to Australia for a little while with Aunt Jenny. It was good to see my friends. But I missed Paul and Grandpère too much. I missed the castle, the village, France itself. I couldn't settle down back in my old life. I had moved on.

And so I came back to France. I enrolled in an International Baccalaureate by correspondence. It's not easy. But I work hard at it. Paul helps me a lot, and Grand-père too. I think I'm going to do okay in it, actually. Imagine that!

I don't think I want to go to university, though. I mean, not straightaway. After my exams are over, I want to go travelling with Paul. We'll just take our backpacks and set off, for all sorts of wonderful places, like Greece and Italy and Russia and India and Kenya and Mexico – and oh, everywhere! It'll be such fun. I can't wait. I've even half-thought I could write a travel blog while we're away. Not on my old Three Wishes blog, for which I've written the last post. But a completely new one, called *Away on The Magic Carpet*. What do you think?

Grand-père says jokingly he should be insulted, that all these plans I'm making mean that I can't wait to shake the dust of this place off my feet and take off far from him. Then he laughs when I protest and says that's what he loves about me, his dear little Rose with all her thorns out, and so easily teased.

Grand-père's very happy these days, and to be perfectly honest it's not just because of me being around, though I know he likes that. Another woman has come into his life. Well, *back* into it, actually. Yes, that's right, my grandmother. Caroline du Merle, or rather, Orazio. A few weeks after everything happened, she rang up, out of the blue. She came round to see us, and she stayed talking for ages. And I discovered she wasn't the flighty, selfish woman I'd thought she was. Neither was she the poor sad creature I'd imagined after I saw her photographs. She was – well, she was herself, actually. I still don't quite know what I

323

think of her, but I can see how happy Grand-père is when she visits, and that's good enough for me.

And what about Aunt Jenny? How does she feel about all this, about me going off and leaving her? And my friends? Well, actually, Aunt Jenny's here a lot of the time, too. She wasn't quite sure that she could cope permanently with life in France, but she just loves to pop over for holidays. She's really racking up the frequent-flyer points! And something really exciting happened the time before last. My grandmother happened to be there and she got talking to Aunt Jenny. Turned out that my grandmother knows people in the TV business, and when she saw Aunt Jenny's designs, she was really enthusiastic, saying she would introduce her to someone she knew who specialised in period productions. Anyway, she did, and the upshot of it was that Aunt Jenny got an interview, and now she's been contracted to do the costumes for an entire new TV series! It's like her dream job and she's just over the moon about it. And she's going to have to stay in France for a good long period of time to do that too, which is just excellent. She's here now, in Albi, actually, having lunch with the producer, who's flown down from Paris especially to see her to talk over final designs.

As to my friends – well, that's what I'm about to do. Go to the airport, with Paul, to pick them up. Yes, Portia and Alice and Maddy are arriving at Toulouse airport today, at the start of a few weeks' holiday with us. They're going to stay at the castle. They're going to be at my eighteenth birthday party tomorrow. It was Grand-père's idea. 'You've talked a lot about your friends back in Australia. You must miss them, no? Would you like to invite them to your party?'

'Oh yes!' I cried. 'That would be wonderful! Let's send them an invitation!' Then I thought again. 'Trouble is, I don't suppose they'll be able to come. Well, Portia might, her family's well-off. And maybe Maddy. But Alice's mother is on her own and quite poor.'

'Bah, when we send an invitation, we mean it seriously,' said Grand-père, with an airy wave of the hand. 'We will send them plane tickets as well. What do you say?'

'Oh, Grand-père!' I flew at him, and hugged him. 'You're so generous!'

He smiled. 'What's the good of money,' he said, 'if it can't be used to spread a little joy around you?'

Well, that was that. You can't imagine how excited my friends were, when I told them. Or maybe you can! Their parents were a bit wary at first but when Grand-père talked to them and Aunt Jenny explained it all, they readily agreed. I've been getting the most excited emails from the girls all the last few weeks, agonising about what they would be wearing at the party and what else they needed to bring and did Paul have any gorgeous brothers or cousins or friends (that was Alice, of course! She always asks straight out what the others are thinking!). They panic about not speaking French well enough and about the food and whether they'll like it and all sorts of stuff. But they can't wait. And neither can I!

Tomorrow will be my eighteenth birthday party. The ballroom will be filled with light, and the band will be playing, and lovely, elegant food laid on trestle tables, and the dance floor inviting us, and everyone dressed up and looking a million dollars. It'll be so different from my seventeenth birthday, which was hardly marked at all, because everyone was still in shock, especially me. This time it'll be wonderful! There'll be heaps of people there, not only my family and Paul's and my friends, but most of the village, and Monsieur Janvier and his family, and even Madame Colzac. I think of the lovely dress I'll wear, that silver one I bought in Paris last year, which will see its first outing tomorrow. I'll wear my magic silver shoes that did bring true love to me, and a gorgeous white beaded stole that once belonged to my great-grandmother Rose, and which Grand-père and I found in a trunk in the attic. I'll wear my blackbird brooch, the only thing my father had kept from his old life, and my mother's opal ring, which Aunt Jenny passed on to me, and the silver bracelet Paul's given me, which has our names engraved on it.

I think of all those things, but I think most of all of the fact that I'll be with all the people I love most in all of the world. People from my old life, people from my new life, all together. I think how lucky I am, and that sometimes wishes do come true, and that life can have its own brilliant magic, even outside of fairytales.

And then I look at my watch and see it's time to go. I'll put down my pen and close this book in a few seconds. But I still have a few more words to write. The traditional kinds of words you do write, after a story like this.

And they lived happily ever after.

If you're feeling brave, you can visit Koschei's blog at
http://koscheithedread.blogspot.com

Pop Princess

Isabelle Merlin

A ticket to a millionaire lifestyle . . .
or a one-way trip to the underworld?

It's a simple twist of fate that catapults Australian teenager
Lucie Rees from her ordinary life in an ordinary town to a
strange, exciting job in Paris as friend to ultra-famous but
troubled young pop star Arizona Kingdom. But it is more
than a simple twist of fate that will see Lucie entangled in
mysterious happenings that soon put her in terrible
danger.

Who can she trust? Will the holiday of a lifetime in
Paris turn into her last days on earth?

Available at all good retailers